BLAKE

BLAKE

or

The Huts of America

A novel by Martin R. Delany

With an introduction

by Floyd J. Miller

BEACON PRESS BOSTON

Beacon Press
25 Beacon Street
Boston, Massachusetts 02108-2800

Beacon Press books
are published under the auspices of
the Unitarian Universalist Association of Congregations.

96 95 94 93 92 91 90 89   9 8 7 6 5 4 3 2

LCN 79-119677
ISBN 0-8070-6419-X

CONTENTS

Contents

A NOTE ON THIS EDITION

This is the first publication of *Blake; or the Huts of America* in book form. Approximately eighty chapters comprise the complete novel, which appeared serially in *The Weekly Anglo-African* from November 26, 1861, until late May, 1862. Chapters 1-23 and 29-31 of this edition have long been known to specialists because of their publication in *The Anglo-African Magazine* between January and July, 1859. The 1859 volume of this magazine has recently been reprinted by Arno Press. Chapters 24-28 and 32-74 of this edition were found in *The Weekly Anglo-African* and are republished here for the first time. The complete novel contains perhaps six chapters that have not yet been uncovered; these undoubtedly appeared in the first four issues of *The Weekly Anglo-African* of May, 1862. Beacon Press would appreciate any information pertaining to their location.

This edition follows the original except for minor changes which have been made for the sake of clarity: typographical errors and obvious misspellings have been corrected, and the punctuation has been modernized. In addition, the numbering of the chapters has been altered: chapters in Parts I and II are here numbered consecutively to eliminate unnecessary complexity and to avoid the confusion existing in Part I of the original, where two sections labeled "Chapter 28" appear. Finally, the editor's notes appear at the end of this book; all notes in the text are by Martin R. Delany.

F.J.M.

Introduction

BY FLOYD J. MILLER

"I beg to call your attention to the Story of 'Blake or the Huts of America' now being published in the 'Anglo-African Magazine ' " Martin R. Delany wrote the noted abolitionist William Lloyd Garrison from a New York boardinghouse in February 1859. In the midst of a lengthy and frustrating attempt to raise money for a proposed African exploring venture (on which he would leave May 24, bound for Liberia), Delany added this plea in his letter to Garrison: "I am anxious to get a good publishing house to take it, as I know I could make a penny by it, and the chances for a Negro in this department are so small, that unless some disinterested competent persons would indirectly aid in such a step, I almost despair of any chance."[1]

Any efforts Garrison may have made clearly did not succeed, for *Blake* was never printed in book form. Twenty-six chapters were printed in *The Anglo-African Magazine* from January to July, 1859. Although the magazine continued to appear monthly until March, 1860, no further installments of Delany's novel were printed. Whether Delany lost confidence in the magazine, or, as is more likely, he did not wish to see his work published while he was out of the country, is not known. Whatever the reasons, the entire novel was not printed until the fall of 1861 when *The Weekly Anglo-African*, edited by Robert Hamilton, whose brother had published the magazine, ran a complete version of *Blake* in consecutive weekly installments from November 26, 1861, until most probably May 24, 1862.[2] Beset by constant financial difficulties, Hamilton apparently looked upon *Blake* as a circulation-builder. As Delany's nationalistic orientation was congenial to the newspaper's attitudes and Hamilton had previously run William Wells Brown's *Miralda; or, the Beautiful*

Quadroon (an updated and more militant version of Brown's *Clotel, or, the President's Daughter* which had originally been published in England in 1853), Hamilton was not afraid to experiment with that rare commodity—fiction by a black author.[3]

If one views *Clotel* and *Miralda* as a single novel, then Delany's *Blake* becomes the third novel written by an Afro-American. (Frank Webb's *The Garies and their Friends* was published in England in 1857.[4]) Its fragmentary appearance in 1859, however, marked the first novelistic offering of a black writer to be published in the United States. Regardless of chronological primacy, however, Delany's novel is clearly the most important black novel of this period and, for the social historian, one of the most significant and revealing novels ever written by an Afro-American. Avoiding the sentimentality of the "tragic mulatto" theme which intrigued both Brown and Webb, Delany focused sharply on the political and social milieu of the 1850s: slavery as an institution, Cuba as the prime interest of Southern expansionists, the "practicality" of militant slave revolution, and, most importantly, the psychological liberation possible through collective action.

Despite its relevance, *Blake* was generally ignored. There was apparently little, if any, commentary on Delany's work. This was partly because the complete novel was printed in 1861 and 1862: the Civil War had begun; little attention was given to the question of annexing Cuba; and the possibility of large-scale slave rebellion was dwarfed by the more immediate issues arising out of the war. In the light of this overt indifference, it is impossible to gauge what impact *Blake* may have had upon Northern black communities; newspaper comment during this period was devoted to the war itself, the Haytian emigration movement, and attempts to push the national administration to faster action on emancipation and the enlistment of black soldiers. Although a black actor, Melachi Dunmore, contemplated dramatizing Delany's novel, this was never seriously undertaken—and *Blake* was quickly forgotten.[5]

To a large extent, *Blake* is important because of its author's prominence. Unlike Brown, who served as a notable antislavery lecturer and author during the decades prior to the war (and whose reputation rests largely upon his antebellum activities), Delany's career spanned four decades of antebellum agitation, Civil War recruiting and soldiering, Freedmen's Bureau activity and Reconstruction politics. Moreover, although an author of some ability, Delany clearly subordinated his writings to his own ideological orientation, and consequently his only fictional effort marks the artistic epitome of a social and political position—that is, the creative offering of an activist rather than the political expressions of an artist. And finally, it is this nationalistic bent throughout his career which gave Delany a prominence among blacks exceeded by few Afro-Americans of his generation.

Born of a free mother and a slave father in Charlestown, Virginia (now West Virginia), on May 6, 1812, Delany claimed to be a descendant of West African native chieftains.[6] He received a scanty education in Charlestown before his mother took her family to Chambersburg, Pennsylvania, in 1822, where they were later joined by Delany's father. In 1831, Delany, then 19, left Chambersburg and traveled over the mountains to Pittsburgh where he found work as a barber and continued his education—studying at a school run by the Rev. Lewis Woodson, a black Methodist minister who had recently moved to Pittsburgh from Ohio. Delany spent twenty-five years in Pittsburgh, dividing his work between moral reform, abolitionism, newspaper editing. From 1843 to 1847, he edited *The Mystery,* one of the very few black newspapers of the period, and for a year and a half, from late 1847 until the middle of 1849, Delany co-edited *The North Star* with Frederick Douglass. In this role Delany was generally on the road, delivering antislavery lectures, enlisting subscriptions and writing long and occasionally revealing letters to *The North Star* describing his work. His attitudes during this period were not unlike those of many other black abolitionists: an awareness of the stridency of Northern prejudice against free blacks, a stress on the necessity for black communities to develop their own sense of pride and community awareness (translated into a "self-help" philosophy which Delany, along with Douglass and many others, promulgated long before Booker T. Washington) and, finally, a sense of moral rectitude at once patronizing toward those of his race unable to achieve personal righteousness and also imitative of the general nineteenth-century concern with moral virtue and ethical grace.

By 1852, no longer associated with Douglass and having flirted with the idea of a Northern American union of blacks (a progenitor of his later separatist ideas), Delany published one of the most significant and also neglected books by a free black prior to the Civil War—*The Condition, Elevation, Emigration, and Destiny of the Colored People of the United States, Politically Considered.*[7] Here Delany enunciated his break with the antiemigration position dominant among abolitionists by advocating Central American emigration as well as the establishment of a Central and South American "nation" which would, by its economic and political potency, contribute to the downfall of American slavery. He did, however, maintain the anti-Liberian position held by most abolitionists. More important in an immediate sense, Delany attacked the prejudice and social and economic discrimination practiced by white abolitionists, and for this he was attacked or ignored by most major abolitionists—white and black—as an apostate. (His charges, obviously impolitic at the time, have recently been substantiated by historians.) Delany's book, however, was more than a polemical tour de force which set him apart from his fellows: it was a careful and revealing sociological examination of elements within the free black communities of the North. For this reason, if for no other, it is significant.

From 1852 through February of 1856, when he moved to Chatham, Canada West, Delany continued to practice medicine in Pittsburgh (as he had done since the 1840s when he upgraded his profession from "cupper and leecher" to physician) while espousing what had become an outspoken emigrationist position. He argued the cause of Central American emigration throughout 1853 and 1854 and in August, 1854, led a National Emigration Convention of some 100-odd delegates in a four-day meeting in Cleveland. His paper, "Political Destiny of the Colored Race on the American Continent," was read at the convention; the essay combined a strong advocacy of Central American emigration (and nationhood) with a nod in the direction of Canadian land investment.[8] Distinguishing between emigration and colonization, Delany continued to attack the American Colonization Society and its Liberian offspring, culminating his anti-Liberian crusade by writing an introduction to William Nesbit's *Four Months in Liberia,* an "expose" of conditions in the infant republic published in 1855 by a short-term emigrant from Pennsylvania.[9]

The apogee of Delany's nationalist and emigrationist interests came, however, with his African trip of 1859 and 1860—a trip which began, ironically, on Liberian soil. (The trip also enabled Delany to be out of the country during John Brown's raid on Harpers Ferry; in May, 1858, he had participated in a Provisional Constitutional Convention at Chatham which discussed the possibility of an attack.[10]) From Liberia, Delany traveled first to Lagos and then Abbeokuta where he met his colleague, Robert Campbell, a young Jamaican who had taught at the Institute for Colored Youth in Philadelphia and who, with Delany, comprised the "Niger Valley Exploring Party." At Abbeokuta in late December, 1859, Delany and Campbell signed a treaty with a group of native chiefs. The terms of the treaty were later to be disputed (and, in fact, abrogated by the Alake of Abbeokuta in February, 1861); however, it is clear that Delany and Campbell were contemplating the "select emigration" of blacks from Canada and the United States and the establishment of a colony in the Abbeokuta area. Their plans beyond the establishment of their settlement were, of course, both vague and grandiose, often encapsulating the rhetoric of both the colonizationists and the English philanthropic imperialists. Essentially the Delany-Campbell plan of a nuclear settlement envisioned the eventual spread of Christianity and civilization (identical concepts in much of the African-development talk of the day) along with commerce, which was to serve as the catalyst necessary for Christian civilization to take root. Cotton was to be the prime factor behind the commercial development (or exploitation) of West Africa. Yet cotton was also to serve as an abolitionist weapon: the development of a ready supply of the staple in West Africa would undermine the American South's economic superstructure by providing English manufacturers (and perhaps others, such as the abolitionist sympathizer Edward Atkinson of Boston) with an alternate source of raw cotton. For Delany especially, the cotton-Christianity-civilization triad represented the benign forces which would be released by an African or black nationalist state gestating in the Niger Valley area around Abbeokuta.[11]

Delany's dream of an African settlement (and of his own personal emigration) did not come to pass. In 1861, having returned to Canada after a seven-month fund-raising lecture tour in England (during which his presence at the International Statistical Congress brought embarrassment to the Buchanan administration[12]), Delany organized a proposed colony of Canadian blacks. Support was promised by the

African Aid Society of England, and the Rev. William King, the leader of the Elgin community at Buxton, near Chatham, acted as an intermediary to expedite the settlement. Unfortunately for Delany, the planned settlement was lost in the increasingly complex web of British imperial designs upon West Africa—especially the rivalry between the British missionaries in Abbeokuta and the English traders centered at Lagos. In the end, the Alake of Abbeokuta, with the sanction of the Rev. Henry Townsend of the Church Missionary Society, denied the terms of the Delany-Campbell treaty; the African Aid Society retreated, and Delany, although still speaking of African emigration, turned his sights elsewhere.[13]

Delany's activities during the Civil War are for the most part lost in obscurity. He continued to lecture on Africa throughout 1862 and into 1863 but increasingly turned his attention to the Civil War and the role of blacks in securing their own freedom. By the middle of 1863, Delany was recruiting black soldiers for various state military units. In February, 1865, after the Lincoln administration had made minor forays in the direction of enrolling black officers (in the medical corps), Delany spoke, according to his own testimony, first with the President and then Secretary of War Stanton. On February 26, 1865, he was commissioned the first black Major in the United States Army.[14]

Unlike Lincoln's decision to employ black troops, Delany's commission apparently was not a major policy innovation, but rather an outgrowth of previous developments pointing toward the increased role of Afro-Americans both in the war effort and in what Lincoln thought would soon be the "restoration" of the Union. For the black community, however, Delany's commission was greeted with the applause and the Major, as he was now to be called, returned to the pantheon of black heroes. (Portraits of Delany in full regalia were sold through *The Weekly Anglo-African* for twenty-five cents.) After a visit to his family, now living in Xenia, Ohio, and several speeches to packed houses in New York, Delany joined General Rufus Saxton's command post at Charleston, South Carolina, in April, 1865, as a general recruiter of black soldiers. His military role was minimal at this late date in the war, and it was as a mass educator and politicizer that Delany was to serve in the closing days of the war and the first days of the confusion which followed. In July he was transferred to the newly established Freedmen's Bureau and assigned to Hilton Head on the Sea Islands as a subassistant commissioner, a position he held until August, 1868, when he was mustered out of the service.[15] As an agent for the Freedmen's Bureau, Delany strongly supported the freedmen's attempts to retain land previously granted to them and also embodied his land proposals with exhortations to collective action independent of the white presence—both malevolent and salutory—hovering over the Sea Islands. (For this he was criticized by both Laura Towne, one of the more perceptive and humane of the Northern "schoolmarms," and General James Scott Fullerton, an advance man for President Andrew Johnson's attempts to destroy the Bureau and to eliminate more radical agents such as Delany.[16])

Delany's Freedmen's Bureau career was not one of consistent radicalism. In part this must have been due to the insecurity engendered by Fullerton's charges (an insecurity well warranted in the light of the replacement of the abolitionist Rufus Saxton as assistant commissioner of the Bureau for South Carolina and Georgia by Robert Scott, who—although perhaps not as partisan toward ex-Confederates as Johnson might have preferred—lacked the commitment to racial equality which marked Saxton's tenure.) In addition, Delany's attitudes toward radical economic change were, at best, ambivalent. He was, after all, committed to nineteenth-century capitalism; his continual espousal throughout his career of self-help views and of the necessity for Afro-Americans to develop commercial aptitudes prevented him from wholeheartedly endorsing the "proletariat economics" necessary for meaningful economic and social restructuring beneficial to the freedmen. For instance, when, in December, 1865, and January, 1866, Delany investigated what proved to be unfounded rumours of insurrectionary activity among the Sea Island freedmen, his response, while sympathetic to the freedmen, fell far short of endorsing their demands for the confiscation of the planters' lands. Rather, Delany reiterated his "triple alliance" plan in which capital (from the North), land (belonging to the white South), and labor (provided by the freedmen) would divide profits equally. However, Delany hoped that the freedmen could accrue sufficient capital to purchase land from the planters. In this expectation, he established an agency to act as an economic intermediary between cotton merchants and the freedmen. Although charged with irregularities in

October, 1866, Delany was cleared when it became obvious that he was attempting to insure that the freedmen received a fair price for their cotton while also teaching them efficient business practices.[17]

Delany also embroiled himself in another controversy, one revealing the ambivalence of his attitudes toward the new political equality blacks were then laboriously constructing (imperfectly, as events would prove) in both North and South. In 1867, after Wendell Phillips had proposed the Republican Party nominate a black man for vice-president, Delany wrote *The New York Tribune* to express his opposition. Neither whites nor blacks were ready for a black vice-president, he argued, resting his rationale largely upon a gradualist philosophy which stressed familiar nineteenth-century homilies: education, moral rectitude and economic self-sufficiency.[18]

Delany's residence in the South did not end with his departure from the Freedmen's Bureau. After an unsuccessful attempt to secure the post of Minister Resident and Consul General to Liberia in 1869, he remained active in South Carolina politics throughout the remaining years of Reconstruction. His role here again was contradictory. At times, especially in the early 1870s, he supported black political participation and the election of black officeholders within the framework of the dominant Republican party.[19] In 1874, however, he bolted from the party and ran for lieutenant-governor on an independent ticket which was supported by dissident (although not necessarily reform-minded) Republicans and some white conservatives. Defeated in a close race by the black incumbent, Richard Gleaves, Delany returned to the Republican party in 1875 and was appointed a trial-justice in Charleston County. Removed later that year in the midst of charges of petty theft committed several years earlier (a charge which although substantially accurate was minor and was motivated by the political ambitions of his detractors), Delany turned to the "redeeming" Democratic party and Wade Hampton in the ferociously-contested gubernatorial election of 1876. His apostasy—from the point of view of most blacks—led to virulent hostility and sparked the Cainhoy riot in September, 1876. After Hampton's victory, Delany was again appointed a trial-justice in Charleston. As the more moderate elements within the state's Democratic Party lost sway, Delany became expendable. He was removed from office in 1878 at which time, powerless and apparently destitute, he turned toward Africa once again.[20]

The story of the Liberian Exodus Joint Stock Steamship Company and its ill-fated ship, the *Azor,* has been told before. Briefly, the company was formed by a group of Charleston-based blacks as an outgrowth of "Liberia fever" which was developing in South Carolina in the summer of 1877. Early in 1878 the company purchased the *Azor,* whose maiden voyage in the spring was a disaster for both the emigrants and the company. To what extent Delany, at one time the treasurer of the company, was responsible for the debacle is impossible to determine and probably of little pertinence. Nevertheless, after his most serious attempt at "black capitalism" had failed, he spent his remaining years attempting to secure a federal appointment as minister to Liberia (he was turned down, largely because of his advanced age); campaigning for John Dezendorf, a white Republican congressman in Virginia; and lecturing. He also published, in 1879, a brief and revealing work on ethnology; here he reversed the arguments of racist theorists and also maintained the pure-blooded African to be racially superior to the mulatto. In January, 1885, having returned to his family in Xenia, Ohio, the previous month, Martin R. Delany died at the age of 72.[21]

Blake; or the Huts of America represents the culmination of Delany's prewar thinking. In a sense "culmination" is a misnomer; "accumulation" being more accurate, since the novel includes bits and pieces drawn from diverse experiences dating as far back as 1840 and focuses upon specific political concerns (for instance, Southern interest in the annexation of Cuba) which were not of uniform importance to Delany throughout the antebellum period. The novel's larger, ideological concerns are more omnipresent; yet the very persistence of certain themes also indicates an accumulation of commitment toward particular stances.

Exactly when Delany began *Blake* must remain conjecture; however, the earliest date in the novel is November 29, 1852, and it is likely he began formulating his story—in mind, if not on paper—sometime late in 1852 or in 1853. At this time, Delany's short career at Harvard Medical School had run its course: he had attended the school during the fall semester of 1850 and left sometime in the winter of 1851, probably at the close of the term. In addition, his *The Condition, Elevation, Emigration, and Destiny of the Colored People of the United States, Politically Considered* had placed him at odds with most white and black abolitionists.[22] Probably the most significant factor, however, in Delany's decision to write *Blake* was Harriet Beecher Stowe's runaway success with *Uncle Tom's Cabin* in 1852. Although Delany never claimed *Blake* to be an answer to Mrs. Stowe's best seller, in theme and content, he is clearly writing the antithesis to Mrs. Stowe's picture of a mulatto hero (Delany preferring a black protagonist), slave docility, Christian endurance and Liberia as the ultimate destination of the successful fugitive slave. (This point has been recognized by Sterling A. Brown, Arthur P. Davis and Ulysses Lee in *The Negro Caravan* when they dispute Vernon Loggins' description of *The Anglo-African Magazine's* fragmentary version of *Blake* as "among the numerous analogues of *Uncle Tom's Cabin*."[23]) In addition, Delany resented Mrs. Stowe's prominence as an interpreter of the Afro-American slave experience to both whites and blacks. This resentment surfaced in the spring of 1853 in several letters to *Frederick Douglass' Paper* in which Delany criticized Mrs. Stowe for her colonizationist sentiments as well as for her prospective role in founding an Industrial School for blacks.[24] The latter proved to be abortive.

If, however, Delany began *Blake* sometime in 1852 or 1853, it is also obvious that he wrote part of the novel much later. He refers to the Dred Scott decision of 1857 at one point (although he subsequently reverts to an 1853 date). Still later in the novel there is evidence that Delany either wrote or reworked a section dealing with the African coast he had seen on his trip in 1859 and 1860. Most likely, however, Delany wrote most of the novel while in Canada from 1856 to 1859, and probably his desire for funds to finance his expedition to Africa motivated his interest in publishing *Blake* as his letter to William Lloyd Garrison suggests.

The story concerns Henrico Blacus, later to be known as Blake, a pure black West Indian who, under false pretenses, is pirated away from his home and brought as a slave (renamed Henry Holland) to the Red River region of Louisiana. There he marries another slave, Maggie, fathered by her owner, Colonel Stephen Franks. After Maggie is sold to the wife of a Northern judge who takes her to Cuba, Henry escapes from the Franks plantation and makes a whirlwind tour of the South during which he spreads his plan of unified rebellion against the Slave Power. Henry then returns to the Franks plantation and aids several slaves in escaping and in following the North Star safely to Canada. At this point, Delany veered away from what was, in part, a conventional story of the breaking-up of a slave family, escape and the long trek north. (The plotted rebellion, of course, was far from conventional.) In Part II, Henry sails to Cuba as a manservant of an American entourage, finds Maggie, and buys her freedom. Now emerging as Blake, he becomes General of a black insurrectionary force and, with the constant aid and poetic encouragement of Placido, the Cuban poet-rebel, plans the overthrow of the Cuban government and the repulsion of Americans intent upon precipitating the annexation of the island by the United States.

As a montage of personal observations and experience, contemporary political debate and incidents drawn from slave narratives, *Blake* is a much more complex (and truthful) rendering of mid-nineteenth century black experience than either *Uncle Tom's Cabin* or William Wells Brown's *Clotel.* Much of Part I (which traces Henry Holland's peregrinations through the South and Southwest) was drawn from a trip Delany made to Louisiana, Arkansas and Texas in 1839-1840. The character of Henry himself may have been inspired in part by the fourteen-year-old Jamaican boy, Alexander Hendrickure, who was kidnapped and brought to Pittsburgh where he was rescued by Delany and several other blacks in May, 1853. Finally, Delany's description of the difficulties in traveling through Ohio was also based upon personal experience. He had, on several occasions, lectured in Ohio and while in Marseilles, Ohio, as part of his tour for *The North Star* in 1848, he was mobbed, but escaped without injury.[25]

Some of the specific plot devices in *Blake* may have been drawn directly from the slave narratives. During Henry's escape from the plantation he carried a bridle enabling him to claim he was searching for his master's horse; this was almost identical to the strategem used by Henry Bibb during one of his many flights from slavery. The plotted slave revolt in the South has some similarities to a much smaller rebellion led by Lew Cheney in Louisiana in 1837 which Solomon Northrup recounts in his *Twelve Years a Slave.*[26] Moreover, the

Red River region of Louisiana, which Delany used as the locale for his intensive examination of plantation conditions, serves as an important backdrop for detailed accounts of the functioning of slavery as an institution in Northrup's and Bibb's narratives as well as Brown's *Clotel*. Other incidents in *Blake* show that Delany was well acquainted with several of the existing narratives as well as the fugitive-slave lore which circulated widely within both abolitionist circles and the abolitionist press.

It is, however, Delany's expansive treatment of Cuba which is the most unusual section of the novel and where he breaks with the more traditional abolitionist concerns. Based entirely on whatever reading about Cuban history and society he was able to do, Delany's treatment of Cuba reflects an uncanny accuracy in portraying Cuban slavery and the complex racial composition of Cuban society as well as the interrelationships between Cuban political developments and the interests of both Southern expansionists and Cuban exiles such as Narciso Lopez, who was garroted by Spanish authorities after leading an unsuccessful attack upon the western coast of Cuba in late summer of 1851. Many of Delany's own attitudes regarding the Southern threat to Cuban independence (and to the emancipation of slaves in Cuba) were outlined in a series of articles he wrote for *The North Star* in 1849. In these articles Delany recognized what he would incorporate into fictional form in *Blake*: the fear of both Southern annexationists and Cuban exiles that Spain would, by liberalizing restrictions upon blacks and concurrently restricting the freedom of slaveholders, eventually "Africanize" Cuba.[27] (The liberal policies of Captain General Juan de la Pezuela in 1854 represented to Southerners and many Cuban slaveholders the most serious of the "Africanization" threats.[28]) In *Blake,* as in his *North Star* articles, Delany turned these fears on their heads and argued that Cuban blacks should take charge of their own revolution—that is, free themselves—and implicitly suggests that a black Cuba will lead to the downfall of slavery in the United States. (Delany and many others argued a similar position concerning the prospective role of a black nation in Africa: that an independent African nation, by the demonstration of its capacity for independence and self-elevation, would lead to the eventual downfall of Southern slavery. The agent here, of course, was to be cotton: the development of an alternate source of cotton in Africa would undercut traditional dependency upon the South's cotton supply.)

Although his picture of Cuba is generally accurate in broad outlines, Delany juggled some of the details to fit his own narrative and ideological purposes. For example, his clearly didactic portrayal of the Creoles subordinating their own biases for the greater good of a black-led rebellion is at variance with the large numbers of Creoles who in actuality feared "Africanization." Moreover he uses actual events and people anachronistically to draw the dynamics of Cuban society more sharply than would otherwise be possible. Thus Placido becomes the muse of a rebellion set sometime in the 1850s, although the real poet-rebel was executed in 1844. Furthermore, Delany's treatment of Southern annexationists, Cuban exiles, and the colonial government compresses into a short period developments occurring over almost a decade.

But *Blake* is more than merely a socio-historical account of Southern slavery and Cuban society in the 1850s. It serves, as Delany obviously intended it to do, as the vehicle for the expression of a racial philosophy as radical today as it was when originally conceived. Central to the novel is a racial consciousness which is expressed in a variety of ways. First, there is Delany's antiwhite posture in which "candlefaces" and "alabasters" appear to be equivalents of contemporary "honkies" and in which Blake declares: "I am for war—war upon the whites." Equally significant is the affirmation of blackness which is expressed through the use of a pure black as the protagonist and in a persistent attack upon those mulattoes who, by following the racist practices of whites, degraded and abused pure-blooded blacks. Consequently, Delany depicts a mulatto slave-owner, discusses the antiblack practices of the mixed-blood Brown Fellowship Society of Charleston and shows on two occasions mulattoes attempting to capture Henry.[29]

Racial consciousness, however, meant more to Delany than direct and indirect affirmations of blackness. It clearly involved a self-consciousness conceived in terms of self-reliance and self-elevation. As a Cuban of mixed blood tells Placido: "I never before felt as proud of my black, as I did of my white blood. . . . How sensibly I feel, that a people never entertain proper opinions of themselves, until they begin to act for themselves." More explicitly, the slave-owner Albertis speaks in terms strikingly similar to many of Delany's pronouncements of the 1850s when he comments on the possibility of England providing aid to rebellious blacks: "The English must see that something is done before they'll recognize the doer. Until the Negro does something, the English will let him remain as he is . . ."[30]

This emphasis upon the necessity for blacks to demonstrate their independence and initiative is even more overt in Delany's treatment of religion. Reiterating ideas which he had developed earlier, Delany argues through Henry that blacks have too often confused physical and spiritual concerns, waiting for divine intervention in secular affairs rather than assuming full responsibility themselves for alleviating their condition. In discussing Southern slavery, Delany uses Henry to argue that the Christianity of the slaves is also that Christianity of the masters and shows what William Wells Brown and others also depicted: that slaveholders relied upon a bastardized form of Christianity to indoctrinate slaves with servility and docility. These religious (or antireligious) themes are maintained throughout the novel. There is, however, a certain amount of ambivalence: Henry does pray for divine guidance in time of crisis, and the necessity for religious faith is from time to time affirmed. Yet the dominant tone admonishes blacks from relying too heavily upon the religion of their masters.[31]

As Delany sees religion destroying the independence and self-reliance of blacks, he also recognizes in *Blake* the potentially crippling effects of slavery. This is not to say that he would agree with Stanley Elkins' portrayal of the "samboized," docile slave who had internalized his master's expectations. Rather, while conscious of the debilitating effects of servitude, Delany also recognizes what the historian Sterling Stuckey has recently expressed: "that slaves were able to fashion a life style and set of values—an ethos—which prevented them from being imprisoned altogether by the definitions which the larger society sought to impose."[32] In sum, Delany's portrayal of slavery in *Blake* encompasses both Nat Turner and Sambo: he is aware of the possibility of "samboization" while also perceiving the potential for rebellion within every slave.

If *Blake* speaks directly to current debates over the nature of slavery, the novel also speaks to Delany's own generation on the nature of separatism and nationalism. Although muting the emigrationist sentiments which he proclaimed frequently throughout most of the 1850s, Delany's advocacy of a black-controlled Cuba fits comfortably with the nationalistic thrust of his thought during the decade. To this extent, Delany had sharply broken with the more integrationist, antiemigrationist Afro-Americans such as Frederick Douglass who were arguing, in general, that blacks should remain in the United States and combat both slavery and Northern discrimination. Delany's stress in *Blake* on self-reliance, upon blacks' leading their own rebellions and avoiding undue dependence upon whites and white institutions, while not completely divorced from the thinking of leaders such as Douglass, does, nevertheless, sharply demonstrate the strength of his commitment to nationalism.

Yet the contours of the nationalism which he developed in his novel forcefully answer the charges of those abolitionists, black and white, who felt that Delany's emigrationist and nationalist positions marked a retreat from the struggle against oppression and degradation in the South. For while developing his nationalistic philosophy in the words and deeds of Henry/Blake and Placido, Delany's stress on slave rebellions in both the South and in Cuba points to his deep concern with the emancipation of the slaves.

Unfortunately we do not know how Delany concluded his novel—whether the rebellion in Cuba was successful and whether it spread to the Southern United States. Yet the very inconclusiveness of the novel as it now exists—the rebellion in process—is perhaps more relevant today than any ending Delany could possibly have conceived.

Notes to Introduction

1 Delany to William Lloyd Garrison, New York, February 19, 1859, William Lloyd Garrison Papers (Boston Public Library).

2 Issues of *The Weekly Anglo-African* from August 10, 1861, through April 26, 1862, are located in the Library of Congress. However, a copy of the June 7, 1862, issue in the Cornell University Library includes the second chapter of another serialized story. Presumably, then, *Blake* was concluded two weeks earlier—or May 24.

3 Hamilton asked Gerrit Smith for financial assistance in a letter from New York, January 23, 1862, Gerrit Smith Papers (Syracuse University Library). Brown's *Miralda; or, the Beautiful Quadroon* had been printed in *The Weekly Anglo-African* from November 30, 1860, through March 16, 1861. The original 1853 version, *Clotel, or, the President's Daughter,* has recently been republished by Arno Press.

4 This also has been recently reprinted by Arno Press.

5 *The Weekly Anglo-African,* January 18, 1862, p. 2.

6 Delany is one of the few nineteenth-century black figures to have received biographical treatment. See Frank A. Rollin, *pseud.* (Francis E. Rollin Whipper), *Life and Public Services of Martin R. Delany* . . . (Boston, 1868), which is helpful despite major omissions and errors. This will soon be supplanted by biographies by Victor Ullman and Dorothy Sterling, the latter for younger readers. The sketch given in the introduction is drawn from the editor's research in progress.

7 *The Voice of the Fugitive,* September 24, 1851; Delany's book is now available in an Arno Press reprint.

8 This was originally printed in the *Proceedings of the National Emigration Convention . . . at Cleveland, . . . the 24th, 25th and 26th of August, 1854* (Pittsburg, 1854), pp. 33-70, and was reprinted in *Report of the Select Committee on Emancipation and Colonization,* House Report No. 148, 37th Cong., 2d sess., Vol. IV (Washington, 1862), pp. 37-59, and in Rollin, pp. 327-367.

9 *Four Months in Liberia; or African Colonization Exposed* (Pittsburgh, 1855).

10 Although Brown apparently did not discuss specific plans at the convention, it was generally understood that a raid would be made upon the slave states. Only Delany would later maintain otherwise. Compare Delany's account in Rollin, pp. 87-88, with James Cleland Hamilton, "John Brown

in Canada," in *The Canadian Magazine*, IV (November, 1894), p. 134, and Richard J. Hinton, *John Brown and His Men* (New York, 1894), pp. 176-177, 182-185.

11 Hollis R. Lynch, "Pan-Negro Nationalism in the New World," in *Boston University Papers on Africa*, II (1966), pp. 163-171; A. H. M. Kirk-Green, "America in the Niger Valley: A Colonization Centenary," in *Phylon*, XXIII (Fall, 1962), pp. 225-239; M. R. Delany, *Official Report of the Niger Valley Exploring Party* (New York, 1861); Robert Campbell, *A Pilgrimmage to My Motherland* (New York, 1861); J. F. Ade Ajayi, *Christian Missions in Nigeria, 1841-1891* (London, 1965), pp. 191-193. Delany's and Campbell's accounts have been reprinted in a single volume, *Search for a Place; Black Separatism and Africa, 1860* (Ann Arbor, 1969); this includes an excellent introduction by Howard H. Bell.

12 At the opening session of the Congress in London in July, 1860, Delany's presence was publicly called to the attention of the American minister to England, George Dallas, by Lord Brougham, the aging British abolitionist. Delany responded to this by assuring Lord Brougham "that I am a man." Although the official American representative to the Congress withdrew, Dallas did not answer either Delany or Lord Brougham and for this he was rebuked by Secretary of State Cass. *Douglass' Monthly*, September, 1860, p. 334; Sister Therese A. Donovan, "Difficulties of a Diplomat: George Mifflin Dallas in London," in the *Pennsylvania Magazine of History and Biography*, XCLL (October, 1968), pp. 428-431.

13 Lord Alfred Churchill to William King, London, March 9, 1861, King Papers (Public Archives of Canada); *Chatham Tri-Weekly Planet*, April 8, 1861, p. 2; Ajayi, pp. 191-193.

14 Rollin, pp. 141-174; *The Anglo-African*, April 18, 1863, p. 1; May 2, 1863, p. 3; November 28, 1863, p. 2; September 10, 1864, p. 1. See also Delany's letter to Secretary of War Edwin Stanton, Chicago, December 15, 1863 (National Archives).

15 Rollin, pp. 176-301; *The Anglo-African*, March 4, 1865, p. 2; March 11, 1865, p. 2; March 18, 1865, p. 1; April 1, 1865, pp. 2,3; April 8, 1865, p. 1; *Xenia Sentinel*, March 17, 1865, p. 3.

16 *Letters and Diary of Laura M. Towne*, edited by Rupert Sargent Holland (Cambridge, 1912), p. 165; Fullerton to O. O. Howard, Hilton Head, S.C., July 20, 1865, Howard Papers (Bowdoin College Library).

17 Rollin, pp. 243-253; W. L. M. Burger, Assistant Adjutant General, to Major General Rufus Saxton, Charleston, December 21, 1865; Delany to Burger, Port Royal, S.C., March 5, 1866—Record Group 393, Department of the South (National Archives); Report of B. F. Foust, Hilton Head, S.C., October 29, 1866; Delany to Lieutenant Colonel H. W. Smith, Port Royal, October 30, 1866—Record Group 105, Bureau of Refugees, Freedmen, and Abandoned Lands, South Carolina (National Archives).

18 *New York Tribune*, August 6, 1867, p. 1; Joel Williamson, *After Slavery; The Negro in South Carolina During Reconstruction, 1861-1877* (Chapel Hill, 1965), p. 357.

19 See Delany's application to President Grant for the Liberian position, Washington, D.C., October 18, 1869, and three accompanying petitions of recommendation—all in Record Group 59 (National Archives).

20 Williamson, 353-354; D. H. Chamberlain to Delany, Columbia, S.C., March 4, 1876, Governor Chamberlain Letterbooks (South Carolina Department of Archives and History); Hampton M. Jarrell, *Wade Hampton and the Negro: The Road Not Taken* (Columbia, 1950), p. 69; *Charleston News and Courier*, April 5, 1878, p. 4; Delany to William Coppinger, Charleston, August 18, 1880, American Colonization Society Papers, 240: 130 (Library of Congress).

21 George Brown Tindall, *South Carolina Negroes, 1877-1900* (Columbia, 1952), pp. 153-168; Coppinger to Delany, Washington, D.C., March 23, 1882; Coppinger to John H. B. Latrobe, Washington, D.C., March 23, 1882—American Colonization Society Letterbooks; John E. Bruce, "Address read before Negro Academy, July 5, 1920," p. 4, Bruce Papers (Schomburg Branch, New York Public Library); Martin R. Delany, *Principia of Ethnology* . . . (Philadelphia, 1879); *Xenia Daily Gazette*, January 24, 1885.

22 William Montague Cobb, "Martin Robison Delany," in *Journal of the National Medical Association*, XLIV (May, 1952), 232-238; see, for instance, *The Pennsylvania Freeman*, April 29, 1852, p. 70.

23 Sterling A. Brown, Arthur P. Davis and Ulysses Lee, *The Negro Caravan; Writings by American Negroes* (New York, 1941), pp. 138-139; Vernon Loggins, *The Negro Author: His Development in America* (New York, 1931), pp. 185-186.

24 See *Frederick Douglass' Paper*, April 1, 1853, p. 2; April 29, 1853, p. 3; May 6, 1853, p. 3. Delany, however, had apparently revised his attitude toward Mrs. Stowe by the time *The Weekly Anglo-African* printed his entire novel because each week's offering was headed by a poem by Mrs. Stowe—one poem for all the chapters in Part I and another for the chapters in Part II.

25 Rollin, pp. 46-48; *Frederick Douglass' Paper*, June 17, 1853, p. 1; *The North Star*, July 14, 1848, pp. 2-3.

26 *Narrative of the Life and Adventures of Henry Bibb* in *Puttin' On Ole Massa*, edited by Gilbert Osofsky (New York, 1969), p. 66; Solomon Northrup, *Twelve Years a Slave* (reprint ed., Baton Rouge, La., 1968), pp. 188-189.

27 *The North Star*, April 27, 1849, p. 2; July 20, 1849, p. 3.

28 C. Stanley Urban, "The Africanization of Cuba Scare," in the *Hispanic American Historical Review*, XXXVII (February, 1957), 29-45.

29 See below, pp. 253, 290, 109-111, 70-72, 116.

30 See also, pp. 262, 184-185, below.

31 *The North Star*, March 23, 1849, p. 2; April 13, 1849, p. 2; April 20, 1849, p. 2; Delany, *The Condition, Elevation, Emigration, and Destiny of the Colored People of the United States* (Philadelphia, 1852), pp. 37-40;

William Wells Brown, *Clotel, or, the President's Daughter* (London, 1853), pp. 88-100.

32 Stanley Elkins, *Slavery; A Problem in American Institutional and Intellectual Life* (Chicago, 1959); Sterling Stuckey, "Through the Prism of Folklore: The Black Ethos in Slavery," in *The Massachusetts Review*, IX (Summer, 1968), p. 418.

PART I

By myself, the Lord of Ages,
I have sworn to right the wrong,
I have pledged my word unbroken,
For the weak against the strong.

H. Beecher Stowe

CHAPTER 1

The Project

On one of those exciting occasions during a contest for the presidency of the United States, a number of gentlemen met in the city of Baltimore. They were few in number, and appeared little concerned about the affairs of the general government. Though men of intelligence, their time and attention appeared to be entirely absorbed in an adventure of self-interest. They met for the purpose of completing arrangements for refitting the old ship "Merchantman," which then lay in the harbor near Fell's Point. Colonel Stephen Franks, Major James Armsted, Captain Richard Paul, and Captain George Royer composed those who represented the American side—Captain Juan Garcia and Captain Jose Castello, those of Cuban interest.

Here a conversation ensued upon what seemed a point of vital importance to the company; it related to the place best suited for the completion of their arrangements. The Americans insisted on Baltimore as affording the greatest facilities, and having done more for the encouragement and protection of the trade than any other known place, whilst the Cubans, on the other side, urged their objections on the ground that the continual increase of liberal principles in the various political parties, which were fast ushering into existence, made the objection beyond a controversy. Havana was contended for as a point best suited for adjusting their arrangements, and that too with many apparent reasons; but for some cause, the preference for Baltimore prevailed.

Subsequently to the adjustment of their affairs by the most complete arrangement for refitting the vessel, Colonel Franks took leave of the party for his home in the distant state of Mississippi.

CHAPTER 2

Colonel Franks at Home

On the return of Colonel Stephen Franks to his home at Natchez, he met there Mrs. Arabella, the wife of Judge Ballard, an eminent jurist of one of the Northern States. She had arrived but a day before him, on a visit to some relatives, of whom Mrs. Franks was one. The conversation, as is customary on the meeting of Americans residing in such distant latitudes, readily turned on the general policy of the country.

Mrs. Ballard possessed the highest intelligence, and Mrs. Maria Franks was among the most accomplished of Southern ladies.

"Tell me, Madam Ballard, how will the North go in the present issue?" enquired Franks.

"Give yourself no concern about that, Colonel," replied Mrs. Ballard, "you will find the North true to the country."

"What you consider true, may be false—that is, it might be true to you, and false to us," continued he.

"You do not understand me, Colonel," she rejoined, "we can have no interests separate from yours; you know the time-honored motto, 'united we stand,' and so forth, must apply to the American people under every policy in every section of the Union."

"So it should, but amidst the general clamor in the contest for ascendancy, may you not lose sight of this important point?"

"How can we? You, I'm sure, Colonel, know very well that in our country commercial interests have taken precedence of all others, which is a sufficient guarantee of our fidelity to the South."

"That may be, madam, but we are still apprehensive."

"Well, sir, we certainly do not know what more to do to give you assurance of our sincerity. We have as a plight of faith yielded Boston, New York, and Philadelphia—the intelligence and wealth of the North—in carrying out the Compromise measures for the interests of the South; can we do more?"

"True, Madam Ballard, true! I yield the controversy. You have already done more than we of the South expected. I now remember that the Judge himself tried the first case under the Act, in your city, by which the measures were tested."

"He did, sir, and if you will not consider me unwomanly by telling you, desired me, on coming here, to seek every opportunity to give the fullest assurance that the judiciary are sound on that question. Indeed, so far as an individual might be concerned, his interests in another direction—as you know—place him beyond suspicion," concluded Mrs. Ballard.

"I am satisfied, madam, and by your permission, arrest the conversation. My acknowledgements, madam!" bowed the Colonel, with true Southern courtesy.

"Maria, my dear, you look careworn; are you indisposed?" inquired Franks of his wife, who during conversation sat silent.

"Not physically, Colonel," replied she, "but——"

Just at this moment a servant, throwing open the door, announced dinner.

Besides a sprightly black boy of some ten years of age, there was in attendance a prepossessing, handsome maidservant, who generally kept, as much as the occasion would permit, behind the chair of her mistress. A mutual attachment appeared to exist between them, the maid apparently disinclined to leave the mistress, who seemed to keep her as near her person as possible.

Now and again the fat cook, Mammy Judy, would appear at the door of the dining room bearing a fresh supply for the table, who with a slight nod of the head, accompanied with an affectionate smile and the word "Maggie," indicated a tie much closer than that of mere fellow servants.

Maggie had long been the favorite maidservant of her mistress, having attained the position through merit. She was also nurse and foster mother to the two last children of Mrs. Franks, and loved them, to all appearance, as her own. The children reciprocated this affection, calling her "Mammy."

Mammy Judy, who for years had occupied this position, ceded it to her daughter; she preferring, in consequence of age, the less active life of the culinary department.

The boy Tony would frequently cast a comic look upon Mrs. Ballard, then imploringly gaze in the face of his mistress. So intent was he in this, that twice did his master admonish him by a nod of the head.

"My dear," said the Colonel, "you are dull today; pray tell me what makes you sad?"

"I am not bodily afflicted, Colonel Franks, but my spirit is heavy," she replied.

"How so? What is the matter?"

"That will be best answered at another time and place, Colonel."

Giving his head an unconscious scratch accompanied with a slight twitch of the corner of the mouth, Franks seemed to comprehend the whole of it.

On one of her Northern tours to the watering places—during a summer season some two years previous, having with her Maggie the favorite—Mrs. Franks visited the family of the Judge, at which time Mrs. Ballard first saw the maid. She was a dark mulatto of a rich, yellow, autumnlike complexion, with a matchless, cushionlike head of hair, neither straight nor curly, but handsomer than either.

Mrs. Franks was herself a handsome lady of some thirty-five summers, but ten years less in appearance, a little above medium height, between the majestic and graceful, raven-black hair, and dark, expressive eyes. Yet it often had been whispered that in beauty the maid equalled if not excelled the mistress. Her age was twenty-eight.

The conduct of Mrs. Franks toward her servant was more like that of an elder sister than a mistress, and the mistress and maid sometimes wore dresses cut from the same web of cloth. Mrs. Franks would frequently adjust the dress and see that the hair of her maid was properly arranged. This to Mrs. Ballard was as unusual as it was an objectionable sight, especially as she imagined there was an air of hauteur in her demeanor. It was then she determined to subdue her spirit.

Acting from this impulse, several times in her absence, Mrs. Ballard took occasion to administer to the maid severities she had never experienced at the hands of her mistress, giving her at one time a severe slap on the cheek, calling her an "impudent jade."

At this, Mrs. Franks, on learning, was quite surprised; but on finding that the maid gave no just cause for it, took no further notice of it, designedly evading the matter. But before leaving, Mrs. Ballard gave her no rest until she gave her the most positive assurance that she would part with the maid on her next visit to Natchez. And thus she is found pressing her suit at the residence of the Mississippi planter.

CHAPTER 3

The Fate of Maggie

After dinner Colonel Franks again pressed the inquiry concerning the disposition of his lady. At this time the maid was in the culinary department taking her dinner. The children having been served, she preferred the company of her old mother whom she loved, the children hanging around, and upon her lap. There was no servant save the boy Tony present in the parlor.

"I can't, I won't let her go! she's a dear good girl!" replied Mrs. Franks. "The children are attached to her, and so am I; let Minny or any other of them go—but do not, for Heaven's sake, tear Maggie from me!"

"Maria, my dear, you've certainly lost your balance of mind! Do try and compose yourself," admonished the Colonel. "There's certainly no disposition to do contrary to your desires; try and be a little reasonable."

"I'm sure, cousin, I see no cause for your importunity. No one that I know of designs to hurt the Negro girl. I'm sure it's not me!" impatiently remarked Mrs. Ballard.

During this, the boy had several times gone into the hall, looking toward the kitchen, then meaningly into the parlor as if something unusual were going on.

Mammy Judy becoming suspicious, went into the hall and stood close beside the parlor door, listening at the conversation.

"Cousin, if you will listen for a moment, I wish to say a word to you," said Mrs. Ballard. "The Judge, as you know, has a countryseat in Cuba near the city of Havana, where we design making every year our winter retreat. As we cannot take with us either free Negroes or white servants, on account of the existing restrictions, I must have a slave, and of course I prefer a well-trained one, as I know all yours to be. The price will be no object; as I know it will be none to you, it shall be none to me."

"I will not consent to part with her, cousin Arabella, and it is useless to press the matter any further!" emphatically replied Mrs. Franks.

"I am sure, cousin Maria, it was well understood between the Colonel and the Judge, that I was to have one of your best-trained maidservants!" continued Mrs. Ballard.

"The Colonel and the Judge! If any such understanding exist, it is without my knowledge and consent, and ——"

"It is true, my dear," interposed the Colonel, "but ——"

"Then," replied she, "heaven grant that I may go too! from——"

"Pah, pah! cousin Maria Franks, I'm really astonished at you to take on so about a Negro girl! You really appear to have lost your reason. I would not behave so for all the Negroes in Mississippi."

"My dear," said Franks, "I have been watching the conduct of that girl for some time past; she is becoming both disobedient and unruly, and as I have made it a rule of my life never to keep a disobedient servant, the sooner we part with her the better. As I never whip my servants, I do not want to depart from my rule in her case."

Maggie was true to her womanhood, and loyal to her mistress, having more than once communicated to her ears facts the sounds of which reflected no credit in his. For several repulses such as this, it was that she became obnoxious to her master.

"Cousin Maria, you certainly have forgotten; I'm sure, when last at the North, you promised in presence of the girl, that I was to have her, and I'm certain she's expecting it," explained Mrs. Ballard.

"This I admit," replied Mrs. Franks, "but you very well know, cousin Arabella, that that promise was a mere ruse, to reconcile an uneasiness which you informed me you discovered in her, after overhearing a conversation between her and some free Negroes, at Saratoga Springs."

"Well, cousin, you can do as you please," concluded Mrs. Ballard.

"Colonel, I'm weary of this conversation. What am I to expect?" enquired Mrs. Franks.

"It's a settled point, my dear, she must be sold!" decisively replied Franks.

"Then I must hereafter be disrespected by our own slaves! You know, Colonel, that I gave my word to Henry, her husband, your most worthy servant, that his wife should be here on his return. He had some misgiving that she was to be taken to Cuba before his return, when I assured him that she should be here. How can I bear to meet this poor creature, who places every confidence in what we tell him? He'll surely be frantic."

"Nonsense, cousin, nonsense," sneered Mrs. Ballard. "Frantic, indeed! Why you speak of your Negro slaves as if speaking of equals.

Make him know that whatever you order, he must be contented with."

"I'll soon settle the matter with him, should he dare show any feelings about it!" interposed Franks. "When do you look for him, Maria?"

"I'm sure, Colonel, you know more about the matter than I do. Immediately after you left, he took the horses to Baton Rouge, where at the last accounts he was waiting the conclusion of the races. Judge Dilbreath had entered them according to your request—one horse for each day's races. I look for him every day. Then there are more than him to reconcile. There's old Mammy Judy, who will run mad about her. You know, Colonel, she thought so much of her, that she might be treated tenderly the old creature gave up her situation in the house as nurse and foster mother to our children, going into the kitchen to do the harder work."

"Well, my dear, we'll detain your cousin till he comes. I'll telegraph the Judge that, if not yet left, to start him home immediately."

"Colonel, that will be still worse, to let him witness her departure; I would much rather she'd leave before his return. Poor thing!" she sighed.

"Then she may go!" replied he.

"And what of poor old mammy and his boy?"

"I'll soon settle the matter with old Judy."

Mrs. Franks looking him imploringly in the face, let drop her head, burying her face in the palms of her hands. Soon it was found necessary to place her under the care of a physician.

Old Mammy Judy had long since beckoned her daughter, where both stood in breathless silence catching every word that passed.

At the conclusion, Maggie, clasping her hands, exclaimed in suppressed tones, "O mammy, O mammy! what shall I do? O, is there no hope for me? Can't you beg master—can't you save me!"

"Look to de Laud, my chile! Him ony able to bring yeh out mo' nah conkeh!" was the prayerful advice of the woe-stricken old mother. Both, hastening into the kitchen, falling upon their knees, invoked aloud the God of the oppressed.

Hearing in that direction an unusual noise, Franks hastened past the kitchen door, dropping his head, and clearing his throat as he went along. This brought the slaves to an ordinary mood, who trembled at his approach.

CHAPTER 4

Departure of Maggie

The countryseat of Franks, or the "great house" of the cotton plantation, was but a short distance from the city. Mrs. Franks, by the advice of her physician, was removed there to avoid the disturbance of the town, when at the same time Mrs. Ballard left with her slave Maggie en route for Baltimore, whither she designed leaving her until ready to sail for Cuba.

"Fahwell, my chile! fahwell; may God A'mighty be wid you!" were the parting words of the poor old slave, who with streaming eyes gazed upon her parting child for the last time.

"O mammy! Can't you save me? O Lord, what shall I do? O my husband! O my poor child! O my! O my!" were the only words, the sounds of which died upon the breeze, as the cab hastily bore her to a steamer then lying at the wharf.

Poor old Mammy Judy sat at the kitchen door with elbows resting upon her knee, side of the face resting in the palm of the hand, tears streaming down, with a rocking motion, noticing nothing about her, but in sorrow moaning just distinctly enough to be understood: "Po' me! Po' me! Po' me!"

The sight was enough to move the heart of anyone, and it so affected Franks that he wished he had "never owned a Negro."

Daddy Joe, the husband of Mammy Judy, was a field hand on the cotton place, visiting his wife at the town residence every Saturday night. Colonel Franks was a fine, grave, senatorial-looking man, of medium height, inclined to corpulency, black hair, slightly grey, and regarded by his slaves as a good master, and religiously as one of the best of men.

On their arrival at the great house, those working nearest gathered around the carriage, among whom was Daddy Joe.

"Wat a mautta wid missus?" was the general inquiry of the gang.

"Your mistress is sick, boys," replied the master.

"Maus, whah's Margot?" enquired the old man, on seeing his mistress carried into the house without the attendance of her favorite maidservant.

"She's in town, Joe," replied Franks.

"How's Judy, seh?"

"Judy is well."

"Tank'e seh!" politely concluded the old man, with a bow, turning away in the direction of his work—with a countenance expressive of anything but satisfaction—from the interview.

The slaves, from their condition, are suspicious; any evasion or seeming design at suppressing the information sought by them frequently arouses their greatest apprehension.

Not unfrequently the mere countenance, a look, a word, or laugh of the master, is an unerring foreboding of misfortune to the slave. Ever on the watch for these things, they learn to read them with astonishing precision.

This day was Friday, and the old slave consoled himself with the thought that on the next evening he would be able to see and know for himself the true state of things about his master's residence in town. The few hours intervening were spent with great anxiety, which was even observed by his fellow slaves.

At last came Saturday evening and with it, immediately after sunset, Daddy Joe made his appearance at the hall door of the great house, tarrying only long enough to inquire "How's missus?" and receive the reply, "she's better," when a few moments found him quite out of sight, striding his way down the lane toward the road to the city.

The sudden and unexpected fate of Maggie had been noised among the slaves throughout the entire neighborhood; many who had the opportunity of doing so, repairing to the house to learn the facts.

In the lower part of the town, bordering on the river there is a depot or receptacle for the slave gangs brought by professional traders. This part of the town is known as "Natchez-under-the-Hill."[1] It is customary among the slaves when any of their number are sold, to say that they are gone "under the hill," and their common salutation through the day was that "Franks' Mag had gone under the hill."

As with quickened steps Daddy Joe approached the town, his most fearful apprehensions became terribly realized when meeting a slave who informed him that "Margot had gone under the hill." Falling upon his knees, in the fence corner, the old man raised his voice in supplication of Divine aid: "O Laud! dow has promis' in dine own wud, to be a fadah to de fadaless, an' husban to de widah! O Laud, let dy wud run an' be glorify! Sof'en de haud haut ob de presseh, an' let my po' chile cum back! an'——"

"Stop that noise there, old nigger!" ordered a patrol approaching him. "Who's boy are you?"

"Sahvant, mausta!" saluted the old slave, "I b'long to cunel Frank, seh!"

"Is this old Joe?"

"Dis is me maus Johnny."

"You had better trudge along home then, as it's likely old Judy wants to see you about this time."

"Tank'e seh," replied the old man, with a bow, feeling grateful that he was permitted to proceed.

"Devilish good, religious old Negro," he remarked to his associates, as the old man left them in the road.

A few minutes more, and Daddy Joe entered the kitchen door at his master's residence. Mammy Judy, on seeing him, gave vent afresh to bitter wailing, when the emotion became painfully mutual.

"O husban'! Husban! Onah po' chile is gone!" exclaimed the old woman, clasping him around the neck.

"Laud! dy will be done!" exclaimed he. "Ole umin, look to de Laud! as he am suffishen fah all tings"; both, falling on their knees, breathed in silence their desires to God.

"How long! How long! O Laud how long!" was the supplicating cry of the old woman being overcome with devotion and sorrow.

Taking the little grandchild in his arms, "Po' chile," said the old man, "I wish yeh had nebeh been baun!" impressing upon it kisses whilst it slept.

After a fervant and earnest prayer to God for protection to themselves, little grandson Joe, the return of his mother their only child, and blessings upon their master and the recovery of their mistress, the poor old slaves retired to rest for the evening, to forget their sorrows in the respite of sleep.

CHAPTER 5

A Vacancy

This morning the sun rose with that beauty known to a Southern sky in the last month of autumn. The day was Sabbath, and with it was ushered in every reminiscence common to the customs of that day and locality.

That she might spend the day at church for the diversion of her mind, Mrs. Franks was brought in to her city residence; and Natchez, which is usually gay, seemed more so on this day than on former occasions.

When the bells began to signal the hour of worship, the fashionable people seemed en masse to crowd the streets. The carriages ran in every direction, bearing happy hearts and cheerful faces to the various places of worship—there to lay their offerings on the altar of the Most High for the blessings they enjoyed, whilst peering over every gate, out of every alley, or every kitchen door, could be seen the faithful black servants who, staying at home to prepare them food and attend to other domestic duties, were satisfied to look smilingly upon their masters and families as they rode along, without for a moment dreaming that they had a right to worship the same God, with the same promise of life and salvation.

"God bless you, missus! Pray fah me," was the honest request of many a simplehearted slave who dared not aspire to the enjoyment of praying for himself in the Temple of the living God.

But amidst these scenes of gaiety and pleasure, there was one much devoted to her church who could not be happy that day, as there to her was a seeming vacancy which could not be filled—the seat of her favorite maidservant. The Colonel, as a husband and father, was affectionate and indulgent; but his slave had offended, disobeyed his commands, and consequently, had to be properly punished, or he be disrespected by his own servants. The will of the master being absolute, his commands should be enforced, let them be what they may, and the consequences what they would. If slavery be right, the master is justifiable in enforcing obedience to his will; deny him this, and you at once deprive him of the right to hold a slave—the one is a necessary sequence of the other. Upon this principle Colonel Franks acted, and the premise justified the conclusion.

When the carriage drove to the door, Mrs. Franks wept out most bitterly, refusing to enter because her favorite maid could not be an incumbent. Fears being entertained of seriousness in her case, it was thought advisable to let her remain quietly at home.

Daddy Joe and Mammy Judy were anxious spectators of all that transpired at the door of the mansion, and that night, on retiring to their humble bed, earnestly petitioned at the altar of Grace that the Lord would continue upon her his afflictions until their master, convinced of his wrongs, would order the return of their child.

This the Colonel would have most willingly done without the petition of Joe or Judy, but the case had gone too far, the offense was too great, and consequently there could be no reconsideration.

"Poor things," muttered Mrs. Franks in a delirium, "she served him right! And this her only offense! Yes, she was true to me!"

Little Joe, the son of Maggie, in consequence of her position to the white children—from whom her separation had been concealed—had been constantly with his grandmother, and called her "mammy." Accustomed to being without her, he was well satisfied so long as permitted to be with the old woman Judy.

So soon as her condition would permit, Mrs. Franks was returned to her countryseat to avoid the contingencies of the city.

CHAPTER 6

Henry's Return

Early on Monday morning, a steamer was heard puffing up the Mississippi. Many who reside near the river, by custom can tell the name of every approaching boat by the peculiar sound of the steampipe, the one in the present instance being the "Sultana."

Daddy Joe had risen and just leaving for the plantation, but stopped a moment to be certain.

"Hush!" admonished Mammy Judy. "Hush! Sho chile, do'n yeh heah how she hollah? Sholy dat's de wat's name! wat dat yeh call eh? 'Suckana,' wat not; sho! I ain' gwine bautha my head long so—sho! See, ole man see! Dah she come! See dat now! I tole yeh so, but yeh uden bleve me!" And the old man and woman stood for some minutes in breathless silence, although the boat must have been some five miles distant, as the escape of steam can be heard on the western waters a great way off.

The approach toward sunrise admonished Daddy Joe of demands for him at the cotton farm, when after bidding "good monin' ole umin," he hurried to the daily task which lay before him.

Mammy Judy had learned—by the boy Tony—that Henry was expected on the "Sultana," and at the approach of every steamer, her head had been thrust out of the door or window to catch a distinct sound. In motionless attitude after the departure of her husband this morning, the old woman stood awaiting the steamer, when presently the boat arrived. But then to be certain that it was the expected vessel—now came the suspense.

The old woman was soon relieved from this most disagreeable of all emotions, by the cry of newsboys returning from the wharf: " 'Ere's the 'Picayune,' 'Atlas,' 'Delta'! Lates' news from New Orleans by the swift steamer 'Sultana'!"

"Dah now!" exclaimed Mammy Judy in soliloquy. "Dah now! I tole yeh so!—de wat's name come!" Hurrying into the kitchen, she waited with anxiety the arrival of Henry.

Busying about the breakfast for herself and other servants about the house—the white members of the family all being absent—Mammy Judy for a time lost sight of the expected arrival. Soon however, a hasty footstep arrested her attention, when on looking around it proved to be Henry who came smiling up the yard.

"How'd you do, mammy! How's Mag' and the boy?" inquired he, grasping the old woman by the hand.

She burst into a flood of tears, throwing herself upon him.

"What is the matter!" exclaimed Henry. "Is Maggie dead?"

"No chile," with increased sobs she replied, "much betteh she wah."

"My God! Has she disgraced herself?"

"No chile, may be betteh she dun so, den she bin heah now an' not sole. Maus Stephen sell eh case she!—I dun'o, reckon dat's da reason."

"What!—Do you tell me, mammy, she had better disgraced herself than been sold! By the——!"

"So, Henry! yeh ain't gwine swah! hope yeh ain' gwine lose yeh 'ligion? Do'n do so; put yeh trus' in de Laud, he is suffishen fah all!"

"Don't tell me about religion! What's religion to me? My wife is sold away from me by a man who is one of the leading members of the very church to which both she and I belong! Put my trust in the Lord! I have done so all my life nearly, and of what use is it to me? My wife is sold from me just the same as if I didn't. I'll——"

"Come, come, Henry, yeh mus'n talk so; we is po' weak an' bline cretehs, an' cah see de way uh da Laud. He move' in a mystus way, his wundahs to puhfaum."

"So he may, and what is all that to me? I don't gain anything by it, and——"

"Stop, Henry, stop! Ain' de Laud bless yo' soul? Ain' he take yeh foot out de miah an' clay, an' gib yeh hope da uddah side dis vale ub teahs?"

"I'm tired looking the other side; I want a hope this side of the vale of tears. I want something on this earth as well as a promise of things in another world. I and my wife have been both robbed of our liberty, and you want me to be satisfied with a hope of heaven. I won't do any such thing; I have waited long enough on heavenly promises; I'll wait no longer. I——"

"Henry, wat de mauttah wid yeh? I neveh heah yeh talk so fo'—yeh sin in de sight ub God; yeh gone clean back, I reckon. De good Book tell us, a tousan' yeahs wid man, am but a day wid de Laud. Boy, yeh got wait de Laud own pinted time."

"Well, mammy, it is useless for me to stand here and have the same gospel preached into my ears by you, that I have all my life time heard from my enslavers. My mind is made up, my course is laid out, and if life last, I'll carry it out. I'll go out to the place today, and let them know that I have returned."

"Sho boy! What yeh gwine do, bun house down? Bettah put yeh trus' in de Laud!" concluded the old woman.

"You have too much religion, mammy, for me to tell you what I intend doing," said Henry in conclusion.

After taking up his little son, impressing on his lips and cheeks kisses for himself and tears for his mother, the intelligent slave left the abode of the careworn old woman, for that of his master at the cotton place.

Henry was a black—a pure Negro—handsome, manly and intelligent, in size comparing well with his master, but neither so fleshy nor heavy built in person. A man of good literary attainments—unknown to Colonel Franks, though he was aware he could read and write—having been educated in the West Indies, and decoyed away when young. His affection for wife and child was not excelled by Colonel Franks's for his. He was bold, determined and courageous, but always mild, gentle and courteous, though impulsive when an occasion demanded his opposition.

Going immediately to the place, he presented himself before his master. Much conversation ensued concerning the business which had been entrusted to his charge, all of which was satisfactorily transacted, and full explanations concerning the horses, but not a word was uttered concerning the fate of Maggie, the Colonel barely remarking "your mistress is unwell."

After conversing till a late hour, Henry was assigned a bed in the great house, but sleep was far from his eyes. He turned and changed upon his bed with restlessness and anxiety, impatiently awaiting a return of the morning.

CHAPTER 7

Master and Slave

Early on Tuesday morning, in obedience to his master's orders, Henry was on his way to the city to get the house in readiness for the reception of his mistress, Mrs. Franks having improved in three or four days. Mammy Judy had not yet risen when he knocked at the door.

"Hi Henry! yeh heah ready! huccum yeh git up so soon; arter some mischif I reckon? Do'n reckon yeh arter any good!" saluted Mammy Judy.

"No, mammy," replied he, "no mischief, but like a good slave such as you wish me to be, come to obey my master's will, just what you like to see."

"Sho boy! none yeh nonsens'; huccum I want yeh bey maus Stephen? Git dat nonsens' in yeh head las' night long so, I reckon! Wat dat yeh gwine do now?"

"I have come to dust and air the mansion for their reception. They have sold my wife away from me, and who else would do her work?" This reply excited the apprehension of Mammy Judy.

"Wat yeh gwine do, Henry? Yeh arter no good; yeh ain' gwine 'tack maus Stephen, is yeh?"

"What do you mean, mammy, strike him?"

"Yes! Reckon yeh ain' gwine hit 'im?"

"Curse——!"

"Henry, Henry, membeh wat ye 'fess! Fah de Laud sake, yeh ain' gwine take to swahin?" interupted the old woman.

"I make no profession, mammy. I once did believe in religion, but now I have no confidence in it. My faith has been wrecked on the stony hearts of such pretended Christians as Stephen Franks, while passing through the stormy sea of trouble and oppression! And——"

"Hay, boy! yeh is gittin high! Yeh call maussa 'Stephen'?"

"Yes, and I'll never call him 'master' again, except when compelled to do so."

"Bettah g'long ten' t' de house fo' wite folks come, an' nebeh mine talkin' 'bout fightin' 'long wid maus Stephen. Wat yeh gwine do wid white folks? Sho!"

"I don't intend to fight him, Mammy Judy, but I'll attack him concerning my wife, if the words be my last! Yes, I'll——!" and, pressing his lips to suppress the words, the outraged man turned away from the old slave mother with such feelings as only an intelligent slave could realize.

The orders of the morning were barely executed when the carriage came to the door. The bright eyes of the footboy Tony sparkled when he saw Henry approaching the carriage.

"Well, Henry! Ready for us?" enquired his master.

"Yes, sir," was the simple reply. "Mistress!" he saluted, politely bowing as he took her hand to assist her from the carriage.

"Come, Henry my man, get out the riding horses," ordered Franks after a little rest.

"Yes, sir."

A horse for the Colonel and lady each was soon in readiness at the door, but none for himself, it always having been the custom in their morning rides, for the maid and manservant to accompany the mistress and master.

"Ready, did you say?" enquired Franks on seeing but two horses standing at the stile.

"Yes, sir."

"Where's the other horse?"

"What for, sir?"

"What for? Yourself, to be sure!"

"Colonel Franks!" said Henry, looking him sternly in the face. "When I last rode that horse in company with you and lady, my wife was at my side, and I will not now go without her! Pardon me—my life for it, I won't go!"

"Not another word, you black imp!" exclaimed Franks, with an uplifted staff in a rage, "or I'll strike you down in an instant!"

"Strike away if you will, sir, I don't care—I won't go without my wife!"

"You impudent scoundrel! I'll soon put an end to your conduct! I'll put you on the auction block, and sell you to the Negro-traders."

"Just as soon as you please sir, the sooner the better, as I don' want to live with you any longer!"

"Hold your tongue, sir, or I'll cut it out of your head! You ungrateful black dog! Really, things have come to a pretty pass when I must take impudence off my own Negro! By gracious!—God forgive me for the expression—I'll sell every Negro I have first! I'll dispose of him to the hardest Negro-trader I can find!" said Franks in a rage.

"You may do your mightiest, Colonel Franks. I'm not your slave, nor never was and you know it! And but for my wife and her people, I never would have stayed with you till now. I was decoyed away when young, and then became entangled in such domestic relations as to induce me to remain with you; but now the tie is broken! I know that the odds are against me, but never mind!"

"Do you threaten me, sir! Hold your tongue, or I'll take your life instantly, you villain!"

"No, sir, I don' threaten you, Colonel Franks, but I do say that I won't be treated like a dog. You sold my wife away from me, after always promising that she should be free. And more than that, you sold her because——! And now you talk about whipping me. Shoot me, sell me, or do anything else you please, but don't lay your hands on me, as I will not suffer you to whip me!"

Running up to his chamber, Colonel Franks seized a revolver, when Mrs. Franks, grasping hold of his arm, exclaimed, "Colonel! what does all this mean?"

"Mean, my dear? It's rebellion! A plot—this is but the shadow of a cloud that's fast gathering around us! I see it plainly, I see it!" responded the Colonel, starting for the stairs.

"Stop, Colonel!" admonished his lady. "I hope you'll not be rash. For Heaven's sake, do not stain your hands in blood!"

"I do not mean to, my dear! I take this for protection!" Franks hastening down stairs, when Henry had gone into the back part of the premises.

"Dah now! Dah now!" exclaimed Mammy Judy as Henry entered the kitchen. "See wat dis gwine back done foh yeh! Bettah put yo' trus' in de Laud! Henry, yeh gone clean back t' de wuhl ghin, yeh knows it!"

"You're mistaken, Mammy; I do trust the Lord as much as ever, but I now understand him better than I use to, that's all. I dont intend to be made a fool of any longer by false preaching."

"Henry!" interrogated Daddy Joe—who, apprehending difficulties in the case, had managed to get back to the house. "Yeh gwine lose all yo' 'ligion? Wat yeh mean, boy!"

"Religion!" replied Henry rebukingly. "That's always the cry with black people. Tell me nothing about religion when the very man who hands you the bread at communion has sold your daughter away from you!"

"Den yeh 'fen' God case man 'fen' yeh! Take cah, Henry, take cah! mine wat yeh 'bout; God is lookin' at yeh, an' if yeh no' willin' trus' 'im, yeh need'n call on 'im in time o' trouble."

"I dont intend, unless He does more for me then than He has done before. 'Time of need!' If ever man needed His assistance, I'm sure I need it now."

"Yeh do'n know wat yeh need; de Laud knows bes'. On'y trus' in 'im, an' 'e bring yeh out mo' nah conkah. By de help o' God I's heah dis day, to gib yeh cumfut!"

"I have trusted in Him, Daddy Joe, all my life, as I told Mammy Judy this morning, but——"

"Ah boy, yeh's gwine back! Dat on't do Henry, dat on't do!"

"Going back from what? My oppressor's religion! If I could only get rid of his inflictions as easily as I can his religion, I would be this day a free man, when you might then talk to me about 'trusting.' "

"Dis, Henry, am one uh de ways ob de Laud; 'e fus 'flicks us an' den he bless us."

"Then it's a way I don't like."

"Mine how yeh talk, boy! 'God moves in a myst'us way His wundahs to pehfaum,' an——"

"He moves too slow for me, Daddy Joe; I'm tired waiting so——"

"Come Henry, I hab no sich talk like dat! yeh is gittin' rale weaked; yeh gwine let de debil take full 'session on yeh! Take cah boy, mine how yeh talk!"

"It is not wickedness, Daddy Joe; you don't understand these things at all. If a thousand years with us is but a day with God, do you think that I am required to wait all that time?"

"Don't, Henry, don't! De wud say 'stan' still an' see de salbation.' "

"That's no talk for me, Daddy Joe; I've been 'standing still' long enough—I'll 'stand still' no longer."

"Den yeh no call t' bey God wud? Take cah boy, take cah!"

"Yes I have, and I intend to obey it, but that part was intended for the Jews, a people long since dead. I'll obey that intended for me."

"How yeh gwine bey it?"

" 'Now is the accepted time, today is the day of salvation.' So you see, Daddy Joe, this is very different to standing still."

"Ah boy, I's feahd yeh's losen yeh 'ligion!"

"I tell you once for all, Daddy Joe, that I'm not only 'losing' but I have altogether lost my faith in the religion of my oppressors. As they are our religious teachers, my estimate of the thing they give is no greater than it is for those who give it."

With elbows upon his knees, and face resting in the palms of his hands, Daddy Joe for some time sat with his eyes steadily fixed on the floor, whilst Ailcey who for a part of the time had been an auditor to the conversation, went into the house about her domestic duties.

"Never mind, Henry! I hope it will not always be so with you. You have been kind and faithful to me and the Colonel, and I'll do anything I can for you!" sympathetically said Mrs. Franks, who, having been a concealed spectator of the interview between Henry and the old people, had just appeared before them.

Wiping away the emblems of grief which stole down his face, with a deep-toned voice upgushing from the recesses of a more than iron-pierced soul, he enquired, "Madam, what can you do! Where is my wife?" To this, Mrs. Franks gave a deep sigh. "Never mind, never mind!" continued he, "yes, I will mind, and by——!"

"O! Henry, I hope you've not taken to swearing! I do hope you will not give over to wickedness! Our afflictions should only make our faith the stronger."

" 'Wickedness.' Let the righteous correct the wicked, and the Christian condemn the sinner!"

"That is uncharitable in you, Henry! As you know I have always treated you kindly, and God forbid that I should consider myself any less than a Christian! And I claim as much at least for the Colonel, though like frail mortals he is liable to err at times."

"Madam!" said he with suppressed emotion—starting back a pace or two—"Do you think there is anything either in or out of hell so wicked, as that which Colonel Franks has done to my wife, and now about to do to me? For myself I care not—my wife!"

"Henry!" said Mrs. Franks, gently placing her hand upon his shoulder. "There is yet a hope left for you, and you will be faithful enough, I know, not to implicate any person. It is this: Mrs. Van Winter, a true friend of your race, is shortly going to Cuba on a visit, and I will arrange with her to purchase you through an agent on the day of your sale, and by that means you can get to Cuba, where probably you may be fortunate enough to get the master of your wife to become your purchaser."

"Then I have two chances!" replied Henry.

Just then Ailcey, thrusting her head in the door, requested the presence of her mistress in the parlor.

CHAPTER 8

The Sale

"Dah now, dah now!" exclaimed Mammy Judy. "Jis wat ole man been tellin' on yeh! Yeh go out yandah, yeh kick up yeh heel, git yeh head clean full proclamation an' sich like dat, an' let debil fool yeh, den go fool long wid wite folks long so, sho! Bettah go 'bout yeh bisness; been sahvin' God right, yeh no call t'do so eh reckon!"

"I don't care what comes! my course is laid out and my determination fixed, and nothing they can do can alter it. So you and Daddy

Joe, mammy, had just as well quit your preaching to me the religion you have got from your oppressors."

"Soul-driveh git yeh, yeh cah git way fom dem eh doh recken! Sho chile, yeh ain' dat mighty!" admonished Mammy Judy.

"Henry, my chile, look to de Laud! Look to de Laud! Case 'e 'lone am able t' bah us up in ouah trouble! An——"

"Go directly sir, to Captain John Harris' office and ask him to call immediately to see me at my house!" ordered Franks.

Politely bowing, Henry immediately left the premises on his errand.

"Laud a' messy maus Stephen!" exclaimed Mammy Judy, on hearing the name of John Harris the Negro-trader. "Hope yeh arteh no haum! Gwine sell all on us to de tradehs?"

"Hoot-toot, hoot-toot! Judy, give yourself no uneasiness about that till you have some cause for it. So you and Joe may rest contented, Judy," admonished Franks.

"Tank'e maus Stephen! Case ah heahn yeh tell Henry dat yeh sell de las' nig——"

"Hush, ole umin, hush! Yeh tongue too long! Put yeh trus' in de Laud!" interrupted Daddy Joe.

"I treat my black folks well," replied Franks, "and all they have to——"

Here the doorbell having been rung, he was interrupted with a message from Ailcey, that a gentleman awaited his presence in the parlor.

At the moment which the Colonel left the kitchen, Henry stepped over the stile into the yard, which at once disclosed who the gentleman was to whom the master had been summoned. Henry passed directly around and behind the house.

"See, ole man, see! Reckon 'e gwine dah now!" whispered Mammy Judy, on seeing Henry pass through the yard without going into the kitchen.

"Whah?" enquired Daddy Joe.

"Dun'o out yandah, whah 'e gwine way from wite folks!" she replied.

The interview between Franks and the trader Harris was not over half an hour duration, the trader retiring, Franks being prompt and decisive in all of his transactions, making little ceremony.

So soon as the front door was closed, Ailcey smiling bore into the kitchen a half-pint glass of brandy, saying that her master had sent it to the old people.

The old man received it with compliments to his master, pouring it into a black jug in which there was both tansy and garlic, highly recommending it as a "bitters" and certain antidote for worms, for which purpose he and the old woman took of it as long as it lasted, though neither had been troubled with that particular disease since the days of their childhood.

"Wat de gwine do wid yeh meh son?" enquired Mammy Judy as Henry entered the kitchen.

"Sell me to the soul-drivers! what else would they do?"

"Yeh gwin 'tay 'bout till de git yeh?"

"I shant move a step! and let them do their——"

"Maus wants to see yeh in da front house, Henry," interrupted Ailcey, he immediately obeying the summons.

"Heah dat now!" said mammy Judy, as Henry followed the maid out of the kitchen.

"Carry this note, sir, directly to Captain Jack Harris!" ordered Franks, handing to Henry a sealed note. Receiving it, he bowed politely, going out of the front door, directly to the slave prison of Harris.

"Eh heh! I see," said Harris on opening the note, "Colonel Frank's boy; walk in here," passing through the office into a room which proved to be the first department of the slave prison. "No common Negro, I see! You're a shade higher. A pretty deep shade too! Can read, write, cipher; a good religious fellow, and has a Christian and sir name. The devil you say! Who's your father? Can you preach?"

"I have never tried," was the only reply.

"Have you ever been a member of Congress?" continued Harris with ridicule.

To this Henry made no reply.

"Wont answer, hey! Beneath your dignity. I understand that you're of that class of gentry who dont speak to common folks! You're not quite well enough dressed for a gentleman of your cloth. Here! Mr. Henry, I'll present you with a set of ruffles: give yourself no trouble sir, as I'll dress you! I'm here for that purpose," said Harris, fastening upon the wrists of the manly bondman a heavy pair of handcuffs.

"You hurt my wrist!" admonished Henry.

"New clothing will be a little tight when first put on. Now sir!" continued the trader, taking him to the back door and pointing into the yard at the slave gang there confined. "As you have been respectably dressed, walk out and enjoy yourself among the ladies and gentlemen there; you'll find them quite a select company."

Shortly after this the sound of the bellringer's voice was heard—a sound which usually spread terror among the slaves: "Will be sold this afternoon at three o'clock by public outcry, at the slave prison of Captain John Harris, a likely choice Negro fellow, the best trained body servant in the state, trained to the business by the most accomplished lady and gentleman Negro-trainers in the Mississippi Valley. Sale positive without a proviso."

"Dah, dah! Did'n eh tell yeh so? Ole man, ole man! heah dat now! Come heah. Dat jis what I been tellin on im, but 'e uden bleve me!" ejaculated old Mammy Judy on hearing the bell ring and the handbill read.

Falling upon their knees, the two old slaves prayed fervently to God, thanking him that it was as "well with them" as it was.

"Bless de Laud! My soul is happy!" cried out Mammy Judy being overcome with devotion, clapping her hands.

"Tang God, fah wat I feels in my soul!" responded Daddy Joe.

Rising from their knees with tears trickling down their cheeks, the old slaves endeavored to ease their troubled souls by singing,

> Oh, when shall my sorrows subside,
> And when shall my troubles be ended;
> And when to the bosom of Christ be conveyed,
> To the mansions of joy and bliss;
> To the mansions of joy and bliss!

"Wuhthy to be praise! Blessed be de name uh de Laud! Po' black folks, de Laud o'ny knows sats t' come ob us!" exclaimed Mammy Judy.

"Look to de Laud ole umin, 'e's able t' bah us out mo' neh conkeh. Keep de monin' stah in sight!" advised Daddy Joe.

"Yes, ole man, yes, dat I done dis many long day, an' ah ain' gwine lose sight uh it now! No, God bein' my helpeh, I is gwine keep my eyes right on it, dat I is!"

As the hour of three drew near, many there were going in the direction of the slave prison, a large number of persons having assembled at the sale.

"Draw near, gentlemen, draw near!" cried Harris. "The hour of sale is arrived: a positive sale with no proviso, cash down, or no sale at all!" A general laugh succeeded the introduction of the auctioneer.

"Come up here my lad!" continued the auctioneer, wielding a long red rawhide. "Mount this block, stand beside me, an' let's see which is the best looking man! We have met before, but I never had the pleasure of introducing you. Gentlemen one and all, I take pleasure in introducing to you Henry—pardon me, sir—Mr. Henry Holland, I believe—am I right, sir?—Mr. Henry Holland, a good looking fellow you will admit.

"I am offered one thousand dollars; one thousand dollars for the best looking Negro in all Mississippi! If all the negro boys in the state was as good looking as him, I'd give two thousand dollars for 'em all myself!" This caused another laugh. "Who'll give me one thousand five——"

Just then a shower of rain came on.

"Gentlemen!" exclaimed the auctioneer. "Without a place can be obtained large enough to shelter the people here assembled, the sale will have to be postponed. This is a proviso we couldn't foresee, an' therefore is not responsible for it." There was another hearty laugh.

A whisper went through the crowd, when presently a gentleman came forward, saying that those concerned had kindly tendered the use of the church which stood nearby, in which to continue the sale.

"Here we are again, gentlemen! Who bids five hundred more for the likely Negro fellow? I am offered fifteen hundred dollars for the finest Negro servant in the state! Come, my boy, bestir yourself an' don't stan' there like a statute; can't you give us a jig? whistle us a song! I forgot, the Negro fellow is religious; by the by, an excellent recommendation, gentlemen. Perhaps he'll give us a sermon. Say, git up there old fellow, an' hold forth. Can't you give us a sermon on Abolition? I'm only offered fifteen hundred dollars for the likely Negro boy! Fifteen, sixteen, sixteen hundred, just agoing at—eighteen, eighteen, nineteen hundred, nineteen hundred! Just agoing at nineteen hundred dollars for the best body servant in the state; just agoing at nineteen and without a better bid I'll—— Going! Going! Go——!"

Just at this point a note was passed up the aisle to the auctioneer, who after reading it said, "Gentlemen! Circumstances beyond my control make it necessary that the sale be postponed until one day next week; the time of continuance will be duly announced," when, bowing, he left the stand.

"That's another proviso not in the original bill!" exclaimed a voice as the auctioneer left the stand, at which there were peals of laughter.

To secure himself against contingency, Harris immediately delivered Henry over to Franks.

There were present at the sale, Crow, Slider, Walker, Borbridge, Simpson, Hurst, Spangler and Williams, all noted slave traders, eager to purchase, some on their return home, and some with their gangs en route for the Southern markets.

The note handed the auctioneer read thus:

CAPT. HARRIS:—Having learned that there are private individuals at the sale, who design purchasing my Negro man, Harry, for his own personal advantage, you will peremptorily postpone the sale—making such apology as the occasion demands—and effect a private sale with Richard Crow, Esq., who offers me two thousand dollars for him. Let the boy return to me. Believe me to be,

Very Respectfully,
STEPHEN FRANKS

Capt. John Harris
   Natchez, Nov. 29th, 1852.

"Now, sir," said Franks to Henry, who had barely reached the house from the auction block, "take this pass and go to Jackson and Wood-ville, or anywhere else you wish to see your friends, so that you be back against Monday afternoon. I ordered a postponement of the sale, thinking that I would try you awhile longer, as I never had cause before to part with you. Now see if you can't be a better boy!"

Eagerly taking the note, thanking him with a low bow, turning away, Henry opened the paper, which read:

Permit the bearer my boy Henry, sometimes calling himself Henry Holland—a kind of negro pride he has—to pass and repass wherever he wants to go, he behaving himself properly.

STEPHEN FRANKS

To all whom it may concern.
   Natchez, Nov. 29th, 1852.

Carefully depositing the charte volante in his pocket wallet, Henry quietly entered the hut[2] of Mammy Judy and Daddy Joe.

CHAPTER 9

The Runaway

"De Laud's good—bless his name!" exclaimed Mammy Judy wringing her hands as Henry entered their hut. " 'e heahs de prahs ob 'is chilen. Yeh hab reason t' tang God yeh is heah dis day!"

"Yes Henry, see wat de Laud's done fah yeh. Tis true's I's heah dis day! Tang God fah dat!" added Daddy Joe.

"I think," replied he, after listening with patience to the old people, "I have reason to thank our Ailcey and Van Winter's Biddy; they, it seems to me, should have some credit in the matter."

"Sho boy, g'long whah yeh gwine! Yo' backslidin' gwine git yeh in trouble ghin eh reckon?" replied Mammy Judy.

Having heard the conversation between her mistress and Henry, Ailcey, as a secret, informed Van Winter's Derba, who informed her fellow servant Biddy, who imparted it to her acquaintance Nelly, the slave of esquire Potter, Nelly informing her mistress, who told the 'Squire, who led Franks into the secret of the whole matter.

"Mus'n blame me, Henry!" said Ailcey in an undertone. "I did'n mean de wite folks to know wat I tole Derba, nor she di'n mean it nuther, but dat devil, Pottah's Nell! us gals mean da fus time we ketch uh out, to duck uh in da rivah! She's rale wite folk's nigga, dat's jus' wat she is. Nevah mine, we'll ketch her yit!"

"I don't blame you Ailcey, nor either of Mrs. Van Winter's girls, as I know that you are my friends, neither of whom would do anything knowingly to injure me. I know Ailcey that you are a good girl, and believe you would tell me——"

"Yes Henry, I is yo' fren' an' come to tell yeh now wat da wite folks goin' to do."

"What is it Ailcey; what do you know?"

"Wy dat ugly ole devil Dick Crow—God fah gim me! But I hate 'im so, case he nothin' but po' wite man, no how—I know 'im he come from Fagina on——"

"Never mind his origin, Ailcey, tell me what you know concerning his visit in the house."

"I is goin' to, but da ugly ole devil, I hates 'im so! Maus Stephen had 'im in da pahla, an' 'e sole yeh to 'im, dat ugly ole po' wite devil, fah—God knows how much—a hole heap a money; 'two' somethin.' "

"I know what it was, two thousand dollars, for that was his selling price to Jack Harris."

"Yes, dat was da sum, Henry."

"I am satisfied as to how much he can be relied on. Even was I to take the advice of the old people here, and become reconciled to drag out a miserable life of degradation and bondage under them, I would not be permitted to do so by this man, who seeks every opportunity to crush out my lingering manhood, and reduce my free spirit to the submission of a slave. He cannot do it, I will not submit to it, and I defy his power to make me submit."

"Laus a messy, Henry, yeh free man! huccum yeh not tell me long'o? Sho boy, bettah go long whah yeh gwine, out yandah, an' not fool long wid wite folks!" said Mammy Judy with surprise, "wat bring yeh heah anyhow?"

"That's best known to myself, mammy."

"Wat make yeh keep heah so long den, dat yeh ain' gone fo' dis?"

"Your questions become rather pressing, mammy; I can't tell you that either."

"Laud, Laud, Laud! So yeh free man? Well, well, well!"

"Once for all, I now tell you old people what I never told you before, nor never expected to tell you under such circumstances; that I never intend to serve any white man again. I'll die first!"

"De Laud a' messy on my po' soul! An' huccum yeh not gone befo'?"

"Carrying out the principles and advice of you old people 'standing still, to see the salvation.' But with me, 'now is the accepted time, today is the day of salvation.' "

"Well, well, well!" sighed Mammy Judy.

"I am satisfied that I am sold, and the wretch who did it seeks to conceal his perfidy by deception. Now if ever you old people did anything in your lives, you must do it now."

"Wat dat yeh want wid us?"

"Why, if you'll go, I'll take you on Saturday night, and make our escape to a free country."

"Wat place yeh call dat?"

"Canada!" replied Henry, with emotion.

"How fah yeh gwine take me?" earnestly enquired the old woman.

"I can't just now tell the distance, probably some two or three thousand miles from here, the way we'd have to go."

"De Laus a messy on me! An' wat yeh gwine do wid little Joe; ain gwine leave 'im behine?"

"No, Mammy Judy, I'd bury him in the bottom of the river first! I intend carrying him in a bundle on my back, as the Indians carry their babies."

"Wat yeh gwine do fah money; yeh ain' gwine rob folks on de road?"

"No mammy, I'll starve first. Have you and Daddy Joe saved nothing from your black-eye peas and poultry selling for many years?"

"Ole man, how much in dat pot undeh de flo' dah; how long since yeh count it?"

"Don'o," replied Daddy Joe, "las' time ah count it, da wah faughty guinea* uh sich a mauttah, an' ah put in some six-seven guinea mo' since dat."

"Then you have some two hundred and fifty dollars in money."

"Dat do yeh?" enquired Mammy Judy.

"Yes, that of itself is enough, but——"

"Den take it an' go long whah yeh gwine; we ole folks too ole fah gwine headlong out yandah an' don'o whah we gwine. Sho boy! take de money an' g'long!" decisively replied the old woman after all her inquisitiveness.

"If you don't know, I do, mammy, and that will answer for all."

"Dat ain' gwine do us. We ole folks ain' politishon an' undestan' de graumma uh dese places, an' w'en we git dah den maybe do'n like it an cahn' git back. Sho chile, so long whah yeh gwine!"

---

*"Guinea" with the slave, is a five-dollar gold piece.

"What do you say, Daddy Joe? Whatever you have to say, must be said quick, as time with me is precious."

"We is too ole dis time a day, chile, t'go way out yauah de Laud knows whah; bettah whah we is."

"You'll not be too old to go if these whites once take a notion to sell you. What will you do then?"

"Trus' to de Laud!"

"Yes, the same old slave song—'Trust to the Lord.' Then I must go, and——"

"Ain' yeh gwine take de money, Henry?" interrupted the old woman.

"No, mammy, since you will not go, I leave it for you and Daddy Joe, as you may yet have use for it, or those may desire to use it who better understand what use to make of it than you and Daddy Joe seem willing to be instructed in."

"Den yeh 'ont have de money?"

"I thank you and Daddy most kindly, Mammy Judy, for your offer, and only refuse because I have two hundred guineas about me."

"Sho boy, yeh got all dat, no call t'want dat little we got. Whah yeh git all dat money? Do'n reckon yeh gwine tell me! Did'n steal from maus Stephen, do'n reckon?"

"No, mammy, I'm incapable of stealing from any one, but I have, from time to time, taken by littles, some of the earnings due me for more than eighteen years' service to this man Franks, which at the low rate of two hundred dollars a year, would amount to sixteen hundred dollars more than I secured, exclusive of the interest, which would have more than supplied my clothing, to say nothing of the injury done me by degrading me as a slave. 'Steal' indeed! I would that when I had an opportunity, I had taken fifty thousand instead of two. I am to understand you old people as positively declining to go, am I?"

"No, no, chile, we cahn go! We put ouh trus' in de Laud, he bring us out mo' nah conkah."

"Then from this time hence, I become a runaway. Take care of my poor boy while he's with you. When I leave the swamps, or where I'll go, will never be known to you. Should my boy be suddenly missed, and you find three notches cut in the bark of the big willow tree, on the side away from your hut, then give yourself no uneasiness; but if you don't find these notches in the tree, then I know nothing about him. Goodbye!" And Henry strode directly for the road to Woodville.

"Fahwell me son, fahwell, an' may God a'mighty go wid you! May de Laud guide an' 'tect yeh on de way!"

The child, contrary to his custom, commenced crying, desiring to see Mamma Maggie and Dadda Henry. Every effort to quiet him was unavailing. This brought sorrow to the old people's hearts and tears to their eyes, which they endeavored to soothe in a touching lamentation:

> See wives and husbands torn apart,
> Their children's screams, they grieve my heart.
>> They are torn away to Georgia!
>> Come and go along with me—
>> They are torn away to Georgia!
>> Go sound the Jubilee!

CHAPTER 10

Merry Making

The day is Saturday, a part of which is given by many liberal masters to their slaves, the afternoon being spent as a holiday, or in vending such little marketable commodities as they might by chance possess.

As a token of gratitude, it is customary in many parts of the South for the slaves to invite their masters to their entertainments. This evening presented such an occasion on the premises of Colonel Stephen Franks.

This day Mammy Judy was extremely busy, for in addition to the responsibility of the culinary department, there was her calico habit to be done up—she would not let Potter's Milly look any better than herself—and an old suit of the young master George's clothes had to be patched and darned a little before little Joe could favorably compare with Craig's Sooky's little Dick. And the cast-off linen given to her husband for the occasion might require a "little doing up."

"Wat missus sen' dis shut heah wid de bres all full dis debilment an' nonsense fah?" said Mammy Judy, holding up the garment, looking at the ruffles. "Sho! Missus mus' be crack, sen' dis heah! Ole man ain' gwine sen' he soul to de ole boy puttin' on dis debilment!" And she hastened away with the shirt, stating to her mistress her religious objections. Mrs. Franks smiled as she took the garment, telling her that the objections could be easily removed by taking off the ruffles.

"Dat look sumphen like!" remarked the old woman, when Ailcey handed her the shirt with the ruffles removed.

"Sen' dat debilment an' nonsense heah! Sho!" And carrying it away smiling, she laid it upon the bed.

The feast of the evening was such as Mammy Judy was capable of preparing when in her best humor, consisting of all the delicacies usually served up on the occasion of corn huskings in the grain-growing region.

Conscious that he was not entitled to their gratitude, Colonel Franks declined to honor the entertainment, though the invitation was a ruse to deceive him, as he had attempted to deceive them.

The evening brought with it much of life's variety, as may be seen among the slave population of the South. There were Potter's slaves, and the people of Mrs. Van Winter, also those of Major Craig, and Dr. Denny, all dressed neatly, and seemingly very happy.

Ailcey was quite the pride of the evening, in an old gauze orange dress of her mistress, and felt that she deserved to be well thought of, as proving herself the friend of Henry, the son-in-law of Daddy Joe and Mammy Judy, the heads of the entertainment. Mammy Judy and Potter's Milly were both looking matronly in their calico gowns and towlinen aprons, and Daddy Joe was the honored and observed of the party, in an old black suit with an abundance of surplus.

"He'p yeh se'f, chilen!" said Mammy Judy, after the table had been blessed by Daddy Joe. "Henry ain' gwine be heah, 'e gone to Wood-ville uh some whah dah, kick'n up 'e heel. Come, chilen, eat haughty, mo' whah dis come f'om. He'p yeh se'f now do'n——"

"I is, Aun' Judy; I likes dis heah kine a witals!" drawled out Potter's Nelse, reaching over for the fifth or sixth time. "Dis am good shaut cake!"

"O mammy, look at Jilson!" exclaimed Ailcey, as a huge, rough field hand—who refused to go to the table with the company, but sat sulkily by himself in one corner—was just walking away, with two whole "cakes" of bread under his arm.

"Wat yeh gwine do wid dat bread, Jilson?" enquired the old woman.

"I gwine eat it, dat wat I gwine do wid it! I ain' had no w'eat bread dis two hauvest!" he having come from Virginia, where such articles of food on harvest occasion were generally allowed the slave.

"Big hog, so 'e is!" rebukingly said Ailcey, when she saw that Jilson was determined in his purpose.

"Nebeh mine dat childen, plenty mo!" responded Mammy Judy.

"Ole umin, dat chile in de way dah; de gals haudly tu'n roun," suggested Daddy Joe, on seeing the pallet of little Joe crowded upon as the girls were leaving the table, seating themselves around the room.

"Ailcey, my chile, jes' run up to de hut wid 'im, 'an lay 'im in de bed; ef yeh fuhd, Van Wintah' Ben go wid yeh; ah knows 'e likes to go wid de gals," said Mammy Judy.

Taking up his hat with a bland smile, Ben obeyed orders without a demur.

The entertainment was held at the extreme end of a two-acre lot in the old slave quarters, while the hut of Mammy Judy was near the great house. Ailcey thought she espied a person retreat into the shrubbery and, startled, she went to the back door of the hut, but Ben hooted at the idea of any person out and about on such an occasion, except indeed it was Jilson with his bread. The child being carefully placed in bed, Ailcey and her protector were soon mingled with the merry slaves.

There were three persons generally quite prominent among the slaves of the neighborhood, missed on this occasion; Franks' Charles, Denny's Sam, and Potter's Andy; Sam being confined to bed by sickness.

"Ailcey, whah's Chaules—huccum 'e not heah?" enquired Mammy Judy.

"Endeed, I dun'o mammy."

"Huccum Pottah's Andy ain' heah muddah?"

"Andy a' home tonight, Aun' Judy, an' uh dun'o whah 'e is," replied Winny.

"Gone headlong out yandah, arteh no good, uh doh reckon, an' Chaules 'e gone dah too," replied the old woman.

"Da ain' nothin' mattah wid dis crowd, Aun' Judy," complimented Nelse as he sat beside Derba. At this expression Mammy Judy gave a deep sigh, on the thought of her absent daughter.

"Come, chilen," suggested Mammy Judy, "yeh all eat mighty hauty, an' been mighty merry, an' 'joy yehse'f much; we now sing praise to de Laud fah wat 'e done fah us," raising a hymn in which all earnestly joined:

Oh! Jesus, Jesus is my friend,
He'll be my helper to the end, . . .

"Young folk, yeh all bettah git ready now an' go, fo' de patrollas come out. Yeh all 'joy yeh se'f much, now time yeh gone. Hope yeh all sauv God Sunday. Ole man fo' de all gone, hab wud uh prah," advised the old woman; the following being sung in conclusion:

The Lord is here, and the Lord is all around us;
Canaan, Canaan's a very happy home—
O, glory! O, glory! O, glory! God is here,

when the gathering dispersed, the slaves going cheerfully to their homes.

"Come ole man, yeh got mautch? light sum dem shavens dah, quick. Ah cah fine de chile heah on dis bed!" said Mammy Judy, on entering the hut and feeling about in the dark for little Joe. "Ailcey, wat yeh done wid de chile?"

"E's dah, Mammy Judy, I lain 'im on de bed, ah spose 'e roll off." The shavings being lit, here was no child to be found.

"My Laud, ole man! whah's de chile? Wat dis mean! O, whah's my po' chile gone; my po' baby!" exclaimed Mammy Judy, wringing her hands in distress.

"Stay, ole 'umin! De tree! De tree!" When, going out in the dark, feeling the trunk of the willow, three notches in the bark were distinct to the touch.

"Ole 'umin!" exclaimed Daddy Joe in a suppressed voice, hastening into the hut. "It am he, it am Henry got 'im!"

"Tang God, den my po' baby safe!" responded Mammy Judy, when they raised their voices in praise of thankfulness:

'O, who's like Jesus!
Hallelujah! praise ye the Lord;
O, who's like Jesus!
Hallelujah! love and serve the Lord!'

Falling upon their knees, the old man offered an earnest, heartful prayer to God, asking his guardianship through the night, and protection through the day, especially upon their heartbroken daughter, their runaway son-in-law, and the little grandson, when the two old people retired to rest with spirits mingled with joy, sorrow, hope, and fear; Ailcey going into the great house.

CHAPTER 11

A Shadow

"Ah, boys! Here you are, true to your promise," said Henry, as he entered a covert in the thicket adjacent the cotton place, late on Sunday evening, "have you been waiting long?"

"Not very," replied Andy, "not mo' dan two-three ouahs."

"I was fearful you would not come, or if you did before me, that you would grow weary, and leave."

"Yeh no call to doubt us Henry, case yeh fine us true as ole steel!"

"I know it," answered he, "but you know, Andy, that when a slave is once sold at auction, all respect for him——"

"O pshaw! we ain' goin' to heah nothin' like dat a tall! case——"

"No!" interrupted Charles, "all you got to do Henry, is to tell we boys what you want, an' we're your men."

"That's the talk for me!"

"Well, what you doin' here?" enquired Charles.

"W'at brought yeh back from Jackson so soon?" further enquired Andy.

"How did you get word to meet me here?"

"By Ailcey; she give me the stone, an' I give it to Andy, an' we both sent one apiece back. Didn't you git 'em?"

"Yes, that's the way I knew you intended to meet me," replied Henry.

"So we thought," said Charles, "but tell us, Henry, what you want us to do."

"I suppose you know all about the sale, that they had me on the auction block, but ordered a postponement, and——"

"That's the very pint we can't understand, although I'm in the same family with you," interrupted Charles.

"But tell us Henry, what yeh doin' here?" impatiently enquired Andy.

"Yes," added Charles, "we want to know."

"Well, I'm a runaway, and from this time forth, I swear—I do it religiously—that I'll never again serve any white man living!"

"That's the pint I wanted to git at before," explained Charles, "as I can't understan' why you run away, after your release from Jack Harris, an'——"

"Nah, I nuthah!" interrupted Andy.

"It seems to me," continued Charles, "that I'd 'ave went before they 'tempted to sell me, an' that you're safer now than before they had you on the block."

"Dat's da way I look at it," responded Andy.

"The stopping of the sale was to deceive his wife, mammy, and Daddy Joe, as he had privately disposed of me to a regular soul-driver by the name of Crow."

"I knows Dick Crow," said Andy, " 'e come f'om Faginy, whah I did, da same town."

"So Ailcey said of him. Then you know him without any description from me," replied Henry.

"Yes 'n deed! an' I knows 'im to be a inhuman, mean, dead-po' white man, dat's wat I does."

"Well, I was privately sold to him for two thousand dollars, then ordered back to Franks, as though I was still his slave, and by him given a pass, and requested to go to Woodville where there were arrangements to seize me and hold me, till Crow ordered me, which was to have been on Tuesday evening. Crow is not aware of me having been given a pass; Franks gave it to deceive his wife, in case of my not returning, to make the impression that I had run away, when in reality I was sold to the trader."

"Then our people had their merrymaking all for nothin'," said Charles, "an' Franks got what 'e didn't deserve—their praise."

"No, the merrymaking was only to deceive Franks, that I might have time to get away. Daddy Joe, Mammy Judy, and Ailcey knew all about it, and proposed the feast to deceive him."

"Dat's good! Sarve 'im right, da 'sarned ole scamp!" rejoined Andy.

"It couldn't be better!" responded Charles.

"Henry uh wish we was in yo' place an' you none da wus by it," said Andy.

"Never mind, boys, give yourselves no uneasiness, as it wont be long before we'll all be together."

"You think so, Henry?" asked Charles.

"Well uh hope so, but den body can haudly 'spect it," responded Andy.

"Boys," said Henry, with great caution and much emotion, "I am now about to approach an important subject and as I have always found you true to me—and you can only be true to me by being true to yourselves—I shall not hesitate to impart it! But for Heaven's sake!—perhaps I had better not!"

"Keep nothin' back, Henry," said Charles, "as you know that we boys 'll die by our principles, that's settled!"

"Yes, I wants to die right now by mine; right heah, now!" sanctioned Andy.

"Well it is this—close, boys! close!" when they gathered in a huddle, beneath an underbush, upon their knees, "you both go with me, but not now. I——"

"Why not now?" anxiously enquired Charles.

"Dat's wat I like to know!" responded Andy.

"Stop, boys, till I explain. The plans are mine and you must allow me to know more about them than you. Just here, for once, the slave-holding preacher's advice to the black man is appropriate, 'Stand still and see the salvation.'"

"Then let us hear it, Henry," asked Charles.

"Fah God sake!" said Andy, "let us heah w'at it is, anyhow, Henry; yeh keep a body in 'spence so long, till I's mose crazy to heah it. Dat's no way!"

"You shall have it, but I approach it with caution! Nay, with fear and trembling, at the thought of what has been the fate of all previous matters of this kind. I approach it with religious fear, and hardly think us fit for the task; at least, I know I am not. But as no one has ever originated, or given us anything of the kind, I suppose I may venture."

"Tell it! tell it!" urged both in a whisper.

"Andy," said Henry, "let us have a word of prayer first!" when they bowed low, with their heads to the ground, Andy, who was a preacher of the Baptist pursuasion among his slave brethren, offering a solemn and affecting prayer, in whispers to the Most High, to give them knowledge and courage in the undertaking, and success in the effort.

Rising from their knees, Andy commenced an anthem, by which he appeared to be much affected, in the following words:

About our future destiny,
There need be none debate—
Whilst we ride on the tide,
With our Captain and his mate.

Clasping each other by the hand, standing in a band together, as a plight of their union and fidelity to each other, Henry said, "I now impart to you the secret, it is this: I have laid a scheme, and matured a plan for a general insurrection of the slaves in every state, and the successful overthrow of slavery!"

"Amen!" exclaimed Charles.

"God grant it!" responded Andy.

"Tell us, Henry, how's dis to be carried out?" enquired Andy.

"That's the thing which most concerns me, as it seems that it would be hard to do in the present ignorant state of our people in the slave States," replied Charles.

"Dat's jis wat I feah!" said Andy.

"This difficulty is obviated. It is so simple that the most stupid among the slaves will understand it as well as if he had been instructed for a year."

"What!" exclaimed Charles.

"Let's heah dat aghin!" asked Andy.

"It is so just as I told you! So simple is it that the trees of the forest or an orchard illustrate it; flocks of birds or domestic cattle, fields of corn, hemp, or sugar cane; tobacco, rice, or cotton, the whistling of the wind, rustling of the leaves, flashing of lightning, roaring of thunder, and running of streams all keep it constantly before their eyes and in their memory, so that they can't forget it if they would."

"Are we to know it now?" enquired Charles.

"I'm boun' to know it dis night befo' I goes home, 'case I been longin' fah ole Pottah dis many day, an' uh mos' think uh got 'im now!"

"Yes boys, you've to know it before we part, but——"

"That's the talk!" said Charles.

"Good nuff talk fah me!" responded Andy.

"As I was about to say, such is the character of this organization, that punishment and misery are made the instruments for its propagation, so——"

"I can't understan' that part——"

"You know nothing at all about it Charles, and you must——"

"Stan' still an' see da salvation!" interrupted Andy.

"Amen!" responded Charles.

"God help you so to do, brethren!" admonished Henry.

"Go on Henry tell us! give it to us!" they urged.

"Every blow you receive from the oppressor impresses the organization upon your mind, making it so clear that even Whitehead's Jack could understand it as well as his master."

"We are satisfied! The secret, the secret!" they importuned.

"Well then, first to prayer, and then to the organization. Andy!" said Henry, nodding to him, when they again bowed low with their heads to the ground, whilst each breathed a silent prayer, which was ended with "Amen" by Andy.

Whilst yet upon their knees, Henry imparted to them the secrets of his organization.

"O, dat's da thing!" exclaimed Andy.

"Capital, capital!" responded Charles. "What fools we was that we didn't know it long ago!"

"I is mad wid myse'f now!" said Andy.

"Well, well, well! Surely God must be in the work," continued Charles.

" 'E's heah; Heaven's nigh! Ah feels it! It's right heah!" responded Andy, placing his hand upon his chest, the tears trickling down his cheeks.

"Brethren," asked Henry, "do you understand it?"

"Understand it? Why, a child could understand, it's so easy!" replied Charles.

"Yes," added Andy, "ah not only undestan' myse'f, but wid da knowledge I has uv it, ah could make Whitehead's Jack a Moses!"

"Stand still, then, and see!" said he.

"Dat's good Bible talk!" responded Andy.

"Well, what is we to do?" enquired Charles.

"You must now go on and organize continually. It makes no difference when, nor where you are, so that the slaves are true and trustworthy, as the scheme is adapted to all times and places."

"How we gwine do Henry, 'bout gittin' da things 'mong da boys?" enquired Andy,

"All you have to do, is to find one good man or woman—I dont care which, so that they prove to be the right person—on a single plantation, and hold a seclusion and impart the secret to them, and make them the organizers for their own plantation, and they in like manner impart it to some other next to them, and so on. In this way it will spread like smallpox among them."

"Henry, you is fit fah leadah ah see," complimentingly said Andy.

"I greatly mistrust myself, brethren, but if I can't command, I can at least plan."

"Is they anything else for us to do Henry?" enquired Charles.

"Yes, a very important part of your duties has yet to be stated. I now go as a runaway, and will be suspected of lurking about in the thickets, swamps and caves; then to make the ruse complete, just as often as you think it necessary, to make a good impression, you must kill a shoat, take a lamb, pig, turkey, goose, chickens, ham of bacon from the smoke house, a loaf of bread or crock of butter from the spring house, and throw them down into the old waste well at the back of the old quarters, always leaving the heads of the fowls lying about and the blood of the larger animals. Everything that is missed dont hesitate to lay it upon me, as a runaway, it will only cause them to have the less suspicion of your having such a design."

"That's it—the very thing!" said Charles. "An it so happens that they's an ole waste well on both Franks' and Potter's places, one for both of us."

"I hope Andy, you have no religious objections to this?"

"It's a paut ah my 'ligion Henry, to do whateveh I bleve right, an' shall sholy do dis, God being my helpah!"

"Now he's talkin!" said Charles.

"You must make your religion subserve your interests, as your oppressors do theirs!" advised Henry. "They use the Scriptures to make you submit, by preaching to you the texts of 'obedience to your masters' and 'standing still to see the salavation,' and we must now begin to understand the Bible so as to make it of interest to us."

"Dat's gospel talk," sanctioned Andy. "Is da anything else yeh want tell us boss—I calls 'im boss, 'case 'e aint nothing else but 'boss'—so we can make 'ase an' git to wuck? 'case I feels like goin' at 'em now, me!"

"Having accomplished our object, I think I have done, and must leave you tomorrow."

"When shall we hear from you, Henry?" enquired Charles.

"Not until you shall see me again; when that will be, I don't know. You may see me in six months, and might not not in eighteen. I am determined, now that I am driven to it, to complete an organization in every slave state before I return, and have fixed two years as my utmost limit."

"Henry, tell me before we part, do you know anything about little Joe?" enquired Charles.

"I do!"

"Wha's da chile?" enquired Andy.

"He's safe enough, on his way to Canada!" at which Charles and Andy laughed.

"Little Joe is on 'is way to Canada?" said Andy. "Mighty young travelah!"

"Yes," replied Henry with a smile.

"You're a-joking Henry?" said Charles, enquiringly.

"I am serious, brethren," replied he. "I do not joke in matters of this kind. I smiled because of Andy's surprise."

"How did 'e go?" further enquired Andy.

"In company with his 'mother' who was waiting on her 'mistress!' " replied he quaintly.

"Eh heh!" exclaimed Andy. "I knows all 'bout it now; but whah'd da 'mammy' come from?"

"I found one!"

"Aint 'e high!" said Andy.

"Well, brethren, my time is drawing to a close," said Henry, rising to his feet.

"O!" exclaimed Andy. "Ah like to forgot, has yeh any money Henry?"

"Have either of you any?"

"We has."

"How much?"

"I got two-three hundred dollahs!" replied Andy.

"An' so has I, Henry!" added Charles.

"Then keep it, as I have two thousand dollars now around my waist, and you'll find use for all you've got, and more, as you will before long have an opportunity of testing. Keep this studiously in mind and impress it as an important part of the scheme of organization, that they must have money, if they want to get free. Money will obtain them everything necessary by which to obtain their liberty. The money is within all of their reach if they only knew it was right to take it. God told the Egyptian slaves to 'borrow from their neighbors'—meaning their oppressors—'all their jewels;' meaning to take their money and wealth wherever they could lay hands upon it, and depart from Egypt. So you must teach them to take all the money they can get from their masters, to enable them to make the strike without a failure.[3] I'll show you when we leave for the North, what money will do for you, right here in Mississippi. Bear this in mind; it is your certain passport through the white gap, as I term it."

"I means to take all ah can git; I bin doin' dat dis some time. Ev'ry time ole Pottah leave 'is money pus, I borrys some, an' e' all'as lays it on Miss Mary, but 'e think so much uh huh, dat anything she do is right wid 'im. Ef 'e 'spected me, an' Miss Mary say 'twant me, dat would be 'nough fah 'im."

"That's right!" said Henry. "I see you have been putting your own interpretation on the Scriptures, Andy, and as Charles will now have to take my place, he'll have still a much better opportunity than you, to "borrow from his master.' "

"You needn't fear, I'll make good use of my time!" replied Charles.

The slaves now fell upon their knees in silent communion, all being affected to the shedding of tears, a period being put to their devotion by a sorrowful trembling of Henry's voice singing to the following touching words:

Farewell, farewell, farewell!
My loving friends farewell!
Farewell old comrades in the cause,
I leave you here, and journey on;
And if I never more return,
Farewell, I'm bound to meet you there! [4]

"One word before we part," said Charles. "If we never should see you again, I suppose you intend to push on this scheme?"

"Yes!"

"Insurrection shall be my theme!
   My watchword 'Freedom or the grave!'
Until from Rappahannock's stream,
   To where the Cuato* waters lave,
One simultaneous war cry
   Shall burst upon the midnight air!
And rouse the tyrant but to sigh—
   Mid sadness, wailing, and despair!"

Grasping each eagerly by the hand, the tears gushing from his eyes, with an humble bow, he bid them finally "farewell!" and the runaway was off through the forest.

CHAPTER 12

The Discovery

"It can't be; I won't believe it!" said Franks at the breakfast table on Sunday morning, after hearing that little Joe was missed. "He certainly must be lost in the shrubbery."

After breakfast a thorough search was made, none being more industrious than Ailcey in hunting the little fugitive, but without success.

"When was he last seen?" enquired Franks.

"He wah put to bed las' night while we wuh at de suppeh seh!" replied Ailcey.

"There's something wrong about this thing, Mrs. Franks, and I'll be hanged if I don't ferret out the whole before I'm done with it!" said the Colonel.

"I hope you don't suspect me as——"

"Nonsense! my dear, not at all—nothing of the sort, but I do suspect respectable parties in another direction."

"Gracious, Colonel! Whom have you reference to? I'm sure I can't imagine."

"Well, well, we shall see! Ailcey, call Judy."

*A river in Cuba.

"Maus Stephen, yeh sen' fah me?" enquired the old woman, puffing and blowing.

"Yes, Judy. Do you know anything about little Joe? I want you to tell me the truth!" sternly enquired Franks.

"Maus Stephen! I cah lie! so long as yeh had me, yu nah missus neveh knows me tell lie. No, bless de Laud! Ah sen' my soul to de ole boy dat way? No maus Stephen, ah uhdn give wat I feels in my soul——"

"Well never mind, Judy, about your soul, but tell us about——"

"Ah! maus Stephen, ah 'spects to shout wen de wul's on fiah! an——"

"Tell us about the boy, Judy, and we'll hear about your religion another time."

"If you give her a little time, Colonel, I think she'll be able to tell about him!" suggested Mrs. Franks on seeing the old woman weeping.

"Sho, mammy!" said Ailcey in a whisper with a nudge, standing behind her, "wat yeh stan' heah cryin' befo' dese ole wite folks fah!"

"Come, come, Judy! what are you crying about! let us hear quickly what you've got to say. Don't be frightened!"

"No maus Stephen, I's not feahed; ah could run tru troop a hosses an' face de debil! My soul's happy, my soul's on fiah! Whoo! Blessed Jesus! Ride on, King!" when the old woman tossed and tumbled about so dexterously, that the master and mistress considered themselves lucky in getting out of the way.

"The old thing's crazy! We'll not be able to get anything out of her, Mrs. Franks."

"No maus Stephen, blessed be God a'mighty! I's not crazy, but sobeh as a judge! An——"

"Then let us hear about little Joe, as you can understand so well what is said around you, and let us have no more of your whooping and nonsense, distracting the neighborhood!"

"Blessed God! Blessed God! Laud sen' a nudah gale! O, fah a nudah showeh!"

"I really believe she's crazy! We've now been here over an hour, and no nearer the information than before."

"I think she's better now!" said Mrs. Franks.

"Judy, can you compose yourself long enough to answer my questions?" enquired Franks.

"O yes, mausta! ah knows wat I's 'bout, but w'en mausta Jesus calls, ebry body mus' stan' back, case 'e's 'bove all!"

"That's all right, Judy, all right; but let us hear about little Joe—do you know anything about him, where he is, or how he was taken away?"

" 'E wah dah Sattiday night, maus Stephen."

"What time, Judy, on Saturday evening was he there?"

"W'en da wah eatin suppeh, seh."

"How do you know, when you were at the lower quarters, and he in your hut?"

" 'E wah put to bed den."

"Who put him to bed—you?"

"No, seh, Ailcey."

"Ailcey—who went with her, any one?"

"Yes seh, Van Wintah Ben went wid uh."

"Van Winter's Ben! I thought we'd get at the thieves presently; I knew I'd ferret it out! Well now, Judy, I ask you as a Christian, and expect you to act with me as one Christian with another—has not Mrs. Van Winter been talking to you about this boy?"

"No seh, nebeh!"

"Nor to Henry?"

"No seh!"

"Did not she, to your knowledge, send Ben there that night to steal away little Joe?"

"No, seh!"

"Did you not hear Ailcey tell some one, or talking in her sleep, say that Mrs. Van Winter had something to do with the abduction of that boy?"

"Maus Stephen, ah do'n undehstan' dat duckin uh duckshun, dat w'at yeh call it—dat big wud!"

"O! 'abduction' means stealing away a person, Judy."

"Case ah waun gwine tell nothin 'bout it."

"Well, what do you know, Judy?"

"As dah's wud a troof in me, ah knows nothin' 'bout it."

"Well, Judy, you can go now. She's an honest old creature, I believe!" said Franks, as the old fat cook turned away.

"Yes, poor old black fat thing! She's religious to a fault," replied Mrs. Franks.

"Well, Ailcey, what do you know about it?" enquired the master.

"Nothin' seh, o'ny Mammy Judy ask me toat 'im up to da hut an' put 'im in bed."

"Well, did you do it?"

"Yes, seh!"

"Did Ben go with you?"

"Yes, seh!"

"Did he return with you to the lower quarters?"

"Yes, seh!"

"Did he not go back again, or did he remain in the house?"

" 'E stay in."

"Did you not see some one lurking about the house when you took the boy up to the hut?"

"Ah tot ah heahn some un in da bushes, but Ben say 'twan no one."

"Now Ailcey, don't you know who that was?"

"No, seh!"

"Was'nt it old Joe?"

"No, seh, lef' 'im in de low quahteh."

"Was it Henry?"

"Dun no, seh!"

"Wasn't it Mrs. Van Winter's——"

"Why Colonel!" exclaimed Mrs. Franks with surprise.

"Negroes, I mean! You didn't let me finish the sentence, my dear!" explained he, correcting his error.

"Ah dun'o, seh!"

"Now tell me candidly, my girl, who and what you thought it was at the time?"

"Ah do'n like to tell!" replied the girl, looking down.

"Tell, Ailcey! Who do you think it was, and what they were after?" enquired Mrs. Franks.

"Ah do'n waun tell, missus!"

"Tell, you goose you! did you see any one?" continued Franks.

"Ah jis glance 'em."

"Was the person close to you?" further enquired Mrs. Franks.

"Yes, um, da toched me on da shouldeh an' run."

"Well, why don't you tell then, Ailcey, who you thought it was, and what they were after, you stubborn jade you, speak!" stormed Franks, stamping his foot.

"Don't get out of temper, Colonel! make some allowance for her under the circumstances. Now tell, Ailcey, what you thought at the time?" mildly asked Mrs. Franks.

"Ah tho't t'wah maus Stephen afteh me."

"Well, if you know nothing about it, you may go now!" gruffly replied her master. "These Negroes are not to be trusted. They will endeavor to screen each other if they have the least chance to do so. I'll sell that girl!"

"Colonel, don't be hasty in this matter, I beg of you!" said Mrs. Franks earnestly.

"I mean to let her go to the man she most hates, that's Crow."

"Why do you think she hates Crow so badly?"

"By the side looks she gives him when he comes into the house."

"I pray you then, Colonel, to attempt no more auction sales, and you may avoid unpleasant association in that direction."

"Yes, by the by, speaking of the auction, I really believe Mrs. Van Winter had something to do with the abduction of that little Negro."

"I think you do her wrong, Colonel Franks; she's our friend, and aside from this, I don't think her capable of such a thing."

"Such friendship is worse than open enmity, my dear, and should be studiously shunned."

"I must acquit her, Colonel, of all agency in this matter."

"Well, mark what I tell you, Mrs. Franks, you'll yet hear more of it, and that too at no distant day."

"Well it may be, but I can't think so."

"May be!" I'm sure so. And more: I believe that boy has been induced to take advantage of my clemency, and run away. I'll make an example of him, because what one Negro succeeds in doing, another will attempt. I'll have him at any cost. Let him go on this way and there won't be a Negro in the neighborhood presently."

"Whom do you mean, Colonel?"

"I mean that ingrate Henry, that's who."

"Henry gone!"

"I have no doubt of it at all, as he had a pass to Woodville and Jackson; and now that the boy is stolen by someone, I've no doubt himself. I might have had some leniency towards him had he not committed a theft, a crime of all others the most detestable in my estimation."

"And Henry is really gone?" with surprise again enquired Mrs. Franks.

"He is, my dear, and you appear to be quite inquisitive about it!" remarked Franks as he thought he observed a concealed smile upon her lips.

"I am inquisitive, Colonel, because whatever interests you should interest me."

"By Monday evening, hanged if I don't know all about this thing. Ailcey, call Charles to get my saddle horse!"

"Charles ain' heah, maus Stephen."

"Where's old Joe?"

"At de hut, seh."

"Tell him to saddle Oscar immediately, and bring him to the door."

"Yes, seh!" replied the girl, lightly tripping away.

The horse was soon at the door, and with his rider cantering away.

"Tony, what is Mammy Judy about?" enquired Mrs. Franks as evening approached.

"She's sif'en meal, missus, to make mush fah ouah suppah."

"You must tell mammy not to forget me, Tony, in the distribution of her mush and milk."

"Yes, missus, ah tell uh right now!" when away ran Tony bearing the message, eager as are all children to be the agents of an act of kindness.

Mammy Judy, smiling, received the message with the assurance of "Yes, dat she shall hab much as she want!" when, turning about, she gave strict orders that Ailcey neglect not to have a china bowl in readiness to receive the first installment of the hasty pudding.

The hut of Mammy Judy served as a sort of headquarters on Saturday and Sunday evenings for the slaves from the plantation, and those in town belonging to the "estate," who this evening enjoyed a hearty laugh at the expense of Daddy Joe.

Slaves are not generally supplied with light in their huts; consequently, except from the fat of their meat and that gathered about the kitchen with which they make a "lamp," and the use of pinewood tapers, they eat and do everything about their dwellings in the dark.

Hasty pudding for the evening being the bill of fare, all sat patiently awaiting the summon of Mammy Judy, some on blocks, some on logs of wood, some on slab benches, some on inverted buckets and half-barrel wash tubs, and whatever was convenient, while many of the girls and other young people were seated on the floor around against the wall.

"Hush, chilen!" admonished Mammy Judy, after carefully seeing that each one down to Tony had been served with a quota from the kettle.

"Laud, make us truly tankful fah wat we 'bout to 'ceive!" petitioned Daddy Joe with uplifted hands. "Top dah wid yo' nause an' nonsense ole people cah heah deh yeahs to eat!" admonished the old man as he took the pewter dish between his knees and commenced an earnest discussion of its contents. "Do'n yeh heah me say hush dah? Do'n yeh heah!"

"Joe!" was the authoritative voice from without.

"Sah!"

"Take my horse to the stable!"

"Yes, sah!" responded the old man, sitting down his bowl of mush and milk on the hearth in the corner of the jam. "Do'n any on yeh toch dat, yeh heah?"

"We ain gwine to, Daddy Joe," replied the young people.

"Huccum de young folks, gwine eat yo' mush and milk? Sho, ole man, g'long whah yeh gwine, ad' let young folk 'lone!" retorted Mammy Judy.

On returning from the stable, in his hurry the old man took up the bowl of a young man who sat it on his stool for the moment.

"Yoheh, Daddy Joe, dat my mush!" said the young man.

"Huccum dis yone?" replied the old man.

"Wy, ah put it dah; yeh put yone in de chimbly connoh."

"Ah! Dat eh did!" exclaimed he, taking up the bowl eating heartily. "Wat dat yeh all been doin' heah? Some on yeh young folks been prankin' long wid dis mush an' milk!" continued the old man, champing and chewing in a manner which indicated something more solid than mush and milk.

"Deed we did'n, Daddy Joe; did'n do nothin' to yo' mush an' milk, so we did'n!" replied Ailcey, whose word was always sufficient with the old people.

"Hi, what dis in heah! Sumpen mighty crisp!" said Daddy Joe, still eating heartily and now and again blowing something from his mouth like coarse meal husks. "Sumpen heah mighty crisp, ah tells yeh! Ole umin, light dat pine knot dah; so dahk yeh cah'n see to talk. Git light dah quick ole umin! Sumpen heah mighty crisp in dis mush an' milk!—Mighty crisp!"

"Good Laud! see dah now! Ah tole yeh so!" exclaimed Mammy Judy when, on producing a light, the bowl was found to be partially filled with large black house roaches.

"Reckon Daddy Joe do'n tank'im fah dat!" said little Tony, referring to the blessing of the old man; amidst an outburst of tittering and snickering among the young people.

Daddy Joe lost his supper, when the slaves retired for the evening.

CHAPTER 13

Perplexity

Early on Monday morning Colonel Franks arose to start for Woodville and Jackson in search of the fugitive.

"My dear, is Ailcey up? Please call Tony," said Mrs. Franks, the boy soon appearing before his mistress. "Tony, call Ailcey," continued she, "your master is up and going to the country."

"Missus Ailcey ain' dah!" replied the boy, returning in haste from the nursery.

"Certainly she is; did you go into the nursery?"

"Yes, um!"

"Are the children there?"

"Yes, um, boph on 'em."

"Then she can't be far—she'll be in presently."

"Missus, she ain' come yit," repeated the boy after a short absence.

"Did you look in the nursery again?"

"Yes, um!"

"Are the children still in bed?"

"Yes, um, boph sleep, only maus George awake."

"You mean one asleep and the other awake!" said Mrs. Franks, smiling.

"Yes um boph wake!" replied the boy.

"Didn't you tell me, Tony, that your master George only was awake?" asked the mistress.

"Miss Matha sleep fus, den she wake up and talk to maus George," explained the boy, his master laughing, declared that a Negro's skull was too thick to comprehend anything.

"Don't mistake yourself, Colonel!" replied Mrs. Franks. "That boy is anything but a blockhead, mind that!"

"My dear, can't you see something about that girl?" said the Colonel.

"Run quickly, Tony, and see if Ailcey is in the hut," bade Mrs. Franks.

"Dear me," continued she, "since the missing of little Joe, she's all gossip, and we needn't expect much of her until the thing has died away."

"She'll not gossip after today, my dear!" replied the Colonel decisively, "as I'm determined to put her in my pocket in time, before she is decoyed away by that ungrateful wretch, who is doubtless ready for anything, however vile, for revenge."

Ailcey was a handsome black girl, graceful and intelligent, but having been raised on the place, had not the opportunity of a house maid for refinement. The Colonel, having had a favorable opinion of her as a servant, frequently requested that she be taken from the field, long before it had been done. This had not the most favorable impression upon the mind of his lady, who since the morning of the interview, the day before, had completely turned against the girl.

Mrs. Franks was an amiable lady and lenient mistress, but did a slave offend, she might be expected to act as a mistress; and still more, she was a woman; but concerning Ailcey she was mistaken, as a better and more pure-hearted female slave there was not to be found; and as true to her mistress and her honor, as was Maggie herself.

"Missus, she ain't dare nudder! aun' Judy ain seed 'er from las' night!" said the boy who came running up the stairs.

"Then call Charles immediately!" ordered she; when away went he and shortly came Charles.

"Servant, mist'ess!" saluted Charles, as he entered her presence.

"Charles, do you know anything of Ailcey?" enquired she.

"No mist'ess I don't."

"When did you see her last?"

"Last night, ma'm."

"Was she in company with anyone?"

"Yes ma'm, Potter's Rachel."

"What time in the evening was it, Charles?"

"After seven o'clock, ma'm."

"O, she was home after that and went to bed in the nursery, where she has been sleeping for several nights."

"My dear, this thing must be probed to the bottom at once! things are taking such a strange course, that we don't know whom to trust. I'll be hanged if I understand it!" The carriage being ordered, they went directly down to 'squire Potter's.

"Good morning Mrs. Potter!—you will pardon us for the intrusion at so early an hour, but as the errand may concern us all, I'll not stop to be ceremonious—do I find the 'squire in?"

The answer being in the affirmative, a servant being in attendance, the old gentleman soon made his appearance.

"Good morning, Colonel and Madam Franks!" saluted he.

"Good morning, 'squire! I shan't be ceremonious, and to give you a history of my errand, and to make a short story of a long one, we'll 'make a lump job of it,' to use a homely phrase."

"I know the 'squire will be interested!" added Mrs. Franks.

"No doubt of it at all, ma'm!" replied Mrs. Potter, who seemed to anticipate them.

"It is this," resumed the Colonel. "On Friday I gave my boy Henry verbal permission to go to the country, when he pretended to leave. On Saturday evening during the Negro-gathering at the old quarters, my little Negro boy Joe was stolen away, and on last evening, our Negro girl Ailcey the nurse, cleared out, and it seems was last seen in company with your Negro girl Rachel."

"Titus, call Rachel there! No doubt but white men are at the bottom of it," said Potter.

"Missus, heah I is!" drawled the girl awkwardly, with a curtsy.

"Speak to your master there; he wants you," ordered Mrs. Potter.

"Mausta!" saluted the girl.

"Rachel, my girl, I want you to tell me, were you with Colonel Franks' black girl Ailcey on last evening?"

"Yes seh, I wah."

"Where, Rachel?" continued the master.

"Heah seh, at ouah house."

"Where did you go to?"

"We go down to docteh Denny."

"What for—what took you down to Dr. Denny's, Rachel?"

"Went 'long wid Ailcey."

"What did Ailcey go there for—do you know?"

"Went dah to see Craig' Polly."

"Craig's Polly, which of Mr. Craig's Negro girls is that?"

"Dat un w'ot mos' white."

"Well, was Polly there?"

"She waun dah w'en we go, but she soon come."

"Why did you go to Dr. Denny's to meet Polly?"

"Ailcey say Polly go'n to meet uh dah."

"Well, did they leave there when you did?"

"Yes, seh."

"Where did you go to then?"

"I come home, seh."

"Where did they go?"

"Da say da go'n down undah da Hill."

"Who else was with them besides you?"

"No un, seh."

"Was there no man with them, when they left for under the Hill?"

"No, seh."

"Did you see no man about at all, Rachel?"

"No, seh."

"Now don't be afraid to tell: was there no white person at all spoke to you when together last night?"

"None but some white gent'men come up an' want walk wid us, same like da al'as do we black girls w'en we go out."

"Did the girls seem to be acquainted and glad to see them?"

"No seh, the girls run, and da gent'men cus——"

"Never mind that, Rachel, you can go now," concluded her master.

"Well, 'squire, hanged if this thing mus'nt be stopped! Four slaves in less than that many days gone from under our very eyes, and we unable to detect them! It's insufferable, and I believe whites to be at the head of it! I have my suspicions on a party who stands high in the community, and——"

"Now Colonel, if you please!" interrupted Mrs. Franks.

"Well, I suppose we'll have for the present to pass that by," replied he.

"Indeed, something really should be done!" said the 'squire.

"Yes, and that quickly, if we would keep our Negroes to prevent us from starving."

"I think the thing should at once be seen into; what say you, Colonel?"

"As I have several miles to ride this morning," said Franks, looking at his watch, it now being past nine o'clock, "I must leave so as to be back in the evening. Any steps that may be taken before my return, you have the free use of my name. Good morning!"

A few minutes and the Colonel was at his own door, astride of a horse, and on his way to Woodville.

CHAPTER 14

Gad and Gossip

This day the hut of Mammy Judy seemed to be the licensed resort for all the slaves of the town; and even many whites were seen occasionally to drop in and out, as they passed along. Everyone knew the residence of Colonel Franks, and many of the dusky inhabitants of the place were solely indebted to the purse-proud occupants of the "great house" for their introduction to that part of Mississippi.

For years he and Major Armsted were the only reliable traders upon whom could be depended for a choice gang of field Negroes and other marketable people. And not only this section, but the whole Mississippi Valley to some extent was to them indebted. First as young men the agents of Woolford, in maturer age their names became as household words and known as the great proprietary Mississippi or Georgia Negro-traders.

Domestic service seemed for the time suspended, and little required at home to do, as the day was spent as a kind of gala-day, in going about from place to place talking of everything.

Among the foremost of these was Mammy Judy, for although she partially did, and was expected to stay and be at home today, and act as an oracle, yet she merely stole a little time to run over to Mrs. Van Winter's, step in at 'squire Potter's to speak a word to Milly, drop by Dr. Denny's, and just poke in her head at Craig's a moment.

"Ah been tellin' on 'em so! All along ah been tellin' on 'em, but da uden bleve me!" soliloquized Mammy Judy, when the first dash of news through the boy Tony reached her, that Ailcey had gone and taken with her some of 'squire Potter's people, several of Dr. Denny's, a gang of Craig's, and half of Van Winter's. "Dat jis wat ah been tellin' on 'em all along, but da uden bleve me!" concluded she.

"Yeah heah de news!" exclaimed Potter's Minney to Van Winter's Biddy.

"I heah dat Ailcey gone!" replied Biddy.

"Dat all; no mo?" enquired the girl with a high turban of Madras on her head.

"I heahn little Joe go too!"

"Didn yeh heah dot Denny' Sookey, an' Craig' Polly, took a whole heap uh Potteh' people an' clah'd out wid two po' white mens, an' dat da all seen comin' out Van Winteh de old ablish'neh, soon in de monin' fo' day?"

"No!" replied the good-natured, simple-hearted Biddy, "I did'n!"

"Yes, sho's yeh baun dat true, case uhly dis monin' cunel Frank' an' lady come see mausta—and yeh know 'e squiah an' make de law—an' mauster ghin 'em papehs, an' da go arter de Judge to put heh in jail!"

"Take who to jail?"

"Wy, dat ole ablish'neh, Miss Van Winteh! Ah wish da all dead, dese ole ablish'nehs, case da steal us an' sell us down souph to haud maustas, w'en we got good places. Any how she go'n to jail, an' I's glad!"

Looking seriously at her, Biddy gave a long sigh, saying nothing to commit herself, but going home, communicated directly to her mistress that which she heard, as Mrs. Van Winter was by all regarded as a friend to the Negro race, and at that time the subject of strong suspicion among the slaveholders of the neighborhood.

Eager to gad and gossip, from place to place the girl Minney passed about relating the same to each and all with whom she chanced to converse, they imparting to others the same strange story, until reaching the ears of intelligent whites who had heard no other version, it spread through the city as a statement of fact.

Learning as many did by sending to the house, that the Colonel that day had gone in search of his slaves, the statement was confirmed as having come from Mrs. Franks, who was known to be a firm friend of Mrs. Van Winter.

"Upon my word!" said Captain Grason on meeting Sheriff Hughes. "Sheriff, things are coming to a pretty pass!"

"What's that, Captain?" enquired the Sheriff.

"Have you not heard the news yet, concerning the Negroes?"

"Why, no! I've been away to Vicksburg the last ten days, and just getting back."

"O, Heavens! we're no longer safe in our own houses. Why, sir, we're about being overwhelmed by an infamous class of persons who live in our midst, and eat at our tables!"

"You surprise me, Captain! what's the matter?"

"Sir, it would take a week to relate the particulars, but our slaves are running off by wholesale. On Sunday night a parcel of Colonel Franks' Negroes left, a lot of Dr. Denny's, some of 'squire Potter's, and a gang of Craig's, aided by white men, whom together with the Negroes were seen before day in the morning coming out of the widow Van Winters, who was afterwards arrested, and since taken before the judge on a writ of habeas corpus, but the circumstances against her being so strong she was remanded for trial, which so far strengthens the accusation. I know not where this thing will end!"

"Surprising indeed, sir!" replied Hughes. "I had not heard of it before, but shall immediately repair to her house, and learn all the facts in the case. I am well acquainted with Mrs. Van Winter—in fact she is a relation of my wife—and must hasten. Good day, sir!"

On ringing the bell, a quick step brought a person to the door, when on being opened, the Sheriff found himself in the warm embraces of the kind-hearted and affectionate Mrs. Van Winter herself.

After the usual civilities, she was the first to introduce the subject, informing him of their loss by their mutual friends Colonel Franks and lady, with others, and no surprise was greater than that on hearing the story current concerning herself.

Mammy Judy was as busy as she well could be, in hearing and telling news among the slaves who continually came and went through the day. So overwhelmed with excitement was she, that she had little else to say in making a period, then "All a long ah been tellin' on yeh so, but yeh uden bleve me!"

Among the many who thronged the hut was Potter's Milly. She in person is black, stout and fat, bearing a striking resemblance to the matronly old occupant Mammy Judy. For two hours or more letting a number come in, gossip, and pass out, only to be immediately succeeded by another; who like the old country woman who for the first time in visiting London all day stood upon the sidewalk of the principal thoroughfare waiting till the crowd of people and cavalcade of vehicles passed, before she made the attempt to cross the street; she sat waiting till a moment would occur by which in private to impart a secret to her friend alone. That moment did at last arrive.

"Judy!" said the old woman in a whisper. "Ah been waitin' all day long to see yeh fah sumpen' ticlar!"

"W'at dat, Milly?" whispered Mammy Judy scarcely above her breath.

"I's gwine too!" and she hurried away to prepare supper for the white folks, before they missed her, though she had been absent full two hours and a half, another thirty minutes being required for the fat old woman to reach the house.

"Heah dat now!" whispered Mammy Judy. "Ah tole yeh so!"

"Well, my dear, not a word of that graceless dog, the little Negro, nor that girl," said Franks who had just returned from the country, "but I am fully compensated for the disappointment, on learning of the arrest and imprisonment of that——!"

"Who, Colonel?" interrupted his wife.

"I hope after this you'll be willing to set some estimation on my judgment—I mean your friend Mrs. Van Winter the abolitionist!"

"I beg your pardon, Colonel, as nothing is farther from the truth! From whom did you receive that intelligence?"

"I met Captain Grason on his way to Woodville, who informed me that it was current in town, and you had corroborated the statement. Did you see him?"

"Nothing of the kind, sir, and it has not been more than half an hour since Mrs. Van Winter left here, who heartily sympathizes with us, though she has her strange notions that black people have as much right to freedom as white."

"Well, my dear, we'll drop the subject!" concluded the Colonel with much apparent disappointment.

The leading gentlemen of the town and neighborhood assembled inaugurating the strictest vigilant police regulations, when after free and frequent potations of brandy and water, of which there was no scarcity about the Colonel's mansion, the company separated, being much higher spirited, if not better satisfied, than when they met in council.

This evening Charles and Andy met each other in the street, but in consequence of the strict injunction on the slaves by the patrol law recently instituted, they only made signs as they passed, intending to meet at a designated point. But the patrol reconnoitred so closely in their track, they were driven entirely from their purpose, retiring to their homes for the night.

CHAPTER 15

Interchange of Opinion

The landing of a steamer on her downward trip brought Judge Ballard and Major Armsted to Natchez. The Judge had come to examine the country, purchase a cotton farm, and complete the arrangements of an interest in the "Merchantman." Already the proprietor of a large estate in Cuba, he was desirous of possessing a Mississippi cotton place. Disappointed by the absence of his wife abroad, he was satisfied to know that her object was accomplished.

Major Armsted was a man of ripe intelligence, acquired by years of rigid experience and close observation, rather than literary culture, though his educational attainments as a business man were quite respectable. He for years had been the partner in business with Colonel Stephen Franks. In Baltimore, Washington City, Annapolis, Richmond, Norfolk, Charlestown, and Winchester, Virginia, a prison or receptacle for coffle-gangs of slaves purchased and sold in the market, comprised their principal places of business in the slave-growing states of the Union.

The Major was a great jester, full of humor, and fond of a good joke, ever ready to give and take such even from a slave. A great common sense man, by strict attention to men and things, and general observation, had become a philosopher among his fellows.

"Quite happy to meet you, Judge, in these parts!" greeted Franks. "Wonder you could find your way so far south, especially at such a period, these being election times!"

"Don't matter a bit, as he's not up for anything I believe just now, except for Negro-trading! And in that he is quite a proselyte, and heretic to the teachings of his Northern faith!" jocosely remarked Armsted.

"Don't mistake me, gentlemen, because it was the incident of my life to be born in a nonslaveholding state. I'm certain that I am not at all understood as I should be on this question!" earnestly replied the Judge.

"The North has given you a bad name, Judge, and it's difficult to separate yourself now from it, holding the position that you do, as one of her ablest jurists," said Armsted.

"Well, gentlemen!" seriously replied the Judge. "As regards my opinion of Negro slavery, the circumstances which brought me here, my large interest and responsibility in the slave-labor products of Cuba, should be, I think, sufficient evidence of my fidelity to Southern principles, to say nothing of my official records, which modesty should forbid my reference to."

"Certainly, certainly, Judge! The Colonel is at fault. He has lost sight of the fact that you it was who seized the first runaway Negro by the throat and held him by the compromise grasp until we Southern gentlemen sent for him and had him brought back!"

"Good, good, by hookie!" replied the Colonel, rubbing his hands together.

"I hope I'm understood, gentlemen!" seriously remarked the Judge.

"I think so, Judge, I think so!" replied Armsted, evidently designing a full commitment on the part of the Judge. "And if not, a little explanation will set us right."

"It is true that I have not before been engaged in the slave trade, because until recently I had conscientious scruples about the thing—and I suppose I'm allowed the right of conscience as well as other folks," smilingly said the Judge, "never having purchased but for peopling my own plantation. But a little sober reflection set me right on that point. It is plain that the right to buy implies the right to hold, also to sell; and if there be right in the one, there is in the other; the premise being right, the conclusion follows as a matter of course. I have therefore determined, not only to buy and hold, but buy and sell also. As I have heretofore been interested for the trade I will become interested in it."

"Capital, capital, by George! That's conclusive. Charles! A pitcher of cool water here; Judge, take another glass of brandy."

"Good, very good!" said Armsted. "So far, but there is such a thing as feeding out of two cribs—present company, you know, and so—

ahem!—therefore we should like to hear the Judge's opinion of equality, what it means anyhow. I'm anxious to learn some of the doctrines of human rights, not knowing how soon I may be called upon to practice them, as I may yet marry some little Yankee girl, full of her Puritan notions. And I'm told an old bachelor 'can't come it' up that way, except he has a 'pocket full of rocks,' and can talk philanthropy like old Wilberforce."

"Here, gentlemen, I beg to make an episode, before replying to Major Armsted," suggested the Judge. "His jest concerning the Yankee girl reminds me—and I hope it may not be amiss in saying so—that my lady is the daughter of a clergyman, brought up amidst the sand of New England, and I think I'll not have to go from the present company to prove her a good slaveholder. So the Major may see that we northerners are not all alike."

"How about the Compromise measures, Judge? Stand up to the thing all through, and no flinching."

"My opinion, sir, is a matter of record, being the first judge before whom a case was tested, which resulted in favor of the South. And I go further than this; I hold as a just construction of the law, that not only has the slaveholder a right to reclaim his slave when and wherever found, but by its provision every free black in the country, North and South, are liable to enslavement by any white person. They are free-men by sufferance or slaves-at-large, whom any white person may claim at discretion. It was a just decision of the Supreme Court—though I was in advance of it by action—that persons of African descent have no rights that white men are bound to respect!"[5]

"Judge Ballard, with this explanation, I am satisfied; indeed as a Southern man I would say, that you've conceded all that I could ask, and more than we expected. But this is a legal disquisition; what is your private opinion respecting the justice of the measures?"

"I think them right, sir, according to our system of government."

"But how will you get away from your representative system, Judge? In this your blacks are either voters, or reckoned among the inhabitants."

"Very well, sir, they stand in the same relation as your Negroes. In some of the states they are permitted to vote, but can't be voted for, and this leaves them without any political rights at all. Suffrage, sir, is one thing, franchisement another; the one a mere privilege—a thing permitted—the other a right inherent, that which is inviolable—cannot be interfered with. And my good sir, enumeration is a national measure, for which we are not sectionally responsible."

"Well, Judge, I'm compelled to admit that you are a very good Southerner; upon the whole, you are severe upon the Negroes; you seem to allow them no chance."

"I like Negroes well enough in their place!"

"How can you reconcile yourself to the state of things in Cuba, where the blacks enter largely into the social system?"

"I don't like it at all, and never could become reconciled to the state of things there. I consider that colony as it now stands, a moral pestilence, a blighting curse, and it is useless to endeavor to disguise the fact; Cuba must cease to be a Spanish colony, and become American territory. Those mongrel Creoles are incapable of self-government, and should be compelled to submit to the United States."

"Well, Judge, admit the latter part of that, as I rather guess we are all of the same way of thinking—how do you manage to get on with society when you are there?"

"I cannot for a moment tolerate it! One of the hateful customs of the place is that you must exchange civilities with whomsoever solicits it, consequently, the most stupid and ugly Negro you meet in the street may ask for a 'light' from your cigar."

"I know it, and I invariably comply with the request. How do you act in such cases?"

"I invariably comply, but as invariably throw away my cigar! If this were all, it would not be so bad, but then the idea of meeting Negroes and mulattoes at the levees of the Captain General is intolerable! It will never do to permit this state of things so near our own shores."

"Why throw away the cigar, Judge? What objection could there be to it because a negro took a light from it?"

"Because they are certain to take hold of it with their black fingers!"

"Just as I've always heard, Judge Ballard. You Northerners are a great deal more fastidious about Negroes than we of the South, and you'll pardon me if I add, 'more nice than wise,' to use a homily. Did ever it occur to you that black fingers made that cigar, before it entered your white lips!—all tobacco preparations being worked by

Negro hands in Cuba—and very frequently in closing up the wrapper, they draw it through their lips to give it tenacity."

"The deuce! Is that a fact, Major!"

"Does that surprise you, Judge? I'm sure the victuals you eat is cooked by black hands, the bread kneaded and made by black hands, and the sugar and molasses you use, all pass through black hands, or rather the hands of Negroes pass through them; at least you could not refrain from thinking so, had you seen them as I have frequently, with arms full length immersed in molasses."

"Well, Major, truly there are some things we are obliged to swallow, and I suppose these are among them."

"Though a Judge, Your Honor, you perceive that there are some things you have not learned."

"True, Major, true; and I like the Negro well enough in his place, but there is a disposition peculiar to the race, to shove themselves into the notice of the whites."

"Not peculiar to them, Judge, but common to mankind. The black man desires association with the white, because the latter is regarded his superior. In the South it is the poor white man with the wealthy, and in Europe the common with the gentlefolks. In the North you have not made these distinctions among the whites, which prevents you from noticing this trait among yourselves."

"Tell me, Major, as you seem so well to understand them, why a Negro swells so soon into importance?"

"Simply because he's just like you, Judge, and I! It is simply a manifestation of human nature in an humble position, the same as that developed in the breast of a conqueror. Our strictures are not just on this unfortunate race, as we condemn in them that which we approve in ourselves. Southerner as I am, I can joke with a slave just because he is a man; some of them indeed, fine warmhearted fellows, and intelligent, as was the Colonel's Henry."

"I can't swallow that, Major! Joking with a Negro is rather too large a dose for me!"

"Let me give you an idea of my feeling about these things: I have on my place two good-natured black fellows, full of pranks and jokes— Bob and Jef. Passing along one morning Jef was approaching me, when just as we met and I was about to give him the time of day, he made a sudden halt, placing himself in the attitude of a pugilist, grasping the muscle of his left arm, looking me full in the eyes exclaimed, 'Maus Army, my arm aches for you!' when stepping aside he gave the path for me to pass by."

"Did you not rebuke him for the impudence?"

"I laid my hand upon his shoulders as we passed, and gave him a laugh instead. At another time, passing along in company, Bob was righting up a section of fence, when Jef came along. 'How is yeh, Jef?' saluted Bob, without a response. Supposing he had not seen me, I halloed out: 'How are you Jef!' but to this, he made no reply. A gentleman in company with me who enjoyed the joke, said: 'Why Jef, you appear to be above speaking to your old friends!' Throwing his head slightly down with a rocking motion in his walk, elongating his mouth after the manner of a sausage—which by the way needed no improvement in that direction—in a tone of importance still looking down he exclaimed, 'I totes a meat!' He had indeed, a fine gammon on his shoulder from which that evening, he doubtless intended a good supper with his wife, which made him feel important, just as Judge Ballard feels, when he receives the news that 'sugar is up,' and contemplates large profits from his crop of that season."

"I'll be plagued, Major, if your love of the ludicrous don't induce you to give the freest possible license to your Negroes! I wonder they respect you!"

"One thing, Judge, I have learned by my intercourse with men, that pleasantry is the life and soul of the social system; and good treatment begets more labor from the slave than bad. A smile from the master is better than cross looks, and one crack of a joke with him is worth a hundred cracks of the whip. Only confide in him, and let him be satisfied that you respect him as a man, he'll work himself to death to prove his worthiness."

"After all, Major, you still hold them as slaves, though you claim for them the common rights of other people!"

"Certainly! And I would just as readily hold a white as a black in slavery, were it the custom and policy of the country to do so. It is all a matter of self-interest with me; and though I am morally opposed to slavery, yet while the thing exists, I may as well profit by it, as others."

"Well, Major," concluded the Judge, "let us drop the subject, and I hope that the free interchange of opinion will prove no detriment to our future prospects and continued friendship."

"Not at all, sir, not at all!" concluded the Major with a smile.

CHAPTER 16

Solicitude and Amusement

Mrs. Franks sought the earliest opportunity for an interview with the Major concerning her favorite, Maggie. The children now missed her, little George [6] continued fretful, and her own troubled soul was pressed with anxiety.

On conversing with the Major, to her great surprise she learned that the maid had been sold to a stranger, which intelligence he received from Mrs. Ballard herself, whom he met on the quay as he left Havana. The purchaser was a planter formerly of Louisiana, a bachelor by the name of Peter Labonier. This person resided twelve miles from Havana, the proprietor of a sugar estate.

The apprehension of Mrs. Franks, on learning these facts, were aroused to a point of fearful anxiety. These fears were mitigated by the probable chance, in her favor by a change of owners, as his first day's possession of her, turned him entirely against her. He would thus most probably part with her, which favored the desires of Mrs. Franks.

She urged upon the Major as a favor to herself, to procure the release of Maggie, by his purchase and enfranchisement with free papers of unconditional emancipation.

To this Major Armsted gave the fullest assurance, at the earliest possible opportunity. The company were to meet at no distant day, when he hoped to execute the orders.

"How did you leave cousin Arabella, Judge?" enquired Mrs. Franks, as he and the Colonel entered the parlor directly from the back porch, where they had been engaged for the last two hours in close conversation.

"Very well, Maria, when last heard from; a letter reaching me just before I left by the kindness of our mutual friend the Major. By the way, your girl and she did not get on so well, I be——!"

An admonitory look from Franks arrested the subject before the sentence was completed.

Every reference to the subject was carefully avoided, though the Colonel ventured to declare that henceforth towards his servants, instead of leniency, he intended severity. They were becoming every day more and more troublesome, and less reliable. He intended, in the language of his friend the Judge, to "lay upon them a heavy hand" in future.

"I know your sentiments on this point," he said in reply to an admonition from Armsted, "and I used to entertain the same views, but experience has taught me better."

"I shall not argue the point Colonel, but let you have your own way!" replied Armsted.

"Well, Judge, as you wish to become a Southerner, you must first 'see the sights,' as children say, and learn to get used to them. I wish you to ride out with me to Captain Grason's, and you'll see some rare sport; the most amusing thing I ever witnessed," suggested Franks.

"What is it?" enquired the Major.

"The effect is lost by previous knowledge of the thing," replied he. "This will suit you, Armsted, as you're fond of Negro jokes."

"Then, Colonel, let's be off," urged the Major.

"Off it is!" replied Franks, as he invited the gentlemen to take a seat in the carriage already at the door.

"Halloo, halloo, here you are, Colonel! Why Major Armsted, old fellow, 'pon my word!" saluted Grason, grasping Armsted by the hand as they entered the porch.

"Judge Ballard, sir," said Armsted.

"Just in time for dinner, gentlemen! Be seated," invited he, holding the Judge by the hand. "Welcome to Mississippi, Sir! What's up, gentlemen?"

"We've come out to witness some rare sport the Colonel has been telling us about," replied the Major.

"Blamed if I don't think the Colonel will have me advertised as a showman presently! I've got a queer animal here; I'll show him to you after dinner," rejoined Grason. "Gentlemen, help yourself to brandy and water."

Dinner over, the gentlemen walked into the pleasure grounds, in the rear of the mansion.

"Nelse, where is Rube? Call him!" said Grason to a slave lad, brother to the boy he sent for.

Shortly there came forward, a small black boy about eleven years of age, thin visage, projecting upper teeth, rather ghastly consumptive look, and emaciated condition. The child trembled with fear as he approached the group.

"Now gentlemen," said Grason, "I'm going to show you a sight!" having in his hand a long whip, the cracking of which he commenced, as a ringmaster in the circus.

The child gave him a look never to be forgotten; a look beseeching mercy and compassion. But the decree was made, and though humanity quailed in dejected supplication before him, the command was imperative, with no living hand to stay the pending consequences. He must submit to his fate, and pass through the ordeal of training.

"Wat maus gwine do wid me now? I know wat maus gwine do," said this miserable child, "he gwine make me see sights!" when going down on his hands and feet, he commenced trotting around like an animal.

"Now gentlemen, look!" said Grason. "He'll whistle, sing songs, hymns, pray, swear like a trooper, laugh, and cry, all under the same state of feelings."

With a peculiar swing of the whip, bringing the lash down upon a certain spot on the exposed skin, the whole person being prepared for the purpose, the boy commenced to whistle almost like a thrush; another cut changed it to a song, another to a hymn, then a pitiful prayer, when he gave utterance to oaths which would make a Christian shudder, after which he laughed outright; then from the fullness of his soul he cried:

"O maussa, I's sick! Please stop little!" casting up gobs of hemorrhage.*

Franks stood looking on with unmoved muscles. Armsted stood aside whittling a stick; but when Ballard saw, at every cut the flesh turn open in gashes streaming down with gore, till at last in agony he appealed for mercy, he involuntarily found his hand with a grasp on the whip, arresting its further application.

"Not quite a Southerner yet Judge, if you can't stand that!" said Franks on seeing him wiping away the tears.

---

*This is a true Mississippi scene.

"Gentlemen, help yourself to brandy and water. The little Negro don't stand it nigh so well as formerly. He used to be a trump!"

"Well, Colonel," said the Judge, "as I have to leave for Jackson this evening, I suggest that we return to the city."

The company now left Grason's, Franks for the enjoyment of home, Ballard and Armsted for Jackson, and the poor boy Reuben, from hemorrhage of the lungs, that evening left time for eternity.

CHAPTER 17

Henry at Large

On leaving the plantation carrying them hanging upon his arm, thrown across his shoulders, and in his hands Henry had a bridle, halter, blanket, girt, and horsewhip, the emblems of a faithful servant in discharge of his master's business.

By shrewdness and discretion—such was his management as he passed along—that he could tell the name of each place and proprietor long before he reached them. Being a scholar, he carefully kept a record of the plantations he had passed, that when accosted by a white, as an overseer or patrol, he invariably pretended to belong to a back estate, in search of his master's racehorse. If crossing a field, he was taking a near cut; but if met in a wood, the animal was in the forest, as being a great leaper no fence could debar him, though the forest was fenced and posted. The blanket, a substitute for a saddle, was in reality carried for a bed.

With speed unfaltering and spirits unflinching, his first great strive was to reach the Red River, to escape from his own state as quickly as possible. Proceeding on in the direction of the Red River country, he met with no obstruction except in one instance, when he left his assailant quietly upon the earth. A few days after an inquest was held upon the body of a deceased overseer—verdict of the Jury, "By hands unknown."

On approaching the river, after crossing a number of streams, as the Yazoo, Ouchita, and such, he was brought to sad reflections. A dread came over him, difficulties lay before him, dangers stood staring him in the face at every step he took. Here for the first time since his maturity of manhood responsibilities rose up in a shape of which he had no conception. A mighty undertaking, such as had never before been ventured upon, and the duty devolving upon him, was too much for a slave with no other aid than the aspirations of his soul panting for liberty. Reflecting upon the peaceful hours he once enjoyed as a professing Christian, and the distance which slavery had driven him from its peaceful portals, here in the wilderness, determining to renew his faith and dependence upon Divine aid, when falling upon his knees he opened his heart to God, as a tenement of the Holy Spirit.

"Arm of the Lord, awake! Renew my faith, confirm my hope, perfect me in love. Give strength, give courage, guide and protect my pathway, and direct me in my course!" Springing to his feet as if a weight had fallen from him, he stood up a new man.

The river is narrow, the water red as if colored by iron rust, the channel winding. Beyond this river lie his hopes, the broad plains of Louisiana with a hundred thousand bondsmen seeming anxiously to await him.

Standing upon a high bank of the stream, contemplating his mission, a feeling of humbleness and a sensibility of unworthiness impressed him, and that religious sentiment which once gave comfort to his soul now inspiring anew his breast, Henry raised in solemn tones amidst the lonely wilderness:

> Could I but climb where Moses stood,
>   And view the landscape o'er;
> Not Jordan's streams, nor death's cold flood,
>   Could drive me from the shore!

To the right of where he stood was a cove, formed by the washing of the stream at high water, which ran quite into the thicket, into which the sun shone through a space among the high trees.

While thus standing and contemplating his position, the water being too deep to wade, and on account of numerous sharks and alligators, too dangerous to swim, his attention was attracted by the sound of a steamer coming up the channel. Running into the cove to shield himself, a singular noise disturbed him, when to his terror he found himself amidst a squad of huge alligators, which sought the advantages of the sunshine.

His first impulse was to surrender himself to his fate and be devoured, as in the rear and either side the bank was perpendicular, escape being impossible except by the way he entered, to do which would have exposed him to the view of the boat, which could not have been avoided. Meantime the frightful animals were crawling over and among each other, at a fearful rate.

Seizing the fragment of a limb which lay in the cove, beating upon the ground and yelling like a madman, giving them all possible space, the beasts were frightened at such a rate, that they reached the water in less time than Henry reached the bank. Receding into the forest, he thus escaped the observation of the passing steamer, his escape serving to strengthen his fate in a renewed determination of spiritual dependence.

While gazing upon the stream in solemn reflection for Divine aid to direct him, logs came floating down, which suggested a proximity to the raft with which sections of that stream is filled, when going but a short distance up, he crossed in safety to the Louisiana side. His faith was now fully established, and thenceforth, Henry was full of hope and confident of success.

Reaching Alexandria with no obstruction, his first secret meeting was held in the hut of aunt Dilly. Here he found them all ready for an issue.

"An dis you, chile?" said the old woman, stooping with age, sitting on a low stool in the chimney corner. "Dis many day, I heahn on yeh!" though Henry had just entered on his mission. From Alexandria he passed rapidly on to Latuer's, making no immediate stops, preferring to organize at the more prominent places.

This is a mulatto planter, said to have come from the isle of Guadaloupe. Riding down the road upon a pony at a quick gallop was a mulatto youth, a son of the planter, an old black man on foot keeping close to the horse's heels.

"Whose boy are you?" enquired the young mulatto, who had just dismounted, the old servant holding his pony.

"I'm in search of master's race horse."

"What is your name?" further enquired the young mulatto.

"Gilbert, sir."

"What do you want?"

"I am hungry, sir."

"Dolly," said he to an old black woman at the woodpile, "show this man into the Negro quarter, and give him something to eat; give him a cup of milk. Do you like milk, my man?"

"Yes, sir, I have no choice when hungry; anything will do."

"Da is none heah but claubah, maus Eugene," replied the old cook.

"Give him that," said the young master. "You people like that kind of stuff I believe; our Negroes like it."

"Yes, sir," replied Henry when the lad left.

"God knows 'e needn' talk 'bout wat we po' black folks eat, case da don' ghin us nothin' else but dat an' caun bread," muttered the old woman.

"Don't they treat you well, aunty?" enquired Henry.

"God on'y knows, my chile, wat we suffeh."

"Who was that old man who ran behind your master's horse?"

"Dat Nathan, my husban'."

"Do they treat him well, aunty?"

"No, chile, wus an' any dog, da beat 'im foh little an nothin'."

"Is uncle Nathan religious?"

"Yes, chile, ole man an' I's been sahvin' God dis many day, fo yeh baun! Wen any one on 'em in de house git sick, den da sen foh 'uncle Nathan' come pray foh dem; 'uncle Nathan' mighty good den!"

"Do you know that the Latuers are colored people?"

"Yes, chile; God bless yeh soul yes! Case huh mammy ony dead two-three yehs, an' she black as me."

"How did they treat her?"

"Not berry well; she nus da childen; an eat in a house arter all done."

"What did Latuer's children call her?"

"Da call huh 'mammy' same like wite folks childen call de nus."

"Can you tell me, aunty, why they treat you people so badly, knowing themselves to be colored, and some of the slaves related to them?"

"God bless yeh, hunny, de wite folks, dese plantehs make 'em so; da run heah, an' tell 'em da mus'n treat deh niggers well, case da spile 'em."

"Do the white planters frequently visit here?"

"Yes, hunny, yes, da heah some on 'em all de time eatin' an' drinkin' long wid de old man; da on'y tryin' git wat little 'e got, dat all! Da 'tend to be great frien' de ole man; but laws a massy, hunny, I doh mine dese wite folks no how!"

"Does your master ever go to their houses and eat with them?"

"Yes, chile, some time 'e go, but den half on 'em got nothin' fit to eat; da hab fat poke an' bean, caun cake an' sich like, dat all da got, some on 'em."

"Does Mr. Latuer give them better at his table?"

"Laws, hunny, yes; yes'n deed, chile! 'E got mutton—some time whole sheep mos'—fowl, pig, an' ebery tum ting a nuddeh, 'e got so much ting dah, I haudly know wat cook fus."

"Do the white planters associate with the family of Latuer?"

"One on 'em, ten 'e coatin de dahta; I don't recon 'e gwine hab heh. Da cah fool long wid 'Toyeh's gals dat way."

"Whose girls, Metoyers?"

"Yes, chile."

"Do you mean the wealthy planters of that name?"

"Dat same, chile.'

"Well, I want to understand you; you don't mean to say that they are colored people?"

"Yes, hunny, yes; da good culed folks anybody. Some five-six boys' an five-six gals on 'em; da all rich."

"How do they treat their slaves?"

"Da boys all mighty haud maustas, de gals all mighty good; sahvants all like 'em."

"You seem to understand these people very well, aunty. Now please tell me what kind of masters are generally in the Red River country."

"Haud 'nough, chile, haud 'nough, God on'y knows!"

"Do the colored masters treat theirs generally worse than the whites?"

"No, hunny, 'bout da same."

"That's just what I want to know. What are the usual allowances for slaves?"

"Da 'low de fiel' han' two suit a yeah; foh umin one long linen coat,* make suit; an' foh man, pantaloon an' jacket."

"How about eating?"

"Half-peck meal ah day foh family uh fo!"

---

*Coat—a term used by slaves for frock.

"What about weekly privileges? Do you have Saturday to yourselves?"

"Laud, honny, no! No, chile, no! Da do'n 'low us no time, 'tall. Da 'low us ebery uddeh Sunday wash ouh close; dat all de time we git."

"Then you don't get to sell anything for yourselves?"

"No, hunny, no. Da don' 'low pig, chicken, tucky, goose, bean, pea, tateh, nothin' else."

"Well, aunty. I'm glad to meet you, and as evening's drawing nigh, I must see your husband a little, then go."

"God bless yeh, chile, whah ebeh yeh go! Yeh ain' arteh no race-hos, dat yeh ain't."

"You got something to eat, my man, did you?" enquired the lad Eugene, at the conclusion of his interview with uncle Nathan.

"I did, sir, and feasted well!" replied Henry in conclusion. "Good bye!" and he left for the next plantation suited to his objects.

"God bless de baby!" said old aunt Dolly as uncle Nathan entered the hut, referring to Henry.

"Ah, chile!" replied the old man with tears in his eyes; "my yeahs has heahn dis day!"

CHAPTER 18

Fleeting Shadows

In high spirits Henry left the plantation of Latuer, after sowing seeds from which in due season, he anticipated an abundant harvest. He found the old man Nathan all that could be desired, and equal to the task of propagating the scheme. His soul swelled with exultation on receiving the tidings, declaring that though nearly eighty years of age, he never felt before an implied meaning, in the promise of the Lord.

"Now Laud!" with uplifted hand exclaimed he at the conclusion of the interview. "My eyes has seen, and meh yeahs heahn, an' now Laud! I's willin' to stan' still an' see dy salvation!"

On went Henry to Metoyers, visiting the places of four brothers, having taken those of the white planters intervening, all without detection or suspicion of being a stranger.

Stopping among the people of Colonel Hopkins at Grantico summit, here as at Latuer's and all intermediate places, he found the people patiently looking for a promised redemption. Here a pet female slave, Silva, espied him and gave the alarm that a strange black was lurking among the Negro quarters, which compelled him to retirement sooner than intended.

Among the people of Dickson at Pine Bluff, he found the best of spirits. There was Newman, a young slave man born without arms, who was ready any moment for a strike.

"How could you fight?" said Henry. "You have no arms!"

"I am compelled to pick with my toes, a hundred pound of cotton a day,* and I can sit on a stool and touch off a cannon!" said this promising young man whose heart panted with an unsuppressed throb for liberty.

Heeley's, Harrison's, and Hickman's slaves were fearfully and pitiably dejected. Much effort was required to effect a seclusion, and more to stimulate them to action. The continual dread "that maus wont let us!" seemed as immovably fixed as the words were constantly repeated; and it was not until an occasion for another subject of inquest, in the person of a pest of an old black slave man, that an organization was effected.

Approaching Crane's on Little River, the slaves were returning from the field to the gin. Many—being females, some of whom were very handsome—had just emptied their baskets. So little clothing had they, and so loosely hung the tattered fragments about them, that they covered themselves behind the large empty baskets tilted over on the side, to shield their person from exposure.

The overseer engaged in another direction, the master absent, and the family at the great house, a good opportunity presented for an inspection of affairs.

"How do you do, young woman?" saluted Henry.

"How de do, sir!" replied a sprightly, comely young mulatto girl, who stood behind her basket with not three yards of cloth in the tattered relic of the only garment she had on.

"Who owns this place?"

"Mr. Crane, sir," she politely replied with a smile.

"How many slaves has he?"

"I don'o, some say five 'a six hunded."

"Do they all work on this place?"

*At the age of thirteen his daily task was 36 lbs. with his toes. This fact was received from the master by the writer.

"No, sir, he got two-three places."

"How many on this place?"

"Oveh a hundred an' fifty."

"What allowances have you?"

"None, sir."

"What! no Saturday to yourselves?"

"No, sir."

"They allow you Sundays, I suppose."

"No, sir, we work all day ev'ry Sunday."

"How late do you work?"

"Till we can' see to pick no mo' cotton; but w'en its moon light we pick till ten o'clock at night."

"What time do you get to wash your clothes?"

"None, sir; da on'y 'low us one suit ev'ry New Yehs day,* an' us gals take it off every Satady night aftah de men all gone to bed and wash it fah Sunday."

"Why do you want clean clothes on Sunday, if you have to work on that day?"

"It's de Laud's day, an' we wa to be clean, and we feel betteh."

"How do the men do for clean clothes?"

"We wash de men's clothes afteh da go to bed."

"And you say you are only allowed one suit a year? Now, young woman, I don't know your name but——"

"Nancy, sir."

"Well, Nancy, speak plainly, and dont be backward; what does your one suit consist of?"

"A frock, sir, made out er coarse tow linen."

"Only one piece, and no underclothes at all?"

"Dat's all, sir!" replied she modestly looking down and drawing the basket, which sufficiently screened her, still closer to her person.

"Is that which you have on a sample of the goods your clothes are made of?"

"Yes, sir, dis is da kine."

"I would like to see some other of your girls."

"Stop, sir, I go call Susan!" when, gathering up and drawing around and before her a surplus of the back section, the only remaining sound remnant of the narrow tattered garment that she wore, off she ran

---

*Some Red River planters do not allow their slaves but one suit a year.

behind the gin, where lay in the sun, a number of girls to rest themselves during their hour of "spell."

"Susan!" she exclaimed rather loudly. "I do'n want you gals!" she pleasantly admonished, as the whole twelve or fifteen rose from their resting place, and came hurriedly around the building, Nancy and Susan in the lead. They instinctively as did Nancy, drew their garments around and about them, on coming in sight of the stranger. Standing on the outside of the fence, Henry politely bowed as they approached.

"Dis is Susan, sir!" said Nancy, introducing her friend with bland simplicity.

"How de do, sir!" saluted she, a modest and intelligent, very pretty young black girl, of good address.

"Well, Susan!" replied Henry. "I don't want anything but to see you girls; but I will ask you this question: how many suits of clothes do they give you a year?"

"One, sir."

"How many pieces make a suit?"

"Jus' one frock," and they simultaneously commenced drawing still closer before, the remnant of coarse garment, which hung in tatters about them.

"Don't you have shoes and stockings in winter?"

"We no call foh shoes, case 'taint cole much; on'y some time little fros'."

"How late in the evening do you work?"

"Da fiel' han's dah," pointing to those returning to the field, "da work till bedtime, but we gals heah, we work in de gin, and spell each other ev'ey twelve ouahs."

"You're at leisure now; who fills your places?"

"Nutha set a' han's go to work, fo' you come."

"How much cotton do they pick for a task?"

"Each one mus' pick big basket full, an' fetch it in f'om da fiel' to de gin, else da git thirty lashes."

"How much must the women pick as a task?"

"De same as de men."

"That can't be possible!" said Henry, looking over the fence down upon their baskets. "How much do they hold?"

"I dis membeh sir, but good 'eal."

"I see on each basket marked 225 pounds; is that the quantity they hold?"

"Yes, sir, dat's it."

"All mus' be in gin certain ouah else da git whipped; sometime de men help 'em."

"How can they do this when they have their own to carry?"

"Da put derse on de head, an' ketch holt one side de women basket. Sometimes they leave part in de fiel', an' go back afteh it."

"Do you get plenty to eat?"

"No, sir, da feeds us po'ly; sometime, we do'n have mo'n half nough!"

"Did you girls ever work in the field?"

"O yes, sir! all uv us, on'y we wan't strong nough to fetch in ouh cotton, den da put us in de gin."

"Where would you rather; in the gin or in the field?"

"If 'twant foh carryin' cotton, we'a rather work in de fiel'."

"Why so, girls?"

"Case den da would'n be so many ole wite plantehs come an' look at us, like we was show!"

"Who sees that the tasks are all done in the field?"

"Da Driveh."

"Is he a white man?"

"No sir, black."

"Is he a free man?"

"No, sir, slave."

"Have you no white overseer?"

"Yes, sir, Mr. Dorman."

"Where is Dorman when you are at work."

"He out at de fiel too."

"What is he doing there?"

"He watch Jesse, da drivah."

"Is Jesse a pretty good fellow?"

"No, sir, he treat black folks like dog, he all de time beat 'em, when da no call to do it."

"How did he treat you girls when you worked in the field?"

"He beat us if we jist git little behind de rest in pickin'! Da wite folks make 'im bad."

"Point him out to me and after tonight, he'll never whip another."

"Now, girls, I see that you are smart intelligent young women, and I want you to tell me why it is, that your master keeps you all here at work in the gin, when he could get high prices for you, and supply your places with common cheap hands at half the money?"

"Case we gals won' go! Da been mo'n a dozen plantehs heah lookin' at us, an' want to buy us foh house keepehs, an' we wont go; we die fus!" said Susan with a shudder.

"Yes," repeated Nancy, with equal emotion, "we die fus!"

"How can you prevent it, girls; won't your master sell you against your will?"

"Yes, sir, he would, but da plantehs da don't want us widout we willin' to go."

"I see! Well girls, I believe I'm done with you; but before leaving let me ask you, is there among your men, a real clever good trusty man? I don't care either old or young, though I prefer an old or middle-aged man."

"O yes, sir," replied Nancy, "da is some mong 'em."

"Give me the name of one," said Henry, at which request Nancy and Susan looked hesitatingly at each other.

"Don't be backward," admonished he, "as I shan't make a bad use of it." But still they hesitated, when after another admonition Nancy said, "Dare's uncle Joe——"

"No, uncle Moses, uncle Moses!" in a suppressed tone interrupted the other girls.

"Who is uncle Moses?" enquired Henry.

"He' my fatha," replied Susan, "an——"

"My uncle!" interrupted Nancy.

"Then you two are cousins?"

"Yes, sir, huh fatha an my motha is brotha an sisteh," replied Nancy.

"Is he a religious man, girls?"

"Yes, sir, he used to preach but'e do'n preach now," explained Susan.

"Why?"

"Case da 'ligions people wo'n heah im now."

"Who, colored people?"

"Yes, sir."

"When did they stop hearing him preach?"

"Good while ago."

"Where at?"

"Down in da bush meetin', at da Baptism."

"He's a Baptist then—what did he do?"

Again became Susan and Nancy more perplexed than before, the other girls in this instance failing to come to their relief.

"What did he do girls? Let me know it quick, as I must be off!"

"Da say—da say—I do'n want tell you!" replied Susan hesitating, with much feeling.

"What is it girls, can't some of you tell me?" earnestly enquired Henry.

"Da say befo' 'e come heah way down in Fagina, he kill a man, ole po' wite ovehseeah!"

"Is that it, girls?" enquired he.

"Yes, sir!" they simultaneously replied.

"Then he's the very man I want to see!" said Henry. "Now don't forget what I say to you; tell him that a man will meet him tonight below here on the river side, just where the carcass of an ox lies in the verge of the thicket. Tell him to listen and when I'm ready, I'll give the signal of a runaway—the screech of the panther*—when he must immediately obey the summons. One word more, and I'll leave you. Every one of you as you have so praiseworthily concluded, die before surrendering to such base purposes as that for which this man who holds you wishes to dispose of you. Girls, you will see me no more. Fare——"

"Yo' name sir, yo' name!" they all exclaimed.

"My name is—Farewell, girls, farewell!"——when Henry darted in the thickest of the forest, leaving the squad of young maiden slaves in a state of bewildering inquiry concerning the singular black man.

The next day Jesse the driver was missed, and never after heard of. On inquiry being made of the old man Moses concerning the stranger, all that could be elicited was, "Stan' still child'en, and see da salvation uv da Laud!"

*This outlandish yell is given by runaway slaves in imitation of what they consider the screech of the panther, so as to frighten people, thus—"Who-wee!" dwelling long on both syllables.

CHAPTER 19
Come What Will

Leaving the plantation of Crane with high hopes and great confidence in the integrity of uncle Moses and the maiden gang of cotton girls, Henry turned his course in a retrograde direction so as again to take the stream of Red River, Little River, where he then was, being but a branch of that water.

Just below its confluence with the larger stream, at the moment when he reached the junction, a steam cotton trader hove in view. There was no alternative but to stand like a freeman, or suddenly escape into the forest, thus creating suspicions and fears, as but a few days previous a French planter of the neighborhood lost a desperate slave, who became a terror to the country around. The master was compelled to go continually armed, as also other white neighbors, and all were afraid after nightfall to pass out the threshold of their own doors. Permission was given to every white man to shoot him if ever seen within rifle shot, which facts having learned the evening before, Henry was armed with this precaution.

His dress being that of a racegroom—small leather cap with long front piece, neat fitting roundabout, high boots drawn over the pantaloon legs, with blanket, girth, halter, whip and bridle—Henry stood upon the shore awaiting the vessel.

"Well boy!" hailed the captain as the line was thrown out, which he caught, making fast at the root of a tree. "Do you wish to come aboard?"

"Good man!" approvingly cried the mate, at the expert manner which he caught the line and tied the sailor knot.

"Have you ever steamboated, my man?" continued the captain.

"Yes, sir," replied Henry.

"Where?"

"On the Upper and Lower Mississippi, sir."

"Whom do you know as masters of steamers on the Upper Mississippi?"

"Captains Thogmorton, Price, Swan, and ——"

"Stop, stop! That'll do," interrupted the captain, "you know the master of every steamer in the trade, I believe. Now who in the Lower trade?"

"Captains Scott, Hart, and——"

"What's Captain Hart's Christian name?" interrupted the captain.

"Jesse, sir."

"That'll do, by George you know everybody! Do you want to ship?"

"No, sir."

"What are you doing here?"

"I'm hunting master's stray racehorse."

"Your master's race horse! Are you a slave boy?"

"Yes, sir."

"How did you come to be on the Mississippi River?"

"I hired my time, sir."

"Yes, yes, boy, I see!"

"Who is your master?"

"Colonel Sheldon; I used to belong to Major Gilmore."

"Are you the boy Nepp, the great horse trainer the Major used to own?"

"No, sir, I'm his son."

"Are you as good at training horses as the old chap?"

"They call me better, sir."

"Then you're worth your weight in gold. Will your master sell you?"

"I don't know, sir."

"How did your horse come to get away?"

"He was bought from the Major by Colonel Sheldon to run at the great Green Wood Races, Texas, and while training he managed to get away, leaping the fences, and taking to the forest."

"Then you're Major Tom's race rider Gilbert! You're a valuable boy; I wonder the Major parted with you."

The bell having rung for dinner, the captain left, Henry going to the deck.

Among those on deck was a bright mulatto young man, who immediately recognized Henry as having seen him on the Upper Mississippi, he being a free man. On going up to him, Henry observed that he was laden with heavy manacles.

"Have I not seen you somewhere before?" enquired he.

"Yes; my name is Lewis Grimes, you saw me on the Upper Mississippi," replied the young man. "Your name is Henry Holland!"

"What have you been doing?" enquired Henry, on seeing the hand-cuffs.

"Nothing at all!" replied he with eyes flashing resentment and suffused with tears.

"What does this mean?" continued he, pointing at the handcuffs.

"I am stolen and now being taken to Texas, where I am to be enslaved for life!" replied Lewis sobbing aloud.[7]

"Who did this vile deed?" continued Henry in a low tone of voice, pressing his lips to suppress his feelings.

"One Dr. Johns of Texas, now a passenger on this boat!"

"Was that the person who placed a glass to your lips which you refused, just as I came aboard?"

"Yes, that's the man."

"Why don't you leave him instantly?" said Henry, his breast heaving with emotion.

"Because he always handcuffs me before the boat lands, keeping me so during the time she lies ashore."

"Why don't you jump overboard when the boat is under way?"

"Because he guards me with a heavy loaded rifle, and I can't get a chance."

"He 'guards' you! 'You can't get a chance!' Are there no nights, and does he never sleep?"

"Yes, but he makes me sleep in the stateroom with him, keeping his rifle at his bedside."

"Are you never awake when he's asleep?"

"Often, but I'm afraid to stir lest he wakens."

"Well don't you submit, die first if thereby you must take another into eternity with you! Were it my case and he ever went to sleep where I was, he'd never waken in this world!"

"I never thought of that before, I shall take your advice the first opportunity. Good-bye sir!" hastily said the young man, as the bell tapped a signal to start, and Henry stepped on shore.

"Let go that line!" sternly commanded the captain, Henry obeying orders on the shore, when the boat glided steadily up the stream, seemingly in unison with the lively though rude and sorrowful song of the black firemen—

I'm a-goin' to Texas—O! O-O-O!
I'm a-goin' to Texas—O! O-O-O!

Having in consequence of the scarcity of spring houses and larders along his way in so level and thinly settled country, Henry took in his pouch from the cook of the boat an ample supply of provisions for the suceeding four or five days. Thus provided for, standing upon the bank for a few minutes, with steady gaz. listening to the sad song of his oppressed brethren as they left the spot, and reflecting still more on the miserable fate of the young mulatto freeman Lewis Grimes held by the slave-holder Dr. Johns of Texas, he, with renewed energy, determined that nothing short of an interference by Divine Providence should stop his plans and progress. In soliloquy said Henry, "Yes!

If every foe stood martialed in the van,
I'd fight them single combat, man to man!"

and again he started with a manly will, as fixed and determined in his purpose as though no obstructions lay in his pathway.

From plantation to plantation did he go, sowing the seeds of future devastation and ruin to the master and redemption to the slave, an antecedent more terrible in its anticipation than the warning voice of the destroying Angel in commanding the slaughter of the firstborn of Egypt. Himself careworn, distressed and hungry, who just being supplied with nourishment for the system, Henry went forth a welcome messenger, casting his bread upon the turbid waters of oppression, in hopes of finding it after many days.

Holding but one seclusion on each plantation, his progress was consequently very rapid, in whatever direction he went.

With a bold stride from Louisiana, he went into Texas. Here he soon met with the man of his wishes. This presented in the person of Sampson, on the cotton place of proprietor Richardson. The master here, though represented wealthy, with an accomplished and handsome young daughter, was a silly, stupid old dolt, an inordinate blabber and wine bibber. The number of his slaves was said to be great and he the owner of three plantations, one in Alabama, and the others in Texas.

Sampson was a black, tall, stoutly built, and manly, possessing much general intelligence, and a good-looking person. His wife a neat, intelligent, handsome little woman, the complexion of himself, was the mother of a most interesting family of five pretty children, three boys and two girls. This family entered at once into the soul of his mission, seeming to have anticipated it.

With an amply supply of means,* buried in a convenient well-marked spot, he only awaited a favorable opportunity to effect his escape from slavery. With what anxiety did that wife gaze smilingly in his face, and a boy and girl cling tightly each to a knee, as this husband and father in whispers recounted his plans and determination of carrying them out. The scheme of Henry was at once committed to his confidence, and he requested to impart them wherever he went.

Richardson was a sportsman and Sampson his body servant, they traveled through every part of the country, thus affording the greatest opportunity for propagating the measures of the secret organization. From Portland in Maine to Galveston in Texas, Sampson was as familiar as a civil engineer.

"Sampson, Sampson, stand by me! Stand by me, my man; stand at your master's back!" was the language of this sottish old imbecile he kept continually reveling at a gambling table, and who from excessive fatigue would sometimes squat or sit down upon the floor behind him. "Sampson, Sampson! are you there? Stand by your master, Sampson!" again would he exclaim, so soon as the tall commanding form of his black protector was missed from his sight.

Sampson and his wife were both pious people, believing much in the Providence of God, he, as he said having recently had it "shown to" him—meaning a presentiment—that a messenger would come to him and reveal the plan of deliverance.

"I am glad to see that you have money," said Henry, "you are thereby well qualified for your mission. With money you may effect your escape almost at any time. Your most difficult point is an elevated obstruction, a mighty hill, a mountain; but through that hill there is a gap, and money is your passport through that White Gap to freedom. Mark that! It is the great range of White mountains and White river which are before you, and the White Gap that you must pass through to reach the haven of safety. Money alone will carry you through the White mountains or across the White river to liberty."

"Brother, my eyes is open, and my way clear!" responded Sampson to this advice.

---

*This person had really $2,000 in gold, securely hid away unknown to any person but his wife, until showing it to the writer.

"Then," said Henry, "you are ready to 'rise and shine' for——"

"My light has come!—" interrupted Sampson. "But——"

"The glory of God is not yet shed abroad!"* concluded Henry, who fell upon Sampson's neck with tears of joy in meeting unexpectedly one of his race so intelligent in that region of country.

Sampson and wife Dursie, taking Henry by the hand wept aloud, looking upon him as the messenger of deliverance foreshown to them.

Kneeling down a fervent prayer was offered by Sampson for Henry's protection by the way, and final success in his "mighty plans," with many Amens and "God grants," by Dursie.

Partaking of a sumptuous fare on 'ash cake and sweet milk—a dainty diet with many slaves—and bidding with a trembling voice and tearful eye a final "Farewell!" in six hours he had left the state of Texas to the consequences of a deep-laid scheme for a terrible insurrection.

CHAPTER 20

Advent Among the Indians

From Texas Henry went into the Indian Nation near Fort Towson, Arkansas.

"Make yourself at home, sir," invited Mr. Culver, the intelligent old Chief of the United Nation, "and Josephus will attend to you," referring to his nephew Josephus Braser, an educated young chief and counselor among his people.

"You are slaveholders, I see, Mr. Culver!" said Henry.

"We are, sir, but not like the white men," he replied.

"How many do you hold?"

"About two hundred on my two plantations."

"I can't well understand how a man like you can reconcile your principles with the holding of slaves and——"[8]

"We have had enough of that!" exclaimed Dr. Donald, with a tone of threatening authority.

"Hold your breath, sir, else I'll stop it!" in a rage replied the young chief.

"Sir," responded the Doctor, "I was not speaking to you, but only speaking to that Negro!"

*A real incident which took place between a slave and a free black adviser.

"You're a fool!" roared Braser, springing to his feet.

"Come, come, gentlemen!" admonished the old Chief. "I think you are both going mad! I hope you'll behave something better."

"Well, uncle, I can't endure him! he assumes so much authority!" replied he. "He'll make the Indians slaves just now, then Negroes will have no friends."

Donald was a white man, married among the Indians a sister of the old Chief and aunt to the young, for the sake of her wealth and a home. A physician without talents, he was unable to make a business and unwilling to work.

"Mr. Bras——"

"I want nothing more of you," interrupted Braser, "and don't——"

"Josephus, Josephus!" interrupted the old chief. "You will surely let the Doctor speak!"

Donald stood pale and trembling before the young Choctaw born to command, when receiving no favor he left the company muttering "nigger!"

"Now you see," said Mr. Culver as the Doctor left the room, "the difference between a white man and Indian holding slaves. Indian work side by side with black man, eat with him, drink with him, rest with him and both lay down in shade together; white man even won't let you talk! In our Nation Indian and black all marry together. Indian like black man very much, ony he don't fight 'nough. Black man in Florida fight much, and Indian like 'im heap!"[9]

"You make, sir, a slight mistake about my people. They would fight if in their own country they were united as the Indians here, and not scattered thousands of miles apart as they are. You should also remember that the Africans have never permitted a subjugation of their country by foreigners as the Indians have theirs, and Africa today is still peopled by Africans, whilst America, the home of the Indian—who is fast passing away—is now possessed and ruled by foreigners."

"True, true!" said the old Chief, looking down reflectingly. "Too true! I had not thought that way before. Do you think the white man couldn't take Africa if he wanted?"

"He might by a combination, and I still am doubtful whether then he could if the Africans were determined as formerly to keep him out. You will also remember, that the whites came in small numbers to

America, and then drove the Indians from their own soil, whilst the blacks got in Africa as slaves, are taken by their own native conquerors, and sold to white men as prisoners of war."

"That is true, sir, true!" sighed the old Chief. "The Indian, like game before the bow, is passing away before the gun of the white man!"

"What I now most wish to learn is, whether in case that the blacks should rise, they may have hope or fear from the Indian?" asked Henry.

"I'm an old mouthpiece, been puffing out smoke and talk many seasons for the entertainment of the young and benefit of all who come among us. The squaws of the great men among the Indians in Florida were black women, and the squaws of the black men were Indian women. You see the vine that winds around and holds us together. Don't cut it, but let it grow till bimeby, it git so stout and strong, with many, very many little branches attached, that you can't separate them. I now reach to you the pipe of peace and hold out the olive-branch of hope! Go on young man, go on. If you want white man to love you, you must fight im!" concluded the intelligent old Choctaw.

"Then, sir, I shall rest contented, and impart to you the object of my mission," replied Henry.

"Ah hah!" exclaimed the old chief after an hour's seclusion with him. "Ah hah! Indian have something like that long-go. I wonder your people ain't got it before! That what make Indian strong; that what make Indian and black man in Florida hold together. Go on young man, go on! may the Great Spirit make you brave!" exhorted Mr. Culver, when the parties retired for the evening, Henry rooming with the young warrior Braser.

By the aid of the young Chief and kindness of his uncle the venerable old brave, Henry was conducted quite through the nation on a pony placed at his service, affording to him an ample opportunity of examining into the condition of things. He left the settlement with the regrets of the people, being the only instance in which his seclusions were held with the master instead of the slave.

CHAPTER 21

What Not

Leaving the United Nation of Chickasaw and Choctaw Indians, Henry continued his travel in this the roughest, apparently, of all the states. Armed with bowie knives and revolvers openly carried belted around the person, he who displays the greatest number of deadly weapons seems to be considered the greatest man. The most fearful incivility and absence of refinement was apparent throughout this region. Neither the robes of state nor gown of authority is sufficient to check the vengeance of awakened wrath in Arkansas. Law is but a fable, its ministration a farce, and the pillars of justice but as stubble before the approach of these legal invaders.

Hurriedly passing on in the darkness of the night, Henry suddenly came upon a procession in the wilderness, slowly and silently marching on, the cortege consisting principally of horsemen, there being but one vehicle, advanced by four men on horseback. Their conversation seemed at intervals of low, muttering, awestricken voices. The vehicle was closely covered, and of a sad, heavy sound by the rattling of the wheels upon the unfinished path of the great Arkansas road. Here he sat in silence listening, waiting for the passage of the solemn procession, but a short distance from whence in the thicket stood the hut of the slave to whom he was sent.

"Ole umin! done yeh heah some 'un trampin' round de house? Hush! evedroppehs 'bout!" admonished Uncle Jerry.

"Who dat?" enquired Aunt Rachel, as Henry softly rapped at the back window.

"A friend!" was the reply.

"What saut frien' dat go sneak roun' people back windah stid comin' to de doh!"

"Hush, ole umin, yeh too fas'! how yeh know who 'tis? Frien', come roun' to de doh," said the old man.

Passing quickly around, the door was opened, a blazing hot fire shining full in his face, the old man holding in his hand a heavy iron poker in the attitude of defence.

"Is dis you, my frien'?" enquired Uncle Jerry, to whom Henry was an entire stranger.

"Yes, uncle, this is me," replied he.

"God bless yeh, honey! come in; we didn know 'twos you, chile! God bless de baby!" added Aunt Rachel. "Ole man, heah yeh comin' an' we been lookin' all day long. Dis evenin' I git some suppeh, an' I don'o if yeh come uh no."

"How did you know I was coming, aunty?"

"O! honey, da tell us," replied she.

"Who told you?"

"De folks up dah."

"Up where?"

"Up dah, 'mong de Injins, chile."

"Indians told you?"

"No, honey; some de black folks, da all'as gwine back and for'ard, and da lahn heap from dem up dah; an' da make 'ase an' tell us."

"Can you get word from each other so far apart, that easy?"

"Yes 'ndeed, honey! some on 'em all de time gwine; wite folks know nothin' 'bout it. Some time some on 'em gone two-three day, an' ain miss; white folks tink da in the woods choppin'."

"Why, that's the very thing! you're ahead of all the other states. You folks in Arkansas must be pretty well organized already."

"Wat dat yeh mean, chile, dat 'organ' so?"

"I mean by that, aunty, a good general secret understanding among yourselves."

"Ah, chile! dat da is. Da comin' all de time, ole man hardly time to eat mou'full wen 'e come in de hut night."

"Tell me, aunty, why people like you and uncle here, who seem to be at the head of these secrets, are not more cautious with me, a stranger?"

"Ole umin, I lisenin at yeh!" said Uncle Jerry, after enough had been told to betray them; but the old people well understood each other, Aunt Rachel by mutual consent being the mouthpiece.

"How we knows you!" rejoined the old woman. "Wy, chile, yeh got mahk dat so soon as we put eye on yeh, we knows yeh. Huccum yeh tink we gwine tell yeh so much wen we don'o who yeh is? Sho, chile, we ain't dat big fool!"

"Then you know my errand among you, aunty?"

"Yes, meh son, dat we does, an' we long been waitin' foh some sich like you to come 'mong us. We thang God dis night in ouh soul! We long been lookin' foh ye, chile!" replied Uncle Jerry.

"You are closely watched in this state, I should think, uncle."

"Yes, chile, de patrolas da all de time out an' gwine in de quahtehs an' huntin' up black folks wid der 'nigga-dogs' as da call 'em."

"I suppose you people scarcely ever get a chance to go anywhere, then?"

"God bless yeh, honey, da blacks do'n mine dem noh der 'nigga-dogs' nutha. Patrolas feahd uh de black folks, an' da black folks charm de dogs, so da cahn heht 'em," said Aunt Rachel.

"I see you understand yourselves! Now, what is my best way to get along through the state?"

"Keep in de thicket, chile, as da patrolas feahd to go in de woods, da feahd runaway ketch 'em! Keep in da woods, chile, an' da ain' goin' dah bit! Da talk big, and sen' der dog, but da ain' goin' honey!" continued the old woman.

"Ah spose, meh son, yeh know how to chaum dogs?" enquired Uncle Jerry.

"I understand the mixed bull, but not the full-bred Cuba dog," replied Henry.

"Well, chile, da keep boph kine heah, de bull dog an' bloodhoun' an' fo' yeh go, I lahn yeh how to fix 'em all! Da come sneakin' up to yeh! da cahn bite yeh!"

"Thank you, Uncle Jerry! I'll try and do as much for you in some way."

"Yeh no call foh dat, meh son; it ain' nothin' mo' nah onh——"

"Hush! ole man; ain' dat dem?" admonished Aunt Rachel, in a whisper, as she went to the door, thrusting out her head in the dark.

"Who? Patrols?" with anxiety enquired Henry.

"No, chile, de man da kill down yondah; all day long da been lookin' foh 'em to come."

"A procession passed just before I came to your door, which I took for a funeral."

"Yes, chile, dat's it, da kill im down dah."

On enquiry, it appeared that in the senate a misunderstanding on the rules of order and parliamentary usage occurred, when the Speaker, conceiving himself insulted by the senator who had the floor, deliberately arose from his chair, when approaching the senator, drove a bowie knife through his body from the chest, which laid him a corpse upon the senate floor.

"There he is! There he is!" stormed the assassin, pointing with defiance at the lifeless body, his hand still reeking with blood. "I did it!" slapping his hand upon his own breast in triumph of his victory.

They had just returned with the body of the assassinated statesman to the wretched home of his distracted family, some ten miles beyond the hut of Uncle Jerry.

"Is this the way they treat each other, aunty?"

"Yes, chile, wus den dat! da kill one-notha in cole blood, sometime at de table eatin'. Da all'as choppin' up some on 'em."

"Then you black people must have a poor chance among them, if this is the way they do each other!"

"Mighty po', honey; mighty po' indeed!" replied Uncle Jerry.

"Well, uncle, it's now time I was doing something; I've been here some time resting. Aunty, see to your windows and door; are there any cracks in the walls!"

"No, honey, da dob good!" whispered the old woman as a well-patched, covering quilt to shield the door was hung, covering nearly one side of the hut, and a thickly-patched linsey gown fully shielded the only window of four eight-by-ten lights.

These precautions taken, they drew together in a corner between the head of the bed and well-daubed wall to hold their seclusion.

"Laud!" exclaimed Uncle Jerry, after the secrets were fully imparted to them. "Make beah dine all-conquering ahm! strike off de chains dat dy people may go free! Come, Laud, a little nigh, eh!"

"Honah to 'is name!" concorded Aunt Rachel. "Wuthy all praise! Tang God fah wat I seen an' heahn dis night! dis night long to be membed! Meh soul feels it! It is heah!" pressing her hand upon her breast, exclaimed she.

"Amen! Laud heah de cry uh dy childen! Anseh prah!" responded the old man, in tears; when Aunt Rachel in a grain of sorrowful pathos, sung to the expressive words in the slaves' lament:

"In eighteen hundred and twenty-three
They said their people should be free!
  It is wrote in Jeremiah,
  Come and go along with me!
  It is wrote in Jeremiah,
  Go sound the Jubilee!"

At the conclusion of the last line, a sudden sharp rap at the door startled them, when the old woman, hastening, took down the quilt, enquiring, "Who dat?"

"Open the door, Rachel!" was the reply, in an authoritative tone from a posse of patrols, who on going their evening rounds were attracted to the place by the old people's devotion, and stood sometime listening around the hut.

"You seem to be happy here, Jerry," said Ralph Jordon, the head of the party. "What boy is this you have here?"

"Major Morgan's sir," replied Henry, referring to the proprietor of the next plantation above.

"I don't remember seeing you before, boy," continued Jordon.

"No, sir; lately got me," explained Henry.

"Aye, aye, boy; a preacher, I suppose."

"No, sir."

"No, Maus Rafe, dis brotheh no preacheh; but 'e is 'logious, and come to gib us little comfit, an' bless God I feels it now; dat I does, blessed be God!" said the old woman.

"Well, Rachel, that's all right enough; but, my boy, its high time that you were getting towards home. You've not yet learned our rules here; where are you from?"

"Louisiana, sir."

"Yes, yes, that explains it. Louisiana Negroes are permitted to go out at a much later hour than our Negroes."

"Maus Rafe, ah hope yah let de brotheh eat a mouph'l wid us fo' go?"

"O yes, Rachel! give the boy something to eat before he goes; I suppose the 'laborer is worthy of his hire,' " looking with a smile at his comrades.

"Yes 'ndeed, seh, dat he is!" replied the old woman with emphasis.

"Rachel, I smell something good! What have you here, spare rib?" enquired Ralph Jordon, walking to the table and lifting up a clean check apron which the old woman had hurriedly thrown over it to screen her homely food from the view of the gentlemen patrols. "Good! spare rib and ash cake, gentlemen! What's better? Rachel, give us some seats here!" continued Ralph.

Hurrying about, the old woman made out to seat the uninvited guests with a half barrel tub, an old split bottom chair, and a short slab bench, which accommodated two.

"By gum! This is fine," said Ralph Jordon, smacking his mouth, and tearing at a rib. "Gentlemen, help yourselves to some spirits," setting on the table a large flask of Jamaica rum, just taken from his lips.

"Nothing better," replied Tom Hammond; "give me at any time the cooking in the Negro quarters before your great-house dainties."

"So say I," sanctioned Zack Hite, champing like a hungry man. "The Negroes live a great deal better than we do."

"Much better, sir, much better," replied Ralph. "Rachel, don't you nor Jerry ever take any spirits?"

"No, Maus Rafe, not any," replied the old woman.

"May be your friend there will take a little."

"I don't drink, sir," said Henry.

Rising from the homely meal at the humble board of Aunt Rachel and Uncle Jerry, they emptied their pockets of crackers, cold biscuits and cheese, giving the old man a plug of honey-cured tobacco, to be divided between himself and wife, in lieu of what they had, without invitation, taken the liberty of eating. The patrol this evening were composed of the better class of persons, principally business men, two of whom, being lawyers who went out that evening for a mere "frolic among the Negroes."

Receiving the parting hand, accompanied with a "good bye, honey!" and "God bless yeh, meh son!" from the old people, Henry left the hut to continue his course through the forest. Hearing persons approaching, he stepped aside from the road to conceal himself, when two parties at the junction of two roads met each other, coming to a stand.

"What's up tonight, Colonel?" enquired one.

"Nothing but the raffle."

"Are you going?"

"Yes, the whole party here; won't you go?"

"I dun'o; what's the chances?"

"Five dollars only."

"Five dollars a chance! What the deuce is the prize!"

"Oh, there's several for the same money."

"What are they?"

"That fine horse and buggy of Colonel Sprout, a mare and colt, a little Negro girl ten years of age, and a trail of four of the finest Negro-dogs in the state."

"Hallo! all them; why, how many chances, in the name of gracious, are there?"

"Only a hundred and fifty."

"Seven hundred and fifty dollars for the whole; that's cheap. But, then, all can't win, and it must be a loss to somebody."

"Will you go, Cap'n?"

"Well, I don't care—go it is!" when the parties started in the direction of the sport, Henry following to reconnoiter them.

On approaching the tavern, the rafflers, who waited the rest of the company to gather, could be seen and heard through the uncurtained windows and the door, which was frequently opened, standing around a blazing hot fire, and in groups over the barroom floor, amusing themselves with jests and laughter. Henry stood in the verge of the forest in a position to view the whole of their proceedings.

Presently there was a rush out of doors with glee and merriment. Old Colonel Sprout was bringing out his dogs, to test their quality previous to the raffle.

"Now, gentlemen!" exclaimed he, "them is the best trained dogs in this part of the state. Be dad, they's the bes' dogs in the country. When you say 'nigger,' you needn't fear they'll ever go after anything but a nigger."

"Come, Colonel, give them a trial; we must have something going on to kill time," suggested one of the party.

"But what will he try 'em on?" said another; "there's no niggers to hunt."

"Send them out, and let them find one, be George; what else would you have them do?" replied a third.

"Where the deuce will they get one?" rejoined a fourth.

"Just as a hunting dog finds any other game," answered a fifth; "where else?"

"O, by golly, gentlemen, you need's give yourselves no uneasiness about the game. They'll find a nigger, once started if they have to break into some Negro quarter and drag 'm out o' bed. No mistake 'bout them, I tell you, gentlemen," boasted Sprout.

"But won't a nigger hurt 'em when he knows he's not a runaway?" enquired Richard Rester Rutherford.

"What, a nigger hurt a bloodhound! By, gracious, they're fearder of a bloodhound than they is of the devil himself! Them dogs is dogs, gentlemen, an' no mistake; they is by gracious!" declared Sprout.

"Well, let them loose, Colonel, and let's have a little sport, at any rate!" said Ralph Jordon, the patrol, who had just arrived; "we're in for a spree tonight, anyhow."

"Here, Caesar, Major, Jowler, here Pup! Niggers about! Seek out!" hissed the Colonel, with a snap of the finger, pointing toward the thicket, in the direction of which was Henry. With a yelp which sent a shudder through the crowd, the dogs started in full chase for the forest.

"By George, Colonel, that's too bad! Call them back!" said Ralph Jordon, as the savage brutes bounded in search of a victim.

"By thunder, gentlemen, it's too late! they'll have a nigger before they stop. They'll taste the blood of some poor black devil before they git back!" declared Sprout.

Having heard every word that passed between them, in breathless silence Henry waited the approach of the animals. The yelping now became more anxious and eager, until at last it was heard as a short, impatient, fretful whining, indicating a near approach to their prey, when growing less and less, they ceased entirely to be heard.

"What the Harry does it mean! the dogs has ceased to bay!" remarked Colonel Sprout.

"Maybe they caught a nigger," replied John Spangler.

"It might be a Tartar!" rejoined Ralph Jordon.

"Maybe a nigger caught them!" said the Sheriff of the county, who was present to superintend the raffle, and receive the proceeds of the hazard.

"What!" exclaimed the old gentleman, to enhance the value of the prizes. "What! My Caesar, Major, Jowler, and Pup, the best dogs in all Arkansas!—A nigger kill them! No, gentlemen, once let loose an' on their trail, an' they's not a gang o' niggers to be found out at night they couldn't devour! Them dogs! Hanged if they didn't eat a nigger quicker as they'd swaller a piece o' meat!"

"Then they're the dogs for me!" replied the Sheriff.

"And me," added Spangle, a noted agent for catching runaway slaves.

"The raffle, the raffle!" exclaimed several voices eager for a chance, estimating at once the value of the dogs above the aggregate amount of the stakes.

"But the dogs, the dogs, gentlemen! They're not here! Give us the dogs first," suggested an eager candidate for competition in the prizes.

"No matter, gentlemen; be sartin," said the Colonel, "when they's done they'll come back agin."

"But how will they be managed in attacking strange Negroes?" enquired Ralph Jordon.

"O, the command of any white man is sufficient to call 'em off, an' they's plenty o' them all'as wherever you find niggers."

"Then, Colonel, we're to understand you to mean, that white men can't live without niggers."

"I'll be hanged, gentlemen, if it don't seem so, for wherever you find one you'll all'as find tother, they's so fully mixed up with us in all our relations!" peals of laughter following the explanation.

"Come, Colonel, I'll be hanged if we stand that, except you stand treat!" said Ralph.

"Stand what? Let us understand you; what'd I say?"

"What did you say? why, by George, you tell us flatly that we are related to niggers!"

"Then, gentlemen, I'll stand treat; for on that question I'll be consarned if some of us don't have to knock under!" at which there were deafening roars of laughter, the crowd rushing into the barroom, crying, "Treat! Treat!! That's too good to be lost!"

Next day after the raffle, the winners having presented the prizes back to their former owner, it was whispered about that the dogs had been found dead in the woods, the mare and colt were astray, the little slave girl was in a pulmonary decline, the buggy had been upset and badly worsted the day before the raffle, and the horse had the distemper; upon which information the whole party met at a convenient place on a fixed day, going out to his house in a body, who ate, drank, and caroused at his expense during the day and evening.

"Sprout," said Ralph Jordon, "with your uniform benevolence, generosity and candor, how did you ever manage to depart so far from your old principles and rule of doing things? I can't understand it."

"How so? Explain yourself," replied Sprout.

"Why you always give rather than take advantage, your house and means always being open to the needy, even those with whom you are unacquainted."

"I'm sure I ain't departed one whit from my old rule," said Sprout; "I saw you was all strangers to the thing, an' I took you in; I'm blamed if I didn't!" the crowd shouting with laughter.

"One word, Sprout," said Jordon. "When the dogs ceased baying, didn't you suspect something wrong?"

"I know'd at once when they stopped that they was defeated; but I thought they'd pitched headlong into a old wellhole some sixty foot deep, where the walls has tumbled in, an' made it some twenty foot wide at the top. I lis'ened every minute 'spectin' to hear a devil of a whinin' 'mong 'em' but I was disapinted."

"Well, its a blamed pity, anyhow, that such fine animals were killed; and no clue as yet, I believe, to the perpetration of the deed," said the Sheriff.

"They was, indeed," replied Sprout, "as good a breed o' dogs as ever was, an' if they'd a been trained right, nothin' could a come up with them; but consarn their picters, it serves 'em right, as they wos the cussedest cowards I ever seed! 'Sarn them, if a nigger ony done so—jis' made a pass at 'em, an' I'll be hanged if they didn't yelp like wild cats, an almost kill 'emselves runin' away!" at which explanation the peals of laughter were deafening.

"Let's stay a week, stay a week, gentlemen!" exclaimed Ralph Jordon, in a convulsion of laughter.

"Be gracious, gentlemen!" concluded Sprout. "If you stay till eternity it won't alter the case one whit; case, the mare an' colt's lost, the black gal's no use to anybody, the buggy's all smashed up, the hos' is got the distemper, and the dogs is dead as thunder!"

With a boisterous roar, the party, already nearly exhausted with laughter, commenced gathering their hats and cloaks, and left the premises declaring never again to be caught at a raffling wherein was interested Colonel Joel Sprout.

The dogs were the best animals of the kind, and quickly trailed out their game; but Henry, with a well-aimed weapon, slew each ferocious beast as it approached him, leaving them weltering in their own blood instead of feasting on his, as would have been the case had he not overpowered them. The rest of the prizes were also valuable and in good order, and the story which found currency depreciating them, had its origin in the brain and interest of Colonel Sprout, which resulted, as designed, entirely in his favor.

Hastening on to the Fulton landing Henry reached it at half-past two o'clock in the morning, just in time to board a steamer on the downward trip, which barely touched the shore to pick up a package. Knowing him by reputation as a great horse master, the captain received him cheerfully, believing him to have been, from what he had learned, to the Texas races with horses for his master.

Being now at ease, and faring upon the best the vessel could afford, after a little delay along the cotton trading coast, Henry was safely landed in the portentous city of New Orleans.

CHAPTER 22

New Orleans

The season is the holidays, it is evening, and the night is beautiful. The moon, which in Louisiana is always an object of impressive interest, even to the slave as well as those of enlightened and scientific intelligence, the influence of whose soft and mellow light seems ever like the enchanting effect of some invisible being, to impart inspiration— now being shed from the crescent of the first day of the last quarter, appeared more interesting and charming than ever.

Though the cannon at the old fort in the Lower Faubourg had fired the significant warning, admonishing the slaves as well as free blacks to limit their movement, still there were passing to and fro with seeming indifference Negroes, both free and slaves, as well as the whites and Creole quadroons, fearlessly along the public highways, in seeming defiance of the established usage of Negro limitation.

This was the evening of the day of Mardi Gras, and from long-established and time-honored custom, the celebration which commenced in the morning was now being consummated by games, shows, exhibitions, theatrical performances, festivals, masquerade balls, and numerous entertainments and gatherings in the evening. It was on this account that the Negroes had been allowed such unlimited privileges this evening.

Nor were they remiss to the utmost extent of its advantages.

The city which always at this season of the year is lively, and Chartier street [10] gay and fashionable, at this time appeared more lively, gay and fashionable than usual. This fashionable thoroughfare, the pride of the city, was thronged with people, presenting complexions of every shade and color. Now could be seen and realized the expressive description in the popular song of the vocalist Cargill:

> I suppose you've heard how New Orleans
>   Is famed for wealth and beauty;
> There's girls of every hue, it seems,
>   From snowy white to sooty.

The extensive shops and fancy stores presented the presence behind their counters as saleswomen in attendance of numerous females, black, white, mulatto and quadroon, politely bowing, curtsying, and rubbing their hands, in accents of broken English inviting to purchase all who enter the threshold, or even look in at the door:

"Wat fa you want something? Walk in, sire, I vill sell you one nice present fa one young lady."

And so with many who stood or sat along the streets and at the store doors, curtsying and smiling they give the civil banter:

"Come, sire, I sell you one pretty ting."

The fancy stores and toy shops on this occasion were crowded seemingly to their greatest capacity. Here might be seen the fashionable young white lady of French or American extraction, and there the handsome, and frequently beautiful maiden of African origin, mulatto, quadroon, or sterling black, all fondly interchanging civilities, and receiving some memento or keepsake from the hand of an acquaintance. Many lively jests and impressive flings of delicate civility noted the greetings of the passersby. Freedom seemed as though for once enshielded by her sacred robes and crowned with cap and wand in hand, to go forth untrammeled through the highways of the town.[11] Along the private streets, sitting under the verandas, in the doors with half-closed jalousies, or promenading unconcernedly the public ways, mournfully humming in solace or chanting in lively glee, could be seen and heard many a Creole, male or female, black, white or mixed race, sometimes in reverential praise of

Father, Son and Holy Ghost—
Madonna, and the Heavenly Host!

in sentimental reflection on some pleasant social relations, or the sad reminiscence of ill-treatment or loss by death of some loved one, or worse than death, the relentless and insatiable demands of slavery.

In the distance, on the levee or in the harbor among the steamers, the songs of the boatmen were incessant. Every few hours landing, loading and unloading, the glee of these men of sorrow was touchingly appropriate and impressive. Men of sorrow they are in reality; for if there be a class of men anywhere to be found, whose sentiments of song and words of lament are made to reach the sympathies of others, the black slave-boatmen of the Mississippi river is that class. Placed in positions the most favorable to witness the pleasures enjoyed by others, the tendency is only to augment their own wretchedness.[12]

Fastened by the unyielding links of the iron cable of despotism, reconciling themselves to a lifelong misery, they are seemingly contented by soothing their sorrows with songs and sentiments of apparently cheerful but in reality wailing lamentations. The most attracting lament of the evening was sung to words, a stanza of which is presented in pathos of delicate tenderness, which is but a spray from the stream which gushed out in insuppressible jets from the agitated fountains of their souls, as if in unison with the restless current of the great river upon which they were compelled to toil, their troubled waters could not be quieted. In the capacity of leader, as is their custom, one poor fellow in pitiful tones led off the song of the evening:

Way down upon the Mobile river,
  Close to Mobile bay;
There's where my thoughts is running ever,
  All through the livelong day:
There I've a good and fond old mother,
  Though she is a slave;

There I've a sister and a brother,
  Lying in their peaceful graves.

Then in chorus joined the whole company——

O, could I somehow a'nother,
  Drive these tears way;
When I think about my poor old mother,
  Down upon the Mobile bay.[13]

Standing in the midst of and contemplating such scenes as these, it was that Henry determined to finish his mission in the city and leave it by the earliest conveyance over Pontchartrain for Alabama—Mobile being the point at which he aimed. Swiftly as the current of the fleeting Mississippi was time passing by, and many states lay in expanse before him, all of which, by the admonishing impulses of the dearest relations, he was compelled to pass over as a messenger of light and destruction.

Light, of necessity, had to be imparted to the darkened region of the obscure intellects of the slaves, to arouse them from their benighted condition to one of moral responsibility, to make them sensible that liberty was legitimately and essentially theirs, without which there was no distinction between them and the brute. Following as a necessary consequence would be the destruction of oppression and ignorance.

Alone and friendless, without a home, a fugitive from slavery, a child of misfortune and outcast upon the world, floating on the cold surface of chance, now in the midst of a great city of opulence, surrounded by the most despotic restrictions upon his race, with renewed determination Henry declared that nothing short of an unforeseen Providence should impede his progress in the spread of secret organization among the slaves. So aroused, he immediately started for a house in the Lower Faubourg.

"My frien', who yeh lookin' foh?" kindly enquired a cautious black man, standing concealed in the shrubbery near the door of a low, tile-covered house standing back in the yard.

"A friend," replied Henry.

"Wat's 'is name?" continued the man.

"I do not rightly know."

"Would yeh know it ef yeh heahed it, my fren'?"

"I think I would."

"Is it Seth?"

"That's the very name!" said Henry.

"Wat yeh want wid 'im, my fren'?"

"I want to see him."

"I spose yeh do, fren'; but dat ain' answer my questin' yet. Wat yeh want wid 'em?"

"I would rather see him, then I'll be better able to answer."

"My fren'," replied the man, meaningly, "ah see da is somethin' in yeh; come in!" giving a significant cough before placing his finger on the latchstring.

On entering, from the number and arrangement of the seats, there was evidence of an anticipated gathering; but the evening being that of the Mardi Gras, there was nothing remarkable in this. Out from another room came a sharp, observing, shrewd little dark brown-skin woman, called in that community a griffe. Bowing, sidling and curtsying, she smilingly came forward.

"Wat brotha dis, Seth?" enquired she.

"Ah don'o," carelessly replied he with a signal of caution, which was not required in her case.

"Ah!" exclaimed Henry. "This is Mr. Seth! I'm glad to see you."

After a little conversation, in which freely participated Mrs. Seth, who evidently was deservingly the leading spirit of the evening, they soon became reconciled to the character and mission of their unexpected and self-invited guest.

"Phebe, go tell 'em," said Seth; when lightly tripping away she entered the door of the other room, which after a few moments' delay was partially opened, and by a singular and peculiar signal, Seth and the stranger were invited in. Here sat in one of the most secret and romantic-looking rooms, a party of fifteen, the representatives of the heads of that many plantations, who that night had gathered for the portentious purpose of a final decision on the hour to strike the first blow. On entering, Henry stood a little in check.

"Trus' 'em!" said Seth. "Yeh fine 'em da right saut uh boys—true to deh own color! Da come fom fifteen diffent plantation."

"They're the men for me!" replied Henry, looking around the room. "Is the house all safe?"

"Yes brotha, all safe an' soun', an' a big dog in da yahd, so dat no one can come neah widout ouah knowin' it."

"First, then, to prayer, and next to seclusion," said Henry, looking at Seth to lead in prayer.

"Brotha, gib us wud a' prah," said Seth to Henry, as the party on their knees bowed low their heads to the floor.

"I am not fit, brother, for a spiritual leader; my warfare is not Heavenly, but earthly; I have not to do with angels, but with men; not with righteousness, but wickedness. Call upon some brother who has more of the grace of God than I. If I ever were a Christian, slavery has made me a sinner; if I had been an angel, it would have made me a devil! I feel more like cursing than praying—may God forgive me! Pray for me, brethren!"

"Brotha Kits, gib us wud a prah, my brotha!" said Seth to an athletic, powerful black man.

"Its not fah ouah many wuds, noah long prah—ouah 'pinion uh ouah self, nah sich like, dat Dou anseh us; but de 'cerity ob ouah hahts an ouah 'tentions. Bless de young man dat come 'mong us; make 'im fit fah 'is day, time, an' genration! Dou knows, Laud, dat fah wat we 'semble; anseh dis ouah 'tition, an' gib us token ob Dine 'probation!" petitioned Kits, slapping his hand at the conclusion down upon and splitting open a pine table before him.

"Amen," responded the gathering.

"Let da wud run an' be glorify!" exclaimed Nathan Seth.

The splitting of the table was regarded as ominous, but of doubtful signification, the major part considering it as rather unfavorable. Making no delay, lest a despondency ensue through fear and superstition, Henry at once entered into seclusion, completing an organization.

"God sen' yeh had come along dis way befo'!" exclaimed Phebe Seth.

"God grant 'e had!" responded Nathan.

"My Laud! I feels like a Sampson! ah feels like gwine up to take de city mehself!" cried out Kits, standing erect in the floor with fists clenched, muscles braced, eyes shut, and head thrown back.

"Yes, yes!" exclaimed Phebe. "Blessed be God, brotha Kits, da King is in da camp!"

"Powah, powah!" responded Seth. "Da King is heah!"

"Praise 'is name!" shouted Phebe clapping and rubbing her hands. "Fah wat I feels an' da knowledge I has receive dis night! I been all my days in darkness till now! I feels we shall be a people yit! Thang' God, thang God!" when she skidded over the floor from side to side, keeping time with a tune sung to the words—

"We'll honor our Lord and Master;
We'll honor our Lord and King;
We'll honor our Lord and Master,
And bow at His command!
O! brothers, did you hear the news?
Lovely Jesus is coming!
If ever I get to the house of the Lord,
I'll never come back any more."

"It's good to be heah!" shouted Seth.

"Ah! dat it is, brotha Seth!" responded Kits. "Da Laud is nigh, dat 'e is! 'e promise whahsomeveh two-three 'semble, to be in da mids' and dat to bless 'em, an' 'is promise not in vain, case 'e heah tonight!"

At the moment which Phebe took her seat, nearly exhausted with exercise, a loud rap at the door, preceded by the signal for the evening, alarmed the party.

"Come in, brotha Tib—come quick, if yeh comin!" bade Seth, in a low voice hastily, as he partially opened the door, peeping out into the other room.

"O, pshaw!" exclaimed Phebe, as she and her husband yet whispered; "I wish he stay away. I sho nobody want 'em! he all'as half drunk anyhow. Good ev'nin', brotha Tib. How yeh been sense we see yeh early paut da night?"

"Reasable, sistah—reasable, thang God. Well, what yeh all 'cided on? I say dis night now au neveh!" said Tib, evidently bent on mischief.

"Foolishness, foolishness!" replied Phebe. "It make me mad see people make fool uh demself! I wish 'e stay home an' not bothen heah!"

"Ah, 'spose I got right to speak as well as da rest on yeh! Yeh all ain' dat high yit to keep body fom talkin', ah 'spose. Betta wait tell yeh git free fo' ye 'temp' scrow oveh people dat way! I kin go out yeh house!" retorted the mischievous man, determined on distracting their plans.

"Nobody odeh yeh out, but I like see people have sense, specially befo' strangehs! an' know how behave demself!"

"I is gwine out yeh house," gruffly replied the man.

"My friend," said Henry, "listen a moment to me. You are not yet ready for a strike; you are not yet ready to do anything effective. You have barely taken the first step in the matter, and ——"

"Strangeh!" interrupted the distracter. "Ah don'o yeh name, yeh strangeh to me—I see yeh talk 'bout 'step'; how many step man got take fo' 'e kin walk? I likes to know dat! Tell me that fus, den yeh may ax me what yeh choose!"

"You must have all the necessary means, my brother," persuasively resumed Henry, "for the accomplishment of your ends. Intelligence among yourself on everything pertaining to your designs and project. You must know what, how, and when to do. Have all the instrumentalities necessary for an effective effort, before making the attempt. Without this, you will fail, utterly fail!"

"Den ef we got wait all dat time, we neveh be free!" gruffly replied he. "I goes in foh dis night! I say dis night! Who goes——"

"Shet yo' big mouth! Sit down! Now make a fool o' yo'self!" exclaimed several voices with impatience, which evidently only tended to increase the mischief.

"Dis night, dis night au neveh!" boisterously yelled the now infuriated man at the top of his voice. "Now's da time!" when he commenced shuffling about over the floor, stamping and singing at the top of his voice—

Come all my brethren, let us take a rest,
While the moon shines bright and clear;
Old master died and left us all at last,
And has gone at the bar to appear!
Old master's dead and lying in his grave;
And our blood will now cease to flow;
He will no more tramp on the neck of the slave,
For he's gone where slaveholders go!
Hang up the shovel and the hoe—o—o—o!
I don't care whether I work or no!

Old master's gone to the slaveholders rest—
He's gone where they all ought to go!

pointing down and concluding with an expression which indicated anything but a religious feeling.

"Shame so it is dat he's lowed to do so! I wish I was man foh 'im, I'd make 'im fly!" said Phebe much alarmed, as she heard the great dog in the yard, which had been so trained as to know the family visitors, whining and manifesting an uneasiness unusual with him. On going to the back door, a person suddenly retreated into the shrubbery, jumping the fence, and disappearing.

Soon, however, there was an angry low heavy growling of the dog, with suppressed efforts to bark, apparently prevented by fear on the part of the animal. This was succeeded by cracking in the bushes, dull heavy footsteps, cautious whispering, and stillness.

"Hush! Listen!" admonished Phebe. "What is dat? Wy don't Tyger bark? I don't understan' it! Seth, go out and see, will you? Wy don't some you men make dat fool stop? I wish I was man, I'd break 'is neck, so I would!" during which the betrayer was shuffling, dancing, and singing at such a pitch as to attract attention from without.

Seth seizing him from behind by a firm grasp of the collar with both hands, Tib sprang forward, slipping easily out of it, leaving the overcoat suspended in his assailant's hands, displaying studded around his waist a formidable array of deathly weapons, when rushing out of the front door, he in terrible accents exclaimed—

"Insurrection! Insurrection! Death to every white!"

With a sudden spring of their rattles, the gendarmes, who in cloisters had surrounded the house, and by constant menacing gestures with their maces kept the great dog, which stood back in a corner, in a snarling position in fear, arrested the miscreant, taking him directly to the old fort calaboose. In the midst of the confusion which necessarily ensued, Henry, Seth, and Phebe, Kits and fellow-leaders from the fifteen plantations, immediately fled, all having passes for the day and evening, which fully protected them in any part of the city away from the scene of disturbance.

Intelligence soon reached all parts of the city, that an extensive plot for rebellion of the slaves had been timely detected. The place was at once thrown into a state of intense excitement, the military called into requisition, dragoons flying in every direction, cannon from the old fort sending forth hourly through the night, thundering peals to give assurance of their sufficiency, and the infantry on duty traversing the streets, stimulating with martial air with voluntary vocalists, who readily joined in chorus to the memorable citing words in the Southern States of—

Go tell Jack Coleman,
The Negroes are arising!

Alarm and consternation succeeded pleasure and repose, sleep for the time seemed to have departed from the eyes of the inhabitants, men, women and children ran every direction through the streets, seeming determined if they were to be massacred, that it should be done in the open highways rather than secretly in their own houses. The commotion thus continued till the morning; meanwhile editors, journalists, reporters, and correspondents, all were busily on the alert, digesting such information as would form an item of news for the press, or a standing reminiscence for historical reference in the future.

CHAPTER 23

The Rebel Blacks

For the remainder of the night secreting themselves in Conti and Burgundi streets, the rebel proprietors of the house in which was laid the plot for the destruction of the city were safe until the morning, their insurrectionary companions having effected a safe retreat to the respective plantations to which they belonged that evening.

Jason and Phebe Seth were the hired slaves of their own time from a widower master, a wealthy retired attorney at Baton Rouge, whose only concern about them was to call every ninety days at the counter of the Canal Bank of New Orleans, and receive the price of their hire, which was there safely deposited to his credit by the industrious and faithful servants. The house in which the rebels met had been hired for the occasion, being furnished rooms kept for transient accommodation.

On the earliest conveyance destined for the City of Mobile, Henry left, who, before he fled, admonished as his parting counsel, to "stand still and see the salvation"; the next day being noted by General Ransom, as an incident in his history, to receive a formal visit of a fortnight's sojourn, in the person of his slaves Jason and Phebe Seth.

The inquisition held in the case of the betrayer Tib developed fearful antecedents of extensive arrangements for the destruction of the city by fire and water, thereby compelling the white inhabitants to take refuge in the swamps, whilst the blacks marched up the coast, sweeping the plantations as they went.

Suspicions were fixed upon many, among whom was an unfortunate English schoolteacher, who was arrested and imprisoned, when he died, to the last protesting his innocence. Mr. Farland was a good and bravehearted man, disdaining to appeal for redress to his country, lest it might be regarded as the result of cowardice.

Taking fresh alarm at this incident, the municipal regulations have been most rigid in a system of restriction and espionage toward Negroes and mulattoes, almost destroying their self-respect and manhood, and certainly impairing their usefulness.

CHAPTER 24

A Flying Cloud

Safely in Mobile Henry landed without a question, having on the way purchased of a passenger who was deficient of means to bear expenses, a horse by which he made a daring entry into the place. Mounting the animal which was fully caparisoned, he boldly rode to the principal livery establishment, ordering for it the greatest care until his master's arrival.

Hastening into the country he readily found a friend and seclusion in the hut of Uncle Cesar, on the plantation of Gen. Audly. Making no delay, early next morning he returned to the city to effect a special object. Passing by the stable where the horse had been left, a voice loudly cried out:

"There's that Negro boy, now! Hallo, there, boy! didn't you leave a horse here?"

Heeding not the interrogation, but speedily turning the first corner, Henry hastened away and was soon lost among the inhabitants.

"How yeh do, me frien'?" saluted a black man whom he met in a by-street. "Ar' yeh strangeh?"

"Why?" enquired Henry.

"O, nothin'! On'y I hearn some wite men talkin' j's now, an' da say some strange nigga lef' a hoss dar, an' da blev 'e stole 'em, an' da gwine ketch an' put 'em in de jail."

"If that's all, I live here. Good morning!" rejoined he who soon was making rapid strides in the direction of Georgia.

Every evening found him among the quarters of some plantations, safely secreted in the hut of some faithful, trustworthy slave, with attentive, anxious listeners, ready for an issue. So, on he went with flying haste, from plantation to plantation, till Alabama was left behind him.

In Georgia, though the laws were strict, the Negroes were equally hopeful. Like the old stock of Maryland and Virginia blacks from whom they were descended, they manifested a high degree of intelligence for slaves. Receiving their messenger with open arms, the aim of his advent among them spread like fire in a stubble. Everywhere seclusions were held and organizations completed, till Georgia stands like a city at the base of a burning mountain, threatened with destruction by an overflow of the first outburst of lava from above. Clearing the state without an obstruction, he entered that which of all he most dreaded, the haughty South Carolina.

Here the most relentless hatred appears to exist against the Negro, who seems to be regarded but as an animated thing of convenience or a domesticated animal, reared for the service of his master. The studied policy of the whites evidently is to keep the blacks in subjection and their spirits below a sentiment of self-respect. To impress the Negro with a sense of his own inferiority is a leading precept of their social system; to be white is the only evidence necessary to establish a claim to superiority. To be a "master" in South Carolina is to hold a position of rank and title, and he who approaches this the nearest is heightened at least in his own estimation.

These feelings engendered by the whites have been extensively incorporated with the elements of society among the colored people, giving rise to the "Brown Society" an organized association of mulattos, created by the influence of the whites, for the purpose of preventing pure-blooded Negroes from entering the social circle, or holding intercourse with them. [14]

Here intelligence and virtue are discarded and ignored, when not in conformity with these regulations. A man with the prowess of Memnon, or a woman with the purity of the "black doves" of Ethiopia and charms of the "black virgin" of Solomon, avails them nothing, if the blood of the oppressor, engendered by wrong, predominates not in their veins.

Oppression is the author of all this, and upon the heads of the white masters let the terrible responsibility of this miserable stupidity and ignorance of their mulatto children rest; since to them was left the plan of their social salvation, let upon their consciences rest the penalties of their social damnation.

The transit of the runaway through this state was exceedingly difficult, as no fabrication of which he was capable could save him from the penalties of arrest. To assume freedom would be at once to consign himself to endless bondage, and to acknowledge himself a slave was at once to advertise for a master. His only course of safety was to sleep through the day and travel by night, always keeping to the woods.

At a time just at the peep of day when making rapid strides the baying of hounds and soundings of horns were heard at a distance.

Understanding it to be the sport of the chase, Henry made a hasty retreat to the nearest hiding place which presented, in the hollow of a log. On attempting to creep in a snarl startled him, when out leaped the fox, having counterrun his track several times, and sheltered in a fallen sycamore. Using his remedy for distracting dogs, he succeeded the fox in the sycamore, resting in safety during the day without molestation, though the dogs bayed within thirty yards of him, taking a contrary course by the distraction of their scent.

For every night of sojourn in the state he had a gathering, not one of which was within a hut, so closely were the slaves watched by patrol, and sometimes by mulatto and black overseers. These gatherings were always held in the forest. Many of the confidants of the seclusions were the much-dreaded runaways of the woods, a class of outlawed slaves, who continually seek the lives of their masters.

One day having again sought retreat in a hollow log where he lay sound asleep, the day being chilly, he was awakened by a cold application to his face and neck, which proved to have been made by a rattlesnake of the largest size, having sought the warmth of his bosom.

Henry made a hasty retreat, ever after declining the hollow of a tree. With rapid movements and hasty action, he like a wind cloud flew through the State of South Carolina, who like "a thief in the night" came when least expected.

Henry now entered Charleston, the metropolis, and head of the "Brown Society," the bane and dread of the blacks in the state, an organization formed through the instrumentality of the whites to keep the blacks and mulattos at variance. To such an extent is the error carried, that the members of the association, rather than their freedom would prefer to see the blacks remain in bondage. But many most excellent mulattos and quadroons condemn with execration this auxiliary of oppression. The eye of the intelligent world is on this "Brown Society"; and its members when and wherever seen are scanned with suspicion and distrust. May they not be forgiven for their ignorance when proving by repentance their conviction of wrong?

Lying by till late next morning, he entered the city in daylight, having determined boldly to pass through the street, as he might not be known from any common Negro. Coming to an extensive wood-yard he learned by an old black man who sat at the gate that the proprietors were two colored men, one of whom he pointed out, saying:

"Dat is my mausta."

Approaching a respectable-looking mulatto gentleman standing in conversation with a white, his foot resting on a log:

"Do you wish to hire help, sir?" enquired Henry respectfully touching his cap.

"Take off your hat, boy!" ordered the mulatto gentleman. Obeying the order, he repeated the question.

"Who do you belong to?" enquired the gentleman.

"I am free, sir!" replied he.

"You are a free, boy? Are you not a stranger here?"

"Yes, sir."

"Then you lie, sir," replied the mulatto gentleman, "as you know that no free Negro is permitted to enter this state. You are a runaway, and I'll have you taken up!" at the same time walking through his office looking out at the front door as if for an officer.

Making a hasty retreat, in less than an hour he had left the city, having but a few minutes tarried in the hut of an old black family on the suburb, one of the remaining confidentials and adherents of the memorable South Carolina insurrection, when and to whom he imparted his fearful scheme.

"Ah!" said the old man, throwing his head in the lap of his old wife, with his hands around her neck, both of whom sat near the chimney with the tears coursing down their furrowed cheeks. "Dis many a day I been prayin' dat de Laud sen' a nudder Denmark 'mong us! De Laud now anseh my prar in dis young man! Go on, my son—go on—an' may God A'mighty bress yeh!"

North Carolina was traversed mainly in the night. When approaching the region of the Dismal Swamp, a number of the old confederates of the noted Nat Turner were met with, who hailed the daring young runaway as the harbinger of better days.[15] Many of these are still long-suffering, hard-laboring slaves on the plantations; and some bold, courageous, and fearless adventurers, denizens of the mystical, antiquated, and almost fabulous Dismal Swamp, where for many years they have defied the approach of their pursuers.

Here Henry found himself surrounded by a different atmosphere, an entirely new element. Finding ample scope for undisturbed action through the entire region of the Swamp, he continued to go scattering to the winds and sowing the seeds of a future crop, only to take root in the thick black waters which cover it, to be grown in devastation and reaped in a whirlwind of ruin.

"I been lookin' fah yeh dis many years," said old Gamby Gholar, a noted high conjurer and compeer of Nat Turner, who for more than thirty years has been secluded in the Swamp, "an' been tellin' on 'em dat yeh 'ood come long, but da 'ooden' heah dat I tole 'em! Now da see! Dis many years I been seein' on yeh! Yes, 'ndeed, chile, dat I has!" and he took from a gourd of antiquated appearance which hung against the wall in his hut, many articles of a mysterious character, some resembling bits of woollen yarn, onionskins, oystershells, finger and toenails, eggshells, and scales which he declared to be from very dangerous serpents, but which closely resembled, and were believed to be those of innocent and harmless fish, with broken iron nails.

These he turned over and over again in his hands, closely inspecting them through a fragment of green bottle glass, which he claimed to be a mysterious and precious "blue stone" got at a peculiar and unknown spot in the Swamp, whither by a special faith he was led—and ever after unable to find the same spot—putting them again into the gourd, the end of the neck being cut off so as to form a bottle, he rattled the "goombah," as he termed it, as if endeavoring to frighten his guest. This process ended, he whispered, then sighted into the neck, first with one eye, then with the other, then shook, and so alternately whispering, sighting and shaking, until apparently getting tired, again pouring them out, fumbling among them until finding a forked breast-bone of a small bird, which, muttering to himself, he called the "charm bone of a treefrog."

"Ah," exclaimed Gamby as he selected out the mystic symbol handing it to Henry, "got yeh at las'. Take dis, meh son, an' so long as yeh keep it, da can' haum yeh, dat da can't. Dis woth money, meh son; da ain't many sich like dat in de Swamp! Yeh never want for nothin' so long as yeh keep dat!"

In this fearful abode for years of some of Virginia and North Carolina's boldest black rebels, the names of Nat Turner, Denmark Veezie, and General Gabriel were held by them in sacred reverence; that of Gabriel as a talisman. With delight they recounted the many exploits of whom they conceived to be the greatest men who ever lived, the pretended deeds of whom were fabulous, some of the narrators claiming to have been patriots in the American Revolution.

"Yeh offen hearn on Maudy Ghamus," said an old man stooped with age, having the appearance of a centenarian. "Dat am me—me heah!" continued he, touching himself on the breast. "I's de frien' on Gamby Gholar; an' I an' Gennel Gabel fit in de Malution wah, an' da want no sich fightin' dare as dat in Gabel wah!"

"You were then a soldier in the Revolutionary War for American independence, father?" enquired Henry.

"Gau bress yeh, hunny. Yes, 'ndeed, chile, long 'for yeh baun; dat I did many long day go! Yes, chile, yes!"

"And General Gabriel, too, a soldier of the American Revolution?" replied Henry.

"Ah, chile, dat 'e did fit in de Molution wah, Gabel so, an' 'e fit like mad dog! Wen 'e sturt, chile, da can't stop 'im; da may as well let 'im go long, da can't do nuffin' wid 'im."

Henry subscribed to his eminent qualifications as a warrior, assuring him that those were the kind of fighting men they then needed among the blacks. Maudy Ghamus to this assented, stating that the Swamp contained them in sufficient number to take the whole United States; the only difficulty in the way being that the slaves in the different states could not be convinced of their strength. He had himself for years been an emissary; also, Gamby Gholar, who had gone out among them with sufficient charms to accomplish all they desired, but could not induce the slaves to a general rising.

"Take plenty goomba an' fongosa 'long wid us, an' plant mocasa all along, an' da got nuffin' fah do but come, an' da 'ooden come!" despairingly declared Maudy Ghamus.

Gamby Gholar, Maudy Ghamus, and others were High Conjurors, who as ambassadors from the Swamp, were regularly sent out to create new conjurers, lay charms, take off "spells" that could not be reached by Low Conjurors, and renew the art of all conjurors of seven years existence, at the expiration of which period the virtue was supposed to run out; holding their official position by fourteen years appointments. Through this means the revenue is obtained for keeping up an organized existence in this much-dreaded morass—the Dismal Swamp.

Before Henry left they insisted upon, and anointed him a priest of the order of High Conjurors, and amusing enough it was to him who consented to satisfy the aged devotees of a time-honored superstition among them. Their supreme executive body called the "Head" consists in number of seven aged men, noted for their superior experience and wisdom. Their place of official meeting must be entirely secluded, either in the forest, a gully, secluded hut, an underground room, or a cave.

The seven old men who, with heightened spirits, hailed his advent among them, led Henry to the door of an ample cave—their hollow—at the door of which they were met by a large sluggish, lazily-moving serpent, but so entirely tame and petted that it wagged its tail with fondness toward Maudy as he led the party. The old men, suddenly stopping at the approach of the reptile, stepping back a pace, looked at each other mysteriously shaking their heads:

"Go back!" exclaimed Maudy waving his hand. "Go back, my chile! 'e in terrible rage! 'e got seben long toof, any on 'em kill yeh like flash!" tapping it slightly on the head with a twig of grapevine which he carried in his hand.

Looking at the ugly beast, Henry had determined did it approach to harm, to slay it; but instead, it quietly coiled up and lay at the door as if asleep, which reminded him of queer and unmeaning sounds as they approached, uttered by Gholar, which explained that the animal had been trained to approach when called as any other pet. The "Head" once in session, they created him conjuror of the highest degree known to their art.* With this qualification he was licensed with unlimited power—a power before given no one—to go forth and do wonders. The "Head" seemed, by the unlimited power given him, to place greater reliance in the efforts of Henry for their deliverance than in their own seven heads together.

"Go, my son," said they, "an' may God A'mighty hole up yo' han's an' grant us speedy 'liverence!'"

Being now well refreshed—having rested without the fear of detection—and in the estimation of Gholar, Ghamus and the rest of the "Heads", well qualified to prosecute his project amidst the prayers, blessings, wishes, hopes, fears, pow-wows and promises of a never failing conjuration, and tears of the cloudy inhabitants of this great seclusion, among whom were the frosty-headed, bowed-down old men of the Cave, Henry left that region by his usual stealthy process, reaching Richmond, Virginia, in safety.

CHAPTER 25

Like Father, Like Son

With his usual adroitness, early in the morning, Henry entered Richmond boldly walking through the streets. This place in its municipal regulations, the customs and usages of society, the tastes and assumptious pride of the inhabitants, much resembles Charleston, South Carolina, the latter being a modified model of the former.

The restrictions here concerning Negroes and mulattos are less rigid, as they may be permitted to continue in social or religious gatherings after nine o'clock at night provided a white person be present to

---

*The highest degree known to the art of conjuration in the Dismal Swamp, is Seven-finger High-glister.

inspect their conduct; and may ride in a carriage, smoke a cigar in daylight, or walk with a staff at night.

According to an old-existing custom said to have originated by law, a mulatto or quadroon who proved a white mother were themselves regarded as white: and many availing themselves of the fact, took advantage of it by leaving their connections with the blacks and turning entirely over to the whites. Their children take further advantage of this by intermarrying with the whites, by which their identity becomes extinct, and they enter every position in society both social and political. Some of the proudest American statesmen in either House of the Capital, receive their poetic vigor of imagination from the current of Negro blood flowing in their veins.

Like those of Charleston, some of the light mixed bloods of Richmond hold against the blacks and pure-blooded Negroes the strongest prejudice and hatred, all engendered by the teachings of their Negro-fearing master-fathers. All of the terms and epithets of disparagement commonly used by the whites toward the blacks are as readily applied to them by this class of the mixed bloods. Shy of the blacks and fearful of the whites, they go sneaking about with the countenance of a criminal, of one conscious of having done wrong to his fellows. Spurned by the one and despised by the other, they are the least happy of all the classes. Of this class was Mrs. Pierce, whose daughter stood in the hall door, quite early enjoying the cool air this morning.

"Miss," enquired Henry of the young quadroon lady, "can you inform me where I'll find the house of Mr. Norton, a colored family in this city?" politely raising his cap as he approached her.

With a screech she retreated into the house, exclaiming, that a black Negro at the door had given her impudence. Startled at this alarm so unexpected to him—though somewhat prepared for such from his recent experience in Charleston—Henry made good a most hasty retreat before the father, with a long red "hide" in his hand, could reach the door. The man grimaced, declaring, could he have his way, every black in the country would be sold away to labor.

Finding the house of his friend, he was safely secluded until evening, when developing his scheme, the old material extinguished and left to mould and rot after the demonstration at Southampton, was immediately rekindled, never again to be suppressed until the slaves stood up the equal of the masters. Southampton—the name of Southampton to them was like an electric shock.

"Ah, Laud!" replied Uncle Medly, an old man of ninety-four years, when asked whether or not he would help his brethren in a critical time of need. "Dat I would. Ef I do noffin' else, I pick up dirt an' tro' in der eye!" meaning in that of their masters.

"Glory to God!" exclaimed his wife, an old woman of ninety years.

"Hallelujah!" responded her daughter, the wife of Norton, the man of the house.

"Blessed be God's eternal name!" concluded the man himself. "I've long been praying and looking, but God has answered me at last."

"None could answer it, but a prayer-hearing God!" replied the wife.

"None would answer it, but a prayer-hearing God!" responded the husband.

"None did answer it, but a prayer-hearing God!" exclaimed the woman. "Glory to God! Glory to God! 'Tis none but He can deliver!"

They fell on their knees to pray, when fervent was their devotion; after which Henry left, but on account of a strict existing patrol regulation, was obliged for three days to be in the wood, so closely watched was he. The fourth evening he effected most adroitly an escape from his hiding place, passing through a strong guard of patrol all around him, entering the District of Columbia at early dawn, soon entering the City of Washington.

The slave prison of Williams and Brien conspicuously stood among the edifices; high in the breeze from the flagstaff floated defiantly the National Colors, stars as the pride of the white man, and stripes as the emblem of power over the blacks. At this the fugitive gave a passing glance, but with hurried steps continued his course, not knowing whither he would tarry. He could only breathe in soliloquy, "How long, O Lord of the oppressed, how long shall this thing continue?"

Passing quietly along, gazing in at every door, he came to a stop on the corner of Pennsylvania avenue and Sixth Street. On entering, looking into the establishment, his eye unexpectedly caught that of a person who proved to be a mulatto gentleman, slowly advancing toward the door.

His first impulse was to make a retreat, but fearing the effort would be fatal, bracing his nerves, he stood looking the person full in the face.

"Do you want anything, young man?" enquired the mulatto gentleman, who proved to be the proprietor.

"I am hungry, sir!" Henry quickly replied.

"You're a stranger, then, in the city?"

"I am, sir."

"Never here before?"

"Never before, sir."

"Have you no acquaintance in the place?"

"None at all, sir."

"Then, sir, if you'll come in, I'll see if I can find as much as you can eat." replied the goodhearted man.

Setting him down to a comfortable breakfast, the wife and niece of the proprietor kindly attended upon him, filling his pouch afterwards with sufficient for the day's travel.

Giving him a parting hand, Henry left with, "God Almighty bless the family!" clearing the city in a short time.

"I understand it all," replied the gentleman in response, "and may the same God guide and protect you by the way!" justly regarding him as a fugitive.

The kindness received at the hands of this family* brought tears of gratitude to the eyes of the recipient, especially when remembering his treatment from the same class in Charleston and Richmond. About the same time that Henry left the city, the slave of a distinguished Southern statesman also left Washington and the comforts of home and kindness of his master forever.

From Washington taking a retrograde course purposely to avoid Maryland, where he learned they were already well advised and holding gatherings, the margin of Virginia was cut in this hasty passage, so as to reach more important points for communication. Stealing through the neighborhood and swimming the river, a place was reached called Mud Fort, some four miles distant from Harper's Ferry, situated on the Potomac.

Seeing a white man in a field near by, he passed on as if unconscious of his presence, when the person hailing him in broken English questioned his right to pass.

"I am going to Charleston, sir." replied Henry.

"Vat fahr?" inquired the Dutchman.

"On business." replied he.

---

*This gentleman died on the 15th of June, 1857, in a distant territory, whither he had removed, where his excellent widow, niece and children all reside, well provided for.

"You nagher, you! dat ish not anzer mine question! I does ax you vat fahr you go to Charleston, and you anzer me dat!"

"I told you, sir, that I am going on business."

"You ish von zaucy nagher, andt I bleve you one runaway! Py ching, I vill take you pack!" said the man instantly climbing the fence to get into the road where the runaway stood.

"That will do," exclaimed Henry, "you are near enough—I can bring you down there," at the same time presenting a well-charged six-barrel weapon of death; when the affrighted Dutchman fell on the opposite side of the fence unharmed, and Henry put down his weapon without a fire.

Having lurked till evening in a thicket near by, Charleston was entered near the depot, just at the time when the last train was leaving for Washington. Though small, this place was one of the most difficult in which to promote his object, as the slaves were but comparatively few, difficult to be seen, and those about the depot and house servants, trained to be suspicious and mistrustful of strange blacks, and true and faithful to their masters.[16] Still, he was not remiss in finding a friend and a place for the seclusion.

This place was most admirably adapted for the gathering, being held up a run or little stream, in a bramble thicket on a marshy meadow of the old Brackenridge estate, but a few minutes walk from the town. This evening was that of a strict patrol watch, their headquarters for the night being in Worthington's old mills, from which ran the race, passing near which was the most convenient way to reach the place of gathering for the evening.

While stealthily moving along in the dark, hearing a cracking in the weeds and a soft tramping of feet, Henry secreted himself in a thick high growth of Jamestown weeds along the fence, when he slightly discerned a small body of men as if reconnoitering the neighborhood. Sensible of the precariousness of his condition, the fugitive lie as still as death, lest by dint he might be discovered, as much fear and apprehension then prevaded the community.

Charleston, at best, was a hard place for a Negro, and under the circumstances, had he been discovered, no plea would have saved him. Breathlessly crouched beneath the foliage and thorns of the fetid weed, he was startled by a voice suddenly exclaiming—

"Hallo there! who's that?" which provided to be that of one of the patrol, the posse having just come down the bank of the race from the mill.

"Sahvant, mausta!" was the humble reply.

"Who are you?" further enquired the voice.

"Zack Parker, sir."

"Is that you, old Zack?"

"Yes, mausta—honner bright."

"Come, Zack, you must go with us! Don't you know that Negroes are not allowed to be out at night alone, these times? Come along!" said Davy Hunter.

"Honner bright, maus Davy—honner bright!" continued the old black slave of Colonel Davenport, quietly walking beside them along the mill race, the water of which being both swift and deep. "Maus Davy, I got some mighty good rum here in dis flas'—you gentmen hab some? Mighty good! Mine I tells you, maus Davy—mighty good!"

"Well, Zack, we don't care to take a little," replied Bob Flagg. "Have you had your black mouth to this flask?"

"Honner bright, maus Bobby—honner bright!" replied the old man.

Hunter raised the flask to his mouth, the others gathering around, each to take a draught in turn, when instantly a plunge in the water was heard, and the next moment old Zack Parker was swinging his hat in triumph on the opposite bank of the channel, exclaiming, "Honner bright, gentmen! Honner bright! Happy Jack an' no trouble!"—the last part of the sentence being a cant phrase commonly in use in that part of the country, to indicate a feeling free from all cares.

In a rage the flask was thrown in the dark, and alighted near his feet upright in the tufts of grass, when the old man in turn seizing the vessel, exclaiming aloud, "Yo' heath, gentmen! Yo' good heath!" Then turning it up to his mouth, the sound heard across the stream gave evidence of his enjoyment of the remainder of the contents. "Thank'e, gentmen—good night!" when away went Zack to the disappointment and even amusement of the party.

Taking advantage of this incident, Henry, under a guide, found a place of seclusion, and a small number of good willing spirits ready for the counsel.

"Mine, my chile!" admonished old Aunt Lucy. "Mine hunny, how yeh go long case da all'as lookin' arter black folks."

Taking the nearest course through Worthington's woods, he reached in good time that night the slave quarters of Captain Jack Briscoe and

Major Brack Rutherford. The blacks here were united by the confidential leaders of Moore's people, and altogether they were rather a superior gathering of slaves to any yet met with in Virginia. His mission here soon being accomplished, he moved rapidly on to Slaughter's, Crane's and Washington's old plantations, where he caused a glimmer of light, which until then had never been thought of, much less seen, by them.

The night rounds of the patrol of the immediate neighborhood, caused a hurried retreat from Washington's—the last place at which he stopped—and daybreak the next morning found him in near proximity to Winchester, when he sought and obtained a hiding place in the woods of General Bell.

The people here he found ripe and ready for anything that favored their redemption. Taylor's, Logan's, Whiting's and Tidball's plantations all had crops ready for the harvest.

"An' is dis de young man," asked Uncle Talton, stooped with the age of eighty-nine years, "dat we hearn so much ob, dat's gwine all tru de country 'mong de black folks? Tang God a'mighty for wat I lib to see!" and the old man straightened himself up to his greatest height, resting on his staff, and swinging himself around as if whirling on the heel as children sometimes do, exclaimed in the gladness of his heart and the bouyancy of his spirits at the prospect of freedom before him: "I dont disagard none on 'em," referring to the whites.

"We have only 'regarded' them too long, father," replied Henry with a sigh of sorrow, when he looked upon the poor old time and care-worn slave, whose only hope for freedom rested in his efforts.

"I neber 'spected to see dis! God bless yeh, my son! May God 'long yeh life!" continued the old man, the tears streaming down his cheeks.

"Amen!" sanctioned Uncle Ek.

"God grant it!" replied Uncle Duk.

"May God go wid yeh, my son, wheresomeber yeh go!" exclaimed the old slaves present; when Henry, rising from the block of wood upon which he sat, being moved to tears, reaching out his hand, said, "Well, brethren, mothers, and fathers! My time with you is up, and I must leave you—farewell!" when this faithful messenger of his oppressed brethren, was soon in the woods, making rapid strides towards Western Virginia.

Wheeling, in the extreme Western part of Virginia, was reached by the fugitive, where the slaves, already restless and but few in number in consequence of their close proximity to a free state—Ohio being on the opposite side of the river, on the bank of which the town is situated—could never thereafter become contented.

The "Buckeye State" steamer here passed along on a downward trip, when boarding her as a black passenger, Cincinnati in due season was reached, when the passengers were transferred to the "Telegraph No. 2," destined for Louisville, Kentucky. Here crowding in with the passengers, he went directly to Shippenport, a small place but two miles below—the rapids or falls preventing the large class of steamers from going thence except at the time of high water—the "Crystal Palace," a beautiful packet, was boarded, which swiftly took him to Smithland, at the confluence of the Cumberland and Ohio rivers.

From this point access up the Cumberland was a comparatively easy task, and his advent into Nashville, Tennessee, was as unexpected at this time to the slaves, as it was portentous and ominous to the masters.

There was no difficulty here in finding a seclusion, and the introduction of his subject was like the application of fire to a drought-seasoned stubble field. The harvest was ripe and ready for the scythe, long before the reaper and time for gathering came. In both town and country the disappointment was sad, when told by Henry that the time to strike had not yet come; that they for the present must "Stand still and see the salvation!"

"How long, me son, how long we got wait dis way?" asked Daddy Luu, a good old man and member of a Christian church for upwards of forty years.

"I can't tell exactly, father, but I suppose in this, as in all other good works, the Lord's own annointed time!" replied he.

"An' how long dat gwine be, honey? case I's mighty ti'ed waitin' dis way!" earnestly responded the old man.

"I can't tell you how long, father; God knows best."

"An' how we gwine know w'en 'E is ready?"

"When we are ready, He is ready, and not till then is His time."

"God sen we was ready, now den!" concluded the old man, blinded with tears, and who, from the reverence they had for his age and former good counsel among them, this night was placed at the head of the Gathering.

Carrying with him the prayers and blessings of his people here, Henry made rapid strides throughout this state, sowing in every direction seeds of the crop of a future harvest.

From Tennessee Henry boldly strode into Kentucky, and though there seemed to be a universal desire for freedom, there were few who were willing to strike. To run away, with them, seemed to be the highest conceived idea of their right to liberty. This they were doing, and would continue to do on every favorable opportunity, but their right to freedom by self-resistance, to them was forbidden by the Word of God. Their hopes were based on the long-talked-of promised emancipation in the state. [17]

"What was your dependence," inquired he of an old man verging on the icy surface of ninety winters' slippery pathways, "before you had this promise of emancipation?"

"Wy, dar war Guvneh Metcalf, I sho 'e good to black folks," replied Uncle Winson.

"Well, uncle, tell me, supposing he had not been so, what would you have then done?"

"Wy, chile, I sho 'e raise up dat time 'sides dem maus Henry and maus John."

"But what good have they ever done you? I don't see that you are any better off than had they never lived."

"Ah, chile! Da good to we black folks," continued the old man, with a fixed belief that they were emancipationists and the day of freedom, to the slaves drew near.

Satisfied that self-reliance was the furthest from their thoughts, but impressing them with new ideas concerning their rights, the great-hearted runaway bid them "Good bye, and may God open your eyes to see your own condition!" when in a few minutes Lexington was relieved of an enemy, more potent than the hostile bands of red men who once defied the military powers of Kentucky.

In a few days this astonishing slave was again on the smooth waters of the beautiful Ohio, making speed as fast as the steamer "Queen of the West" could carry him down stream towards Grand Gulf on the great river of the Southwest.

CHAPTER 26

Return to Mississippi

The evening, for the season, was very fine; the sky beautiful; the stars shining unusually bright; while Henry, alone on the hurricane deck of the "Queen of the West," stood in silence abaft the wheel-house, gazing intently at the golden orbs of Heaven. Now shoots a meteor, then seemingly shot a comet, again glistened a brilliant planet which almost startled the gazer; and while he yet stood motionless in wonder looking into the heavens, a blazing star whose scintillations dazzled the sight, and for the moment bewildered the mind, was seen apparently to vibrate in a manner never before observed by him.

At these things Henry was filled with amazement, and disposed to attach more than ordinary importance to them, as having an especial bearing in his case; but the mystery finds interpretation in the fact that the emotions were located in his own brain, and not exhibited by the orbs of Heaven.

Through the water plowed the steamer, the passengers lively and mirthful, sometimes amusingly noisy, whilst the adventurous and heart-stricken fugitive, without a companion or friend with whom to share his grief and sorrows, and aid in untangling his then deranged mind, threw himself in tribulation upon the humble pallet assigned him, there to pour out his spirit in communion with the Comforter of souls on high.

The early rising of the passengers aroused him from apparently an abridged night of intermitting sleep, when creeping away into a by-place, he spent the remainder of the day. Thus by sleeping through the day, and watching in the night—induced by the proximity to his old home—did the runaway spend the time during the first two days of his homeward journey.

Falling into a deep sleep early on the evening of the third day, he was suddenly aroused about eleven o'clock by the harsh singing of the black firemen on the steamer:

Natchez under the Hill!
Natchez under the Hill!

sung to an air with which they ever on the approach of a steamer, greet the place, as seemingly a sorrowful reminiscence of their ill-fated brethren continually sold there; when springing to his feet and hurrying upon deck, he found the vessel full upon the wharf boat stationed at the Natchez landing.

Taking advantage of the moment—passing from the wheelhouse down the ladder to the lower deck—thought by many to have gone forever from the place, Henry effected without detection an easy transit to the wharf, and from thence up the Hill, where again he found himself amid the scenes of his saddest experience, and the origination and organization of the measures upon which were based his brightest hopes and expectations for the redemption of his race in the South.

CHAPTER 27

A Night of Anxiety

On Saturday evening, about half past seven, was it that Henry dared again to approach the residence of Colonel Franks. The family had not yet retired, as the lights still burned brilliantly in the great house, when, secreted in the shrubbery contiguous to the hut of Mammy Judy and Daddy Joe, he lay patiently awaiting the withdrawal in the mansion.

"There's no use in talkin,' Andy, he's gittin' suspicious of us all," said Charles, "as he threatens us all with the traders; an' if Henry don't come soon, I'll have to leave anyhow! But the old people, Andy, I can't think of leavin' them!"

"Do you think da would go if da had a chance, Charles?"

"Go? yes 'ndeed, Andy, they'd go this night if they could git off. Since the sellin' of Maggie, and Henry's talkin' to 'em, and his goin' an' takin' little Joe, and Ailcey, an' Cloe, an' Polly an' all clearin' out, they altered their notion about stayin' with ole Franks."

"Wish we could know when Henry's comin' back. Wonder what 'e is," said Andy.

"Here!" was the reply in a voice so cautiously suppressed, and so familiarly distinct that they at once recognized it to be that of their long-absent and most anxiously looked-for friend. Rushing upon him, they mutually embraced, with tears of joy and anxiety.

"How have you been anyhow, Henry?" exclaimed Charles in a suppressed tone. "I's so glad to see yeh, dat I ain't agwine to speak to yeh, so I ain't!" added Andy.

"Come, brethren, to the woods!" said Henry; when the three went directly to the forest, two and half miles from the city.

"Well now, Henry, tell us all about yourself. What you been doin'?" inquired Charles.

"I know of nothing about myself worth telling," replied he.

"Oh, pshaw! wot saut a way is dat, Henry; yeh wont tell a body nothin'. Pshaw, dats no way," grumbled Andy.

"Yes, Andy, I've much to tell you; but not of myself; 'tis about our poor oppressed people everywhere I've been! But we have not now time for that."

"Why, can't you tell us nothin'?"

"Well, Andy, since you must have something, I'll tell you this much: I've been in the Dismal Swamp among the High Conjurors, and saw the heads, old Maudy Ghamus and Gamby Gholar."

"Hoop! now 'e's a talkin'! Ef 'e wasn't I wouldn't tell yeh so! An' wat da sa to yeh, Henry?"

"They welcomed me as the messenger of their deliverance; and as a test of their gratitude, made me a High Conjuror after their own order."

"O pshaw, Henry! Da done what? Wy, ole feller, yeh is high sho 'nough!"

"What good does it do, Henry, to be a conjuror?" inquired Charles.

"It makes the more ignorant slaves have greater confidence in, and more respect for, their headmen and leaders."

"Oh yes, I see now!" Because I couldn't see why you would submit to become a conjuror if it done no good."

"That's it, Charles! As you know, I'll do anything not morally wrong, to gain our freedom; and to effect this, we must take the slaves, not as we wish them to be, but as we really find them to be."

"You say it gives power, Henry; is there any reality in the art of conjunction?"

"It only makes the slaves afraid of you if you are called a conjuror, that's all!"

"Oh, I understand it well enough now!" concluded Charles.

"I undehstood well 'nough fuss, but I want to know all I could, dat's all!" added Andy. "Ole Maudy's a high feller, aint 'e, Henry?"

"Oh yes! he's the Head," replied Charles.

"No," explained Henry, "he's not now Head, but Gamby Gholar, who has for several years held that important position among them. Their Council consists of Seven, called the 'Heads,' and their Chief is called 'the Head.' Everything among them, in religion, medicine, laws, or politics, of a public character, is carried before the Head in Council to be settled and disposed of."

"Now we understan'," said Andy, "but tell us, Henry, how yeh get 'long 'mong de folks whar yeh bin all dis time?"

"Very well; everywhere except Kentucky, and there you can't move them toward a strike!"

"Kentucky!" rejoined Andy. "I all'as thought dat de slaves in dat state was de bes' treated uv any, an' dat da bin all 'long spectin' to be free."

"That's the very mischief of it, Andy! 'Tis this confounded 'good treatment' and expectation of getting freed by their oppressors, that has been the curse of the slave. All shrewd masters, to keep their slaves in check, promise them their freedom at their, the master's death, as though they were certain to die first. This contents the slave, and makes him obedient and willing to serve and toil on, looking forward to the promised redemption. This is just the case precisely now in Kentucky. It was my case. While Franks treated me well, and made promises of freedom to my wife"—and he gave a deep sigh—"I would doubtless have been with him yet; but his bad treatment—his inhuman treatment of my wife—my poor, poor wife!—poor Maggie! was that which gave me courage, and made me determined to throw off the yoke, let it cost me what it would. Talk to me of a good master! A 'good master' is the very worst of masters. Were they all cruel and inhuman, or could the slaves be made to see their treatment aright, they would not endure their oppression for a single hour!"

"I sees it, I sees it!" replied Andy.

"An' so do I," added Charles, "who couldn't see that?"

"I tells yeh, Henry, it was mighty haud for me to make up my mine to leave ole Potteh; but even sence you an' Chaules an' me made de vow togedder, I got mo' an' mo' to hate 'im. I could chop 'is head off sometime, I get so mad. I bleve I could chop off Miss Mary' head; an' I likes hur; she mighty good to we black folks."

"Pshaw! yes 'ndeed' ole Frank's head would be nothin' for me to chop off; I could chop off mistress head, an' you know she's a good woman; but I mus' be mighty mad fus'!" said Charles.

"That's it, you see. There is no danger that a 'good' master or mistress will ever be harmed by the slaves. There's neither of you, Andy, could muster up courage enough to injure a 'good master' or mistress. And even I now could not have the heart to injure Mrs. Franks," said Henry.

"Now me," replied Charles.

"Yes, 'ndeed, dats a fac', case I knows I couldn' hurt Miss Mary Potteh. I bleve I'd almos' chop off anybody's head if I see 'em 'tempt to hurt 'e!" added Andy; when they heartily laughed at each other.

"Just so!" said Henry. "A slave has no just conception of his own wrongs. Had I dealt with Franks as he deserved, for doing that for which he would have taken the life of any man had it been his case— tearing my wife from my bosom!— the most I could take courage directly to do, was to leave him, and take as many from him as I could induce to go. But maturer reflection drove me to the expedient of avenging the general wrongs of our people, by inducing the slave, in his might, to scatter red ruin throughout the region of the South. But still, I cannot find it in my heart to injure an individual, except in personal conflict."

"An has yeh done it, Henry?" earnestly inquired Andy.

"Yes, Andy; yes, I have done it! and I thank God for it! I have taught the slave that mighty lesson: to strike for Liberty. 'Rather to die as freemen, than live as slaves!' "

"Thang God!" exclaimed Charles.

"Amen!" responded Andy.

"Now, boys, to the most important event of your lives!" said Henry.

"Wat's dat?" asked Andy.

"Why, get ready immediately to leave your oppressors tonight!" replied he.

"Glory to God!" cried Andy.

"Hallelujah!" responded Charles.

"Quietly! Softly! Easy, boys, easy!" admonished Henry, when the party in breathless silence, on tiptoe moved off from the thicket in which they were then seated, toward the city.

It was now one o'clock in the night, and Natchez shrouded in darkness and quiet, when the daring and fearless runaway with his companions, entered the enclosure of the great house grounds, and approached the door of the hut of Daddy Joe and Mammy Judy.

"Who dat! Who dat, I say? Ole man, don' yeh hear some un knockin' at de doh?" with fright said Mammy Judy in a smothered tone, hustling and nudging the old man, who was in a deep sleep, when Henry rapped softly at the door.

"Wat a mautta, ole umin?" after a while inquired the old man, rubbing his eyes.

"Some un at de doh!" she replied.

"Who dar?" inquired Daddy Joe.

"A friend!" replied Henry with suppressed voice.

"Ole man, open de doh quick! I bleve in me soul dat Henry! Open de doh!" said mammy.

On the door being opened, the surprise and joy of the old woman was only equalled by the emotion of her utterance.

"Dar! dar now, ole man! I tole 'em so, but da 'uden bleve me! I tole 'em 'e comin', but da 'uden lis'en to me! Did yeh git 'er, me son? Little Joe cum too? O Laud! whar's my po' chile! What's Margot?"

To evade further inquiry, Henry replied that they were all safe, and hoping to see her and the old man.

"How yeh bin, my chile? I'se glad to see yeh, but mighty sorry eh cum back; case de wite folks say, da once git der hands on yeh da neber let yeh go 'g'in! Potteh, Craig, Denny, and all on 'em, da tryin' to fine whar yeh is, hunny!"

"I am well, mammy, and come now to see what is to be done with you old people," said Henry.

"We 'ont to be hear long, chile; de gwine sell us all to de traders!" replied mammy with a deep sigh.

"Yes chile," added Daddy Joe, "we all gwine to de soul-driveh!"

"You'll go to no soul-drivers!" replied Henry, the flash of whose eyes startled Mammy Judy.

"How yeh gwine help it, chile?" kindly asked Daddy Joe.

"I'll show you. Come, come, mammy! You and daddy get ready, as I've come to take you away, and must be at the river before two o'clock," said Henry, who with a single jerk of a board in the floor of the hut, had reached the hidden treasure of the old people.

"Who gwine wid us, chile?" inquired Mammy Judy.

"Charles, Andy, and his female friend, besides some we shall pick up by the way!" replied Henry.

"Now he's a-talkin'!" jocosely said Charles, looking at Andy with a smile, at the mention of his female friend.

"'E ain' doin' nothin' else!" replied Andy.

"Wat become o' po' little Tony! 'E sleep here tonight case he not berry well. Po' chile!" sighed the old woman.

"We'll take him too, of course; and I would that I could take every slave in Natchez!" replied Henry. "It is now half-past one," said he, looking at his watch, "and against two we must be at the river. Go Andy, and get your friend, and meet us at the old burnt sycamore stump above the ferry. Come mammy and daddy, not a word for your lives!" admonished Henry, when taking their package on his back, and little Tony by the hand, they left forever the great house premises of Colonel Stephen Franks in Natchez.

On approaching the river a group was seen, which proved to consist of Andy, Clara (to whom his integrity was plighted), and the faithful old stump, their guidepost for the evening. Greeting each other with tears of joy and fearful hearts, they passed down to the water's edge, but a few hundred feet below.

The ferry boat in this instance was a lightly built yawl, commanded by a white man; the ferry one of many such selected along the shore, expressly for such occasions.

"Have you a pass?" demanded the boatman as a ruse, lest he might be watched by a concealed party. "Let me see it!"

"Here, sir," said Henry, presenting to him by the light of a match which he held in his hand for the purpose, the face of a half eagle.

"Here is seven of you, an' I can't do it for that!" in an humble undertone supplicating manner, said the man. "I axes that for one!"

The weight of seven half eagles dropped into his hand, caused him eagerly to seize the oars, making the quickest possible time to the opposite side of the river.

CHAPTER 28

Studying Head Work

"Now Henry," said Andy, after finding themselves in a safe place some distance from the landing, "you promise' w'en we stauted to show us de Noth Star—which is it?" On looking up the sky was too much obscured with clouds.

"I can't show it to you now, but when we stop to refresh, I'll then explain it to you," replied he.

"It high time now, chil'en, we had a mou'full to eat ef we got travel dis way!" suggested Mammy Judy, breaking silence for the first time since they left the great house.

"Yes," replied Andy, "Clara and little Tony mus' wan' to eat, an' I knows wat dis chile wants!" touching himself on the breast.

The runaways stopped in the midst of an almost impenetrable thicket, kindled a fire to give them light, where to take their fare of cold meat, bread and butter, and cheese, of which the cellar and pantry of Franks, to which Mammy Judy and Charles had access, afforded an ample supply.

Whilst the others were engaged in refreshing, Henry, aside of a stump, was busily engaged with pencil and paper.

"Whar's Henry, dat 'e ain't hear eatin?" inquired Mammy Judy, looking about among the group.

"I sho, ole umin, 'e's oveh dar by de stump," replied Daddy Joe.

"Wat dat boy doin' dar? Henry, wat yeh doin'? Mus' be studyin' headwuck, I reckon! Sho boy! betteh come 'long an' git a mou'full to eat. Yeh ain' hungry I reckon," said the old woman.

"Henry, we dun eatin' now. You mos' ready to tell us 'bout de Noth Star?" said Andy.

"Yes, I will show you," said Henry, walking forward and setting himself in the center of the group. "You see these seven stars which I've drawn on this piece of paper—numbered 1, 2, 3, 4, 5, 6, 7? From the peculiarity of the shape of their relative position to each other, the group is called the 'Dipper,' because to look at them they look like a dipper or a vessel with a long handle.

"I see it; don't you see dat, Chaules?" said Andy.

"Certainly, anybody could see that," replied Charles.

"Ole umin," said Daddy Joe, "don' yeh see it?"

"Sho', ole man! Ain't I lookin!" replied the old woman.

"You all see it then, do you?" inquired Henry.

"Yes, yes!" was the response.

"Now then," continued Henry; "for an explanation by which you can tell the North Star, when or from whatever place you may see it. The two stars of the Dipper, numbered 6 and 7, are called the pointers, because they point directly to the North Star, a very small, bright star, far off from the pointers, generally seeming by itself, especially when the other stars are not very bright.

"The star numbered 8, above the pointer, a little to the left, is a dim, small star, which at first sight would seem to be in a direct line with it; but by drawing a line through 7 to 8, leaves a space as you see between the star 6 and lower part of the line; or forms an angle (as the 'book men' call it, Andy) of ten degrees. The star number 9 in the distance, and a little to the right, would also seem to be directly opposite the pointers; but by drawing a line through 7 to 9, there is still a space left between the lower end of the line and 6. Now trace the dotted line from 6 through the center of 7, and it leads directly to 10. This is the North Star, the slave's great Guide to Freedom! Do you all now understand it?"

"See it!" replied Andy. "Anybody can't see dat, ain' got sense 'nuff to run away, an' no call to be free, dat's all! I knows all about it. I reckon I a'mos' know it betteh dan you, Henry!"

"Dar, dar, I tole yeh so! I tole yeh dat boy studyin' head wuck, an yeh 'uden bleve me! 'E run about yendeh so much an' kick up 'e heel dat'e talk so much gramma an' wot not, dat body haudly undehstan'! I knows dat 'e bin 'splainin do. Ole man, yeh understan' im?" said Mammy Judy.

"Ah, ole umin, dat I does! An' I' been gone forty years 'ago, I' know'd dis much 'bout it!" replied Daddy Joe.

"Above number 2 the second star of the handle of the Dipper, close to it, you will see by steadily looking, a very small star, which I call the knob or thumb-holt of the handle. You may always tell the Dipper by the knob of the handle; and the North star by the Dipper. The Dipper, during the night you will remember, continues to change its position in relation to the earth, so that it sometimes seems quite upside down."

"See here, Henry, does you know all——"

"Stop, Andy, I've not done yet!" interrupted he.

"Uh, heh!" said Andy.

"When the North star cannot be seen," continued Henry, "you must depend alone upon nature for your guide. Feel, in the dark, around the trunks or bodies of trees, especially oak, and whenever you feel moss on the bark, that side on which the moss grows is always to the north. One more explanation and then we'll go. Do you see this little round metallic box? This is called a——"

"Wat dat you call 'talic, Henry? Sho, boy! yeh head so full ob gramma an' sich like dat yeh don' know how to talk!" interrupted Mammy Judy.

"That only means iron or brass, or some hard thing like that, mammy," explained he. "The little box of which I was speaking has in it what is called a compass. It has a face almost like a clock or watch, with one straight hand which reaches entirely across the face, and turns or shakes whenever you move the box. This hand or finger is a piece of metal called 'loadstone' or 'magnet,' and termed the needle of the compass; and this end with the little cross on it, always points in one direction, and that is to the north. See; it makes no difference which way it is moved, this point of the needle turns back and points that way."

"An mus' ye al'as go de way it pints, Henry?" inquired Andy.

"No; not except you are running away from the South to Canada, or the free States; because both of these places are in the north. But when you know which way the north is, you can easily find any other direction you wish. Notice this, all of you."

"When your face is to the north, your back is to the south; your right hand to the east, and your left to the west. Can you remember this?"

"O yes, easy!" replied Andy.

"Then you will always know which way to go, by the compass showing you which is north," explained Henry.

"What does dese letters roun' hear mean, Henry?" further inquired Andy.

"Only what I have already explained; meaning north, east, west, and south, with their intermediate——"

"Dar!" interrupted Mammy Judy. " 'E gone into big talk g'in! Sho!"

"Intermediate means between, mammy," explained Henry.

"Den ef dat's it, I lis'en at yeh; case I want gwine bautheh my head wid you' jography an' big talk like dat!" replied the old woman.

"What does a compass cost?" inquired Charles, who had been listening with intense interest and breathless silence at the information given by their much-loved fellow bondman.

"One-half a dollar, or four bits, as we call it, so that every slave who will, may get one. Now, I've told you all that's necessary to guide you from a land of slavery and long suffering, to a land of liberty and future happiness. Are you now all satisfied with what you have learned?"

"Chauls, aint 'e high! See here, Henry, does yeh know all dat yeh tell us? Wy, ole feller, you is way up in de hoobanahs! Wy, you is conjure sho'nuff. Ef I only know'd dis befo', ole Potteh neven keep me a day. O, pshaw! I bin gone long 'go!"

"He'll do!" replied Charles.

"Well, well, well!" apostrophized Mammy Judy. "Dat beats all! Sence I was baun, I nebber hear de like. All along I been tellen on yeh, dat 'e got 'is head chuck cleanfull ob cumbustable, an' all dat, but yeh 'ud'n bleve me! Now yeh see!"

"Ole umin, I 'fess dat's all head wuck! Dat beats Punton! dat boy's nigh up to Maudy Ghamus! Dat boy's gwine to be mighty!" with a deep sigh replied Daddy Joe.

"Come, now, let's go!" said Henry.

On rising from where they had all been sitting with fixed attention upon their leader and his instruction, the sky was observed through the only break in the thicket above their heads, when suddenly they simultaneously exclaimed:

"There's the Dipper! there's the North Star!" all pointing directly to the Godlike beacon of liberty to the American slave.

Leaving Mammy Judy and Daddy Joe, Clara and little Tony, who had quite recovered from his indisposition the early part of the night, in charge of a friend who designedly met them on the Louisiana side of the river, with heightened spirits and a new impulse, Henry, Charles and Andy, started on their journey in the direction of their newly described guide, the North Star.

Star of the North thou art not bigger,
  Than the diamond in my ring;
Yet every black star-gazing nigger,
  Looks up to thee as some great thing! [18]

was the apostrophe of an American writer to the sacred orb of
Heaven, which in this case was fully verified.

During the remainder of the night and next day, being Sabbath,
they continued their travel, only resting when overcome wth fatigue.
Continuing in Louisiana by night, and resting by day, Wednesday
morning, before daybreak, brought them to the Arkansas river. At
first they intended to ford, but like the rivers generally of the South,
its depth and other contingencies made it necessary to seek some
other means. After consultation in a canebrake, day beginning to
dawn, walking boldly up to a man just loosening a skiff from its
fastenings, they demanded a passage across the river. This the skiffman refused peremptorily on any pretext, rejecting the sight of a
written pass.

"I want none of yer nigger passes!" angrily said he. "They ain't
none uv 'em good 'or nothin', no how! It's no use to show it to me,
ye's can't git over!"

First looking meaningly and determinedly at Charles and Andy—
biting his lips—then addressing himself to the man, Henry said:

"Then I have one that will pass us!" presenting the unmistaking
evidence of a shining gold eagle, at the sight of which emblem of his
country's liberty, the skiffman's patriotism was at once awakened,
and their right to pass as American freemen indisputable.

A few energetic muscular exertions with the oars, and the sturdy
boatman promptly landed his passengers on the other side of the river.

"Now, gentlm'n, I done the clean thing, didn't I, by jingo! Show me
but half a chance an' I'll ack the man clean out. I dont go in for this
slaveholding o' people in these Newnited States uv the South, nohow,
so I don't. Dog gone it, let every feller have a fair shake!"

Dropping into his hand the ten-dollar gold piece, the man bowed
earnestly, uttering—

"I hope ye's good luck, gent'men! Ye'll al'as fine me ready when
ye's come 'long this way!"

CHAPTER 29

The Fugitives

With much apprehension, Henry and comrades passed hastily through the State of Arkansas, he having previously traversed it partly, had learned sufficient to put him on his guard.

Traveling in the night, to avoid the day, the progress was not equal to the emergency. Though Henry carried a pocket compass, they kept in sight of the Mississippi river, to take their chance of the first steamer passing by.

The third night out, being Monday, at daybreak in the morning, their rest for the day was made at a convenient point within the verge of a forest. Suddenly Charles gave vent to hearty laughter, at a time when all were supposed to be serious, having the evening past, been beset by a train of three Negro-dogs, which, having first been charmed, they slew at the instant; the dogs probably not having been sent on trail of them, but, after the custom of the state, baying on a general round to intimidate the slaves from clandestinely venturing out, and to attack such runaways as might by chance be found in their track.

"Wat's da mauttah, Chauls?" enquired Andy.

"I was just thinking," replied he, "of the sight of three High Conjurers, who if Ghamus and Gholar be true, can do anything they please, having to escape by night, and travel in the wild woods, to evade the pursuit of white men, who do not pretend to know anything about such things."

"Dat's a fack," added Andy, "an' little, scronny triflin' weak, white men at dat—any one uv us heah, ought to whip two or three uv 'em at once. Dares Hugh's a little bit a feller, I could take 'im in one han' an' throw 'im oveh my head, an' ole Pottah, for his pant, he so ole an' good foh nothin, I could whip wid one hand half a dozen like 'im."

"Now you see, boys," said Henry, "how much conjuration and such foolishness and stupidity is worth to the slaves in the South. All that it does, is to put money into the pockets of the pretended conjurer, give him power over others by making them afraid of him; and even old Gamby Gholar and Maudy Ghamus and the rest of the Seven Heads, with all of the High Conjurors in the Dismal Swamp, are depending more upon me to deliver them from their confinement as prisoners in the Swamp and runaway slaves, than all their combined efforts together. I made it a special part of my mission, wherever I went, to enlighten them on this subject."

"I wandah you didn't fend 'em," replied Andy.

"No danger of that, since having so long, to no purpose, depended upon such persons and nonsense, they are sick at heart of them, and waiting willing and ready, for anything which may present for their aid, even to the destruction of their long cherished, silly nonsense of conjuration."

"Thang God foh dat!" concluded Andy.

Charles having fallen asleep, Andy became the sentinel of the party, as it was the arrangement for each one alternately, every two hours during rest, to watch while the other two slept. Henry having next fallen into a doze, Andy heard a cracking among the bushes, when on looking around, two men approached them. Being fatigued, drowsy, and giddy, he became much alarmed, arousing his comrades, all springing to their feet. The men advanced, who, to their gratification proved to be Eli and Ambrose, two Arkansas slaves, who having promised to meet Henry on his return, had effected their escape immediately after first meeting him, lurking in the forest in the direction which he had laid out to take.

Eli was so fair as to be taken, when first seen, to be a white man. Throwing their arms about Henry, they bestowed upon him their blessing and thanks, for his advent into the state as the means of their escape.

While thus exchanging congratulations, the approach upstream of a steamer was heard, and at once Henry devised the expedient, and determined boldly to hail her and demand a passage. Putting Eli forward as the master, Ambrose carrying the portmanteaus which belonged to the two, and the others with bundles in their hands, all rushed to the bank of the river on the verge of the thicket; Eli held up a handkerchief as a signal. The bell tolled, and the yawl immediately lowered, made for the shore. It was agreed that Eli should be known as Major Ely, of Arkansas.[19]

Seeing that blacks were of the company, when the yawl approached, the mate stood upon her forecastle.

"What's the faction here?" cried out the sturdy mate.

"Where are you bound?" enquired Eli.

"For St. Louis."

"Can I get a passage for myself and four Negroes?"

"What's the name, sir?"

"Major Ely, of Arkansas," was the reply.

"Aye, aye, sir, come aboard," said the mate; when, pulling away, the steamer was soon reached, the slaves going to the deck, and the master to the cabin.

On application for a stateroom, the clerk, on learning the name, desired to know his destination.

"The State of Missouri, sir," said Eli, "between the points of the mouth of the Ohio and St. Genevieve."

"Ely," repeated the clerk, "I've heard that name before—it's a Missouri name—any relation to Dr. Ely, Major?"

"Yes, a brother's son," was the prompt reply.

"Yes, yes, I thought I knew the name," replied the clerk. "But the old fellow wasn't quite of your way of thinking concerning Negroes, I believe?"

"No, he is one man, and I'm another, and he may go his way, and I'll go mine," replied Eli.

"That's the right feeling, Major," replied the clerk, "and we would have a much healthier state of politics in the country, if men generally would only agree to act on that principle."

"It has ever been my course," said Eli.

"Peopling a new farm I reckon, Major?"

"Yes, sir."

The master, keeping a close watch upon the slaves, was frequently upon deck among them, and requested that they might be supplied with more than common fare for slaves, he sparing no expense to make them comfortable. The slaves, on their part, appeared to be particularly attached to him, always smiling when he approached, apparently regretting when he left for the cabin.

Meanwhile, the steamer gracefully plowing up the current, making great headway, reached the point desired, when the master and slaves were safely transferred from the steamer to the shore of Missouri.

CHAPTER 30

The Pursuit

The absence of Mammy Judy, Daddy Joe, Charles, and little Tony, on the return early Monday morning of Colonel Franks and lady from the country, unmistakably proved the escape of their slaves, and the further proof of the exit of 'squire Potter's Andy and Beckwith's Clara, with the remembrance of the stampede a few months previously, required no further confirmation of the fact, when the neighborhood again was excited to ferment. The advisory committee was called into immediate council, and ways and means devised for the arrest of the recreant slaves recently left, and to prevent among them the recurrence of such things; a pursuit was at once commenced, which for the three succeeding days was carried in the wrong direction—towards Jackson, whither, it was supposed in the neighborhood, Henry had been lurking previous to the last sally upon their premises, as he had certainly been seen on Saturday evening, coming from the landing.

No traces being found in that direction, the course was changed, the swiftest steamer boarded in pursuit for the Ohio river. This point being reached but a few hours subsequent to that of the fugitives, when learning of their course, the pursuers proceeded toward the place of their destination, on the Mississippi river.

This point being the southern part of Missouri but a short distance above the confluence of the Ohio and Mississippi, the last named river had, of necessity, to be passed, being to the fugitives only practicable by means of a ferry. The ferryman in this instance commanded a horse-boat, he residing on the opposite side of the river. Stepping up to him—a tall, raw-boned athletic, rough looking, bearded fellow—Eli saluted:

"We want to cross the river, sir!"

"Am yers free?" enquired the ferryman.

"Am I free! Are you free?" rejoined Eli.

"Yes, I be's a white man!" replied the boatman.

"And so am I!" retorted Eli. "And you dare not tell me I'm not."

"I'll swong, stranger, yer mus' 'scuse me, as I did n' take notice on yez! But I like to know if them air black folks ye got wey yer am free, cause if they arn't, I be 'sponsible for 'em 'cording to the new law,

139

called, I 'bleve the Nebrasky Complimize Fugintive Slave Act, made down at Californy, last year," apologized and explained the somewhat confused ferryman.

"Yes," replied Henry, "we are free, and if we were not, I do'nt think it any part of your business to know. I thought you were here to carry people across the river."

"But frien'," rejoined the man, "yer don't understan' it. This are a law made by the Newnited States of Ameriky, an' I be 'bliged to fulfill it by ketchin' every fugitive that goes to cross this way, or I mus' pay a thousand dollars, and go to jail till the black folks is got, if that be's never. Yer see yez can't blame me, as I mus' 'bey the laws of Congress I'll swong it be's hardly a fair shake nuther, but I be 'bliged to 'bey the laws, yer know."

"Well sir," replied Henry, "we want to cross the river."

"Let me see yez papers frien'?" asked the ferryman.

"My friend," said Henry, "are you willing to make yourself a watch dog for slaveholders, and do for them that which they would not do for themselves, catch runaway slaves? Don't you know that this is the work which they boast on having the poor white men at the North do for them? Have you not yet learned to attend to your own interests instead of theirs? Here are our free papers," holding out his open hand, in which lay five half eagle pieces.

"Jump aboard!" cried the ferryman. "Quick, quick!" shouted he, as the swift feet of four hourses were heard dashing up the road.

Scarcely had the boat moved from her fastenings, till they had arrived; the riders dismounted, who presenting revolvers, declared upon the boatman's life, instantly, if he did not change the direction of his boat and come back to the Missouri shore. Henry seized a well-charged rifle belonging to the boatman, his comrades each with a well-aimed six-barreled weapon.

"Shoot if you dare!" exclaimd Henry, the slaveholders declining their arms—when, turning to the awestricken ferryman, handing him the twenty-five dollars, said, "your cause is a just one, and your reward is sure; take this money, proceed and you are safe—refuse, and you instantly die!"

"Then I be to do right," declared the boatman, "if I die by it," when applying the whip to the horses, in a few moments landed them on the Illinois shore.

This being the only ferry in the neighborhood, and fearing a bribe or coercion by the people on the Illinois side, or the temptation of a high reward from the slave-catchers, Henry determined on eluding, if possible, every means of pursuit.

"What are your horses worth?" enquired he.

"They can't be no use to your frien' case they is both on 'em bline, an' couldn't travel twenty miles a day, on a stretch!"

"Have you any other horses?"

"They be all the horses I got; I gineraly feed a spell this side. I lives over here—this are my feedin' trip," drawled the boatman.

"What will you take for them?"

"Well, frien', they arn't wuth much to buy, no how, but wuth good lock to me for drawin' the boat over, yer see."

"What did they cost you in buying them?"

"Well, I o'ny giv six-seven dollars apiece, or sich a maiter for 'em' when I got 'em, an' they cos me some two-three dollars, or sich a matter, more to get 'em in pullin' order, yer see."

"Will you sell them to me?"

"I hadn't ort to part wey 'em frien', as I do good lock o' bisness hereabouts wey them air nags, bline as they be."

"Here are thirty dollars for your horses," said Henry, putting into his hand the money in gold pieces, when, unhitching them from their station, leading them out to the side of the boat, he shot them, pushing them over into the river.

"Farewell, my friend," saluted Henry, he and comrades leaving the astonished ferryman gazing after them, whilst the slaveholders on the other shore stood grinding their teeth, grimacing their faces, shaking their fists, with various gesticulations of threat, none of which were either heard, heeded or cared for by the fleeting party, or determined ferryman.

Taking a northeasterly course of Indiana, Andy being an accustomed singer, commenced, in lively glee and cheerful strains, singing to the expressive words:

We are like a band of pilgrims,
  In a strange and foreign land,
With our knapsacks on our shoulders,
  And our cudgels in our hands,

We have many miles before us.
But it lessens not our joys,
We will sing a merry chorus,
For we are the tramping boys.

Then joined in chorus the whole party—

We are all jogging,
Jog, jog, jogging,
And we're all jogging,
We are going to the North!

The Wabash river becoming the next point of obstruction, a ferry, as in the last case, had also to be crossed, the boatman residing on the Indiana side.

"Are you free?" enquired the boatman, as the party of blacks approached.

"We are," was the reply of Henry.

"Where are you from?" continued he.

"We are from home, sir," replied Charles, "and the sooner you take us across the river, just so much sooner will we reach it."

Still doubting their right to pass he asked for their papers, but having by this time become so conversant with the patriotism and fidelity of these men to their country, Charles handing the Indianan a five dollar piece, who on seeing the outstretched wings of the eagle, desired no further evidence of their right to pass, conveying them into the state, contrary to the statutes of the Commonwealth.

On went the happy travelers without hinderance, or molestation, until the middle of the week next ensuing.

CHAPTER 31

The Attack, Resistance, Arrest

The travel for the last ten days had been pleasant, save the necessity in the more southern part of the state, of lying-by through the day and traveling at night—the fugitives cheerful and full of hope, nothing transpiring to mar their happiness, until approaching a village in the center of northern Indiana.

Supposing their proximity to the British Provinces made them safe, with an imprudence not before committed by the discreet runaways, when nearing a blacksmith's shop a mile and a half from the village, Andy in his usual manner, with stentorian voice, commenced the following song:

I'm on my way to Canada,
   That cold and dreary land:
The dire effects of slavery,
   I can no longer stand.
My soul is vexed within me so,
   To think that I'm a slave,
I've now resolved to strike the blow,
   For Freedom or the grave.

All uniting in the chorus,

O, righteous Father
   Wilt thou not pity me;
And aid me on to Canada,
   Where fugitives are free?
I heard old England plainly say,
   If we would all forsake,
Our native land of Slavery,
   And come across the lake.[20]

"There, Ad'line! I golly, don't you hear that?" said Dave Stark-weather, the blacksmith, to his wife, both of whom on hearing the unusual noise of singing, thrust their heads out of the door of a little log hut, stood patiently listening to the song, every word of which they distinctly caught. "Them's fugertive slaves, an' I'll have 'em tuck up; they might have passed, but for their singin' praise to that darned Queen! I can't stan' that no how!"

"No," replied Adaline, "I'm sure I don't see what they sing to her for; she's no 'Merican. We ain't under her now, as we Dave?"

"No we ain't, Ad'line, not sence the battle o' Waterloo, an' I golly, we wouldn't be if we was. The 'Mericans could whip her a darned sight easier now than what they done when they fit her at Waterloo."

"Lah me, Dave, you could whip 'er yourself, she ai'nt bigger nor tother wimin is she?" said Mrs. Starkweather.

"No she ain't, not a darn' bit!" replied he.

"Dave, ask em in the shop to rest," suggested the wife in a hurried whisper, elbowing her husband as the party advanced, having ceased singing so soon as they saw the faces of white persons.

"Travlin', I reckon?" interrogated the blacksmith. "Little tired, I spose?"

"Yes sir, a little so," replied Henry.

"Didn't come far, I 'spect?" continued he.

"Not very," carelessly replied Henry.

"Take seat there, and rest ye little," pointing to a smoothly-worn log, used by the visitors of the shop.

"Thank you," said Henry, "we will," all seating themselves in a row.

"Take little somethin?" asked he; stepping back to a corner, taking out a caddy in the wall, a rather corpulent green bottle, turning it up to his mouth, drenching himself almost to strangulation.

"We don't drink, sir," replied the fugitives.

"Temperance, I reckon?" enquired the smith.

"Rather so," replied Henry.

"Kind o' think we'll have a spell o' weather?"

"Yes," said Andy, "dat's certain; we'll have a spell a weatheh!"

On entering the shop, the person at the bellows, a tall, able-bodied young man, was observed to pass out at the back door, a number of persons of both sexes to come frequently look in, and depart, succeeded by others; no import being attached to this, supposing themselves to be an attraction, partly from their singing, and mainly from their color being a novelty in the neighborhood.

During conversation with the blacksmith, he after eyeing very closely the five strangers, was observed to walk behind the door, stand for some minutes looking as if reading, when resuming his place at the anvil, after which he went out the back door. Curiosity now, with some anxiety induced Henry to look for the cause of it, when with no little alarm, he discovered a handbill fully descriptive of himself and comrades, having been issued in the town of St. Genevieve, offering a heavy reward, particularizing the scene at the Mississippi ferry, the killing of the horses as an aggravated offense, because depriving a poor man of his only means of livelihood, being designed to strengthen inducements to apprehend them, the bill being signed "John Harris."

Evening now ensuing, Henry and comrades, the more easily to pass through the village without attraction, had remained until this hour, resting in the blacksmith shop. Enquiring for some black family in the neighborhood, they were cited to one consisting of an old man and woman, Devan by name, residing on the other side, a short distance from the village.

"Ye'll fine ole Bill of the right stripe," said the blacksmith knowingly. "Ye needn' be feard o' him. Ye'll fine him and ole Sally just what they say they is; I'll go bail for that. The first log hut ye come to after ye leave the village is thern; jist knock at the door, an' ye'll fine ole Bill an' Sally all right blame if ye don't. Jis name me; tell 'em Dave Starkweather sent ye there, an' blamed if ye don't fine things at high water mark; I'm tellin' ye so, blamed if I ain't!" was the recommendatior of the blacksmith.

"Thank you for your kindness," replied Henry, politely bowing as they rose from the log. "Goodbye, sir!"

"Devilish decent lookin' black fellers," said the man of the anvil, complimenting, designedly for them to hear. "Blamed if they ain't as free as we is—I golly they is!"

Without, as they thought, attracting attention, passing through the village a half mile or more, they came to a log hut on the right side of the way.

"How yeh do fren? How yeh come on?" saluted a short, rather corpulent, wheezing old black man. "Come in. Hi! Dahs good many on yeh; ole 'omin come, heah's some frens!" calling his wife Sally, an old woman, shorter in stature, but not less corpulent than he, sitting by a comfortable dry-stump fire.

"How is yeh, frens? How yeh do? come to da fiah, mighty cole!" said the old woman.

"Quite cool," replied Andy, rubbing his hands, spreading them out, protecting his face from the heat.

"Yeh is travelin, I reckon, there is good many go' long heah; we no call t'ask 'em whah da gwine, we knows who da is, case we come from dah. I an, ole man once slave in Faginny; mighty good country fah black folks."

Sally set immediately about preparing something to give her guests a good meal. Henry admonished them against extra trouble, but they insisted on giving them a good supper.

Deeming it more prudent, **the hut** being on the highway, Henry requested to retire until summoned to supper, being shown to the loft attained by a ladder and simple hatchway, the door of which was shut down, and fastened on the lower side.

The floor consisting of rough, unjointed board, containing great cracks through which the light and heat from below passed up, all could be both seen and heard, which transpired below.

Seeing the old man so frequently open and look out at the door, and being suspicious from the movements of the blacksmith and others, Henry affecting to be sleepy, requested Billy and his wife when ready, to awaken them, when after a few minutes, all were snoring as if fast asleep, Henry lying in such a position as through a knothole in the floor, to see every movement in all parts of the room. Directly above him in the rafter within his reach, hung a mowing scythe.

"Now's yeh time, ole man; da all fas' asleep, da snorin' good!" said old Sally, urging Billy to hasten, who immediately left the hut.

The hearts of the fugitives were at once "in their mouths," and with difficulty it was by silently reaching over and heavily pressing upon each of them, Henry succeeded in admonishing each to entire quietness and submission.

Presently entered a white man, who whispering with Sally left the room. Immediately in came old Bill, at the instant of which, Henry found his right hand above him, involuntarily grasped firmly on the snath of the scythe.

"Whah's da?" enquired old Bill, on entering the hut.

"Sho da whah yeh lef' em!" replied the old woman.

"Spose I kin bring 'em in now?" continued old Bill.

"Bring in who?"

"Da white folks: who else I gwine fetch in yeh 'spose?"

"Bettah let em 'tay whah da is, an' let de po' men lone, git sumpen t' eat, an' go 'long whah da gwine!" replied Sally, deceptively.

"Huccum yeh talk dat way? Sho yeh tole me go!" replied Billy.

"Didn' reckon yeh gwine bring 'em on da po' cretahs dis way, fo' da git moufful t' eat an' git way so."

"How I gwine let 'em go now de white folks all out dah? Say Sally? Dat jis what make I tell yeh so!"

"Bettah let white folks 'lone, Willum! dat jis what I been tellin' on yeh. Keep foolin' 'long wid white folks, bym'by da show yeh! I no trus' white man, no how. Sho! da no fren' o' black folks. Bus spose body 'blige keep da right side on 'em long so."

"Ole 'omin," said Bill, "yeh knows we make our livin' by da white folks, an' mus' do what da tell us, so whah's da use talkin' long so. 'Spose da come in now?"

"Sho, I tole yeh de man sleep? gwine bring white folks on 'em so? give po' cretahs nc chance? Go long, do what yeh gwine do; yeh fine out one dese days!" concluded Sally.

Having stealthily risen to their feet standing in a favorable position, Henry in whispers declared to his comrades that with that scythe he intended mowing his way into Canada.

Impatient for their entrance, throwing wide open the door of the hut, which being the signal, in rushed eleven white men, headed by Jud Shirly, constable, Dave Starkweather the blacksmith, and Tom Overton as deputies; George Grove, a respectable well-dressed villager, stood giving general orders.

With light and pistol in hand, Franey, mounting the stairway commanded a surrender. Eli, standing behind the hatchway, struck the candle from his hand, when with a swing of the scythe there was a screech, fall, and groan heard, then with a shout and leap, Henry in the lead, they cleared the stairs to the lower floor, the white men flying in consternation before them, making their way to the village, alarming the inhabitants.

The fugitives fled in great haste continuing their flight for several miles, when becoming worn down and fatigued, retired under cover of a thicket a mile from a stage tavern kept by old Isaac Slusher of German descent.

The villagers following in quick pursuit, every horse which could be readily obtained being put on the chase, the slaves were overtaken, fired upon—a ball lodging in Charles' thigh—overpowered, and arrested. Deeming it, from the number of idlers about the place, and the condition of the stables, much the safest imprisonment, the captives were taken to the tavern of Slusher, to quarter for the night.

On arriving at this place, a shout of triumph rent the air, and a general cry "take them into the barroom for inspection! Hang them! Burn them!" and much more.

Here the captives were derided, scoffed at and ridiculed, turned around, limbs examined, shoved about from side to side, then ordered to sit down on the floor, a noncompliance with which, having arranged themselves for the purpose, at a given signal, a single trip by an equal number of whites, brought the four poor prisoners suddenly to the floor on the broad of their back, their heads striking with great force. At this abuse of helpless men, the shouts of laughter became deafening. It caused them to shun the risk of standing, and keep seated on the floor.

Charles having been wounded, affected inability to stand, but the injury being a flesh wound, was not serious.

"We'll show ye yer places, ye black devils!" said Ned Bradly, a rowdy, drawing back his foot to kick Henry in the face, as he sat upon the floor against the wall, giving him a slight kick in the side as he passed by him.

"Don't do that again, sir!" sternly said Henry, with an expression full of meaning, looking him in the face.

Several feet in an instant were drawn back to kick, when Slusher interfering, said, "Shendlemans! tem black mans ish prishners! You tuz pring tem into mine housh, ant you shandt puse tem dare!" when the rowdies ceased abusing them.

"Well, gentlemen," said Tom Overton, a burly, bullying barroom person, "we'd best git these blacks out of the way, if they's any fun up tonight."

"I cot plendy peds, shendlemans, I ondly vants to know who ish to bay me," replied Slusher.

"I golly," retorted Starkweather, "you needn't give yourself no uneasiness about that Slusher. I think me, and Shirly, and Grove is good for a night's lodging for five niggers, anyhow!"

"I'm in that snap, too!" hallooed out Overton.

"Golly! Yes, Tom, there's you we like to forgot, blamed if we didn't!" responded Starkweather.

"Dat ish all right nough zo far as te plack man's ish gonzern, put ten dare ish to housh vull o' peoples, vot vare must I gheep tem?"

"We four," replied Grove, "will see you paid, who else? Slusher, we want it understood, that we four stand responsible for all expenses incurred this night, in the taking of these Negroes," evidently expecting to receive as they claimed, the reward offered in the advertisement.

"Dat vill too, ten," replied Slusher. "Vell, I ish ready to lite tese black mans to ped."

"No Slusher," interrupted Grove, "that's not the understanding, we don't pay for beds for niggers to sleep in!"

"No, by Molly!" replied Overton. "Dogged if that ain't going a leetle too far! Slusher, you can't choke that down, no how you can fix in. If you do as you please with your own house, these niggers is in our custody, and we'll do as we please with them. We want you to know that we are white men, as well as you are, and can't pay for niggers to sleep in the same house with ourselves."

"Gents," said Ned Bradly, "do you hear that?"

"What?" enquired several voices.

"Why, old Slusher wants to give the niggers a room upstairs with us!"

"With who?" shouted they.

"With us white men."

"No, blamed if he does!" replied Starkweather.

"We won't stand that!" exclaimed several voices.

"Where's Slusher?" enquired Ben West, a discharged stage driver, who hung about the premises, and now figured prominently.

"Here ish me, shendlemans!" answered Slusher, coming from the back part of the house. "Andt you may do as you please midt tem black mans, pud iv you dempt puse me, I vill pudt you all out mine housh!"

"The stable, the stable!" they all cried out. "Put the niggers in the stable, and we'll be satisfied!"

"Tare ish mine staple—you may pud tem vare you blease," replied the old man, "budt you shandt puse me!"

Securely binding them with cords, they were placed in a strongly built log stable closely weather-boarded, having but a door and window below, the latter being closely secured, and the door locked on the outside with a staple and padlock. The upper windows being well secured, the blacks thus locked in, were left to their fate, whilst their captors comfortably housed, were rioting in triumph through the night over the misfortune, and blasted prospects for liberty.

CHAPTER 32

The Escape

This night the inmates of the tavern revelled with intoxication; all within the building, save the exemplary family of the stern old German, Slusher, who peremptorily refused from first to last, to take any part whatever with them, doubtless, being for the evening the victims of excessive indulgence in the beverage of ardent spirits. Now and again one and another of the numerous crowd gathered from the surrounding neighborhood, increasing as the intelligence spread, went alone to the stable to examine the door, reconnoiter the premises, and ascertain that the prisoners were secure. The company getting in such high glee that, fearing a neglect of duty, it became advisable to appoint for the evening a corps of sentinels whose special duty, according to their own arrangements, should be to watch and guard the captives. This special commission being one of pecuniary consideration, Jim Franey, the township constable, the rowdy Ned Bradly, and Ben West the discharged stage driver, who being about the premises, readily accepted the office, entering immediately on the line of duty.

The guard each alternately every fifteen minutes went out to examine the premises, when one and a half of the clock again brought around the period of Ben West's duty. Familiar with the premises and the arrangement of the stables, taking a lantern, West designed closely to inspect their pinions, that no lack of duty on his part might forfeit his claim to the promised compensation.

When placing them in the stable, lights then being in requisition, Henry discovered in a crevice between the wall an the end of the feed-trough a common butcher knife used for the purpose of repairing harness. So soon as the parties left the stable, the captives lying with their heads resting on their bundles, Henry arising, took the knife, cutting loose himself and companions, but leaving the pinions still about their limbs as though fastened, resumed his position upon the bundle of straw. The scythe had been carelessly hung on a section of the worm fence adjoining the barn, near the door of the prison department, their weapons having been taken from them.

"Well, boys," enquired West, holding up the lantern, "you're all here, I see: do you want anything? Take some whiskey!" holding in his hand a quart bottle.

"The rope's too tight around my ankle!" complained Charles. "Its took all the feeling out of my leg."

Dropping upon his knees to loosen the cord, at this moment, Henry standing erect brandishing the keen glistening blade of the knife before him—his companions having sprung to their feet—"Don't you breathe," exclaimed the intrepid unfettered slave, "or I'll bury the blade deep in your bosom! One hour I'll give you for silence, a breach of which will cost your life." Taking a tin cup which West brought into the stable, pouring it full to the brim, "Drink this!" said Henry, compelling the man who was already partially intoxicated, to drink as much as possible, which soon rendered him entirely insensible.

"Come, boys!" exclaimed he, locking the stable, putting the key into his pocket, leaving the intoxicated sentinel prostrated upon the bed of straw intended for them, and leaving the tavern house of the old German Slusher forever behind them.

The next period of watch, West being missed, Ned Bradly, on going to the stable, finding the door locked, reported favorably, supposing it to be still secure. Overton in turn did the same. When drawing near daylight—West still being missed—Franey advised that a search be made for him. The bedrooms, and such places into which he might most probably have retired, were repeatedly searched in vain, as calling at the stable elicited no answer, either from him nor the captives.

The sun was now more than two hours high, and word was received from the village to hasten the criminals in for examination before the magistrate. Determining to break open the door, which being done, Ben West was found outstretched upon the bed of straw, who, with difficulty, was aroused from his stupor. The surprise of the searchers on discovering his condition, was heightened on finding the escape of the fugitives. Disappointment and chagrin now succeeded high hopes and merriment, when a general reaction ran throughout the neighborhood; for the sensation at the escape even became greater than on the instance of the deed of resistance and success of the capture.

Of all the disappointments connected with this affair, there was none to be regretted save that of the old German tavern keeper, Isaac Slusher, who, being the only pecuniary sufferer, the entire crowd revelling at his expense.

"Gonvound dish bishnesh!" exclaimed Slusher with vexation. "Id alwaysh cosht more dan de ding ish wordt. Mine Got! afder dish I'll mindt mine own bishnesh. Iv tem Soudt Amerigans vill gheep niggersh de musht gedch dem demzelve. Mine ligger ish ghon, I losht mine resht, te niggersh rhun avay, an' I nod magk von zent!"

Immediate pursuit was sent out in search of the runaways but without success; for, dashing on, scythe in hand, with daring though peaceable strides through the remainder of the state and that of Michigan, the fugitives reached Detroit without further molestation or question from any source on the right of transit, the inhabitants mistaking them for resident blacks out from their homes in search of employment.

CHAPTER 33

Happy Greeting

After their fortunate escape from the stables of Isaac Slusher in Indiana, Henry and comrades safely landed across the river in Windsor, Essex County, Canada West, being accompanied by a mulatto gentleman resident of Detroit, who from the abundance of his generous heart, with others there, ever stands ready and has proven himself an uncompromising, true and tried friend of his race, and every weary traveler on a fugitive slave pilgrimage, passing that way.[21]

"Is dis Canada? Is dis de good ole British soil we hear so much 'bout way down in Missierppi?" exclaimed Andy. "Is dis free groun'? De lan' whar black folks is free! Thang God a'mighty for dis privilege!" When he fell upon his hands and knees and kissed the earth.

Poor fellow! he little knew the unnatural feelings and course pursued toward his race by many Canadians, those too pretending to be Englishmen by birth, with some of whom the blacks had fought side by side in the memorable crusade made upon that fairest portion of Her Majesty's Colonial Possessions, by Americans in disguise, calling themselves "Patriots." He little knew that while according to fundamental British Law and constitutional rights, all persons are equal in the realm, yet by a systematic course of policy and artifice, his race with few exceptions in some parts, excepting the Eastern

Province, is excluded from the enjoyment and practical exercise of every right, except mere suffrage-voting—even to those of sitting on a jury as its own peer, and the exercise of military duty. He little knew the facts, and as little expected to find such a state of things in the long-talked of and much-loved Canada by the slaves. He knew not that some of high intelligence and educational attainments of his race residing in many parts of the Provinces, were really excluded from and practically denied their rights, and that there was no authority known to the colony to give redress and make restitution on the petition or application of these representative men of his race, which had frequently been done with the reply from the Canadian functionaries that they had no power to reach their case. It had never entered the mind of poor Andy, that in going to Canada in search of freedom, he was then in a country where privileges were denied him which are common to the slave in every Southern state—the right of going into the gallery of a public building—that a few of the most respectable colored ladies of a town in Kent County, desirous through reverence and respect, to see a British Lord Chief Justice on the Bench of Queen's Court, taking seats in the gallery of the court house assigned to females and other visitors, were ruthlessly taken hold of and shown down the stairway by a man and "officer" of the Court of Queen's Bench for that place. Sad would be to him the fact when he heard that the construction given by authority to these grievances, when requested to remedy or remove them, was, that they were "local contingencies to be reached alone by those who inflicted the injuries." An emotion of unutterable indignation would swell the heart of the determined slave, and almost compel him to curse the country of his adoption. But Andy was free—being on British soil—from the bribes of slaveholding influences; where the unhallowed foot of the slavecatcher dare not tread; where no decrees of an American Congress sanctioned by a president born and bred in a free state and himself once a poor apprentice boy in a village, could reach.

Thus far, Andy was happy; happy in the success of their escape, the enlarged hopes of future prospects in the industrial pursuits of life; and happy in the contemplation of meeting and seeing Clara.

There were other joys than those of Andy, and other hopes and anticipations to be realised. Charles, Ambrose, and Eli, who, though with hearts overflowing with gratitude, were silent in holy praise to

heaven, claiming to have emotions equal to his, and conjugal expectations quite as sacred if not yet as binding.

"The first thing now to be done is to find our people!" said Henry
with emotion, after the excess of Andy had ceased.

"Where are they?" inquired the mulatto gentleman. "And what are
their names?"

"Their names at home were Frank's Ailcey, Craig's Polly, and Little
Joe, who left several months ago; and an old man and woman called
Daddy Joe and Mammy Judy; a young woman called Clara Beckwith,
and a little boy named Tony, who came on but a few days before us."

"Come with me, and I'll lead you directly to him!" replied the
mulatto gentlemen; when taking a vehicle, he drove them to the
country a few miles from Windsor, where the parties under feelings
such as never had been experienced by them before, fell into the
embrace of each other.

"Dar now, dar! wat I tell you? Bless de laud, ef dar ain' Chaules an'
Henry!" exclaimed Mammy Judy, clapping her hands, giving vent to
tears which stole in drops from the eyes of all. "My po' chile! My po'
Margot!" continued she in piteous tones as the bold and manly leader
pressed closely to his bosom his boy, who now was the image of his
mother. "My son, did'n yeh hear nothing bout er? did'n yeh not bring
my po' Margot?"

"No, mammy, no! I have not seen and did not bring her! No,
mammy, no! But——!" When Henry became choked with grief which
found an audible response from the heart of every child of sorrow
present.

Clara commenced, seconded by Andy and followed by all except
him the pierce to whose manly heart had caused it, in tones the most
affecting:

O, when shall my sorrow subside!
And when shall my troubles be ended;
And when to the bosom of Christ be conveyed,
To the mansions of joy and bliss!
To the mansions of joy and bliss!

Falling upon their knees, Andy uttered a most fervent prayer, in-
voking Heaven's blessing and aid.

"Amen!" responded Charles.

"Hallelujah!" cried Clara, clapping her hands.

"Glory, glory, glory!" shouted Ailcey.

"O laud! W'en shall I get home!" mourned Mammy Judy.

"Tis good to be here, chilen! 'Tis good to be here!" said Daddy Joe, rubbing his hands quite wet with tears—when all rising to their feet met each other in the mutual embraces of Christian affection, with heaving hearts of sadness.

"We have reason, sir," said Henry addressing himself to the mulatto gentleman who stood a tearful eye witness to the scenes, "we have reason to thank God from the recesses of our hearts for the providential escape we've made from slavery!" which expression was answered only by trickles down the gentleman's cheeks.

The first care of Henry was to invest a portion of the old people's money by the purchase of fifty acres of land with improvements suitable, and provide for the schooling of the children until he should otherwise order. Charles by appointment in which Henry took part, was chosen leader of the runaway party, Andy being the second, Ambrose and Eli respectively the keepers of their money and accounts, Eli being a good penman.

"Now," said Henry, after two days rest, "the time has come and I must leave you! Polly, as you came as the mistress, you must now become the mother and nurse of my poor boy! Take good care of him—mammy will attend to you. Charles, as you have all secured land close to, I want you to stand by the old people; Andy, you, Ambrose, and Eli, stand by Charles and the girls, and you must succeed, as nothing can separate you; your strength depending upon your remaining together."

"Henry, is yeh guine sho' nuff?" earnestly enquired Andy.

"Yes, I must go!"

"Wait little!" replied Andy, when after speaking aside with Eli and Ambrose, calling the girls they all whispered for sometime together; occasional evidence of seriousness, anxiety, and joy marking their expressions of countenance.

The Provincial regulations requiring a license, or three weeks report to a public congregation, and that many sabbaths from the altar of a place of worship to legalise a marriage, and there being now no time for either of these, the mulatto gentleman who was still with them, being a clergyman, declared, that in this case no such restrictions were binding; being originally intended for the whites and the free, and not for the panting runaway slave.

"Thank God for that! That's good talk!" said Charles.

"Ef it aint dat, 'taint nothin! Dat's wat I calls good black talk!" replied Andy, causing the clergyman and all to look at each other with a smile.

The party gathered standing in a semicircle, the clergyman in the center, a hymn being sung and prayer offered—rising to their feet, and an exhortation of comfort and encouragement being given, with the fatherly advice and instructions of their domestic guidance in after life by the aged man of God; the sacred and impressively novel words: "I join you together in the bonds of matrimony!" gave Henry the pleasure before leaving of seeing upon the floor together, Charles and Polly, Andy and Clara, Eli and Ailcey, "as man and wife forever."

"Praise God!" exclaimed poor old mammy, whose heart was most tenderly touched by the scene before her, contrasting it by reflection with the sad reminiscence of her own sorrowful and hopeless union with Daddy Joe, with whom she had lived fifty years as happily as was possible for slaves to do.[22]

"Bless de laud!" responded the old man.

The young wives all gave vent to sobs of sympathy and joy, when the parson as a solace sung in touching sentiments:

Daughters of Zion! awake from thy sadness!
Awake for they foes shall oppress thee no more.
Bright o'er the hills shines the day star of gladness
Arise! for the night of they sorrow is o'er;
Daughters of Zion, awake from thy sadness!
Awake for they foes shall oppress thee no more!

"O glory!" exclaimed Mammy Judy, when the scene becoming most affecting; hugging his boy closely to his bosom, upon whose little cheek and lips he impressed kisses long and affectionate, when laying him in the old woman's cap and kissing little Tony, turning to his friends with a voice the tone of which sent through them a thrill, he said:

"By the instincts of a husband, I'll have her if living! If dead, by impulses of a Heaven-inspired soul, I'll avenge her loss unto death! Farwell, farwell!" the tears streaming as he turned from his child and its grandparents; when but a few minutes found the runaway leader seated in a car at the Windsor depot, from whence he reached the Suspension Bridge at Niagara en route for the Atlantic.

CHAPTER 34

A Novel Adventure

From the Suspension Bridge through the great New York Central Railway to Albany, and thence by the Hudson River, Henry reached the city on the steamer "Hendrick Hudson," in the middle of an afternoon. First securing a boarding house—a new thing to him—he proceeded by direction to an intelligence office, which he found kept by a mulatto gentleman.[23] Here inquiring for a situation as page or valet on a voyage to Cuba, he deposited the required sum, leaving his address as "Gilbert Hopewell, 168 Church St."—changing the name to prevent all traces of himself out of Canada, whither he was known to have gone, to the free states of America, and especially to Cuba whence he was going, the theater of his future actions.

In the evening Henry took a stroll through the great thoroughfare, everything being to him so very novel, that eleven o'clock brought him directly in front of doubtless the handsomest saloon of the kind in the world, situated on the corner of Broadway and Franklin street. Gazing in at the luxurious and fashionable throng and gaieties displayed among the many in groups at the tables, there was one which more than all others attracted his attention, though unconscious at the time of its doing so.

The party consisted of four; a handsome and attractive young lady, accompanied by three gentlemen, all fine looking, attractive persons, wearing the undress uniforms of United States naval officers. The elder of these was a robust, commanding person in appearance, black hair, well mixed with white, seemingly some sixty years of age. One of the young gentlemen was tall, handsome, with raven-black hair, moustache, and eyes; the other, medium height, fair complexion, hair, moustache and whiskers, with blue eyes; while the young lady ranked of medium proportions in height and size, drab hair, fair complexion, plump cheeks and hazel eyes, and neatly dressed in a maroon silk habit, broadly faced in front and cuffed with orange satin, the collar being the same, neatly bound with crimson.

While thus musing over the throng continually passing in and out, unconsciously Henry had his attention so fixed on this group, who were passing out and up Broadway, involuntarily leaving the window through which he had been gazing, he found himself following them in the crowd which throng the street closely, foot to foot.

Detecting himself and about to turn aside, he overheard the elderly gentleman in reply to a question by the lady concerning the great metropolis, say, that in Cuba where in a few days they would be, recreation and pleasure were quite equal to that of New York. Now drawing more closely he learned that the company were destined for Havana, to sail in a few days. His heart beat with joy, when turning and making his way back, he found his boarding house without difficulty.

Henry once more spent a sleepless night, noted by restless anxiety; and the approach of morning seemed to be regulated by the extent of the city. If thoughts could have done it, the great Metropolis would have been reduced to a single block of houses, reducing in like manner the night to a few fleeting moments.

Early in the morning he had risen, and impatiently pacing the floor, imagined that the people of that city were behind the age in rising. Presently the summons came for breakfast, and ere he was seated a note was handed him reading thus:

Intelligence Office—Leonard St.,
New York, March 5th, 1853

Gilbert Hopewell: There is now an opportunity offered to go to Cuba, to attend on a party of four—a lady and three gentlemen—who sail for Havana direct (see Tribune of this morning). Be at my office at half past ten o'clock, and you will learn particulars, which, by that time I will have obtained.

Respectfully,
B. A. P.

Though the delay was but an hour, Henry was restless, and when the time came was punctually in his place. The gentleman who called to meet him at the Intelligence office Henry recognized as one of the party seen the previous evening at the great saloon in Broadway. Arrangements having been completed concerning his attendance and going with them, "Meet me in an hour at the St. Nicholas, and commence your duties immediately," said the gentleman, when politely bowing, Henry turned away with a heart of joy, and full of hope.

Promptly to the time he was at the hotel, arranging for a start; when he found that his duties consisted in attendance particularly on the young lady and one of the young gentlemen, and the other two as occasion might require. The company was composed of Captain Richard Paul, the elderly gentleman; Lieutenant Augustus Seeley, the black-haired; passed Midshipman Lawrence Spencer, the light-haired gentleman, and Miss Cornelia Woodward.

Miss Woodward was modest and retiring, though affable, conversant and easy in manner. In her countenance were pictured an expression of definite anxiety and decisive purpose, which commanded for her the regard and esteem of all whom she approached. Proud without vanity, and graceful without affectation, she gained the esteem of everyone; a lady making the remark that she was one of the most perfect of American young ladies.

After breakfast the next morning they embarked on the steam packet "Isabella," to sail that day at eleven o'clock.

Of the gentlemen, Augustus Seeley gave to Miss Woodward the most attention, though nothing in her manner betrayed attachment except an occasional sigh.

Henry, for the time, appeared to be her main dependence; as shortly after sailing she manifested a disposition to keep in retirement as much as possible. Though a girl of tender affections, delicate sentiments, and elevated Christian graces, Cornelia was evidently inexperienced and unprepared for the deceptious impositions practiced in society. Hence, with the highest hopes and expectations, innocently unaware of the contingencies in life's dangerous pathway, hazarding her destiny on the simple promise of an irresponsible young man, but little more than passed midshipman, she reached the quay at Moro Castle in less than six days from the Port of New York.

PART II

Hear the word!—who fight for freedom!
Shout it in the battle van!
Hope! for bleeding human nature!
Christ the God, is Christ the Man!
H. Beecher Stowe

CHAPTER 35

Cornelia Woodward

"What next?" inquired Seeley of Captain Paul, immediately after refreshing at the "American Hotel," whither they had gone from the vessel.

"I shall take you out directly to see Captain Garcia, one of the finest fellows in the world."

"Is this Emanuel Garcia, the expert fellow so long engaged in the trade, and so hard to catch?"

"The same. He married a sister of Peter Albertis, of New Orleans, formerly a planter on the Louisiana coast."

"Ah hah! All right, then!" replied Seeley.

These expressions Cornelia heard, but without the remotest idea of their real import, regarding them merely as commonplace conversation.

A black driver being summoned with a diligence to the door, in less than five hours the party were enjoying the balmy odors amidst the beautiful shrubbery at the hacienda of Captain Emanuel and Madame Adelaide Garcia.

The greetings between Paul and Garcia were very familiar, having the appearance of old acquaintance and a mature understanding.

In the family on a visit, was a French lady, Madame Celia Bonselle, who for a time had resided in Louisiana, a relative of the Albertises'.

The conduct of Madame Garcia was painful to Cornelia, causing her much embarrassment, there being much close conversation between the gentlemen, in which Adelaide took an active part, for which she received the disapprobation of Madame Bonselle.

"Tomorrow," said Paul, after one of these private conferences, "we repair to Matanzas to examine the craft preparatory to sailing."

"When do you sail, Captain Paul?" earnestly enquired Cornelia.

"I can't just say; it may be in a day or two, and it may be longer."

"Then I'm sure I cannot understand my position, if you are to go off in a day or two!"

"She's not yet acquainted with our nautical customs, but will learn better by-and-by," replied Seeley.

"I hope I may learn nothing worse than that which I already know, I'm afraid to my sorrow!"

"What nonsense, madame, can't you trust your husband?" impatiently admonished the Spaniard.

"You're mistaken, sir; he's not my husband!" exclaimed Cornelia with resentment.

"If not, then I'm wrongly informed; but I still believe that I'm right!" replied Garcia.

"And so do I," sanctioned Adelaide, "for Lieutenant Seeley is incapable of falsehood."

"Do you solemnly tell me that you are not the wife of Lieutenant Seeley?" enquired Garcia.

"Indeed, sir, upon my oath I am not!" replied Cornelia, whose eyes were suffused to blindness with tears.

"Upon my oath, you are then!" maliciously retorted Paul, to the great discomfiture of the almost distracted girl.

"I believe it! I believe it," sanctioned Adelaide, "and nothing can remove any impression!"

"In Heaven's name where am I, and what is to become of me!" exclaimed the poor girl in anguish. "You wrong me! You do me a murderous wrong! I'm incapable of the implied charge upon my reputation; my only sin had been a misplaced affection! Let me tell you my story. I pray you, I beg you, to permit a poor wretch that's soon to become an outcast, to tell her tale of wretchedness and sorrow! O, I beg of you to hear me, ladies of position and happiness! My home is Pennsylvania in America; I had just finished my education in Delaware; went to New York expecting to meet my mother to take me home; met the young man, who under solemn promise of marriage, decoyed me away; I, eluding my dear mother, escaped with him on the vessel. O! This is the truth! This is the truth, and will you for God's sake believe me, if not for my own!"

"She's crazy," angrily replied Seeley, "and utterly irresponsible for what she says!" he and Spencer taking their hats and immediately leaving the room.

"Crazy!" indignantly retorted the intelligent girl. "Call me what you will—mock my distraction—sport with my misfortune—trample upon my feelings, and deride my anguish if you will—but by the purity of unsullied womanhood, you never shall carry out the base designs I'm now satisfied were intended toward me! O, Heaven, I know," said the heart-wrecked girl, falling upon her knees with hands clapped and face upturned in supplication to God, "will protect me! And——"

"So will I!" interrupted Celia Bonselle, choked with feelings of sympathy, at the instant when Seeley and Spencer reentered the room, leaving their hats in the piazza.

"Lieutenant Seeley—I desire a word with you," solicited Madame Bonselle, walking in the direction of the door of the drawing room, the house being a cottage.

"Madam!" exclaimed Seeley, giving vent to an irritable temper now excited to a rage. "Are you the arbiter of my choice and conjugal destiny?"

"I assumed it not, sir! but since I am summoned to do so without my own desire or consent—if I am compelled to sit in judgment on virtue and vice—to decide between innocence and infamy according to justice—then are you, sir, by the righteous decrees of offended morality and insulted womanhood, condemned to obscurity and disgrace!" Then with a spurn and a haughty toss of the head, such as a French lady only can give, she turned away leaving Seeley as motionless as a statue, standing before the gaze of Spencer and now-indignant frown of Madam Garcia.

Paul, who immediately after his attack upon Cornelia, had left the room with Garcia to pace the lawn, now entered, and though himself having induced the two young naval officers to desert their post and go with him into the slave trade, being perfectly conversant with the designs, it having been arranged to decoy the young miss with them as a victim; such was the sympathy manifested by the ladies and Spencer for the soul-tormented girl, that they also became deeply interested in her behalf.

At the instant when the two gentlemen entered, Cornelia left the room, walking through the shrubbery where to sooth her sorrows amidst the eloquent though silent sympathy of the flowers.

Seeley being left without a rallying point, with a seriousness of countenance to him unusual, without a word of reply to what had been said after the current turned against him, slowly retreated from the room. Taking up his hat as he passed through the piazza, raising it to his head as he passed out the door, a billet fell at his feet. Snatching it up and hastening to a secluded spot in the grove, on opening it gave the following lines of touching and chaste appeal to his manhood:

How sweet at close of silent eve
The harp's responsive sound;

How sweet the vows that ne'er deceive,
And deeds by virtue crowned!
How sweet to sit beneath a tree
In some delightful grove;
But O! more soft, more sweet to me
The voice of him I love!
           UNHAPPY CORNELIA.
        Castillan Haciendes, Isle of Cuba,
        March 14, 1853.

This formidable charge discomfited him; it proved the blow which sent the spear to his heart, arousing the languid sensibility of his manhood to honor; when, regardless of paths, forcing his way in the direction from which, but a few moments before, the sound of sobs and bitter wailing had reached his ear, there finding her alone in the densest of the grove, he cast himself at her feet, with tears, upon his knees begging forgiveness for the past, with pledges of honor for the future. The scene was indescribably touching, their sympathy mutual, and the next day before the rays of the sun had ceased their genial influence over the hacienda, Cornelia Woodward and Augustus Seeley were pronounced with holy benediction, to be "man and wife forever!"

CHAPTER 36

Henry at the Hacienda

On arriving at the hacienda, Henry was impressed at the first sight of the mistress, Madam Garcia. In her arms the maid held one child, by the hand another. Besides these there were two others, Ferdinand and Miguel, six and eight years of age—also a little black boy to wait upon and play with the young masters, with whom he then gamboled near by among the flowers.

"What is your name, young woman?" inquired Henry.

"Lotty," was the reply; "what is yours?"

"Gilbert they call me. These are handsome children."

"Yes sir," she indifferently replied with a deep sigh.

"You seem to speak carelessly; don't you like children?"

"I like some children."

"Do you not like these?"

"I might like them, but——"

"What?" interrupted he.

"I'm treated so bad, I don't care anything about them, so I don't."

"Who treats you bad, your mistress?"

"Yes, sir, she beats me like any dog, so she does, and makes master beat me for spite!"

"Have they many slaves besides you?"

"Yes, sir, they have over three hundred on two places; this one here, and the other at Matanzas."

"How are the slaves used here in Cuba? I understand they are well treated."

"'Taint so, sir—these people treat theirs like brutes!"

"What is the name of the little slave there, who plays with his young master?"

"Pomp. They beat and pull him about all the time; and if he don't let them do as they please with him, they go crying to their ma, who whips him severely."

"What are the names of those children, Lotty?"

"The biggest one there is Miguel, the next Ferdinand, the girl Bracinia, and the baby in my arms is Justinia."

"What are their ages?"

"One boy is eight, and the other six; one girl four, and the other not two."

"What is the age of little Pomp, who waits on them, as he seems to be between the two?"

"He is seven years old."

"Lotty, what is your age? You look like a young woman, but you're quite gray and careworn."

"I used to know my age, but since I had so much trouble and came here, they beat me so much over the head till I can't remember hardly anything. I can't tell how old I am!"

"Do the little girls love you as children generally do their nurses?"

"No, sir, they're cross, sassy little brats. They'll pull my hair, scratch my face, and bite me; they go crying to her; then she falls on me and beats me to please them!"

Four o'clock, the dinner hour having arrived, the maid was summoned to duty, and anxious to witness the new order of things, Henry went to await the return of the nurse.

Madame Bonselle was an excellent lady, and loved by all the slaves on the hacienda. Being French, she was an inherent votary of the late revolution and reform, and a believer in the principles espoused by the government of Lamartine, Ludro Rollin and Louis Blanc, and even wore a gold brooch on which the motto was inscribed "Liberte, Eqalite, Fraternite!" the memorable rallying cry of the Liberalists.

After dinner, being seated on the piazza, Lotty on passing with the child in her arms playfully whispered in Madame Bonselle's ear, which the mistress by chance observed.

"A fine girl!" said she smiling as the maid left her.

"She's a forward strap, Madame Bonselle, and I'll break her of it!" replied Madame Garcia.

"I'm sure, Adelaide, she means no harm at all, as you certainly must know!"

"She's entirely spoilt, Celia, since you've been here, with your crazy notions of French equality!"

"We are not accustomed to look upon these poor, unfortunate people with the charity we should, forgetting that naturally they're the same as ourselves."

"Absurd! Celia Bonselle—it's all imagination, as I'm sure the Negroes were made to serve the whites!"

"On this you and I cannot see alike, as I never will sanction such nonsense! God be merciful!" she sighed in conclusion, rising and walking down the lawn, the maid entering the piazza as she left.

"Lot, you strap! How dare you whisper in Madame Bonselle's ear, and that——"

"I'm sure, mistress, I meant no harm! and I didn't know that you saw me, else I wouldn't have done it, indeed I wouldn't. I won't do so any more, if you only spare me this time, and don't whip me before that strange man that came with the Americans! Oh, mistress!" she exclaimed, dropping to her knees, as Madame Garcia sunk the thumb nail deep into her ear, nearly cutting it through, saying:

"Now, take that, you impudent black jade, and begone out of my presence. The next time I'll cut you to pieces!"

The poor thing hastened away sorrowing, silently praying that God would remove her from her sufferings. Sitting some time after this with the children under the shade of orange trees, Henry approaching observing the ear, side of the face and neck much swollen, inquired the cause, she evasively answering that a wasp had stung her.

" 'Twan no wasp sting dat! Missers done it so she did!" explained little Pomp, which was heard by the young masters.

"How dare you say that about ma!" said the child Miguel, grasping the little black boy, who was sitting on the grass at the time, by the hair, jerked him upon his face to the ground saying, "Now, you black!"

Hastening into the house, the child in a whisper acquainted his mother with what had transpired between the man and maidservant, Pomp and himself. No notice whatever was taken of it at the time.

Little Pomp was the son of the slave cook of the family, Abigail; the name of her mistress being a terror to her, as well as to all of the slaves. Night had now somewhat advanced, the guests retired; and the news of the displeasure of the mistress toward Lotty and Pomp having spread through the place, many of the slaves had come from their huts concealing themselves in the shrubbery around the mansion to watch, well knowing that punishment would be the consequence. Lotty had expressed in anguish that she dreaded the approach of night, which induced Henry, who well understood her condition, to remain up until the last, determining to witness all that he could pertaining to Cuban slavery. He had come in search of his poor lost wife, and was anxiously desirous of having some idea of her true condition before reaching her, which he was determined on doing, did she live at all on earth. All was now silent, the slaves awestricken in their hiding places; the nurse, her personal attendant maidservant, and Henry sat in quiet waiting on the back piazza, there seeming at the time not a ripple of air, nor quiver of a leaf to interrupt the monotonous harmony. But the occupants of the piazza were suddenly started by a voice accustomed on such occasions to command, and but too familiar:

"Dilsey, go bring me the cowhide!"* the girl soon returning with the dreadful thing of punishment. "Now call Abigail, and tell her to bring that nigger of hers with her," the servant executing as soon as possible the mistress' order, when the slave-mother and child stood trembling before her. "You are here, my lady, are you!" continued Madame

---

*Cowhide—the name given to a raw-skin whip in America.

Garcia, addressing herself to Lotty. "Stand aside there!" then turning to the mother of the child, she said, "take off his clothes!"

"O, missus!" exclaimed the poor cook, as she laid on the stripes, regardless of the screams of agony uttered by the little one. "Dohn beat my po' chile no mo! here's my back, gib it to me!" A severe cut with the hide across the face instantly silenced the petitions of Abigail, when handing her the whip, she compelled her to scourge her own child till he fell motionless and bleeding at her feet.

"O, Laud!" exclaimed the more than tormented slave-mother. "Wot's to come o' we po' black people! I wish in God I nebeh been baun."

"Not a word of reflection there, you black ape, or I'll have you given ten times as much! Take him out of this!" When as she lugged away her boy, insensible and bloody, the mother gave way to choking sobs of inexpressible grief. To her maid the mistress said, "Poor old black thing! It was natural, I suppose, for her to feel for the little Negro! He'll soon get over it! Now my lady, you may go!" she said, speaking to Lotty. "And the next time I have occasion to use that" (pointing to the bloody whip) "it shall be your time!" Lotty, humbly curtsying, left her presence.

To all this, Henry was a serious spectator, having twice detected himself in an involuntary determination to rush forward and snatch the infernal thing of torture from the hand of the heart-crushed mother. He retired that night with a mind nearer distraction than sanity.

Early next morning he asked, and kindly received, consent to leave for a fortnight, the services of Mrs. Seeley, for the purpose as he stated of visiting some relation in the colony; the Seeleys supposing, as he spoke Castilian well when employed by them, that he was a resident of Cuba.

CHAPTER 37

A Glimmer of Hope

In his conversation with Lotty, Henry had learned of the residence of two families from Louisiana near Matanzas, when on leaving the hacienda of the Garcias, he went directly in search of the Americans. In his stroll, he kept the great roads, because these a Negro might travel without suspicion, besides to have frequently the benefit of the diligence, all of which are driven by blacks; and also because to venture through the plantations would have been hazardous, nearly the whole of which keep Negro-dogs, or bloodhounds with which to run down the slaves.

On approaching his destined point of anxiety, meeting an old black man whom he addressed and was answered in Creole, the following conversation ensued:

"Do you live about here?" asked Henry.

"I do," replied the man.

"Where abouts?"

"On de nex' place."

"Are you a free man?"

"No, my frien', I'se a slave."

"I thought the slaves out this way were not allowed clothes. How's this?" said Henry, speaking knowingly to conceal his being a stranger, by assuming a familiarity with all part of the island; as it is indeed a truth that the slaves in Cuba generally go nude.

"Da's not 'lowed nothin' to put on, only wen de wite folks sen' um out."

"Will you not be allowed, after you get home, to keep those clothes on while attending about the house, and waiting on the white folks?"

"No, seh, no; I has to take 'em off, an' go 'long so, no matter who's dar."

"What is the name of your plantation?"

"Da calls it Lucyana Hacienda."

"What's your master's name?"

"He name Jenkin."

"Is he a Creole?"

"No, he 'Merica man."

"Is he a good master?"

"Ah, God knows bes'. He wus kine a man!"

"Does he keep an overseer?"

"Yes, bless yeh! 'E got two-three places, and ovehseeh on 'em all."

"How many slaves has Jenkin in all?"

"I do' no'; 'e got heap a slaves."

"What does he raise; sugar, coffee, or rice?"

" 'E raise sugar on all of 'em."

"Are the planters generally good or bad to their people?"

"Bad 'nough, bad 'nough!"

"Do you all get much chance to go out at night?"

"No, no, bless yeh! Da all keep bloodhoun' to watch arter an' keep us in."

"What part of America did your master come from?"

"De Lucyana whar I com from."

"Are there any other Louisiana planters near here?"

"Da's one some ten-twenty mile, uh sich a mautta."

"I would like to go and stay with you, or some of your people tonight in their huts."

"Well, meh frien', it is very dange'ous, case de wite folks al'as lookin' 'roun', an' da got bloodhoun' out all night long watchin', and wen strangeh come 'among us, de dog bay roun' de hut till wite folks come."

"Then it must be dangerous to go on the plantations at all."

"Yes, 'ndeed, mighty dange'ous; case da larn de dog, an' sometime 'e so famish' dat 'e break in de hut an' tare our po' children to pieces!"

"I must go with you, let come what will!" concluded Henry.

"Well, me frien', I try an' do all I kin for yeh!" finally replied the old man, conducting him from the main road leading to Matanzas into a road to the right, which led them directly to the place of Jenkin, which they reached in safety sometime after nightfall, the man immediately leaving.

This family proved to be a choice one, on which Henry fixed his memory for future movements, he being then in search of a wife, to him at the time the greatest domestic concern on earth; made no seclusions, nor organized gatherings among his brethren of this class in Cuba. The hut was of superior construction to those of the slaves generally in the colony; the family of a superior order, proved to be native African, having learned English on the coast, French Creole at New Orleans, and Spanish at Cuba; but ten years having elapsed since they were kidnapped, the whole family by chance getting together. Their African name was Oba, the Cuban, Grande. Grande was foreman on the plantation of Jenkin, probably because of his superior intelligence; but most probably because of the fact that from the day of his advent on the place, the bloodhounds were known to fondle with his family, and never could be made to attack or even bay after one of them. This gave them reverence among brother slaves, which must have induced his attainment to this post.

During the night bloodhounds were heard yelping, but none approached the old man Oba's hut.

Secrets were exchanged concerning dog charming between Henry and his new friend Grande, and much information was obtained concerning the character of Cuban planters, as well as the designs of the slaves. They were ripe for a general rising, said the old man, but God only knew where they would find a leader. These things and many more were made known to him during three days' secretion in the family.

"I have been with you three days and nights, Father Oba, and now must think about going," said Henry.

"How, me son, ye 'scape ovesee; that wat trouble me mos'," replied the old man.

"Your good friend Carl who brought me here, told me that Albertis had a plantation not more than ten miles from here."

"Yes, me son, he great frien' to Jenkin. They both 'Merican men."

"Then leave the matter with me, Father Oba, and I'll risk the chance with the overseer."

"What you goin' do, me son?"

"I'm going directly to Jenkin himself."

"Sho, chile, he aint goin' to give you a pass."

"I'll risk the matter; just leave it to me, father."

"Spose he come ax me who you is; what I goin' tell 'im, chile?"

"Just tell him that I called myself a slave from the next plantation; what is the name?"

"Buena Terra Hacienda is the name, me son; the mausta name Faries."

"That's enough, father, I must go. Farewell!" said Henry, directing his course across the place towards the mansion some three miles off.

"Good-bye, me son, good-bye! Sorry you go in daylight, but hope you fool 'im good!" concluded the kind old Father Oba, gazing after him as far as he could see.

It was dinner hour when Henry reached the mansion, and inquired of a servant if Mr. Jenkin were in, being answered in the affirmative.

"Can I see him?" inquired Henry.

"He's engaged with company," replied the servant. "Sit down here under the verandah." Henry, thanking him, took a seat.

The dinner being over, after two hours waiting, the master appeared on the back verandah, preceded by the servant to direct him.

"Well, my boy, to whom do you belong?" saluted Mr. Jenkins.

"I belong to Señor Faries of Buena Terra Hacienda, sir."

"Señor Faries' boy, hey! What is your errand, my boy?"

"To ask, sir, if you have some of the Chinese sugar-cane seed sent you from the patent office in America, that you will oblige him with a small sample."

"Yes, my boy, you shall have them. Stay and take your dinner with my people." Henry, politely bowing, resumed his seat at the withdrawal of the master.

On a visit from America was a gentleman by the name of Postlewaite, formerly of Kentucky, his body servant George, a tall, fine-looking, manly, intelligent fellow, being quite a favorite with his master.

When called, the servant approached with a dejection and submission of manner, which seemed at the moment to affect even the master himself who had caused it.

"George, hold up your head, and don't look down as if you were condemned to be hung!" said Postlewaite; the servant raising his eyes with a look of irrecoverable humiliation.

"Your Negro seems to be pretty well broken; how did you manage it?" remarked Jenkin.

"I did as you advised me; sent him to a professional whipper, who charged him with the misconduct of making free with his master."

"I always thought him the most confounded forward, impudent Negro I ever saw!" said Jenkin.

"You are mistaken, Mr. Jenkin, it was not impudence nor even forwardness, as he was most delicately sensible of what was due to others, especially superiors; but I and he being raised up from childhood together, he was accustomed to look upon and treat me more as a friend and equal, than a master and superior."

"You may thank me, then, Mr. Postlewaite, for the change!"

"Certain it is, sir, that had you not repeatedly called my attention to it, insisting that I must persist in punishment until he was broken, I never should have noticed his conduct."

"Do you think he's completely cured?"

"He's completely broken, sir, and as humble as a dog. The last chastisement that Goodman gave completely reduced him, taking out the last remnant of his manhood, so that he's as spiritless as a kitten!"

"Who was the whipper?"

"Goodman is his name, an American, from Pennsylvania I believe; one of your real poor white men, whom our Negro slaves so much despise and hate to have over them."

"He's certainly the fellow for his work, Mr. Postlewaite; he does it well, I assure you!" concluded Jenkin.

Postlewaite was a man of very generous disposition, and always had been indulgent to his favorite servant George; but as a master, by the force of circumstances was compelled to yield to the whims of those whose judgment, as successful planters, were reqarded as superior.

The seed being obtained, with a note directed to "Señor Faries, Buena Terra Hacienda," Henry left late in the afternoon, making his way toward the hacienda of the anxiously sought-for Peter Albertis.

CHAPTER 38

Impatience

"Good evening, my friend! Is this the hacienda of Señor Peter Albertis?" inquired Henry, who had made good speed of some twelve miles distance since leaving the place of Jenkin; startling a man who stood at the entrance of a large gateway waiting the approach of a herd of goats from an adjoining open plain.

"Dis si his'n," was the reply.

"Is he at home?"

"No; 'e gone 'way."

"When did he go?"

"Dis mornin'."

"Where has he gone?"

" 'E gone to Habana."

"When will he be back?"

"I do'no."

"Have you an overseer?"

"Yes, my fren', dat we has!"

"Where is he?"

" 'E gone to 'Tanzas to de bullfight."

"To Matanzas—when did he start?"

"E jus' gwine long down de road dar now."

"When will he be back?"

"In de mornin'."

"In the morning—why, when does the fight take place?"

"It take place arly, jus' at daybreak; afteh it oveh den he come home."

"Who attends to the place when he and your master are away?"

"Black man name Dominico."

"Is he strict?"

"Ah, my fren', dat 'e is—mighty stric'!"

"Can I see him?"

"I do'no, my fren', if yeh kin or no. Stop, I go see fus!"

"How far is it to his hut?"

"Way up yondeh, 'bout half mile."

"Do you keep Negro-hounds on the place?"

"Yes 'ndeed, dat de am, plenty on 'em!"

"Can't I go with you?"

"No, my fren', betteh stay whar yeh is, 'case de houn 'ont be out dis two hours, sich a matter yit," replied the herdsman, supposing Henry to be afraid of the dogs, about which he cared but little, having fully learned to subdue the most ferocious of them.

The herd, which had been slowly approaching, grazing as they moved, passed through, when the gate was securely locked, and the herdman left with his message for the hut. Half an hour having ensued, the approach of a person was seen at some distance in the clear twilight of a most beautiful West-India evening, which appeared like a shadow. As the figure drew near, Henry receded a few paces close in the corner of a hedge-fence near the gateway, partially screening himself by the overhanging branches.

"Who is here?" inquired a voice in intelligent Creole, as the person came to the gate, discovering no one in waiting.

"A friend!" replied Henry, the man starting at the voice.

"If you be what you say, come forth like a man, and show yourself!" was the reply, Henry immediately coming out from the bramble.

"Is this Dominico?" he inquired of a stalwart, fine looking black man, past the middle of life.

"I answer to that name."

"Can I rest with you tonight?"

"What is your name, and who are you?"

"Jacob, sir," replied Henry, cautiously concealing his nom de plume of "Gilbert," that no traces of his rambling might be detected should he fall in with treacherous blacks disposed to betray him.

"Where are you from, and where do you live?"

"I cannot tell you that."

"What is your errand, then, that you come here at such an hour?"

"If you'll take me to your quarters and have a little talk till I learn more about you, then I may be ready to answer that question."

"My friend, I think I understand you; come with me," concluded Dominico, starting down the lane with his friend.

Henry soon became acquainted with this family, who were true to the cause of their race and people. Dominico and wife were the pride and counsel of all the slaves in their immediate neighborhood. The overseer was passionately fond of sporting, and always sought the absence of the master, who himself resided on the plantation, to indulge in recreation. At such times he left his trust to revel in the games and sports at Matanzas, the most of the master's time being spent at Havana and Principe. The understanding between them seemed mutual, that Henderich, might go when he pleased, which gave an opportunity to the Dominico family to counsel and prepare the slaves for the future.

The man who stood at the gate, apparently awaiting the goatherd to pass, was a good and trusty outpost spy, keeping the herd in check as a ruse. By this arrangement of their duty, even in the absence of the master, the privileges of the whole plantation were left entirely to themselves. This evening presented an especial privilege by the occasion of Henry's visit.

"What sort of a master is Albertis?" inquired he of the intelligent Dominico.

"A mighty hard master indeed when he takes it into his head."

"Does he whip much?"

"When he has been drinking or loses by gambling he is very severe and cruel."

"Does he drink and gamble much?"

"Whenever he's at home and has company. But he's a great deal away, else some of the people wouldn't stand him."

"Where is he from?"

"Louisiana, in America."

"Has he a wife?"

"No indeed; but he's always buying handsome slave girls."

"Why does he buy so many?"

"They don't seem to like 'im. Some won't stay with him, and them that does he soon falls out with. All such he generally sends off to America, where they bring better prices than if he sold 'em here."

"You say some won't stay with him at all?"

"No indeed they won't. The last one he got was a mighty fine woman, I do assure you; she wouldn't even stay in the great house where he was."

"Where did she stay?"

"She stayed with my family, and he couldn't make her go out."

"Did he not punish her very severely for such disobedience?" inquired Henry, becoming almost impatient with anxiety.

"He beat her like a dog; and one evening just at dusk he came in and ordered her to leave and go over to the great house; when she refused, telling him she would not, if he killed her. He then struck her in the breast with his fist, knocking her against me, when I kept her from falling. He next gave her a kick in the side, which brought her with a scream to her knees, where for some time leaning against the bed, she was unable to speak from pain, and when she could speak she screamed whenever she drew her breath; when he ordering her with a dreadful oath to get up; and knowing what he was, as she couldn't she put up her hands to beg him, when he jerked down that piece of iron there, and struck her across the side of the head, nearly splitting the skull, when she fell, we thought, for dead, and he walked indifferently away."

Henry now became so anxious concerning the fate of his wife, that for a time he suspended the inquiry, dreading the conclusion.

"What was the name of this woman?" after some minutes reflection, which had been observed by the family of Dominico, he inquired.

"Lotty, he called her," was the reply; when Henry involuntarily started from his seat to the door, returning again as if unconscious of what he did.

"Where is she now—did he sell her?" with great anxiety he inquired, the emotion being such as to almost betray his interest in her behalf.

"He put her with his sister to break her."

"Who is his sister?" continued Henry with unabated anxiety.

"Madame Garcia, at Castilian Hacienda, near Habana," concluded Dominico, the perspiration breaking upon Henry, who spent a night of torturing impatience.

CHAPTER 39

The Discovery

The morning came and with its dawn Henry was an impatient waiting spectator. Leaving one of the most interesting slave families, he reached the great road leading to Havana, where taking a diligence without interruption, in three days arrived in the precincts of Castilian Hacienda. On arriving at the mansion, the family were all in the garden, recreating among the shrubbery, enjoying an atmosphere freighted with odor, and vibrating with the melody of the feathered inhabitants.

Late that afternoon, a sultry day, in the bower verging on a stream which fell abruptly into a craggy gully, at the extreme back part of the great thicket, sat Captains Garcia and Paul, Lieutenant Seeley and passed Midshipman Spencer, Mesdames Garcia, Bonselle, and Seeley. Henry approached them, made his respects to the gratification of the young Madame Seeley, who had been doubtful of his return; then went where the maid and children were, some distance off, though in sight in a rude pathway leading through a ravine under a rugged fence into the adjacent wildwood.

The maid smiled as he approached, reached out her hand which was prevented from taking his by their being simultaneously raised to absorb with a white handkerchief, the tears which at that moment obscured his sight and dampened his cheeks.

The terribly scourged little Pomp, was dejectedly playing near his young masters Miguel and Ferdinand, and Henry having cast a look upon him, the maid reasonably supposed that his emotion was a manifestation of sympathy for the child. Recovering from the emotion, he quietly stood with eyes fixed upon her.

She had a careworn expression of irreconcilable trouble,

unhappiness and sorrow, sunken eyes, a full suit of crimpy hair, but carelessly worn, well mixed with grey, the scar of a deep cut wound on the right angle of the forehead, and her appearance was that of a woman ten years the senior of his wife.

"Have you any children, Lotty?" said Henry, the first word spoken, after sometime gazing upon her.

"One!" was the only reply, when she turned away with choking emotion.

"What is it, a boy or girl? I mean no harm in asking you."

"Boy, sir," she sobbed.

"Where is he?"

"In Mississippi, in America."

"What is his name?"

"Joe! Oh my dear little Joe!" she replied convulsed with smothered wailing.

"Have you a husband?"

"O! I once had a dear good husband! But O Lord, I'm now a poor wretched woman here in a strange country!"

"Where is your husband?"

"He's there too, in the Mississippi."

"What was your husband's name?"

"Henry Hol——"

"O! My God! Is this my wife!" he exclaimed, at the moment when was heard the frightful yelping of approaching dogs, having in chase a large guana,* which rushing pass, brushed the skirt of her dress, when screaming, Maggie stood supported in the arms of her husband.

"O Henry! O me, what shall I do! O, this ain't you! O, what shall I do! Mistress will kill me! O Henry! O Henry, is this you!"

"Yes, yes, my poor wife! this is your——"

"Do you see that jade?" said Madame Garcia, Henry stopping to catch the words. "In spite of all I can do, she will put on airs in the presence of white persons, and I'm determined to break her, if I have to break her neck!"

"Poor thing, she couldn't help doing so! I'm sure that ugly creature

---

*Guanas are run down by dogs and caught—a South American custom, introduced into Cuba by Brazillian slaves, some of whom when sold carry the young animals with them.

is enough to frighten any one. I'm as afraid of them as death," replied Madame Bonselle.

"She's not afraid of them; she only wants to show herself before that Negro man of Madame Seeley, that's all!"

The game being caught, the baying of the dogs and noisy jabber of the slaves who poured in eager pursuit to the lawn in large numbers, was such that the company retired to the Verandah to escape the annoyance.

"This is your husband, poor outraged suffering one, and he comes to take you, if in doing it, he takes the life of every slaveholder in Cuba!" said Henry, pressing her closely to his bosom.

"O! this can't be you! O my God, I have suffered more than death! How did you come? O my poor child! Where's mammy, did she come too? My poor father!" When with an innocent smile, Maggie gazed in the face of her husband, with eyes immovably fixed.

Gently laying her on the grass under the shade of a tree, the greathearted slave hastened to the rippling stream nearby from which to get water to lave her brow and temples to relieve her of the temporary insanity; when sitting over her in discharge of his duty of love and conjugal affection, he found a solace by the intrusion of tears which freely fell from his eyes.

At these scenes the children were surprised and hastened to their mother to tell their childish story, which only tended to aggravate an offence to her already unpardonable.

"O, you worst of treated women, I'll have revenge for it!" said the half-distracted husband to himself, as he leaned over her, applying the water with his handkerchief.

Presently the child, which till then had been quietly playing on the grass aside of her, began to cry—the larger ones having gone to the house—when Henry took it, holding it on his arm, which only increased its fretfulness. The other children just returning, heard the little sister fretting, while the nurse lay unheeding it, when returning to the house, reported again to their mother concerning her conduct.

The mistress now became impatient and sent her servant Dilsey to summon Lotty to appear immediately before her. The girl returning reported Lotty to be sick. The mistress insisted that it was all affectation, and determined on having her whipped by her master.

Poor Maggie's joys on recovering, were blasted by anticipation of the punishment that awaited her.

"O Lord!" she sighed as the sun declined beneath the horizon; "I dread night coming on! I wish I was dead, so I do; they'll beat me to death!"

"The villain who dares lay hands on you, I'll send into eternity as quick as my arm can execute the deed! And——"

Here he was suddenly interrupted by Dilsey, who was a good girl and a true friend to her people, running hastily into the garden to inform Maggie that Peter Albertis had just arrived from Principe. Clasping her hands and looking Henry in the face, Maggie cried out, "O husband, what will I do?"

"Don't be the least frightened Maggie, my child; I assure you not a hair of your head will be hurt!"

"But he'll take my life, and ——"

"I'll take his first," said Henry so determinedly, that she concluded to say nothing more, lest he might be aggravated to an overt act and blast all hopes, however futile they were.

The arrival of Albertis arrested the anticipated proceedings of the evening, Henry taking advantage of which carefully cautioned his wife, who required no such admonishing, to impart nothing that would in the least betray their relation. They separated for the time, when for the first night in many months, both husband and wife could retire to see each other in the morning.

CHAPTER 40

The Confrontment

Alone, early on Monday morning, ere an inmate of the premises had risen, Henry sat in the bower devising measures and the course to pursue in relation to obtaining his wife. If she could be purchased the money was ready; if not, a determination to have her at any risk had been maturely decided on. Thus was he meditating, when the Seeleys summoned him to domestic duties.

That morning Madame Garcia was stirring unusually early, having much in relation to his unruly servant to report to her brother. The maid was, in her estimation, the worst of beings—stubborn, disobedient, saucy, and wicked—insisting that measures the severest should be taken to check her in time, and subdue her spirit. She had tried every reasonable method to break her, but entirely failed in the effort. She had whipped her, pinched her, goaded her, and even smoked her and burned her with a smoothing iron,* but all had failed to reach her; she was so effectually depraved and obdurate.

"She has been spoilt by her first mistress in her training, and a lifetime will not now correct the error."

"I know of no other remedy, Adelaide, than to sell her immediately off of our hands," replied Peter Albertis to his sister. "She is the stubbornest creature I ever had to deal with. She takes more lashing than a dog; and if you can't break her, she can't be broken."

"There is now an opportunity to do so, Mr. Albertis, as our man Gilbert and she seem much attached; and he may make proposals to buy her," suggested Madame Seeley, intentionally for him to profit by the hint, as he was passing at the time it was spoken.

"I decidedly object to the proposal of Madame Seeley; as she should be allowed no such privileges," readily responded Madame Garcia.

"You can't object if she desire it; so you must make the best of a bad thing, Adelaide," replied Albertis.

"I don't understand you, brother! Do you mean to say that we cannot do as we please with our own Negroes?"

"You may think it hard, but what is law is fair, I suppose. This law gives the slave the right, whenever desirous to leave his master, to make him a tender in Spanish coin, which if he don't accept, on proof of the tender the slave may apply to the parish priest or bishop of the district, who has the right immediately to declare such slave free."[24]

"I'm sure I was not aware of that before."

"Very likely, sister; but that does not make it any the less law."

"And what is the sum that the Negro must offer?"

"Four hundred and fifty dollars, I think."

"If this is the kind of place Cuba is, I don't want to live here! We better go back to Louisiana. Why, your Negro girl cost you more than twice that much!"

"Yes, I paid for her two thousand dollars cash; but it is better to get a part of my money back than lose the whole. The law in its wisdom

---

*This cruelty of fastening slaves in a tight room, smoking them with burning rags, and burning them with a hot smoothing iron, has often been done in the South.

supposes it better to lose our property than our lives; better to let the Negro have his liberty at his own expense at a price fixed by the law, than have him to take his liberty and the Island by violence at the expense of our blood. Those who made the laws could probably see farther than you or I, Adelaide."

"Then if what you say be true, I don't see what's to be gained by staying in such a country. I want to go home!"

"You might not better it by going there, for, as in Cuba, there are also many existing laws of which you know nothing. And respecting the contingencies of insurrection, you are not more safe than here. In New Orleans, as in Havana, the great gun at the fort must at a certain hour every night be fired, to intimidate and keep down the Negroes; and there as here, while you are unsuspectingly sleeping in your quiet bed in seeming safety, a guard for private and public safety must be kept through the night, and even secret guards through the day, to keep in check the disposition to rebellion on the part of the slave population."[25]

"Then indeed must we be in a most dangerous position."

"I know it; but hang it, it can't be helped. We must do the best we can under the circumstances, that's all."

"I wonder all the Negroes in Cuba are not free, since they have the right to purchase themselves."

"They don't all know it; and if they did, few comparatively could raise the means. And even now among those who have the means and desire, a given fee dropped into the hands of certain parties impairs their memory wonderfully, making them forget the existence of such law or the time when to proclaim it.

"I should think that the English, who are such friends to the Negroes, would see that the law was strictly enforced."

"Womanlike Adelaide, you don't understand political matters. The English have nothing to do with it; and they have no more love for Negroes than for other people. They have sympathy for the Negro because he is oppressed: but never help those, in a general sense, who don't help themselves. If the Negroes rise and take off our heads, declaring their independence, the English will be the first to acknowledge it. But they'll never come and cut off our heads, politely handing them to the Negroes. The English must see that something is done before they'll recognize the doer. Until the Negro does something, the English will let him remain as he is; so don't be troubled about English Negro-interference in Cuba, nor your own country."

"Well," said Adelaide with a deep, long sigh, "I wish I was in Louisiana."

Henry having been a secret auditor, found opportunity to impart to his wife the entire conversation between Albertis, his sister, and Cornelia Seeley. He strictly instructed her to preemptorily refuse to live with him an hour longer, and seize an opportunity immediately of confronting him on the subject of her rights.

As if unconscious of the existing state of her feelings, Maggie with the children went sautering into the parlor.

"Well, my girl," saluted Albertis, "are you ready to go home with me?"

"No, sir!"

"Don't want to go, hey! Then we'll find a way to make you!"

"I won't live on your place any more; and there is no use in asking me!"

"Don't let her give such impudence, brother! I'd knock her down first!" interposed Madame Garcia.

"I'll sell you, you impudent strap, to the hardest master I can find!"

"I won't serve any person any more, so I won't! And its no use to talk about selling me!" said Maggie, emboldened at the thought of freedom, knowing that her husband sustained her in it.

"I want none of your impudence here, Lot, and won't take it," reproved Madame Garcia.

"I now demand a bill of sale of you to myself, Mr. Albertis, and tender in Spanish gold four hundred and fifty dollars!" reaching out to him the money in a careless way, which she drew from under her apron.

At this Albertis was surprised, his sister indignant, and the other two ladies highly pleased. The matter was too plain, and no longer to be ignored. Maggie knew her rights, and Albertis discovered it. Dissembling for the moment he said:

"I want more money; that's not half what I paid for you!"

"I make you a legal tender, and I'll give no more!" concluded Maggie, abruptly turning from him and walking out of the room.

"It's all over with her, I see," said Albertis; that Cuban Negro has taught her this!" referring to Henry, who, on account of his fluent Spanish, was not suspected as a stranger.

"And are you going to take so small a sum as that?" inquired Madame Garcia anxiously.

"There is no use, Adelaide, in cutting off one's nose to spite his face; for the truth of the matter is, if I don't hasten to take that sum, she can decline giving me anything at all, and go to the parish priest and be declared free, in spite of all I can say or do!"

"There seems then to be no chance for us Americans here, except in the prospect of a patriotic movement?"

"But little reliance can be placed in them, a set of dissatisfied, irresponsible American intruders, who only stir up strife to the danger of life and property."

"Are not the patriots the Creoles?"

"They assume the name of Creole, but are little short of marauding foreigners. The Negroes are the mainstay of Cuba, and can never be induced to join the patriots, who, as soon as they got the island, would deny the Negroes the rights they now have. I know this information is against me, but you must be made sensible of your true position here, that when trouble comes you may the better be prepared to meet it."

"But why should the Spanish government in the event of a loss of the island, prefer a Negro to a white dominion? This I confess I cannot comprehend."

"Simply because the Negroes are more docile, contented, religious and happy. They are civil, and more easily governed as a race than the Anglo-American; hence they make better subjects, being more submissive than they."

In half an hour after the withdrawal of Maggie from the parlor, Albertis presented the following document, which was hastily executed and delivered.

CASTILIAN HACIENDA,
*ISLE OF CUBA, April 16, 1853.
Received of my girl Lotty, of zambo complexion, calling herself

*The time of Henry's sale in Mississippi, and all of the circumstances, antecede the dates given by several years.

Lotty Holland, formerly my slave, the sum of four hundred and fifty dollars legal tender, as purchase money for herself; by which act she is manumitted,* set free and enfranchised, according to the laws of Cuba, made and provided for in such cases.

SIGNED PETER ALBERTIS
Proprietor of El Paso Hacienda

AUGUSTUS SEELEY,
Witness   CORNELIA SEELEY,
CELIA BONSELLE.

Adelaide Garcia refusing to witness the transaction, had gone into the lawn, while Garcia, Paul, and Spencer, who from the first intended being only silent spectators to the whole, sat intently watching the proceedings.

The long-desired end being attained—the dearest object of his desires, his wife found, her freedom obtained, and having secured this simple Magna Charta of her liberty, Henry was among the happiest of men.

A private interview was had with the Seeleys, in which he made known his intention of leaving them, and they having no idea of the relation between them, supposed his intention was to unite with the maid in wedlock. Intending to leave immediately for America to remain in the country but a fortnight, the Seeleys at once proposed that the two accompany them as man and maidservants, as Seeley had inherited a large estate which for several years had been available. Money to him was not an object, the happiness of his wife being his only concern; and Henry had but to name his terms, which would readily be complied with. This the man, as yet to them unknown, declined; preferring, as he stated, rather for the time to remain awhile at Havana. He proposed to them instead, the arrangement of bringing with them a man and maidservant and two small boys—one the child of the servants and the other a black boy eight years old, no relation, whom they might keep subject to his guardianship, until such times as he should himself have use for him. The man and maidservants

---

*Manumitted, set free and enfranchised—terms used in the free papers of manumitted persons in America.

proposed to be bought, would be left to their own choice. The restrictions being great concerning foreign Negroes and mulattoes, Henry having gone into Cuba as a Creole, that as soon as they boarded the vessel at New York on return, the servants should be claimed as their slaves, the custom being common in America to take slave servants to the free states, their masters instructing them to pass as free people. Madame Seeley was to have the boy as her page, but strictly to instruct him and attend to his morals. The persons would meet the Seeleys in the city, so soon as intelligence reached them through the friend to whom he would give them a note, enclosed to the care of the intelligencer who procured for them his services.

Everything having been well understood, the following is a copy of the notes borne by the hands of the Seeleys, superscribed to the proprietor of the intelligence office:

B. A. P., Esq., New York, U. S.—

DEAR SIR: Enclosed please find two letters, one addressed to our mutual friend, C. R——h, who called to see me; the old veteran in the cause of the runaway slave, which you will please hand to him; and the other to Rev. W. Mon——, of Detroit, Mich.,[26] which you will have mailed to him. Any assistance you can give to Lieutenant Seeley and lady, will very much oblige

Yours respectfully,

GILBERT.

CUBA, April, 1853.

P. S.—You will remember having procured a place for me to go with a party to Cuba, some time since.   G.

The letter addressed to C. R——h, the slave's old friend in New York read thus:

ISLE OF CUBA, April, 1853.

C. R——h—MY DEAR SIR:

This letter is enclosed in a note to our friend, B. A. P., of the intelligence office, in Leonard St.; borne by a gentleman and lady, Lieutenant Augustus Seeley and his wife, Madame Cornelia Seeley, with whom I came to Cuba when I left you. A mulatto man and his wife, a quadroon woman, and two little boys—a small brown child, said to be their own, and a little black boy some eight years of age, no relation to them—will come to you from the neighborhood of Windsor, Canada West, sent on by that excellent, pious friend of the slave and his race, Rev. W. Mon——. Their names are Charles and Polly Tiptoe, who are to come to Cuba as servants to the Seeleys; for whom you need have no fears, as the lieutenant and his excellent lady have proven themselves the best of friends, and worthy of all confidence. Some day perhaps you may be surprised to learn who I am; but until then,

I am very Respect'ly,   GILBERT.

The Detroit letter read:

NEW YORK, April, 1853.

REV. W. MON——MY VERY DEAR FRIEND:

The mere thought of your name produces in me emotions. You will please call over to the settlement as soon as possible, see our people there, and tell Charles Tiptoe and his wife to come immediately and bring my little son, Joe, and little Tony to New York. The particulars will be made known to you hereafter. Console the old people by giving them to understand that I must either have got my wife, or am certain of doing so, else I would not send for the children; and that they will all hear in due season from me. Tell Charles to bring with him all the available money he has, but none of the others must come with him. Love to the old people particularly, also Andy and Clara, Eli, Ailcey and Ambrose. That you may know the letter is genuine, I fix my mark.

Some day, my dearest of friends, I shall be able to do, and you will know me other than as now, your ever indebted and very grateful runaway slave,

HENRY

P.S.—To prevent all traces of me, I assumed the name of Gilbert, my old travelling name after I left you, which is the only name by which I am known here. Should you hereafter hear of my whereabouts, it must be strictly kept to yourself, not even Andy and Eli are to know it till I am ready to inform them.   G.

With cheerfulness receiving this billet addressed to the New York agent, a reciprocal hearty shake of the hands, and wish by the Seeleys for the happy union of Gilbert and Lotty against their return, they left for Havana early next morning en route for New York, there to celebrate their nuptials, and Henry and Maggie in another diligence in the afternoon of the same day, also proceeded direct to the city.

CHAPTER 41

Obscurity

On their arrival in Havana, Henry found lodgings for himself and wife in an obscure but very respectable old black family, consisting of man and wife, with a half-grown adopted daughter, the wife too aged to do the active services of the family; the husband being a stevedore made his means by superintending the loading of vessels at the quay, by the employment of large numbers of men. The house was in an obscure and retired locality, the family being, seemingly, without acquaintances or visitors.

This evening the Omnipotence of God was satisfactorily verified and established to depart from them "no more forever," in the living reality, as they sat together in the neat and comfortable little back room, assigned them in the humble abode of old man Zoda and wife Huldah Ghu.

Here was told that unparalleled tale of sorrow to a husband never expected again to be seen by the wife; and his narrated facts, unequalled in the living history of a slave; concerning the determined efforts of that husband to reach the wife, and rescue her from thralldom at the risk of every consequence.

Goaded and oppressed by a master known to be her own father, under circumstances revolting to humanity, civilization and Christianity, she had been ruthlessly torn from her child, husband and mother, and sold to a foreign land, all because, by the instincts of nature—if by the honor of a wife and womanhood she had not been justified—she repelled him. Sold again to a severe mistress, then to a heartless, cruel man for the worst of designs, by whom she had been almost daily beaten, frequently knocked down, kicked and stamped on, once struck and left for dead; and even smoked and burnt to subdue her. During these sufferings and those untold, her faith had often faltered, and she had staggered at the thought of believing that "God was no respecter of persons."

Maddened to desperation at the tearing away of his wife during his absence from her child and home, he had confronted his master at the hazard of life, been set upon the auction block in the midst of an assemblage of anxious slavetraders, escaped being sold, traversed the greater part of the slaveholding states amid dangers the most imminent; been pursued, taken, and escaped, frequently during which time, he, too, had his faith much shaken, and found his dependence in Divine aid wavering. But God to them, however their unworthiness, had fully made manifest Himself, and established their faith in His promises, by again permitting them to meet each other under circumstances so singular and extraordinary.

The heartbroken look, hopeless countenance, languid eye, and dejected appearance of the gray-haired, apparently aged, sorrow-stricken Lotty, the nurse of Adelaide Garcia, was now succeeded by the buoyant spirit, handsome smile and brilliant-eyed Maggie Holland, though the sunken sockets, and gray-smitten hairs still remained, which time and circumstances would doubtless much improve.

"God be thanked for this privilege!" said Henry, as he sat with his wife leaning upon his knees, looking in his face, her right hand resting on his shoulder, his left supporting her waist.

"God's name be praised!" responded Maggie both laughing and crying at the same time.

Henry here, as rapidly as possible, detailed to her his plans and schemes; and the next day imparted his grand design upon Cuba. At this information she was much alarmed, and could not comprehend that an ordinary man and American slave such as he, should project such an undertaking.

"Never mind, wife, you will know better by-and-by," was the only answer he would give, with a smile, at his wife's searching inquiries.

"Oh, husband don't have anything to do with it; as we are now both free and happy, let us attend to our own affairs. I think you have done enough."

"I am not free, wife, by their acknowledgment, as you are, but have escaped; they can take me whenever they catch me."

"I think, then, you might let them alone."

"As God lives, I will avenge your wrongs; and not until they let us alone—cease to steal away our people from their native country and oppress us in their own—will I let them alone. They shall only live—while I live—under the most alarming apprehensions. Our whole race among them must be brought to this determination, and then, and not til then, will they fear and respect us."

"I don't know, husband, I may be wrong, and I expect you will say so; but I think our people had better not attempt any such thing, but be satisfied as we are among the whites, and God, in His appointed time, will do what is required."

"My dear wife, you have much yet to learn in solving the problem of this great question of the destiny of our race. I'll give you one to work out at your leisure; it is this: Whatever liberty is worth to the whites, it is worth to the blacks; therefore, whatever it cost the whites to obtain it, the blacks would be willing and ready to pay, if they desire it. Work out this question in political arithmetic at your leisure, wife, and by the time you get through and fully understand the rule, then you will be ready to discuss the subject further with me." Maggie smiled and sighed, but said no more on the subject.

CHAPTER 42

The Interview—Blake

Having placed his money in the keeping of his wife, Henry suggested that, having enjoyed a good rest of two days pleasure in her company, a visit in the city to make some acquaintances was indispensable at such a juncture.

His first object was to find the residence of the distinguished poet of Cuba, Placido;[27] being directed to a large building occupied below, in the upper story of which was the study of the poet. On giving a light tap at the door, a voice in a somewhat suppressed but highly musical tone said, "Come in!" On entering: the stare of a person of slender form, lean and sinewy, rather morbid, orange-peel complexion, black hair hanging lively quite to the shoulders, heavy deep brow and full moustache, with great expressive black piercing eyes, with pen in hand, sitting with right side to the table looking over the left shoulder toward the door, occupied the study.

"Be seated, sir!" said the yellow gentleman, as Henry, politely bowing raised his cap, advancing toward the table.

"I am looking, sir, for the proprietor of the room," said Henry.

"I am the person," replied the gentleman.

"The poet, sir, I believe," continued he.

"I may not answer your expectation, sir!" modestly answered the gentleman.

"Your name, sir?" inquired Henry.

"Placido" was the reply; at which Henry rose to his feet, respectfully bowing.

"May I inquire your name?" asked the poet.

"Blacus, sir." replied he.

"A familiar name to me. Many years ago I had a cousin of that name, an active, intelligent youth, the son of a wealthy black tobacco, cigar, and snuff manufacturer, who left school and went to sea, since when his parents still living, who doted in him with high hopes of his future usefulness, have known nothing of him," explained Placido.

"What was his Christian name, sir?"

"Carolus Henrico."

"Cousin, don't you know me?" said Henry in a familiar voice, after nearly twenty years absence. "I am Carolus Henrico Blacus, your cousin and schoolmate, who nineteeen years ago went to the Mediterranean. I dropped Carolus and Anglicized my name to prevent identify, going by the name of Henry Blake."

"Is it delusion or reality!" replied Placido with emotion.

"It is reality. I am the lost boy of Cuba," said Henry, when they mutually rushed into each others arms.

"Where in God's name have you been, cousin Henry—and what have you been doing?"

"My story, Placido, is easily told—the particulars you may get from one who will be more ready than I to give you details."

"Who is that you——"

"I will tell you presently; but first to my story. When I left father's house at the age of seventeen, I went to sea on what I believed to be a Spanish man-of-war. I was put as apprentice, stood before the mast, the ship standing east for the Western coast of Africa, as I thought for the Mediterranean. On arriving on the coast, she put into the Bight of

Benin near Wydah; was freighted with slaves—her true character then being but too well known—when she again put to sea, standing as I thought for Cuba, but instead, put into Key West, where she quickly disposed of her cargo to Americans. My expression of dissatisfaction at being deceived offended the commander, who immediately sold me to a noted trader on the spot—one Colonel Franks, of Mississippi, near Natchez. He seized me under loud and solemn protest, collared and choked me, declaring me to be his slave. By recommendations from the commander, whose name was Maria Gomez, that I would become a good sailor, I was left with him, to return as apprentice to marine services, making three voyages, returning with as many cargoes, once to Brazil, once more to Key West, and once to Matanzas, Cuba, each of which times I was put in irons on landing, and kept in close confinement during the vessel's stay lest I ran away. The last cargo was taken to Key West, where Franks was in waiting, when a final settlement of the affairs resulted in my being taken by him to the United States, and there held as a slave, where in a few years I became enamored with a handsome young slave girl, a daughter of his (the mother being a black slave) married, have one living child, and thus entangled, had only to wait and watch an opportunity for years to do what has just now been affected," narrated Henry to the astonishment of his intelligent auditor, who, during the time, stood pen in hand, with eyes fixed upon him.

"Just God!" exclaimed Placido: "how merciful He is! Who could have believed it! And you are also a sailor, Henry?"

"I am, cousin; and have served the hardest apprenticeship at the business, I do assure you; I have gone through all the grades, from common seaman to first mate, and always on the coast had full command, as no white men manage vessels in the African waters, that being entirely given up to the blacks."

"I really was not aware of that before; you surprise me!" said Placido.

"That is so! Every vessel of every nation, whether trader or man-of-war, so soon as they enter African waters are manned and managed by native blacks, the whites being unable to stand the climate."

"That, then, opens up to me an entirely new field of thought."

"And so it does. It did to me, and I've no doubt it does so to every man of thought, black or white."

"Give me your hand, Henry"—both clasping hands—"now by the instincts of our nature, and mutual sympathy in the common cause of our race, pledge to me on the hazard of our political destiny what you intend to do."

"Placido, the hazard is too much! Were it lost, the price is too great—I could not pay it. But I read across the water, in a Cuba journal at New Orleans, a lyric from your pen, in which the fire of liberty blazed as from the altar of a freeman's heart. I therefore make no hazard when I this to you impart: I have come to Cuba to help to free my race; and that which I desire here to do, I've done in another place."

"Amen!" exclaimed Placido. "Heaven certainly designed it, and directed you here at this most auspicious moment, that the oppressed of Cuba also may 'declare the glory of God!' "

"Have you thought much in that direction, Placido?"

"I have, though I've done but little, and had just finished the last word of the last stanza of a short poem intended to be read at a social gathering to be held at the house of a friend one evening this week, which meets for the express purpose of maturing some plan of action."

"Read it."

"I will; tell me what you think of it:

Were I a slave I would be free!
    I would not live to live a slave;
But rise and strike for liberty,
    For Freedom, or a martyr's grave!

One look upon the bloody scourge,
    Would rouse my soul to brave the fight,
And all that's human in me urge,
    To battle for my innate right!

One look upon the tyrant's chains,
    Would draw my sabre from its sheath,
And drive the hot blood through my veins,
    To rush for liberty or death!

One look upon my tortured wife,

Shrieking beneath the driver's blows,
Would nerve me on to desp'rate strife,
    Nor would I spare her dastard foes!

Arm'd with the vindicating brand,
    For once the tyrant's heart should feel;
No milk-sop plea should stay my hand,
    The slave's great wrong would drive the steel!

Away the unavailing plea!
    Of peace, the tyrant's blood to spare;
If you would set the captive free,
    Teach him for freedom bold to dare!

To throw his galling fetters by,
    To wing the cry on every breath,
Determined manhood's conquering cry,
    For Justice, Liberty, or death! [28]

"If Heaven decreed my advent here—and I believe it did—it was to
have my spirits renewed and soul inspired by that stimulating appeal,
such as before never reached the ear of a poor, weary, faltering
bondman, Placido. I thank God that it has been my lot to hear it,
culled fresh from your fertile brain. Were there but a smoldering
spark nearly extinguished in the smothered embers of my doubts and
fears, it is now kindled into a flame, which can only be quenched by
the regenerating waters of unconditional emancipation."

"Ah, cousin, though you consider us here free—those I mean who
are not the slaves of white man—I do assure you that my soul as much
as yours pants for a draft from the fountain of liberty! We are not
free, but merely exist by suffrance—a miserable life for intelligent
people, to be sure!"

"You, Placido, are the man for the times!"

"Don't flatter, Henry; I'm not."

"You are, and its no flattery to say so. The expression of an honest
conviction is not flattery. When the spirits of the Christian begin to
droop, to hear the word of life is refreshing to the soul. That is
precisely my case at present."

"Then you have the vital spark in you?"

"Ah, Placido, I often think of the peaceful hours I once enjoyed at the common altar of the professing Christian. I then believed in what was popularly termed religion, as practised in all the slave states of America; I was devoted to my church, and loved to hear on a Sabbath the word of God spoken by him whom I believed to be a man of God. But how sadly have I been deceived! I still believe in God, and have faith in His promises; but serving Him in the way that I was, I had only 'the shadow without the substance,' the religion of my oppressors. I thank God that He timely opened my eyes."

"In this, Henry, I believe you are right; I long since saw it, but you are clear on the subject. I had not thought so much as that."

"Then as we agree, let us at once drop the religion of our oppressors, and take the Scriptures for our guide and Christ as our example."

"What difference will that make to us? I merely ask for information, seeing you have matured the subject."

"The difference will be just this, Placido—that we shall not be disciplined in our worship, obedience as slaves to our master, the slaveholders, by associating in our mind with that religion, submission to the oppressor's will."

"I see, Henry, it is plain; and every day convinces me that we have much yet to learn to fit us for freedom."

"I differ with you, Placido; we know enough now, and all that remains to be done, is to make ourselves free, and then put what we know into practice. We know much more than we dare attempt to do. We want space for action—elbow room; and in order to obtain it, we must shove our oppressors out of the way."

"Heaven has indeed, I repeat, decreed your advent here to——"

"Learn of you!" interrupted Henry.

"No; but to teach us just what we needed," replied Placido.

"God grant us, then, a successful harmony of sentiment!" responded Henry.

"Grant that we may see eye to eye!" exclaimed Placido.

"Amen, amen!" concluded Henry when relinquishing hands they mutually clasped, embracing in each others' arms.

"Tell me now, cousin, to whom did you allude when you first came in, as the person from whom I should obtain details of your life?"

"My wife."

"Is she here?"

"She is," replied Henry relating all the particulars of their separation and reunion.

"Where have you got her?"

"At the house of an old family, west of the Plaza; Zoda and Huldah Ghu are their names; the man is a stevedore."

"She must not remain there."

"Why?" asked Henry.

"I deem it an unsafe quarter under the circumstances—that's all," suggested Placido.

"Then she is committed to your charge. Come with me to see her."

"Gladly will I do so; but tell me this before we leave—whither are you bound, cousin?"

"I go directly to Matanzas, to take out a slaver as sailing-master, with the intention of taking her in mid-ocean as a prize for ourselves, as we must have a vessel at our command before we make a strike. She is also freighted with powder for Dahomi, with several fine field pieces, none of which, I learned, were to be disposed of, but safely deposited at the slaver's rendezvous in an island which I know off the African coast, for future use in trade. I am well acquainted with the native Krumen on the coast, many of the heads of whom speak several European tongues, and as sailing-master, I can obtain as many as I wish, who will make a powerful force in carrying out my scheme on the vessel."

"I thank God for this interview. Henry, I thank God. Come, let's go and see your wife," said Placido in conclusion, when they left the poet's study for the hut of Zoda Ghu, back of the Plazas.

CHAPTER 43

Meeting and Greeting

The poet having been introduced as the cousin of Henry, Maggie was without ceremony taken to Henry's father, the uncle of Placido, and there introduced as the wife of an old friend of his, it being understood that Henry was to remain incognito, as they could not possibly have the slightest idea of him. Madam Blake was to remain as a guest, till the return of her husband from a voyage at sea, with which fact the poet was familiar.

Here everything around was strange to Maggie, who found herself suddenly transferred from wretchedness as a slave on the hacienda of Emanuel Garcia, to that of the happiness of a lady in the elegant mansion of one of the wealthiest and most refined black merchants in the West Indies. Everything was kindness and affection, and but for the thought of the absence of her husband for a time, she would have been the happiest of women. But now she had reconciled herself to his course, for since meeting with the poet, she was satisfied that he was not alone in the important scheme for the redemption of his race.

CHAPTER 44

Seeking Employment

With an affectionate leave of his wife, concealing from her his real movement (she rather suspecting his return to America), with sack in hand Blake started ere a member of the family stirred.

Early this morning a soft rap at the door aroused the poet, who lodged in his study.

"It is not possible," said he on opening the door, "you are off already?"

"Yes, cousin, I must be off to meet the vessel in time, as she'll make no delay."

"That's right, but tell me how you know of the situation, when you were here yesterday?"

"I knew the place was vacant and a black preferred to fill it, and none other to take it than myself; whom if they could not secure, they intended to sail without the office being filled."

"That explains. Well, I must say——"

"Goodbye, cousin!" interrupted Blake, reaching out his hand.

"Goodbye!" responded Placido, when soon Blake was in a diligence hastening on towards Matanzas.

The next morning he approached the vessel lying at her moorings in the harbor; a burly Portuguese, an excellent seaman, standing on her quarterdeck.

"Ship ahoy!" cried the black in familiar nautical phrase.

"Aye, aye!" answered the Portuguese.

"Master aboard, sir?"

"I answer to that name; what's the matter?"

"I wish to speak to him."

"Come along, my hardy!" he replied in true sailor language.

Taking from his pocket a certificate of his marine qualifications, obtained when he left the slaver at Florida, and which he always managed to keep from Franks, who had lost sight entirely of it—he presented it, soliciting the situation of sailing-master, having learned that the proprietors preferred black seaman.

"You are the very black that I've been looking for," said the Portuguese.

"Have you known of me before, sir?" enquired Blake with no anxiety.

"No," replied the Portuguese, "but I'm in want of just such a larky as you; a likely good-looking black to wrestle with the storms and uptrip the hurricanes. By your looks a grin from you would fascinate a mermaid; the flash of your eye obscure the most vivid streak of lightning, and the sound of your voice silence the loudest clap of thunder. Have you ever stayed a tempest and quieted the raging seas?"

"No sir," was the simple reply to all this tirade. "You are the master commanding, I believe?"

"No; my name is Señor Jose Castello, first mate of the 'Vulture.' Can you remember that?" assumptiously said the Portuguese in the true style of a slaver.

"I can, sir," answered Blake.

"Can you read?" continued Castello.

"Yes, sir."

"What is your name?"

"Henry, sir," Blake now adopting his own name instead of Gilbert, the name by which he went to Cuba.

"Henry what? can't you afford another name? Your daddy must have been a poor man."

"Blake, sir."

"Ah! I thought you would be able to raise another. Are you English? I see you have an English name."

"African born, sir, and Spanish bred," was the reply.

"How in the name of St. Peter did you come by that English name of yours?"

"Henrico Blacus was my name in Spanish, but being much among the English, they called me Henry Blake."

"Ah ha! I see" replied Castello, with seeming satisfaction from the interview. "Been on the coast, I see by your papers."

"Yes," said Blake, "I have."

"The coast is divided into three trades; ivory, gold, and slave. Which of them have you been in? Do you take?" knowingly explained the Portuguese, concluding with that quaint expression.

"I cannot inform you, sir," replied Blake, seizing the opportunity to gain a point. "In this my honor is at stake; I cannot betray my trust!"

"Good man, and good talk!" exclaimed the Portuguese, who had the employment of the hands on board. "You're the sailing-master of the 'Vulture' at your own wages! Doff duds!"* When making a low bow, wheeling around, going down the gangway to the quay, Blake picked up his luggage which had been left ashore, went on board, entering immediately on duty.

CHAPTER 45

Coastward Bound

The old ship "Merchantman" fitted up at Baltimore and brought to Matanzas, had been changed in name to "Vulture," and a slight alteration from the original intention had been made in the arrangements. Lieutenant Seeley, who was to have filled the post of supercargo, through the influence of his lady abandoned the enterprise entirely; passed Midshipman Spencer being appointed in his place. Captains Paul and Garcia, and Royer and Castello, were to be respectively commanders and mates in the order of the list, to represent their national character, as occasion required them to sail under either American or Spanish colors. The most active preparations were being made, and besides the officers already named, there were thirty other whites, many of whom were Americans, all shipped as

---

*Doff duds—a nautical phrase, meaning "pull off clothes," or "get ready for work."

common seamen, but in reality were supernumeraries retained to meet a contingency and check an emergency such as might ensue, as the real working hands of the vessel were blacks.

All eyes seemed fixed on Blake. His movements were of the most energetic and decisive character, being those of one adapted if not accustomed to give orders. From point to point, giving orders; sometimes scaling the shrouds among the rigging, at another moment mounting the topmasts with an ease and dexterity that astonished the superior officers. An expression of deep concern and anxiety marked the motions of his countenance.

Presently a boy on shore approached, to whom he beckoned, the lad passing quickly up the gangway handing him a note which hastily opening he read, saying in answer, "Tell her I shan't be gone long!" tearing it into fragments and casting them into the water; the boy bowing left the ship.

A fragment of this note fell upon the deck unobserved by Blake, which through curiosity was picked up by Castello, the words on which read:

Faithfully yours to the end of the war
PLACIDO

"A letter from his wife I reckon!" said Captain Paul who had just come on board behind the boy. "I'm glad you secured him, he's a good fellow, all things considered."

"You know him then?" enquired Castello.

"Yes, yes—he came to Cuba with my company."

"What in St. Peter can she mean by this termination of the letter! 'Yours to the end of the war!' This I can't understand: 'Placido,' as its signed, I suppose is her father's name."

"I don't know; his name is Gilbert," replied Paul.

"Gilbert! He shipped as Henry Blake," said Castello.

"No matter; I suppose he wants to conceal his identity in the business!" suggested Paul.

"Yes, yes!" replied Castello. "I noticed he had a good deal of feeling about the thing, and talked about his 'honor' being at stake."

"That explains," said Paul, "why his wife covers herself under a fictitious name, and conceals the business he is in, as if he was going to 'war.' "

"That explains it!" concluded Castello, satisfied with the tattling fragment of the billet.

The vessel was arranged to carry two thousand slaves, with full provisions for a nine months' voyage. All things being in readiness and all hands to their posts, with the Spanish colors flying from the peak, under the stern command of Emanuel Garcia, who boldly stood upon the quarterdeck to take her out of the harbor, she sailed in April, near the first of May, for the Western Coast of Africa.

CHAPTER 46

Trans-Atlantic

Scarcely had the "Vulture" reached the outside of the harbor before Paul appeared with glass in hand, aside of Captain Garcia, at whose orders the Spanish colors were run down and the American hoisted in their stead. Paul was an able and experienced officer, who, according to usage in the trade, had taken this position as protection against the British West India cruisers, it being a disputed point that they have a right to search American vessels for slaves, however suspicious the vessel.[29]

"A fine breeze!" remarked Paul.

"Quite so," replied Garcia, who still stood at his side.

"What do you think of the black?" continued Paul, referring to the sailing-master.

"A strange fellow indeed! I cannot understand him. I hope he may turn out all right. I can't understand as you do that signing of the note sent him, 'till the end of the war.' "

"That may have been caused by the ignorance of his wife who sent it," explained Paul.

"Not a bit of it! I know her well. She's far from being ignorant, and knows only too well what to say and how to say it. Besides, the note was not from her, but the noted Negro or mulatto poet, Placido, an educated fellow who visits among the first white families in Havana, and even attends the levees of the Captain General. I noticed this blunder, but feared to excite the suspicions of Castello and others," explained Garcia.

"Well really, well really!" said Paul with a tuck of the lips and a sigh.

"There's certainly something brewing among the Negroes, as it is not long since much sensation was produced by the appearance of a prayer written by the mulatto poet, in which Heaven was invoked in the name of the slaves of Cuba."

"It then must mean something more than a Negro blunder," remarked Paul.

"I fear so, really; and we should, in self-defence, if nothing more, keep a strict eye upon him and the Negroes on board."

"I'll go bail for that! Blame me if he escapes the sight of my eye!" said Paul. "I can see a nigger through the decks."

"Yes, but you can't regard him as a common Negro, Captain Paul—one who possesses his intelligence—and I shall never forget the shrewdness with which he managed the purchase of the girl Lotty. Peter Albertis is regarded as one of the most discreet men, and anyone who outdoes him is not to be trifled with, I do assure," said Garcia, "but——"

"A sail!" cried a voice from aloft,* Paul immediately sweeping the ocean with his glass.

"What of a sail, Captain Paul?" inquired Spencer just emerging from the companionway.

"I see a vessel in the distance; a brigantine. British flag, by Harry!" replied Paul.

"How does she stem?" asked Garcia.

"She quarters our starboard bow."

During this time the black sailing-master stood upon the forecastle viewing with a steady eye all that passed, while the blacks on board all turned their attention toward him. A change suddenly came over his countenance—a stern look of grim satisfaction; while great anxiety, with flushes of excitement and fear, were apparent among the whites. The secret soon revealed itself. The British cruiser "Sea Gull," which had suspected and been watching the movements of the "Vulture," had now entered chase after her, gaining most rapidly, when the shaft broke, and the screw was disabled for service. On spreading her sails she was found inadequate to vie with the Baltimore clipper, and was consequently left in the distance, while the slaver proudly riding the waves arrogantly defied her approach.

*Slavers always keep a "lookout," aloft, as the person is termed.

"There has something gone wrong about her," said Paul. "As you see she has hoisted the canvas."

"If she could catch us every man would be hung," said Spencer with fright.

"All except the Negroes, you mean. These they'd take to the colonies, and put them in office to rule the whites," sarcastically replied Paul.

The whites raised a shout at the accident to the "Sea Gull," which was then very evident. In this the blacks did not participate, being governed entirely by the apparent feelings of their head on board, upon whom they invariably cast a look at every incident. Did he but smile or give a look of approbation, the bland grin was seen to light up the dark gloom of their sombre faces; but did he look grave or ignore by notice passing events, then they too appeared as sad as pallbearers in a funeral train. All this to the whites was significant and foreboding; but whence the beginning and whither the end, was incomprehensible to them.

The Negroes fully understood themselves, as arrangement had been made with the old stevedore, Zada Ghu, who, in connection with the loading the vessel, also procured for the "Vulture" Negro sailors, which having obtained, were assembled at his house ready to start for Matanzas, when fortunately Blake made his appearance just in time to instruct them. They knew their man, and understood themselves, and, so understanding, acted well their part.

For several hours pushing the chase without advantage, the "Sea Gull" tacked about and was suddenly lost to view. Paul eagerly surveyed the seas, when not but sky and water could be seen. Scaling the shrouds, Blake for an hour or more sat on the mizzenmast scanning the ocean.

The clouds which partially curtained the zenith had disappeared, the sun was fast receding from the horizon, the prospect which had been doubtful now seemed definite, and the beautiful crimson sky splendidly contrasted with the sublimity of the black and gloomy gulf beneath. It was then that the vastness of Omnipotence was felt and realised in all its grandeur; it was then the human heart manifested its most delicate sympathies; it was then that the soul poured forth from its hidden recesses those gifts of God to man; the Divine sentiment of benevolence, philanthropy and charity in tender accents of compassionate regard in Christian solicitude. The soul then dives into the mysteries of godliness or soars to the realms of bliss, when the reflector, for the time, is lost entirely to external objects.

Orders being given for the evening, and Garcia on watch, Paul entered the cabin, taking his seat with more than ordinary soberness, being closely eyed by his ship fellows. Here, quite unexpectedly, he acknowledged his error in a matter which all had forgotten, manifested remorse, making admissions which surprised them all. He renounced the traffic in slaves as vile, accusing parties in New York for his participation in it. They first induced him to engage in it, when, finding it lucrative, he had subsequently made it a livelihood. But he would offend Heaven no longer—he had gone his last voyage, and then would have quit, but could not get from the vessel. He would relinquish all agency as far as he could in the interest of the voyage they were then making.

"At an unguarded moment," said Paul, "when self-interest was all prevalent with me, I suffered myself, through political motives, to be forced into this thing, who, like Satan, not content with his own rebellion against Heaven, but corrupted some of the Angels, dragging them from Paradise with him."*

Spencer, who was young, regretted the part he had taken in the affair at New York, and hoped that one who had proven herself an honor to her sex, whose heart knew nothing but goodness, having, in his estimation, no other attribute than kindness, would forgive him. He had just entered the business of slave trading; knew nothing about it, and should abandon the enterprise on his return, and sooner, did he have an opportunity of leaving the vessel.

So explaining and understanding each other, they went to their berths to await with anxiety a return of morning. But the blacks and Spaniards, though not intended for their ears, had caught every word that fell from the Americans, to the joy of the one, and the sadness of the others. Joy to the Negroes who designed upon the Spaniards and sadness to the Spaniards who feared the Negroes. Though they paced the decks in their respective quarters, as if picket guarding each other, they mutually withdrew for the evening, and rested quietly till duty required their presence.

*The author met with an old slave-trading master of a vessel, who admitted his wrongs, and seemed sorely to repent his great sins.

CHAPTER 47

Significant

Early next morning, the first indication of the kind since the ship set sail, was the attention of the whites being arrested by a merry sea song of the blacks, which they chanted with cheerful glee, and rather portentous mood and decisive air:

My country, the land of my birth,
  Farewell to thy fetters and thee!
The by-word of tyrants—the scorn of the earth,
  A mockery to all thou shalt be!
Hurra, for the sea and its waves!
  Ye billows and surges, all hail!
My brothers henceforth—for ye scorn to be SLAVES,
  As ye toss up your crests to the gale;
Farewell to the land of the blood-hound and chain,
  My path is away o'er the fetterless main!

George Royer, the American mate, full of ardor and patriotism, hastening on deck, commanded immediate silence. Aware of the change that had taken place in his superior, Captain Paul, he felt the more sensible that the song was a taunt by the blacks to the Americans. To this order the Negroes paid little attention, but continued singing the more cheerfully. Startling suspicions at once impressed him that the blacks designed a mutiny with the Negro sailing-master at their head, and Blake now became a dread. Hastening to the master's room and imparting his convictions, Garcia, followed by Captain Paul, who also heard the message, was quickly on the deck.

"Silence!" commanded the Spaniard. "What in the name of St. Joseph does all this mean?" when Blake, raising his hand, the blacks instantly ceased.

"What is the meaning of this disturbance, Blake?" inquired Paul on the Negroes' ceasing.

"There has been none, sir!" was the reply.

"Were not the commands of the second officer, Mr. Royer, disobeyed?" continued Paul.

"They were not, sir. 'Less noise' was the command, and they sung easier though it may have been more cheerfully. My people are merry when they work, especially at sea; and they must not be denied the right to sing, a privilege allowed seamen the world over!"

"Is that all?" asked Paul sharply, who, although declining a participance in the trade of the voyage, still held his commanding authority, representing the American interest.

"It is, sir!" replied Blake with feeling.

"Then I see no cause to fault them! Cheerily, then my lads, cheerily!" said Paul, who went directly to the cabin, when the Negroes at the command of their leader commenced more cheerfully to sing:

O Cuba! 'tis in thee
Dark land of slavery,
    In thee we groan!
Long have our chains been worn,
Long has our grief been borne,

Our flesh has long been torn,
    Even from our bones!
The white man rules the day,

He bears despotic sway,
    O'er all the land;
He wields the tyrant's rod,
Fearless of man or God,
And at his impious nod,
    We fall or stand!
O, shall we longer bleed! [30]

"Do you hear that?" exclaimed Royer, who also had gone to the cabin, but then stood in the companionway in a sulky mood at the course pursued by his superior. "These Negroes are determined on mischief, and we will have to keep a close watch over them, if we wish to keep gashes out of our throats!"

"Let us neither invite nor provoke those gashes to be made, Mr. Royer. Our overzealousness sometimes, in a good or a bad cause, if you please, makes us aggravate the resentment we are endeavoring to stave off."

"Well, time will show who is right!" concluded Royer, pressing his lips to suppress the feeling.

"And so it will as well prove who is wrong!" replied the captain in conclusion.

Subsequently both Garcia and Royer became quite pleasantly disposed, treating with civility and even affability the entire ship's company, frequently jesting with the common seamen with whom they met in the course of their duty. And the Negroes being mostly hired slaves,* and heretofore restricted in their movements about the ship, then boldly walked at will over the vessel, enjoying all the privileges of common seamen. The tone and sentiment of things had changed, and every one felt himself at liberty, and on terms of friendship with his fellows.

Fine weather and fine sailing now sped the vessel swiftly over the bosom of the ocean, each heart rejoicing, and each feeling seemingly satisfied that—

No mail clad serfs, obedient to their lord,
  In grim array the crimson cross demand,
Or gay assemble round the festive board.
  Their chief's retainers—an immortal band.

Though Paul may, and doubtless will be censured for his course, and convicted of timidity and weakness, if not cowardice and want of integrity, but the sequel will prove him to have been right and his course suited to the circumstances.

Among the blacks there was a singular character, comical in appearance, and comic by nature. His wit was surprisingly ready and almost unbounded, and provokingly ludicrous. Irony and satire abounded in almost everything he said, so that he became the attraction of all on board. Both Royer and Castello much disliked him and fain would have summarily disposed of him, had fears not prevented. Gascar was a youth in adolescence, and being of slightly

---

*Slaves are kept and hired to parties by the day or month, as a source of income to their master.

curved spine, with rather long legs and broad shoulders, though low stature—all of which were congenital—when he spoke and looked up, his expression was most striking, and he knew it.

"What are you doing there, you stack of black cats! Get up out of that!" said Royer, as the boy sat on a coil of rope upon the deck.

"Take care dat black cat don't scratch somebody!" responded the boy, throwing up his eyes in Royer's face, at which there was a roar of laughter from the whites present.

"There," said the mate, "you see what I told you, Captain!"

"I see nothing, sir; I see nothing!" tartly replied Paul.

"If I had my way, I'd keep the Negroes in their place!" muttered Royer, which Gascar hearing, as though he had not noticed it, instantly commenced humming, loud enough to be heard by all,

I'm a goin' to Afraka,
Where de white man dare not stay;
I ketch 'im by de collar,
Den de white man holler;
I hit 'im on de pate,
Den I make 'im blate!
I seize 'im by de throat—
Laud!—he beller like a goat!*

Hastening away, Royer declared that the only place where a white man was safe and a Negro taught to know his place, was the United States; and he cared not to go, not to live anywhere else but there. Business alone compelled him to do otherwise, and did he but get back, he would never again leave his native country, as the last few days' experience had taught him no other was equal to it. In his own country a white man was all that he desired to be; and out of it, he was no better than a Negro. Such a state of things would not do for him, and he determined never again to place himself in a position to bear them.

"I see——" said Royer.

"A sail!" cried out Gascar, interrupting the sentence, when every

---

*This song was sung by a little black boy, sitting by himself on a fence in the South, musing.

eye was again strained over the ocean, and anxiety once more arresting their attention.

CHAPTER 48

Making the Coast

This day anxiety pervaded, and every eye was put upon the sketch, not only to get a glimpse of the portentious coast of Africa, but also in fearful anticipation of a pursuit by the British cruiser "Medusa," whose prowess along the Gulf of Guinea was fearfully notorious to the slaves. The Kings of Dahomi and Ashanti were compelled to respect it in a manner which gave terror to the traders. Though every glass at command was levelled at every point of compass over the seas, yet not a sail was descried, and a surmise was justly concluded, that the distant object had its origin in the productive imagination of the comic seaman Gascar. For his imposition the impertinent black would have met at the hands of the crude American a severe chastisement, but the words of the song still rang in his ears, that he was:

Goin' to Afraka
Where de white man dare not stay.

With this impression that "cats" however black, may "scratch" as well as others, the mate was contented to let things take their natural course, provided they grew no worse than they had been. The blacks were now closely watched, their every motion being noticed, and Blake was now looked upon with the greatest possible interest. On sailed the vessel like a goddess of the water, gracefully gliding every wave, riding the high seas like a waterfowl, nothing more transpiring to give alarm save the occasional drolleries of Gascar, which always might be considered ominous.

The "Vulture" now entered the Gulf of Guinea and after several days of fair sailing put into a lagoon in one of the most secluded and least suspected places on the coast. Here was the trading post of the great factor, a noted Portuguese, Ludo Draco, the friend of Geza, King of Dahomi. Near but a short distance from the beach in the thickest of the bush, were situated the barracoons, many in number, being long one-story wooden houses, thatched with grass. One mile from the barracoons, in a beautifully cleared and elevated spot, was the residence of Draco, attained only by narrow footpath, through the densest of the forest.

Scarcely had the vessel moored, till Blake was on shore and off into the forest. Cheers by the clapping of hands and as many grins as claps, were given in approbation of the arrival. The miserable victims who filled these coffleshambles of suffering humanity, having been so taught to do by their relentless and insatiable oppressor.

Garcia was now more at ease, and having observed the unceremonious manner in which the sailing-master left them, he ordered the confinement of the others, to prevent the example being followed. But the blacks fully understood themselves, and did not design leaving the vessel.

The family of Draco consisted of a wife, Zorina, a handsome native African,[31] and two daughters, Angelina and Seraphina, beautiful mulatto children, the former having just completed at Lisbon her education in one of the first convents. The residence was finely furnished, and the family pleasant and agreeable; but the circumstances surrounding them of the horrible manner in which their wealth was acquired, cast a gloom over the dazzling splendor of their gaudy mansion, making the noon day and sunlight of their brilliant abode as dark as midnight obscurity.

In Zorina was that amiable and benevolent expression of countenance, so common to the native women of her race, and which always implies a welcome to the privileges of the house; but yet there was that absence of earnest gratification which usually characterizes those who anticipate gain from their visitors. Affable and sociable, she was still reserved and seriously thoughtful as though some weighty matter was struggling within.* It was the traffic doubtless in human beings, in which her husband was engaged, and already amassed a princely fortune, that disturbed her peace of mind. It was this which like a millstone had sunk deep to the bottom, and troubled the still waters of her peaceful soul.

---

*The character exhibited by the sister of the native wife of a once-noted slave trader on the Coast, whom the writer met in Africa—a very respectable, intelligent, Christian young woman.

Though civilized, in early life a pupil in the Christian Missionary school at Badagry, and a professed convert, with afflictions such as these, Zorina was not the woman she would have been, and could not be such as her husband Ludo Draco desired she should be, a woman devoted as a wife to his pecuniary interests.

"What are the prospects, Don Ludo; have you much stock in trade?" enquired Garcia of the Portuguese, after refreshing with brandy and water.

"Only a moderate supply, señor—some five-and-twenty hundred in the pens—a little more than one good cargo,"* replied Ludo Draco.

"Pretty good stock, Don Ludo! Assorted selection?"

"They are prime what is of them; of both sexes, all sizes; men, women and children; and few or no old Negroes among them, señor."

"What are slaves now worth, Don Ludo?"

"From twenty to forty dollars, señor; wish a large cargo? "

"We have a double decker, and prepared for twenty hundred."

"What's your destination, North or South America?"

"We cleared from Matanzas, but shall import where there is the greatest demand. You have the best knowledge of the markets—where had we best import, Don Ludo?"

"The Brazils are going down; that religious cant and nonsense about philanthropy and human rights has already reached there, and measures and restrictions have been decreed by the National Congress against importation."

"What of Cuba, Don Ludo?"

"A little better, señor, but not what it should be. Taking advantage of the political signs of the time, the prohibition of the trade in Brazil, and the leniency of the home government toward the Negroes in consequence of their insurrectionary tendencies—the Cubans set their own price and pay what they please ahead, because of no competition in the trade. The United States is now decidedly the best market, because the supply is inadequate to the demand of the new territory continually opening up, without a heavy loss to the old states. Indeed the disciplined slave is preferred for the new states from their

---

*They frequently prepare the vessels to carry 2000, which was the case with a slaver taken by the British cruiser, brig "Triton," which the writer saw at Sierra Leone, in April 1860. [32]

experience in labor, while the native African will do better in the old cultivated grounds. An American agency in Cuba is all you require to make the trade a most lucrative one."

"Fine, fine, by St. Joseph!" said Garcia. "Not being in the business for some time, I had lost the run of things. Old Key West, I suppose still holds her own?"

"Key West is all right, señor!" replied Draco.

At the mention of Key West, Royer looked knowlingly at Paul and Garcia with a wink, as to them this was a familiar place of safety in years past; but true to his previous convictions of wrong, Paul preserved his seriousness and ignored a cognizance of the hint.

There was now a great point gained as there had been an unsettled opinion as to the best point to make with their cargo. Captain Emanuel Garcia and his Portuguese mate, Jose Castello, had at the start—previous to the convictions of Paul—insisted on Matanzas as the place, whilst Paul and his American officer only held Cuba as a dernier resort, preferring the United States as the market—Key West being the place of safety.

"I am satisfied," said Garcia, "that the United States is the market. Let us have a full cargo, and as little delay as possible."

At this moment a signal was given by the tapping of the bell suspended above the mansion.

"Gentlemen, a large supply has just arrived rom the interior; walk with me," said Draco; the party going directly to the "barracoons for reception," secluded in a cloister near the mansion, those near the moorings being used only for shipping.

CHAPTER 49

The Slave Factory

"Hark!" exclaimed Angelina, unaccustomed, from her continued absence at school, to such a sound—"What is that I hear?"

"It comes, my child, from the barracoons," explained the mother, with a deep sigh.

"Do you tell me, mother, that wailings come already, since the tapping of that bell? What does it mean?"

"Preparing the slaves, my child, for packing, I suppose."

"How preparing them, mother? What do they do to them?" anxiously inquired the girl.

"They whip and burn them, my child, to make them obey."

"And what do you mean by "packing"?"

"Putting them down in the bottom of the ship, my child, so that they can't move about."

"How can they live this way? Oh, mother, they can't live!"

"They can't live long, my child; but many of them die, when that makes room, and some of them live."

"O horrible!—cruel, cruel!" exclaimed the more than astonished girl. "Pardon me, mother—I cannot help it—and is this my father's business?"

"It is, my daughter," replied the mother, the brightness of whose eyes were glaring with the evidence of sympathy for the sufferings of her people.

"Then forgive me, mother, I receive nothing from this day forth from my father's hand.* He's cruel, and——"

"Stop, my child!" interrupted the mother. "Curse** not him from whose lines you came."

"Forgive me, mother, Heaven forbid! But I cannot consent to go to Madrid to obtain accomplishments at the price of blood. The Lady Superior when at Lisbon, taught me to 'love my neighbor as myself'—that all mankind was my neighbor. I thought I was educated to come home and teach my race."

"My child, you must——"

"Hark! Mother, don't you hear?" again exclaimed the young affrighted girl, when another wailing came, more terrible than the other.

"Have patience, my child."

"I can't, mother—I can't! How can I have patience with such dreadful things as these?"

"God will give you patience, my child. Depend on Him."

---

*The young mulatto daughter of a slave trader on the coast peremptorily refused to leave her people and go with him to Portugal to finish an education.

**The native African is very correct in speech, pronouncing very distinctly any word they learn in other languages. Curse—to speak ill of, by the native African.

"I will depend on Him, and go directly to the spot and beseech Him in mercy for the poor suffering ones. Come and take me to them," she concluded, calling for native servants to carry her after them, as the party had now left the receptacles for the trading posts at the landing on the lagoon, nearly a mile distant.

Soon she arrived near the dreadful scene

Where fiends incarnate—vile confederate band—
Torture with thumscrew, lash, and fire-brand.

This most remarkable spot which for years had sent forth through the world its thousands of victims—a place repulsively noted in the history of wrong—was a dismal nook in the northeastern extremity of the lagoon, extending quite into the bush, forming a cove of complete security and quiet. In this position lay the "Vulture"; and near the barracoons, under cover of seemingly impenetrable undergrowth, sat the beautiful Angelina, the good-hearted natives who bore her there lying at her feet to protect her, as is their custom to strangers in the forest. In this position, quietly inspecting the whole proceedings, her soul became horror-stricken.

"Hark!" again exclaimed Angelina in a suppressed frightened tone, unconscious, seemingly, of the half-dressed natives lying at her feet. "Don't you hear? What in God's name does it mean?"

Scarcely had the awe-stricken girl given utterance, till a heartrending wail sent a thrill through her.

"O! O! O!" was the cry from a hundred voices, as the last torture was inflicted upon them.*

Again came a hissing sound, accompanied by the smell of scorched flesh, with wailing in their native tongues for mercy to God.

"Holy Madonna! Mother of God! Is this the sacrifice, or what is it?"

"Yes," replied a hidden, unknown voice, in chaste and elegant Portuguese—"a sacrifice of burnt offering to the god of Portugal and Spain."

"Good, sir, pray tell me"—looking around she said—"what is this, and where am I?"

---

*One method of torture inflicted by the foreign traders to prevent meeting, is an oblong square piece of iron in a box form, made so as to admit the ends of the middle and ring fingers, when it is driven down as far as it will go, tearing the flesh from the bone as it forces its way.

"Be patient, dear child—be patient, and you shall hear—as from the graves of our forefathers—of untold suffering from this spot—

"A place where demons daring land—
Fiends in bright noon day—and sit
A hellish conclave band to barter
The sons and daughters of our land away."

"May God protect me!" she screamed, and sunk in a swoon, when in an instant the servants bore her in the hammock away.

In parties of ten or more the branding iron was applied in such quick succession, that a sound and smell like that of broiling and scorched flesh was produced. At this last sad act of cruelty, and the voice in explanation of it, the tender and affrighted girl, yielding to frail nature, had sickened and fallen at the root of a tree where she sat, when the first impressions of consciousness found her again at the side of a devoted mother under the roof of the dwelling, fondly ministering to her relief.

"O, mother—O, mother! What an experience have I had this day! O, what my ears have heard!" were the first words of Angelina on recovering.

"Tell me, my child," with native simplicity but earnestness inquired the mother, "what is it?"

"As well may you, mother," replied the excited, intelligent girl, "go

"Ask the whirlwinds why they rove;
The storms their raging showers:
Ask the lightning why they move,
The thunders whence their powers!"

"My child, your head is bad; it is hot; it is not sound. You must keep quiet, my child," anxiously admonished the mother, applying leaves taken from cold water continually to her brow.

"A cup of water, mother; I am sick. Oh, I hear it again! They are burning them alive!" continued she to talk at random, till sleep quieted her voice, whilst the mother stood over her with a calabash of leaves and water anxiously watching every breath she drew.

CHAPTER 50

Before Leaving

The "Vulture" was now freighted, the cargo completed, and eighteen hundred human beings made up the bill of lading. All being ready, Ludo Draco left the vessel for his residence. The better to evade the vigilance of those ever watchful and indomitable guardians of the coast, the British cruisers, it is customary, under favorable circumstances, to leave the factories under cover of night.

It was now the fourth evening, the hour for sailing fast ensuing, up to which time the black sailing-master had not appeared. About him there was much talk, speculation and uneasiness; some suspecting that he might have been the employed spy of the English; while Royer and Costello, the mates, believed that the tendency of the Negro being degeneracy, he having before been on the coast and in the country, must have seized the opportunity of returning to the usages of savage life.

But he had not been far from the vessel since her arrival, but, having a knowledge of the place, had secreted himself near the residence of Draco, that the whole proceedings might be witnessed by him, and he thus become an unexpected auditor of the lamentations of the young and lovely Angelina; first in the mansion—he having stolen in after the trading party left at the sound of the bell—and subsequently under cover of the forest, whither he followed her cortege of carriers.

Midnight had arrived: all was still around and wrapped in silence, nothing disturbing the quietude, save the dashing of the surf against the beach, occasional noise of a night bird, or hideous screech of a distant hyena. No human being was to be seen, except a solitary black watchman moodily crouched upon the quarterdeck, who, though a slave, was as vigilant on duty as the sentinel on a man-of-war. His duty was of two-fold—one for the vessel, and the other entirely foreign to its interest. Presently the form of a person was seen to approach; it was Blake, who, saluting the watchman, took a seat also upon the quarterdeck, the seamen all taking rest at the time, not knowing what hour they would be called to duty.

A scene in the mansion had protracted his stay, although Blake was ready for duty so soon as the vessel was ready to sail. Her stay being but a few short days he had availed himself of the time and communicated with many of the natives opposed to the king, among whom he took his fare and lodging, except when concealed in disguise in the mansion, dressed as a native, being known only to the servants.

Draco, that evening, on entering the house for the first time, from the vessel, was met by his wife in tears, stating that their dear child was dying—when he hastened to her room and found her in a most distressing condition. Looking in his face she gave a silly look, with a smile, then closing her eyes lay as if lifeless.

"O, Don Ludo, my poor child is almost gone!" said Zorina, the silvery tears studding her cheeks like crystal spangles on a velvet cushion; Draco making no reply, but gave a deep sigh.

Suddenly they were startled by a song of lamentation, the most remarkable and pathetic, in which the traffic, gains, and wealth of her father, the punishment, suffering and sorrows of her mother's race, caused by him and a king unworthy to be classed with the race of her mother, were uttered in tones of scathing rebuke. She would that she had not been torn to have been thus distracted, that her mother had never seen her father, and that Dahomi had never existed.

"O, 'tis my mother's race and not his! Yes, 'tis my blood and not his!" she frantically exclaimed, then again sank into stillness, when her mother pressing her hands and cheeks, cried out,

"My child is cold,—she must be dead! My poor child, my poor child! O!"

> Tell me not of my sad lot,
>   Of death's cold cheeks repine,
> Of life's last hope, and endless scope,
>   Of miseries of mine!

"They are nothing, mother, nothing. But you it is who feels as never woman felt, and none to pity. O sister, are you here? Know you pity, mother?" she again exclaimed, interrupting her mother, by stopping her wailing, and recognising her sister Seraphina, who lay at her side from the time she was taken into the mansion on the hammock.

Draco during the time stood in tears over her bed, and when the song and last frantic wail was given, taking his wife by one hand, and his youngest daughter, who lay on the bed beside her sister, by the other, leaning over and impressing kisses long and many upon her cheeks, he promised the distracted Angelina never again to traffic in human beings.

Suddenly springing up in the bed, she sat looking around at each person and object in the room; drawing her hand over her face, and raising her eyelids as if just aroused from a deep sleep, exclaimed:

"What is the matter—is any one sick? Have I been dreaming, or what? I am well now!"* when Blake left the mansion for the vessel, which he reached at so late an hour.

CHAPTER 51

Homeward Bound

This morning at half-past three, a favorable wind having risen, the stern command of Royer was heard preparing to weigh anchor; the blacks being promptly at their post, among whom was Blake. Soon were the white sails spread to the breeze, and the clipper cleaving the waters like a monster of the sea. The day dawned most beautifully; the wind continued fair, and ten o'clock brought every white upon the decks to enjoy the pleasures of the morning. No sickness had pervaded them, and all looked fresh and cheerful. Until then no spiritous liquor was allowed though a large supply was on board. This restriction had only been a precautionary measure, to guard against contingencies until the cargo was obtained, and they homeward bound. But this morning the beverage was in great profusion; the blacks alone being prohibited its use, and among the privileged Royer was a patron. Excited with the ardent liquid, he seemed familiarily at ease, and simply required an occasion to execute his will. Though burly and sulky before, he now became blustering, boisterous and overbearing; and Blake, if none other, seemed to be in imminent danger.

"Where the mischief have you been!" roared the man, almost maddened by a too free indulgence, on seeing Blake on deck for the first time since the vessel moored. "Reveling I suppose back in the

---

*An interesting scene is said to have taken place between the family—which is colored—of a slave trader and himself who had renounced the trade previous to his renouncement and leaving the coast.

bush among the heathen wenches, palming yourself off for a nigger chief? Step light and bestir yourself my larky; you're not now in Africa to give nigger impudence to white men! Get about there, get about! or the knot-end of a tar rope may teach you how they make smart blacks in America."

Blake giving him a look—and such a look!—ascended the shrouds, where seating himself, loitered on the mizenmast. Looking up at him, Royer called out——

"Come down there, you saint of a chimney sweep, or I'll teach you how to——"

"Take care dat sweep don't throw sut in yo' eyes!" interrupted Gascar, who till then had been lost sight of; Royer pretending not to have heard him, though the whites laughed out at the expression from the boy; and the blacks, huddling, whispered together for a time.

"Disperse there, you black clouds! We're not ready for a rain!" again ordered the intoxicated man on seeing the blacks standing together.

"But you may have a storm,"* replied the boy.

"What's that, you lump of charcoal!" rebuked Royer, looking about as if to find a rope's end: "what did you say?"

"Take care dat lump o' charcoal don't burn yeh, sir, dats all!" replied the boy to the utter merriment of Paul and Spencer, though the rest of the whites felt otherwise. Royer pressing his lips made no reply, but doubtless would have severely chastised him had not the presence of Paul, and suspicion of the ultimate intention of the Negroes deterred him.

The morning had passed and it was then about the middle of the afternoon, when Paul and Garcia both appearing on deck ordered an inspection of the hole of the ship for an examination of the slaves therein confined. The hatches being opened, those standing nearest fell back from the stench escaping as if repulsed by an explosion of gas.

"Heavens! there must be a good lot of 'em dead, captain," exclaimed Paul, addressing Garcia as the fumes met them in the face.

---

*A little native Greba boy employed on a vessel on the coast of Africa, 1859, was remarkable for wit and repartee, regarding neither officers nor passenger, but had a ready reply for them.

"I reckon not," answered Garcia, "the stalls only want washing."

"How is this done, captain?" enquired Lawrence Spencer.

"By means of a force pump and hose throwing sea water among them," replied Garcia.

"This I supposed from the manner they are packed; but indeed the business is all so entirely new to me, that I don't pretend to know anything on shipboard, though I've served a long apprenticeship in nautical matters."

The stench having somewhat abated, the officers and others approached the open hatches.

"Blake, my good fellow, I'm glad to see you again at your post; I don't know what that girl of yours would have done had we left you in Africa. I'm fearing she would have charged me with kidnapping you," remarked captain Paul, being the first time he had spoken to him since they left the coast; at which he smilingly made no reply.

"Ah!" replied Royer, affecting pleasantry. "I see what'll make the fellow laugh—talk about his girl. This morning he was as sulky as a black ram, because I told him about the nigger wenches on the coast. I suppose he thinks himself one crust above the black wenches."

Paul looking at Royer, advanced whispering in his ear, "You better treat him well; he's no common Negro, I assure you," to which Royer answered also in a whisper:

"But we're going where he will be common, where every Negro's made to know his place."

"Where is that?" whispered Paul.

"Home, in the United States, where else!" replied Royer.

"Yes, but you're not yet there, and it might be that you'll never reach there!" rejoined he.

"Curse the niggers, I hate 'em!" retorted Royer impatiently.

"That may be, Mr. Royer, but it wasn't the way to show it I'm thinking, by comin' to Africa after 'em," calmly replied Paul.

Abruptly leaving him, Royer advanced to the main hatchway, when Paul following after, they made ready to enter, each officer with a sabre at his side, revolver studded in his belt, and an unsheathed bowie knife in his hand.

"Blake," said Paul, "you better take the lead!" to which Royer readily consented, though opposed to a Negro leading in anything wherein a white man was concerned.

Blake entered the hatch followed by Paul, Garcia, Castello and Royer.

"Merciful God! what a sight," exclaimed Spencer, as he caught the first sight of the half-suffocated beings closely packed in narrow stalls like brutes wallowing in revolting mire.

"In very good condition," replied the Spaniard, "none dead worth naming"; two fine children—a boy and girl of three years of age—having died through the night for want of air and water.

"Stir up here, you nests of black maggots, stir up!" exclaimed Royer, punching with a capstan bar all within his reach to see whether they lived or not.

"Good Heavens!" again exclaimed Spencer. "What a condition they are in. I wonder they're not all dead. How on earth will we ever get them purified?"

"The pump and hose with plenty sea water is all that's required," replied Garcia.

"Yes, give 'em plenty; that'll soon straighten up matters," added Royer. "Stir about there—stir about!" still punching in among them.

Next commenced the washing process, when the double cranked pump was brought into full requisition. The stream was directed by Royer himself, which, regardless of their eyes, was thrown into their faces, when the poor wretches almost dying with thirst, opened their mouths to catch the stream as it played among them, sucking and licking the salt water off of each others heads and shoulders.

During the inspection of the stalls an affecting scene ensued. A fine specimen of a man, tall and athletic, of some forty-five years of age, was cruelly treated by the coarse and ruthless American. On looking imploringly at his abuser, he gave him a punch with the butt end of the bar, drawing blood, which streamed down his face. On again imploring him, Royer screamed—

"Do you look at me that way, you black devil!" when, turning his face away to conceal his grief, the mate gave him another blow on the cheek bone, producing contusion, when the tears stole down his manly face, baptizing with sorrow his bare expanded breast heaving with emotions of despair.

To all this Blake was witness, with a watchful eye and determination more than ever to carry out his objects, observing which in his countenance, the grief-pierced captive cast at him a glance the most impressive.

Leaving this scene of distress, passing to another tier in which were confined principally females, the attention of Blake was attracted by a sprightly, handsome little bright-eyed boy, playing about with as much delight and unconcern as if gamboling with the freedom of a kid over some grassy common in his own loved nativity. He readily recognized in the child the likeness of the noble-looking captive confined in another place, so ruthlessly abused by the heartless American mate, Royer.

While thus standing contemplating with sorrow the scenes around him, his attention was called to a woman, handsome and pleasant, with a meek and humble look, as she sat buried in her living grave. This woman was from Soudan, whose occupation had been that of a vender of "country cloths," as the native dry goods are termed, or as by the Creoles of Louisiana, a "merchant woman." She had been a Mohammedan, but, going into the Eba country to reside, had been converted to Christianity by missionary influence, but sold to Dahomi by the Ibadans, by whom she was taken in warfare.

As Abyssa caught the eye of Blake, she gave him a look which at once riveted his attention. She saw that he was a civilized man, and desired that he should observe her. The look was reciprocated, and as he passed close by where she sat, to get a better observation of her, he startled as his ears caught the whisper in good English—

"Arm of the Lord, awake!"

The commander and party leaving the hold, Blake also went to the deck, relieved from the stench of the great cesspool, and heartrending scenes of the living potter's field.

CHAPTER 52

The Middle Passage

The "Vulture" like a monster was gliding and mounting the then increasing swells of the seas; Blake stood as if unconscious of the presence of those around him, reconnoitering the surrounding waters.

"Did you notice how that stout black fellow and the handsome Negro woman looked at Blake in the hole?" remarked Paul. "You reckon he knows 'em?"

"Negroes all know each other, you know; all uncles and aunts, brothers and sisters, and counsins," replied the American. "I never saw a Negro yet that wasn't acquainted with another Negro you could name; Negroes are all the same everywhere."

"But how do you account for ——"

"A sail!" exclaimed Castello, interrupting Paul.

"A sail, a sail!" rang through the vessel, especially by the Negroes, the blackness of whose faces seemed to glisten with emotion.

"Northeast," remarked Paul, elevating his glass. "European, I reckon."

"Can't tell," said Garcia, following his example, "good way off yet."

"Brig: I reckon she's a man-of-war," continued Paul.

"Can't tell, sir!" replied Castello, exhibiting signs of fear.

During this time the approaching vessel was coursing from northeast to southwest, the "Vulture" from southeast to northwest, their lines of direction forming an X. Whilst every eye with fear was strained at the advancing seaman, suddenly she was seen to tack to the northeast, her direction being such as to have to meet the "Vulture" at a point in a given distance. All now stood in fearful silence waiting an expression from Garcia, who alone of the officers was an experienced slaver.

"Can't be after mischief, I reckon?" enquiringly said Paul, the first to break silence in the anxiously gazing group.

"An infernal fast sailor!" replied Castello.

"No idea what she is?" again enquired Paul.

"Some cussed thief of an Englishman I suppose," said Royer, Garcia giving him a look of caution, to guard against the ear of the Negroes.

The stranger was still advancing, but not near enough to determine what she was, as she carried no color, and all still stood in fear, waiting an opinion from the superior judgment of the Spaniard, when unexpectedly they were startled by a loud exclamation from Gascar—

"Golly, but she come! De old Gull got nothin' to do but flap 'er wings, an' she pick up 'erself an' sails!"

"Shut up there, you black raven! Who asked you for your lip. Begone in an instant, or I'll lash you to the mizzenmast and give you a hundred!" ordered Royer; the boy making away quaintly saying:

"De raven goes; but he croak fo' he did go!"

Royer cast an eye at the blacks who stood on the forcastle quite aside from them—while the whites occupied the quarterdeck—who smiled among themselves at the last repartee of their young fellow seaman.

"Curse the—!" said Royer, scratching his head, but did not for prudential reasons finish the sentence.

All available canvas was given to the winds strongly blowing from the northeast, and speed was now increased at least one fourth. It was evidently decided in the minds of all to be a chase, which could not be concealed, and every tack in nautical science was put to the test. On sped the "Vulture" dashing and splashing like a great living monster of the main, and on came the stranger in the distance riding and gliding the waves like a monstrous waterfowl. The scene increased in interest as the vessels increased their speed, and the Negroes were among the boldest of the crew. But the shades of evening were coming on, and the stranger which was to all appearance fast gaining on them, by illusion of the growing obscurity, seemingly fell back in the distance. The strictest watch was kept, and fearful anticipations troubled the whites during the entire evening.

Emboldened by what was now thought to be an Englishman, the Negroes had determined to have a merry chant. So soon as Blake, who for a short time had withdrawn, made his appearance among them, they commenced in loud tones a glee:

We have hatred dark and deep for the fetter and the thong;
We bring light to prisoned spirits, for the captive wail a song!
We bring light——

"See!" interrupted Blake, as a vivid flash of lightening was seen in the distance, presently followed by a heavy rumbling of thunder.

The glee stopped, the blacks for the night, except those on watch, and the whites separated to rest till aroused in the morning to scenes of a more pleasing prospect, each party in hopes of the other's disappointment.

CHAPTER 53

Middle Passage—Chase Continued

A sail—a sail! a promised prize to hope!
Her nation—flag—how speaks the telescope?
She walks the water like a thing of life,
And seems to dare the elements to strife.
—Byron

This morning ushered in a day of hope and cheerful promise to the mariner. The sun rose beautifully, overspreading by his reflections the expanded surface of the ocean, as if by the skill of some magic touch, changing at once the silvery to a golden hue. While the winds blew constantly—and occasionally moderate—a gale, there was not a cloud in the sky observable, to mar the prospects nor check the progress of a fair sail and passage to all appearance, during the remainder of the voyage. The spirits of all seemed in unison with the prospects of the day, cheerful and happy, all having assembled on the decks in anticipation of something decisive concerning the pursuing vessel the day before. And while thus standing in anxious expectation, the blacks had congregated together mooting a council regardless of their superiors who occupied another position on the same plane with themselves.

The whites were now quite desirous for a chant from the blacks, to divert their attention from the stranger which they expected shortly to make his appearance above the swelling seas. Passing by Gascar who stood alone, Royer desired to know what the blacks were doing so long together, and why they did not entertain the vessel with a merry sea song. Gascar made no reply, but started toward the group wagging his head, which he occasionally touched on one side knowingly with the end of his finger, then stopping, looked back at the mate, then started again.

"What the deal does he mean?" said Royer.

"Headwork!" replied Paul, when there was a laugh at Royer's expense.

"At your old tricks again, Captain Paul? You'll spoil Negroes wherever you go!" retorted Royer. "Negroes should be kept in their place."

"This is not the occasion for talking about 'place,' Mr. Royer," rebuked Captain Paul. "You had better think about fate!"

"I'll teach the black rascal how to behave to white men!" said Royer in reply.

"You'll find it a task, I'm thinking, Mr. Royer!" said Paul.

"There we have it again! Give a nigger his own way and he's of no use to anybody," rejoined Royer.

"Maybe so!" said Paul.

"I know so!" retorted Royer.

"This is no time for cross-firing, Mr. Royer, and the sooner you stop it the better!" rebuked Captain Paul in an authoritative tone.

Seizing a rope's end, Royer, smarting under the rebuke of his superior officer, raised it over the boy, asking why he did not answer him when spoken to—to which the boy made no reply, but raised his head with a straining look over the sides of the deck toward the northwest.

"Answer me instantly!" commanded Royer.

"A sail!" replied the boy, pointing in the direction in which he was looking.

"A sail!" repeated Royer, dropping the rope.

"What is her course?" inquired Garcia, without his glass.

"Direct pursuit!" answered Castello.

"What flag?"

"Red ensign."

"British then, as sure as the world!" exclaimed Garcia.

"Run up the Stars and Stripes," commanded Royer.

"Off with the hatches there, you black devils! Bring out the dead and dying; heave them overboard!" order the heartless Portuguese.

The hatches, which had been for many hours closed, being opened, the blacks fell back, and retreated to escape the pestiferous fumes which met them.

"No running from dead niggers there, you black wolves! Down in the hold like a gang of half-starved hyenas into the grave of an executed thief!" exclaimed the reckless American.

Next came the heaves and sighs, wailing and cries, groaning and moaning of the thirsty, hungry, sick, and dying, in tones of agony, such to rend the soul with anguish to invoke Jehovah why

Is there not some chosen curse—
Some hidden thunder in the stores of heaven,
Red with uncommon wrath, to blast the man
Who gains his fortune from the blood of souls?

"Bring out the dead, dying, and damaged, an' we'll give 'em* a free an' quick passage to kingdom come, in less an' no time. Out with 'em, you black porcupines—out with 'em" again roared the coarse American.

Then came a scene the most terrible. Men, women and children raging with thirst, famished, nauseated with sea sickness, stifled for want of pure air, defiled and covered with loathsomeness, one by one were brought out, till the number of six hundred were thrown into the mighty deep, and sunk to rise no more till summoned by the trump of Heaven in the morning of the General Resurrection of all the dead, to appear before the Eternal Throne of God.

On casting them over, many of the sick and feeble begged in humble supplication to be spared, who, when clinging to the rigging or side of the vessel, had their hold broken by the foot of an officer, and when this was unsuccessful, a blow on the head with a handspike or capstan bar, sent the helpless victim trembling to a watery grave.

"Bear a hand at the pumps there—bear a hand!" ordered the surly Portuguese, the water being directed in constant streams among them, when opening their mouths as before they caught at it to slake their parching palates and stay the perishing threat.

Among those remaining in loathsomeness was Abyssa, the Christian woman of Soudan, who so soon as the black seamen entered, burst into tears of grief, begging for relief from her disgusting condition.**

With glass in hand, standing upon the quarter deck, Royer declared in words of blasphemy and boasting, that the American flag, which

---

*The coarseness and ruthlessness of these persons on slavers are indescribable. Imprecations, blasphemy, and sacriligiousness, they seem to delight in mocking and sporting over the distresses of their victims, even when themselves are in danger.

**Native Africans are very cleanly about their person, bathing generally several times a day.

had never grounded nor cowered before British colors, should not then become their prize. Before an event so humiliating should occur, he would consent to see her scuttled and all go to the depths of the ocean together. With lips pressed together, Blake looked on without an evidence of emotion, but a countenance and expression so determined, that Royer on passing turned about to look at him. Here, too, was Gascar as quiet as Blake was grave, but occasionally casting a look at Royer, which well might have caused him to suspicion the boy for some ill design toward him personally.

Meanwhile the "Vulture" dashed through the water at fourteen knots an hour, with American colors up and Spanish spirits down. All jesting among them had ceased, and even Gascar, who to them had always been a source of merriment, was now compelled to change his mood, which gave him the countenance of deep distress. Castello continued to pace the decks in silence, speaking only when spoken to, and though in reality the bravest man on board among the whites, submitted to his fate, though with grim reluctance.

The blacks were now under a new order of things, the destruction of the captives having frightened them, and all excepting Blake passed under the ordeal of Royer and Garcia's displeasure; with blasphemy ever on his lips, he was ready to abuse and insult the feelings of all to whom he spoke.

Calling them to duty, he abused them for delay in coming, and swore at them for coming when they knew that they had no duty to perform; this state of things continued till chance induced a change. The daring Briton seemed now to fall in the distance beyond the recovery of her former position, taking courage from which, Lawrence Spencer, on behalf of the Americans, raised a national air, joined by his party, to the words:

> The British shot flew hot,
> But the Yankees answered not,
> Till they got within the distance
> They called handyo!
> Says——

"Three times three, for the American flag!" interrupted Royer, when they became uproarious.

Thus escaping capture, by the speed of a superior Baltimore-built slaver, rigged and fitted out in New York for the trade; with a favorable wind, on she sped, clearing the water with nothing unusual occurring excepting every day to throw into the deep some half-a-dozen dead and dying captives taken from the hold, who had perished for want of sustenance in food, water, or air. The whites now were in high hopes and anticipation of pleasant and profitable termination of the voyage.

CHAPTER 54

Storm During Middle Passage

The prospects of the day this morning at sunrise were promising, and the entire ship's company, black and white, were out upon the decks. The Spaniards still exhibited feelings of dissatisfaction, and Royer continued his overbearing assumption. On the quarterdeck were standing the Americans, on the poop the Spaniards, the blacks occupying the forecastle.

While all thus positioned were enjoying the morning sun, looking out upon the ocean, a huge monster appeared in the water off the port bow of the vessel. The creature delighted in playing around and about the ship, diving on one side and coming up on the other, to the amusement and curiosity of the spectators. It was singular in shape, much larger than a grampus, and not so large as a whale. About it there was much cavil, some stating one thing, some another, when Garcia at once pronounced it a "sign of trouble."

The sky was clear—there were no fears of a storm; the cruiser distanced, no fears from her; they were approaching America, with no fears of the blacks. Then there was nothing to apprehend but the Spaniards, upon whom subsequently the eyes of the Americans were naturally turned.

But the weather suddenly changed; and the recently clear sky became decked with clouds and hazy, when the Americans more than ever became interested in the Spaniards. "A sign of trouble" had impressed them, and kept ringing in their ears, till not but trouble could they imagine was before them. In the moment of a serious consultation among them, a voice was heard cry "a weather," instantly succeeded by "a sail." Glasses were immediately leveled, when, just above the horizon, was a steamer to all appearance in direct pursuit. The prospect around had materially changed, the clouds gathered thickly and fast, lowering, seemingly, to the waters, while the steamer approached every minute nearer and nearer. Alarm now succeeded boasting; and fear, arrogant assumption. And whilst such was the case, on their part the Spaniards appeared unchanged by the surrounding circumstances.

This to the Americans was ominous, and caused them apprehension. The slaves at noon but the day before, had been well ventilated, fed, and watered,* and the hatches ordered to be kept partially open, that nothing might occur to hinder their progress. But the steamer still advancing, was fast gaining upon them.

"Examine the hold, and see what them niggers is about!" commanded Royer with a stentorian voice.

"The slaves are restless, Mr. Royer," replied Lawrence Spencer, who, to guard against the stench, had peeped into the hatch.

"What! I'll soon quiet 'em," replied he, who, armed with sword and whip in hand, ordering the whites to follow him, entered the hold, commanding silence.

The slaves confined in the stalls, immediately turned their eyes toward Mendi, [33] the athletic captive so abused by the mate, who then sat in the centre of the hold, loose and entirely out of place.

"I now see the cause of it," remarked George Royer, "he has worked himself out of place, and others want to follow."

Mendi suddenly sprang to his feet, stood with eyes fixed, looking defiant at the whites, then casting a look around upon his fellow captives, he spoke to them in his native Congolese. Royer drew with a brandish his sword, shook with a threat his whip, then gave him a look of authority, and left the hold followed by his companions.

Gaining the decks, and looking up, the skies still angrily threatened a storm, but nothing in comparison with the angry threatening of the dusky faces below.

"Apprehend anything serious?" inquired Paul.

---

*A fact worthy of note is that the captives in a slaver are only fed once a day, and sometimes watered only once.

"No, not any," replied Royer, supposing that the shake of his whip had intimidated the captive Mendi, though he, in reality, was alarmed.

"No danger of 'em gettin' loose, then?" continued Paul.

"None, sir, whatever. All the black rascals require to keep 'em in order is the shake of cowskin over 'em," replied George Royer.

"I'm not so certain about that; but hark!" said Paul, as a crash was heard below decks, like the crushing of boxes.

"The slaves are dissatisfied, and in a muss below, Mr. Royer," exclaimed Tom Hardy, an old American seaman.

"What under the sun is the matter with 'em?" replied the mate.

"They must want water, sir," replied he, just returning from a peep where he saw them sucking the broken glass of wine bottles.

"Just as you might expect! a nigger is all'as after somethin' to eat or drink," replied Royer in a passion. "Give 'em water."

Water was given which they drank, but still were thirsty; food they ate, but yet were hungry. They hungered and thirsted for liberty, heaven's great boon to man. Restlessness, with fierce demonstrations, pervaded the slave department, at which the whites becoming alarmed made serious suggestions to the commander.

"By the winds of Heaven, I'll subdue 'em or die! Follow me!" exclaimed Royer in a torrent of passion entering the hold, armed with sword and revolver.

Mendi on seeing him enter, advanced, stood boldly before him making gestures of the most serious apprehension.

"Rally, men, rally!" sternly commanded Royer, making a rush toward the unmanacled captive, when Tom Hardy, stopping suddenly, shrugged up his shoulders and reached out his hand, which Mendi eagerly grasped.

"Are you dry, old fellow?" inquired the seaman, with suitable gesture, to which he shook his head. "Are you hungry?" continued he, suiting an action to the word; when with a look of contempt the captive smiled. "By daddy, cap'n, this chap seems bent on a muss, an' I'm kind a thinkin' he's able to get up one," concluded he.

"Nonsense, nonsense!" contemptuously bellowed Royer. "He's a nigger, an' I'll teach him his place."

"Ef 'e don't, cap'n," comically replied Hardy, "he'll mock devilish close the man that does."

"Come, boys, come!"

"On deck!" was the stern command of Paul at the instant when the order was about to be given by Royer to rush upon the unmanacled bondman.

"Reef sails."

"Aye, aye, sir!"

"Lively, there, lively!" were commands, answers and orders given, all at the same time by different voices, everything being in the utmost confusion.

A heavy sea now struck the vessel, followed by a blinding flash of lightning and deafening peal of thunder; the "Vulture" dashing, heaving, tossing, plunging, and again mounting the swells as if in defiance of the confusion, roaring of the storm, and threatening danger around.

The contemplation of the scene had now become fearfully interesting. The black and frowning skies and raging hurricane above; the black and frowning slaves with raging passions below, rendered it dreadful without, fearful within, and terrible all around. Whilst captain, mate, and crew were with might and main struggling against the fierce contending elements above, the master spirit of the captives seized the opportunity to release his fellow slaves from their fetters. Armed with a heavy weapon found in the hold, Mendi stood in readiness for the conflict; with which on crushing a box to pieces, billhooks or sugar knives were strewn about the place. Arming his comrades they made ready for a charge.

Standing near to reconnoiter the hatch, an approach from above caused him to recede a pace or two from his position, as Spencer peeped down.

Here he descried the master standing in an attitude of determined resistance, boldly and fearlessly peering at the frowning clouds, as though to invoke the fury of the skies. A dreadful peal of thunder with a fearful flame of lightning just then burst in the elements, causing a glare deep down into the portentous dungeon illuminating his face, who starting stepped back a pace with face upturned to Heaven, falling upon his knees with hands extended in supplication to Jehovah, with great piercing eyes sparkling from under the heavy black brow, presented a sight which struck terror to the heart of the young American passed midshipman.

Pale and trembling he turned away, with faltering speech to describe the scene. Terrible as they might have been, the storm and hurricane above had not produced the trepidation in the young American as did the storm of silent vengeance deeply concealed amidst the fires of the troubled soul of this outraged son of Africa.

"Heavens!" exclaimed Royer at seeing Spencer stand back from the hatch, pale and panic-stricken. "What's the matter?"

"If the storm continues, we are lost!" replied Spencer.

"Death and destruction!" roared Royer. "Will you let a blast of thunder frighten you?"

"You don't understand me sir, the Negroes, the Negroes are——"

"What?"

"Loose!" replied Spencer; when again the thunder pealed as if uttering Heaven's indignation, while the lightning's forked streaks displayed the threatening of its wrath.

The storm raged, the waters dashed, while the vessel like a cork was tossed amidst the furies of the hurricane, and not a sound nor whisper heard but frightful antecedents. Then above the roaring storm might be heard the voice of Royer, with words of startling blasphemy, endeavoring to encourage on to battle the seamen with the elements; when again it might be heard in tones of discouragement but not less blasphemous, calling upon the thunder and lightning to dash in pieces the vessel, rather than it should be taken by a gang of black devils.

"What did you see?" asked Royer when a moment again favored the enquiry.

"That big restless Negro!" replied Spencer tremblingly.

"How did he look?"

"Like the devil just let loose!"

"Let us look again!" said Royer peeping into the hold. "just as I expected! a nigger's always after something to eat or drink. See them drums of figs—yes, there's resons too, and look at the fruits and broken licker bottles scattered round. By the lightning its too bad!"

"Can you see nothing else?" asked Spencer, closely peeping in.

"Stay!" whispered Royer, closely creeping up, laying down and peeping into the hold. "Hark! Still, still! Yes, there he is armed to the teeth, and all his niggers armed. See him, he peeps to see someone—only see his eyes!"

"The vicious devil!" added Spencer. "That look!"

Dark and unearthly is the scowl,
That glares beneath his dusty cowl;
The flash of that dilating eye
Reveals too much of time gone by!
Though——"

"Come, come, Mr. Spencer, this is no time for Shakespeare and nonsense!* I wish men was as good in showin' their bravery, as they is sometimes in showin' their learnin'," rebuked Royer. Spencer laughed at the mention of Shakespeare.

"Well, cap'n, bravery or not, it ain't no chile's play to go in the hold after you black feller, I'm told ye it ain't," suggested Tom Hardy.

Crash, again roared the thunder, as if shattering the skies to pieces, the lightning spreading flashes as though the clouds were in a flame. Startled at this potent mandate from above, captain, mate and all stood in silence at the scene.

"Yo ho! Ho eyo!" could be heard above the winds and dashing spray, the seamen manfully contending against the tempest, being fearfully exposed to the raging, merciless blast above, and the restless and dangerous elements of passion below.

Such was the state of things but twenty-four hours' sail from Matanzas.

Suddenly the winds changed, the clouds began to disperse, the thunder and lightning ceased to be seen and heard. Late in the afternoon a rainbow appeared above the horizon, telling in distant and silent eloquence as a harbinger of gladness, of a brighter prospect to all, as if conscious of the terror which pervaded the enslavers, and the future that awaited the enslaved.

The hatches being secured it was conceded that were it known that the slaves had been rebellious their value would be much depreciated, if not their sale prevented. The agreement was then made to suppress all information concerning their mutinous tendency, and dispose of the cargo as quickly as possible at the barracoons of Matanzas.

Blake during the entire troubles was strangely passive to occurring events below, strictly attending to the duties of his office in silence, except when speaking to a black, or spoken to by a white; but was

*Some young officers at sea are full of levity in times of the greatest danger.

suspicioned by the Americans as being the instigator of the plot, who under ordinary circumstances would have been executed at the yardarm of the vessel. But the Spaniards having accomplished their ends were satisfied, and showed pleasantness, becoming quite affable, they having at the start desired the cargo to be taken to Cuba.

Nothing could be seen of the daring British West India schooner, she having escaped the storm by putting into harbor. Nothing during the night occurred, and at daybreak next morning they hove in sight of the island, and at six o'clock that afternoon the "Vulture" secured her moorings in the bay at Matanzas.

Scarcely had she landed than without waiting for the adjustment of his engagement, Blake went immediately on shore, and was soon lost among the gazing spectators who assembled on the quay at the arrival of the vessel.

CHAPTER 55

The Captives

Next morning at the earliest dawn, when the song of animated nature, birds, reptiles, and insects—which in Cuba generally enliven the night and cheer the spirits with varied tones of discordant harmony—gaye way for the noise and clamor of the designing inhabitants of the port; among the first few who appeared on the quay was a mulatto gentleman.

There was nothing very remarkable about this, because were Cubans classified according to their complexion or race, three out of five of the inhabitants called white would decidedly be claimed by the colored people, though there is a larger number much fairer than those classified and known in the register as colored .[34] To this class belonged the gentleman in question.

Blake, regardless of the injunction of secrecy, had made known the mutinous spirit of the captives, which Placido managed to get into the hands of the hawkers and gossipers of news in Havana. The sales were delayed till late in the day, which brought a large number of human speculators, the design of which was to enhance the price by the competition on change.

To guard against all such contingencies, and prevent a recurrence of the scenes among them at sea, the most restless spirits among the captives were disposed of as soon as possible; the better to ensure which, a private sale had been effected, through a secret agent of Placido, affecting concern for the interest of the traders. But the poet still continued on the ground covertly depreciating the value of the slaves by the circulation of "postscripts" from the "press," giving full particulars of the mutiny at sea.

This reduced the captives to a minimum price, which placed them in the reach of small capitalists, for whom they were purchased by agents, who pretended themselves to be spectators. These agents were among the fairest of the quadroons, high in the esteem and confidence of their people, the entire cargo of captives through them going directly into black families or their friends.

The great scheme through this medium being much enhanced, though the mutiny was unsuccessful, with a cheerful heart and lively spirits, Placido with his choice two, Mendi and Abyssa, left Matanzas directly for Havana.

CHAPTER 56

The Seeleys

Blake, from Matanzas, had gone directly to Havana, where to meet and greet his wife and little son, and the poet, his cousin; still concealing from his father's family his identity; all of whom gave him a hearty welcome.

During his absence Placido had been busy, industriously disseminating the great principles implied in the silence, designed to be put in operation. Both tongue and pen in unison had been mutually engaged, eloquently impressing what the heart and mind conceived. Privately he whispered them in accents softly, meaningly, and confidingly. In poetry he wrote them in sentiments of song, enigmatically, though comprehensively. These words, though softly and fearfully spoken—as if in thunder tones—were indelibly impressed on every heart, while the sentiments of song, like a lightning flash, ran through every mind the length and breadth of the island.

The first care of Blake in his interview with the poet was the release of the captive Mendi, and Abyssa. Mendi was expected to be a powerful accession to their forces, as, being a native chief, he would meet with many of his race whose language he understood, and was thereby better suited to them than many others among them. The mere slave, as such, was deficient in discipline, except that which unfitted him for self-reliance. That was the curse which blighted his moral prospects, the blow which riveted upon him the links of an unyielding chain; the burden which, with mountain weight, pressed his mind to the earth, only to be thrown off by the force of an extraordinary self-exertion, verified the sentiment that—

The day that makes a man a slave,
Takes half his worth away.

The Seeleys had returned from America, after faithfully discharging their trust, bringing with them Charles and Polly, little Joe Blake, and Tony. After his interview with Placido, taking his wife and child, Blake rode out to the residence of the Seeleys, situated some ten miles distant. Mr. Seeley had purchased a fine countryseat called Homewood Grove, and entered in a lucrative shipping business in the city.

The shrubbery and grounds of the place were beautiful, affording ample residence for insects and birds. The meeting and greeting also here were affecting, mutual tears being shed for each other, Polly fell upon her knees with outstretched arms to Blake, and Charles embracing Maggie, laughed and cried, while Tony alternately kissed little Joe and hugged his father around the legs. Nor was Madam Seeley a passive spectator to the touching scenes around her.

The little son of Blake on arrival was received and taken to his mother by Placido, the party who accompanied the Seeleys not having met them till then. Mr. Seeley on going out in the evening to his place, was not remiss in sympathy to the party; Charles, Polly, and the boy remaining with the Seeleys until duties required a change. Blake and family left the seat of Homewood Grove for their residence in Havana.

Tony was becoming a very useful boy as an aid to Madam Seeley, whose attention had been turned to animated nature; the securing of specimens for the cabinet being the function assigned the boy. No naturalist was more assiduous than he, as far as his vocation extended;

not a bird nor insect seeming to escape his notice, nor fail to receive his most earnest gaze; some of which underwent a much closer examination, by an almost unerring direction of a stone from his hand, or a crush under the weight of his great palmleaf hat.

The first day he started on his mission of research, two hours was the time assigned him, with the promise of reward for the faithful discharge of his duty. The time allotted him was now half an hour overdue, but with the delinquency came Tony, who, as a proof of his claim to the reward and ample satisfaction for his tardiness, tumbled at the feet of Madam Seeley a hatful of insects of every kind he met, and an orange sprig well strung with a variety of birds; many among them of the choicest warblers.

"O, cruel, cruel!" exclaimed Madam Seeley as the heap was placed at her feet. "Tony, why did you do so? What made you kill those beautiful birds—and oh! these lovely insects? Look, too, at the butterflies—poor little creatures!"

"Da was singin' an' did'n see me," replied Tony, referring to the birds, "an' I jis sneaked up an' popt 'em."

"O, you cruel boy!" said the madam.

"O, Miss Seeley, dat ain't nothin' to kill a bird! An' dese bugs, I could jis' take an' mash 'em!" replied the boy, looking at the pile of insects, as though he was anxious to jump upon them with both feet.

Madam Seeley, as encouragement, admitted his dexterity and skill in the art of killing, when the boy sauntered away toward the pantry to refresh himself, being well satisfied with his reputation as a naturalist.

CHAPTER 57

Anticipation

"Just in time, Henry!" said Placido, as he entered the house of Junius Blacus, the father of Henry, who had just come from Homewood Grove, taking him by the hand. "I was fearful you wouldn't get here!"

"Why, Placido: what is the anxiety?" enquired he.

"I will tell you—come aside—tomorrow is a gala day, the celebration of the nativity of the Infanta Isabella, by a grand national fete at the palace of the Captain General."

"Thank God! Not only do the heavens, but the earth seems to declare his glory! How singularly He willed it, that I should return just at so auspicious a moment, to be with you in council, Placido!"

"God wills what's best, Henry!" said Placido.

"Then we would what God wills!" replied he.

"Let God's will be done then!" responded the poet.

"Can we not turn the day to our advantage, Placido?"

"Certainly! There's wherein consists the importance of your return from sea at this time. Could we have had the appointment, it could not have been better suited."

"Let us then get ready; the sooner, the better," said Henry. "What have you done?"

"Seeds have been planted in good ground, the hulls bursted, and kernels already sprouted!"

"Then but little time is required to mature the crop for the sickle of the reaper."

"I hope much from tomorrow," suggested Placido.

"We must make much of tomorrow!" replied Blake.

"We can if we will!" added Placido.

"Then we will!" decisively concluded Blake.

"That's just what I desired to hear, cousin Henry. I suppose I may now leave you, and repair to other quarters in the city, that they may be advised fully of the arrangements."

"Have you already made arrangements, cousin?"

"Certainly; did I not tell you?"

"Certainly, you did not! I was expecting to hear something of the kind, but was disappointed."

"Pardon me, General! I——"

"Come, come, Placido! you should not deal in jests of that kind; the thing is too serious for merriment!" interrupted Blake as Placido was about to compliment him.

"I beg your pardon, cousin Henry. I am not jesting, nor can I jest on such a subject, at such a time. And now let me inform you, that we have had our gatherings, held our councils, formed our legions, chosen our leaders, and made Henry Blake General-in-Chief of the army of emancipation of the oppressed men and women of Cuba!" explained Placido.

At the announcement, bracing his arms across his breast, dropping his head, looking down on the floor, Henry stood for some minutes, his wife who entered the room at the moment, throwing herself upon the poet's neck, weeping audibly.

"I only wish I thought myself worthy and competent, but I much doubt my ability, cousin!" replied Blake with much depression of spirits.

"We have examined every point, and weighed the whole matter, cousin: Henry Blake is the man!" rejoined Placido.

"In bondage again! Well, I suppose those who are bound, especially when they seek it, must obey," replied Blake.

"Indeed, Henry, I wouldn't undertake it, so I wouldn't! I would leave that for cousin Placido or some other gentleman here to do. I'm sure you know nothing about such things!" advised Maggie, at which pressing his hand on her cheek, Placido laughed.

"Wife, I must in this, submit entirely to others," said Blake.

"I suppose then I may give up all hope of ever having you with me at all!" she replied with renewed sobs.

"Stop, cousin!" admonished Placido. "You must remember that there's a great difference between Franks' slaves and General Blake and wife. As the former, you were irresponsible, the latter responsible; that was a life of trouble and sorrow, this of care and pleasure. One shuns adventure, the other seeks it; the slaves feels an issue, and the freeman makes it. A slave must have somebody to care for him; a freeman must care for himself and others. The position of a man carries his wife with him; so when he is degraded, she is also, because she cannot rise above his level; but when he is elevated, so is she also; hence, the wife of Henry the slave was Maggie the slave; but the wife of Mr. Henry Blake will be Mrs. Maggie Blake; and the wife of General Blake will be Mrs. General Blake. What objections have you to this, cousin?"

"You must make every allowance for me, cousin Placido, as I have not been long enough in the enjoyment of freedom to have considered these things but I do assure you, that I now understand and appreciate all that you say," replied Maggie with a smile of gratification at the thought.

"Then, cousin, grieve not!" solaced Placido, as he observed the tears stealing down her cheeks. "Your husband is our leader, and as you see the legions advancing, fear not, as you shall hear this song to comfort you, and encourage on the portentous Army of Emancipation:

Be patient in your misery, be meek in your despair,
Be patient, O be patient, suffer on, suffer on!
We are all for freedom, we are all for freedom,
We are for liberty and justice—
And for freedom through the land!
We have hatred dark and deep for the fetter and the thong,
We bring light to prisoned spirits, for the captive wail a song;
We are all for freedom, we are all for freedom,
We're for liberty and justice,
And for freedom through the land!
We are coming, we are coming, and no league with tyrant man,
Is emblazoned on our banner, while Jehovah leads the van!
He is coming on to lead us,
And never means to leave us,
Till he gains us our liberty,
And freedom through the land!"

"God grant," responded Maggie, "that he may be equal to the task!"

"God grant it!" replied Henry.

"What is the policy among us tomorrow in assembling with the public?" enquired Blake.

"To assemble promiscuously among the whites, and segregate as usual in groups by accident."

"That's the idea," concluded Henry, who smiling explained it to his wife, who acknowledged that freedom developed many things she had never before thought of; when Placido hurriedly left them to send the tidings through the city.

CHAPTER 58

Gala Day

This morning was ushered beautifully in, the West India sky being unusually clear, the morning star in its brilliancy adorning the cloudless horizon.

The evening before there was little rest, in consequence of the general noise, hum and din, by passing to and fro of the vehicles, and chatting of the busy people during the night. The hotels too were kept open for the accommodation of the officers of government, and the musicians from Moro Castle, and other bands of music, which from the porticos and corridors, almost incessantly assembled through the night, discoursed to the cheering crowds continually in honor of the Infanta Sovereign of Spain.

The morning brought with it contemplated joy to the minds of the elevated, and sadness of heart to the crushed and oppressed people on the island. Business on such occassions is usually suspended; the soldiers parading with attracting display, are inspected and commanded by the Captain General in person, surrounded by a brilliant and haughty staff of cavaliers. Moro Castle was on this occasion proudly decorated with all the national colors: the Spanish Protective, merchantman, man-of-war, and Spanish flags. From the British and American flagstaff also waved their national pendants.

The Palace of the Captain General was richly decorated with many curious and highly ornamental designs, all having some allusion of historic or political import. The slaves throughout the island were, as is customary on such occasions, given a general holiday, and all within ten leagues of the city poured in from every direction, like the gathering of black and threatening clouds, necessary to a fearful storm; while the cannon from the castle roared in tones as thunder preceding a tempest.

Floating over the surface of the bay with liveliness and gaiety, were numerous pleasure boats kept in constant transit, and among the most exciting of the water pleasures was the regatta, when the quay was thronged with the multitude who bet and bantered various sums, much money being lost and won. Sports of almost every description during the day occupied the attention of the people. In the courts, narrow alleys, and byways might have been seen squads of idle slaves or trifling wayward Creoles and Spaniards, playing at chicken-hazard, pitching quoits on bets, or betting silver at a toss. At many corners of the streets might have been seen crowds in the center of which was a ring, surrounding a dogfight on heavy bets. The bullfight too was in high requisition the day of this national fete.

The next amusement succeeding was the sport of the chase, which consisted in training the bloodhounds exhibited on the parade ground. This sport is such that in the training the slave is sometimes caught and badly lacerated, which produces terror in the black spectators, the object designed by the custom.

Never before had the African race been so united as on that occassion, the free Negroes and mixed free people being in unison and sympathy with each other. During the sport of the chase, it was generally observed by the whites that in the event of a slave being caught, instead of—as formerly—indifference on the part of the blacks, or a shout from a portion of the free colored people present, there were gloomy countenances, sour angry expressions and looks of revenge, with general murmuring, which plainly indicated if not a preconcerted action, at least a general understanding pertaining to that particular amusement. There was a greater tendency to segregation instead of a seeming desire to mingle as formerly among the whites, as masses of the Negroes, mulattoes and quadroons, Indians* and even Chinamen, could be seen together, to all appearance absorbed in conversation on matters disconnected entirely from the occasion of the day.

The National Parade came next in order, being the only exhibition in which the African race took pleasure, they being desirous of witnessing the display of the troops to learn something of the character of the soldiers that might be brought against them. Though not so exciting particularly to the blacks, this was the most grand and imposing scene of the day.

At the sound of the reveille, the troops assembled in military array, presenting a formidable front, the field officers being richly dressed and elegantly mounted on splendid caparisoned, grand, and dashing steeds. Here and there through the field they were flying, inspecting the lines without giving orders, intending it would seem to anticipate by intimidating the Negroes from action. Now and again as though to show the blacks their chance of escape in an attempt at retreat, came an isolated soldier running at the best of speed, who had been loitering away his time in idle gossip, or in a booth regaling a whetted appetite, and thirst with ardent spirits.

In a short time after the reveille, every soldier was in his place, soon after which the salutes from Moro Castle caused everyone to turn in

*For many years the Yucatan Indians taken in war by the Mexicans were sold into Cuba as slaves.

the direction of the city. The Captain General and suit were now approaching, and the populace were frantic to get a sight of his Excellency. With pomp and splendor he entered the parade ground, amidst the deafening shouts of the multitude, his inspection and exercising of the troops consuming the time allotted for his stay.

The troops as an escort to the Governor entered the city late in the afternoon, leaving his Excellency at the Government palace, the thousands who crowded the thorough fares dispersing in every direction, repairing to their homes early to return in the evening, many to gaze upon the splendid illumination by chandeliers of the interior of the residence, others to the Castle to witness a grand display of fireworks and the various amusements and entertainments throughout Havana that night.

Of the thousands thus dispersing, various feelings existed. Some were merry, others sad—some joyful, others mad; some discouraged, others encouraged—some hopeful, others despairing. Among the disappointed should be considered the restless American part of the inhabitants known as "patriots"; the sad and hopeful were the black and colored people who had determined to manage in future their own affairs; there were among this portion of the inhabitants those who determined that for the last time they had looked with passiveness upon the sad scene of training bloodhounds upon the living flesh of their kindred and sporting in luxury on the misfortunes of their race. Whilst reflecting upon these scenes with a sad and heavy heart, they could only discern before them a dark and gloomy pathway, which but now and again was lighted up by the sudden outbursting of a concealed flame, deeply hidden in their breast, flashing as they passed along. But they had one encouragement—a faint, steady light away off in the distance—discernible through the obscurity of space—the Star of Hope—whose cheering rays had reached them, encouraging them onward in their slow but steady march.

To this end, this portion of the population returning to their homes, prepared for an occasion quite different in its bearing to that which would call together the brilliant and imposing assemblage, soon to crowd the splendid apartments in the Palace of the Captain General.

CHAPTER 59

National Fete

The feature of attraction for the evening among the higher classes was the Palace of the Captain General, and while a selection from the elite were alone to be the guests, yet the avenue leading to, and the space in front of, the mansion were thronged by the common people who crowded the passes to get a peep at the rich costumes and gaze in at the windows and doors of the brilliantly illuminated apartments.

At the hour of nine the company commenced to gather, when all that beauty and grandeur could effect, certainly was on the occasion accomplished; by ten o'clock the spacious apartments being crowded with an assemblage that might have graced the palace of an European monarch.

The servants thronged not only their own, but lined the piazzas and walls around the dancing hall; and besides these, the visiting domestics about the palace were also numerous.

There was evident anxiety concerning absent guests, which seemed to be mutual through the assemblage; and the Negro servants on this occasion appeared more than usually observing.

That day was seen on parade several fine looking mulatto officers, the confidants of the Captain General and incognito members of his staff; men upon whom he depended in the event of an outbreak of the American party in Cuba. Juan Montego, Ferdinand Ricardo, Pedro Castina, Stephen Rivera, and the poet Placido were among the foremost of these persons. There were still others of the fairest complexion among the quadroons, who were classed as white, that faithfully adhered to the interests of the African race,* and were ready at any moment to join them. Of the delinquent guests at the Palace, besides the wives and female relatives of many of the gentlemen, there were other ladies expected who failed to appear, of whom may be named Madame Cordora and daughter; Madame Barbosa, and Madame Sebastina, educated, wealthy ladies.

Placido was Poet Laureate to His Excellency, and Pino Golias, a black surgeon, the leading amateur musician, banjoist extraordinary, being the most accomplished banjoist and guitarist in the city.

---

*The term "African race" includes the mixed as well as the pure bloods.

In a group stood Count Alcora, the Captain General; Lady Charlotte, the Countess; and several foreign officials and their ladies, in close conversation. Presently a servant hastily entered, looked around the room in a meaning manner to others, then suddenly left. There being in this nothing to cause suspicion, as it might have been a summons to domestic duty, no particular attention was thereby elicited.

In the hall directly opposite this group stood the servant of an American, intently looking at the company; his wife, the maidservant to her mistress, standing at his side. A servant of the palace was observed to step up, tap him on the shoulder, and was off in an instant, the American servant following; when, after a short interview in the palace park with a concealed group of Negroes, returned and took his wife from the room. At the head of this grave gathering stood the caterer of the police cuisine, Gofer Gondolier. This person was a black, who in boyhood had attended a Spanish grandee to Genoa, where during his stay, his principal recreation was aquatic sports on the gulf, the lad being his principal oarsman—hence the name of Gondolier. The Christian name of the lad was Godfrey, but by singular corruption he was called Gofer—thence Gofer Gondolier became his fixed name. After a hasty counsel, the caterer returned to duty, and the rest of the servants to their places in the room.

Whilst the palace was the scene of life and gaiety, thronged with those in the highest enjoyment of their rights, free to go and come when and where they pleased, all fondly uniting in loyalty and deference to do homage to the sovereign demands of Spain, little dreaming of serious contingencies or trouble, there was at the same time going on in another part of the city an affair, though if not so grand and potent at least it may have been equally as interesting, and in all probability much more portentous than the elevated assemblage at the seat of government of Count Alcora, the Captain General—the proud and haughty military Chief of Cuba.

CHAPTER 60

Great Gathering at Madame Cordora's

But a peep in at this unsuspected gathering would give an idea of its designs and general character.

Among the leading persons were Juan Montego, Ferdinand Ricardo, Pedro Castina, Stephen Rivera, and other noted gentlemen; Madame Cordora and Ambrosina, the wife and daughter of a deceased wealthy mulatto merchant; Madame Cordelia Barbosa, a wealthy young quadroon widow; Madame Evelina Sebastina, a refined wealthy mestizo lady; Carolus Blacus, a wealthy black tobacco dealer; Madame and Señorita Seraphina, his wife and daughter, both accomplished black ladies; Andro Camina and Madame Tripolia and Tripolina, his lady and daughter, a refined family of wealthy blacks, retired on a great fortune; and Justin Pompa, a distinguished black artist of rare accomplishments, composed a part of this unique gathering, many of whom till a late hour at night had been anxiously looked for and expected at the palace of the Captain General to complete the assembly at the national fete.

Among those of note, but humble pretensions, were Mendi, the captive chief; and Abyssa, the trading woman of Soudan.

During the evening a general privilege was extended to any of their race in the confidence of a seclusion, to pass and repass during the gathering. Nor were they in the least slighted. Everything was systematically arranged, the organization being complete. Juan Montego was head of the occasion, and where he presided nothing was neglected; consequently every guest and visitor went through an ordeal of the closest possible inspection.

Abyssa, who had for a long time sat closely eyeing the entire company, involuntarily gave vent to an exclamation of prayer.

"Is she crazy?" inquired Louis Chevora, a wealthy quadroon planter from Principe, who, unaccustomed to such promiscuous mingling with people of every complexion of his race, laughed in ridicule.

"No, she's not crazy; her head is as clear as a sunbeam," tartly replied Montego, who was a great admirer of the simple but great- and good-hearted female African captive.

"You will know before we separate the meaning of that prayer," whispered Castina in the ear of Chevora, who had attended but one gathering, and knew nothing of the seclusions.

It was full the eleventh hour before the gathering was complete, and except at intervals a ballad and guitar accompaniments by the voluntary offering of some young lady present, there had been no music during the evening.

All were now seriously silent; everyone no doubt deeply reflecting on the great event and momentous occasion which had brought them together.

Suddenly, as if by magic, the whole company simultaneously rose to their feet. With silent and suppressed demonstrations, men and women waved hand and handkerchief, Blake and Placido entering at the instant when the amateur orchestra, instrumental and vocal commenced in strains most impressive:

All hail thou true and noble chief,
Who scorned to live a cowering slave;
Thy name shall stand on history's leaf,
Amid the mighty and the brave!

Thy name shall shine a glorious light
To other brave and fearless men,
Who like thyself in freedom's might,
Shall brave the robber in his den;

Thy name shall stand on history's page,
And brighter, brighter, brighter glow,
Throughout all time, through every age,
Till bosoms cease to feel and know.

"Created worth or human woe";
Thy name shall nerve the patriot's hand,
When mid the battle's deadly strife,
The glittering bayonet and brand

Are coming with the stream of life;
When the dark clouds of battle roll,
And slaughter reigns without control,

Thy name shall then fresh life impart
And fire anew each freeman's heart.

Though wealth and power their force combine
To crush thy noble spirit down,
There is above a power divine
Shall bear thee up against their frown.

The effects of the reception ballad was electrical—every kind of demonstration indicating the soul's deep sympathy and heartfelt hatred to oppression, with cautious suppression, was made in silence. There stood Abyssa bathed in tears, moaning with joy in African accents, while Mendi with outstretched arms fell upon his knees in thankfulness to God for what he had witnessed. Louis Chevora, the quadroon planter, unprepared to see a Negro chosen leader of the great scheme of redemption, was singularly embarrassed and awkward.

"Why, I didn't know it was you! I am glad to see you! I wasn't expecting to meet you here!" confusedly expressed the almost bewildered man on being introduced to Blake, whom he had never before seen nor even heard of, as entering the city the evening before and attending but one gathering, he knew nothing of the seclusions, to whom alone the Hero was known.

A general rush was made each seeming to envy the other who succeeded before him in getting a grasp of the hand of Henry Blake, the Leader of the Army of Emancipation and originator of the scheme to redeem them from slavery and an almost helpless degradation. On this occasion Pino Golias proved himself master of the favorite instrument of his father land, the African bango.[35] In solos of strains the sweetest the Spanish guitar proved but a secondary instrument compared with the touching melodies of the pathetic bango in the hands of this Negro artiste.

This instrument, heretofore neglected and despised by the better class among them, at once became the choice—and classically refined by the nearest and dearest historic reminiscences among them, by an association with the evening of the great gathering, from a seclusion of which the momentous question of immediate redemption or an endless degradation and bondage was to be forever settled. From these associations and remembrances, the Nigrition bango could thenceforth be seen in the parlors and drawing rooms of all of the best families of this class of the inhabitants.

The demonstrations to Placido were only less than those given to the Chief, and could they have but given expression to their feelings, a shout would have rent the air for "Blake and Placido" such as never before had been heard in Havana. Singing and executing of the guitar and bango by the Misses Seraphina Blacus and Ambrosina Cordora, both young, handsome, and accomplished, were very much appreciated by the delighted assemblage. These young ladies were great favorites at the Palace of the Captain General, where the pianoforte and their favorite stringed instruments seldom had their equals to execute upon them. The black surgeon Pino Golias was their only rival and superior on these instruments.

Madame Cordora on this occasion was particularly happy, aided in her untiring efforts to make others so, by the generous, greathearted Montego. All that wealth and refinement, modified by simplicity and an entire absence of ostentation and display—except, indeed, the richly furnished mansion and valuable table plate and jewelry so much in taste with Spaniards—could accomplish was contributed. Her own exemplary deportment and high-toned conversation, the edifying discourses of Montego, the elevated influence and demeanor of the Blacus family and such persons, made the assemblage one that bore no disparaging comparison with the splendid fete then being held in gilded drawing rooms of the Government Palace.

To complete the portentous gathering and crown their hopes with the highest expectation, there were Placido the cousin, adviser and counselor, and Henry Blake, the master spirit of the occasion.

The refreshments were simple, mainly consisting of fruits, biscuit, cheese, chocolate, coffee, and cool drinks with no virous beverage at all. There was no empty parade and imitative aping, nor unmeaning pretentions observed in their doings, but all seeming fully to comprehend the importance of the ensemble. They were earnest, firm, and determined; discarding everything which detracted from their object, permitting nothing to interfere. Thus intelligently united, a dangerous material existed in the midst of such an element as Cuba.

In the midst of their enjoyment a person made his appearance at the main door of the drawing rooms causing no little alarm, though they knew he must have been a seclusionist to have passed the scrutiny of Montego and reached where he was. This person was a black, a little above medium height, strong physical conformation, with fine expression of countenance, attired in blue nankin pantaloons, buff vest, white linen jacket, collar of shirt turned over the jacket collar, tied with a broad black ribbon, white half hose, long low quartered black morocco slippers tied with narrow black ribbon, his right hand in which he held a black slouch silk cap, carelessly akimbo, leaning with left shoulder against the door casing. His dress being that of a domestic heightened the suspicion, as he might have been a spy sent by the whites. For this reason he was closely reconnoitered by many who designedly positioned themselves near him.

"This beats the alabasters over yonder all to pieces!" he was heard to say to himself, comparing the gathering with the fete at the palace, as with a bland smile he stood gazing in upon such an assemblage of his own people, as he had never before witnessed.

"Who is that suspicious-looking person peeping into the drawing room?" enquired Julia Chevora, the wife of the Principe planter, addressing herself to Ambrosina, who hastily cited her mother to the supposed intruder.

"Why that is Gofer Gondolier, the caterer of the Palace," replied Madame Cordora, calling the attention of Montego to him.

"Come in Gofer, come in!" invited Montego, approaching where he stood near the door.

"Things look too warm in there for me, Colonel," replied he with a slow and meaning shake of the head, when pointing at a bango lying upon a pier table he continued, "but ef you han' me that thing out here, ef I don't make 'er hum I wouldn't tell you so!" Laughing, Montego turned away, relating to the ladies his short interview with the caterer, speaking highly of his integrity as a man though humbly positioned in life.

"Come in, Gofer Gondolier—feel yourself at home, as I'm sure you are welcomed by everybody here," insisted Madame Cordora, "this is not the Palace of the Captain General filled with whites. Come in and take a seat!" Gofer acknowledged the honor, bowed himself quite into the drawing room.

"Now, Gondolier," said Castina, who sat as guard at the door, on resigning his seat and handing him the sword, "I leave you my post in charge; see that you do your duty!"

"I will sir, and ef a candle face gits by me, it'll not be tell after I knock the light out of it!" drolly replied he, referring to the gendarmes or such other whites as might be out on espionage. "But I got a better thing than this!" he said, holding out and looking at the sword, with a wag of his head.

"What is that curiously constructed instrument you have there, Gofer; will you show it to me?" asked Castina, on seeing under his jacket on the left breast a large weapon.

"O, nothing, sir, but a knife. I thought as you had a gathering tonight that you might have some carving to do, an' as I just finished that business at the Palace, I thought I'd come over and help here," replied he.

"Carving! Do you call that a carving knife?" earnestly enquired Castina, as Gondolier handed him the formidable instrument.

"I do, sir!" replied Gofer.

"Where did you get it?"

"I made it, sir."

"You made it!" with surprise enquired Castina.

"I did, sir, I cut the pattern out of a barrel stave, and had the knife manufactured to order."

"What motives had you in doing so?"

"That on a general rising the blacks in every house might have good weapons without suspicion."

"I can't see how this could be effected without detection, as they must be made and sold by the whites," judiciously replied Castina.

"If you can't, I can, sir, because anything originating among the people about the Palace the Captain General always receives with favor, giving orders to be supplied; and I being his butler and chief caterer, these orders go through me. So you see sir, by making a carving knife, I present something that comes in general use as a domestic and family convenience, with which every person may supply himself without suspicion, especially the blacks, who are not only great imitators of the whites as they say we are, but also great eaters as we know ourselves to be," intelligently explained Gondolier.

"Gracious!" exclaimed Castina, examining the weapon. "What a formidable thing it is to be sure! You must be a man, Gondolier, to have conceived such an idea."

"If I wasn't I wouldn't be here, sir," promptly replied Gofer.

"I mean, sir, that you are worthy to be here!" explained Castina.

"That is just what I mean, sir," continued he. "If the poet hadn't known me to be such, as I was only a domestic in the palace where he and the Colonel were visitors, he never would have admitted me to the gatherings, nor took me into the seclusions."

"You are right, Gondolier, you are right, and shall henceforth hold a place among us higher than the position of caterer at the National Palace; it shall be here!" said Castina, placing his hand upon his breast over his heart.

"Noble fellow!" said Montego to Madame Cordora; "He's worthy of a better position than his former one, and he shall have it."

Madame Cordora herself served up refreshments which were borne to him by her daughter Ambrosina, who with her hand gently resting on his shoulders, sat supporting in her lap a silver plateau, from which he was supplied. These marks of kindness quite surprised Gondolier, who not expecting such notice and attention rising to his feet, bowing expressed acknowledgements for the honor received at their hands.

"But your knife, Señor Gondolier, on this occasion will be of no use to you, there being no meats to carve," said Madame Cordora.

With a significant shake of the head, Gondolier implied that the carving he had reference to was quite of a different kind.

The weapon from its original peculiarity excited much interest and no little alarm among the novices and less experienced among them, especially the female portion. Its breadth was that of the widest common carving knife. He simply called it the "Cuban carver," or "Gondolier's carving knife."

About the first watch of the morning—the hour of one—the seclusion met, holding a Grand Council, consisting of Henry Blake, Placido, Montego, the Blacuses, Carolus and Antonio, Castina, Ricardo, Rivera, Camina, the Captive Chief, Madame Cordora, Maggie Blake, Madame Barbosa, Madame Blacus, Madame Sebastina, Abyssa Soudan, and Madame Camina, the misses being admitted by courtesy, they having the confidence of the seclusion. Gofer Gondolier stationed on the outside of the door, desired, as he said, no better weapon of defence than his own carving knife.

The seclusion was held on the southwest corner of the mansion in an airy attic room, reserved for the purpose, where subsequent to the maturest deliberation, the most concise measures were entered into—Henry Blake presiding, and Placido secretary, completed the organization for the evening. Preliminaries were fully decided on, and a time specified for holding the Grand Official Council of the seclusion, when officers both civil and military for their future government were to be appointed.

At the third watch of the morning as the great bell told three, the seclusion arose, when a social company, unknown to their superiors in society, separated; more portentous to the political interests of Cuba, than any similar gathering in this history of the colony.

CHAPTER 61
The Grand Council

A rain—a gust, a thunder-storm most loud—
Is indicated by this gathering cloud!

It was Sabbath—a beautiful day—the sun bright and cheering; the air cool and refreshing, and the fragrance and odors of flowers, fruits and spices, seemed more exhilirating than at any time before during the season.

The countenances of the inhabitants generally wore a cheerful expression, and though throughout the day the streets were literally crowded, there was less of sports and amusements than usual on this day of the week. The evening was also beautiful, and whilst there was nothing unusual to note its general character, yet to one portion of the inhabitants at least, it became a memorable period in the history of their existence.

This evening, according to appointment, the seclusion met in Grand Council at the house of Madame Cordora. But instead of the attic story, the drawing rooms were occupied, each member in his place—Gofer Gondolier post guard, stationed at the door in the hall.

The provisional organization consisted of Placido, Director of Civil Government; Minister of State, Camina; Minister of Justice, Carolus Blacus; Minister of Foreign Affairs, Castina; Postmaster General, Antonio Blacus; Minister of War and Navy, Montego.

The Army regulations were: Henry Blake, Commander in Chief of the Army of Emancipation; Juan Montego, General of First Division;

Pedro Castina, General of Second Division; Ferdinand Recaud, General Third Division; Stephen Rivera, General of Fourth Division; Gofer Gondolier, Quartermaster General. Thus organized, the oppressed became a dangerous element in the political ingredients of Cuba.

Already the atmosphere of sentiments began to change, the weather of prospects to alter, the sunlight of promise grow dim, the day of anticipation darker, and clouds of the downtrodden were seen in specks, to gather throughout the island. The signs of the public zodiac were warningly significant of an approaching storm, though a great way off, yet the calculation of the political calendar paid no attention to it.

Moved by a solemn sense of the import of the momentous subject before them, and the great responsibility of the undertaking, Blake in a few words thus impressingly addressed them:

"Brethren, sisters, men and women of Cuba!—The like of tonight's gathering, save in a neighboring island years before any of us had an existence, in this region is without a parallel; and as the Lord lives, and my soul bears witness that he does, I will do all that in my power lies to carry out the decrees of this Council!"

"Amen!" responded Placido.

"God grant it," added Gondolier, who had gone inside to hear the address of their Chief.

"Arm of the Lord awake!" cried Abyssa Soudan.

"With strength and power!" responded the Council.

The female members of the Council instantly commenced whispering among themselves, all except Abyssa seeming earnestly engaged. The captive woman noticing them with some embarassment, which the ladies observed, Madame Cordora rose to ask an explanation.

"I should like to be relieved of a difficulty," said this highly intelligent woman, "not only for my own sake, but that of my female colleagues of the Council as well as the general cause in which we are engaged. We have all or most of us been bred Catholic, to believe in the doctrines of the Romish Church. I perceive, however, that a portion of our ceremonies consist of prayers and other formalties, objectionable to us as such. Can we as Catholics, with any degree of propriety consistently with our faith, conform to those observances? I ask only for information, and hope for reasons stated to receive it."

"A word of explanation addressed to your intelligence, Madame Cordora, will suffice I know to set the matter right," said Blake. "I, first a Catholic, and my wife bred as such, are both Baptists; Abyssa Soudan, once a pagan, was in her own native land converted to the Methodist or Wesleyan belief; Madame Sabastina and family are Episcopalians; Camina, from long residence out of the colony, a Presbyterian, and Placido is a believer in the Swedenborgian doctrines. We have all agreed to know no sects, no denomination, and but one religion for the sake of our redemption from bondage and degradation, a faith in a common Savior as an intercessor for our sins; but one God, who is and must be our acknowledged common Father. No religion but that which brings us liberty will we know; no God but He who owns us as his children will we serve. The whites accept of nothing but that which promotes their interests and happiness, socially, politically and religiously. They would discard a religion, tear down a church, overthrow a government, or desert a country, which did not enhance their freedom. In God's great and righteous name, are we not willing to do the same?"

"Yes!" was the unanimous response.

"Our ceremonies, then," continued Blake, "are borrowed from no denomination, creed, nor church: no existing organization, secret, secular, nor religious; but originated by ourselves, adopted to our own condition, circumstances, and wants, founded upon the eternal word of God our Creator, as impressed upon the tablet of each of our hearts. Will this explanation suffice, women of Cuba, sisters in oppression with us? Are you satisfied to act and do our own way regardless of aping our oppressors indiscriminately?"

"We are, we are!" cried out they.

"Amen!" exclaimed the woman of Soudan.

"Amen!" responded the poet.

"Amen!" cried out Madame Cordora.

"Amen!" concluded Montego and the Council. "Amen!"

"Thank God for this interchange of sentiments!" exclaimed Blake. "Thank God! A word more and I have done. In regard to the justice of our course: if we are to consult our oppressors our very assemblage is in violation of the laws of God; because they tell us that the powers that be are ordained of God; hence our Council sitting contrary to the will of these powers, therefore must be against the ordinance of God. Do you see it?"

"We do, we do!" responded many voices.

"And we want no more of their gospel neither," cried out Gofer Gondolier to the amusement of the entire assemblage.

"I rise simply to observe," said Madame Cordora, "that I and the other female members of the Council are satisfied and that henceforth we are willing to go and do our own way, and let our oppressors go and do theirs."

"Then, by God's help, we must succeed," said Blake.

The general interest and anxiety manifested throughout the evening in the multitude of sentiments and opinions interchanged was beyond description. The greatest emotions were frequently demonstrated, with weeping and other evidences of deep impressions made.

"Everything being now settled," said Montego, "I now suggest that the seclusion be formally closed."

"I now remind the Chief that the poet will give the dismissing prayer prepared expressly for the occasion," added Montego, after the ceremony of closing had been gone through with.

At the signal of the Chief, the poet, stepping upon the elevation on which were seated the orchestra, amidst a deathlike silence of anxious listeners and fond admirers, read in a loud, impressive, and solemn manner:

Oh Great Jehovah, God of Love!
Thou monarch of the earth and sky,
Canst thou from thy great throne above
Look down with an unpitying eye!
See Africa's sons and daughters toll,
Day after day, year after year,
Upon this blood bemoistened soil,
And to their cries turn a deaf ear?
Canst thou the white oppressor bless,
With verdant hills and fruitful plains,
Regardless of the slave's distress—
Unmindful of the blackman's chains?
How long, O Lord! ere thou wilt speak
In thy Almighty thundering voice,

To bid the oppressors fetters break,
And Ethiopia's sons rejoice?
How long shall Slavery's iron grip,
And prejudices guilty hand,
Send forth like bloodhounds from the slip
Foul persecutions o'er the land?
How long shall puny mortals dare
To violate Thy just decree,
And force Thy fellow men to wear
The galling chains by land and sea?
Hasten, Oh Lord! the glorious time
When everywhere beneath the skies,
From every land and every clime
Peons to Liberty shall rise!
When the bright sun of Liberty
Shall shine o'er each despotic land;
And all mankind from bondage free,
Adore the wonders of thy hand.

"Arm of the Lord, awake!" cried out Abyssa.

"Amen!" replied Gondolier.

"Ah ha! Dat's de talk!" exclaimed an old domestic, whose head that moment had been thrust in from an adjoining room, where he sat in waiting on Montego.

"I do not wish to be troublesome," interrupted Madame Cordora, rising to her feet, "but I must here ask another explanation. Engaged as we all are in a common cause for liberty and equality, I would not have a difference to be made at the start. The poet in his prayer spoke of Ethiopia's sons; are not some of us left out in the supplication, as I am sure, although identified together, we are not all Ethiopians."

"No," rejoined Placido, "we are not; but necessarily implied in the term, and cannot exist without it."

"How so; I'm sure I cannot understand you!" replied the Madame with surprise.

"I'll explain," said Placido. "I hold that colored persons, whatever the complexion, can only obtain an equality with whites by the descendants of Africa of unmixed blood."

"You surprise me, Señor Placido! I certainly cannot comprehend you. That is a positive admission that the mixed bloods are inferior to the pure-blooded descendants of Africa. I did not expect it to come to this, I think the acknowledgement of an equality of classes is sufficient for any purpose, without having to regard ourselves as inferiors—just what we are all contending against."

"I see you do not understand my position, Madame Cordora; let me make it plain to you," further explained the poet. "The whites assert the natural inferiority of the African as a race: upon this they premise their objections, not only to the blacks, but all who have any affinity with them. You see this position taken by the high Court of America, which declares that persons having African blood in their veins have no rights that white men are bound to respect. Now how are the mixed bloods ever to rise? The thing is plain; it requires no explanation. The instant that an equality of the blacks with the whites is admitted, we being the descendants of the two, must be acknowledged the equals of both. Is not this clear?"

"I certainly see it, Señor Placido, as I never saw it before, and you have given me a greater idea of the relation we sustain to the African race, than I ever had before; and the same certainly obtains in regard to Africa as a country, and her people as a nation or nations."

"Of course it does. Heretofore that country has been regarded as desolate—unadapted to useful cultivation or domestic animals, and consequently, the inhabitants savage, lazy, idle, and incapable of the higher civilization and only fit for bondmen, contributing nothing to the civilized world but that which is extorted from them as slaves. Instead of this, let us prove, not only that the African race is now the principal producer of the greater part of the luxuries of enlightened countries, as various fruits, rice, sugar, coffee, chocolate, cocoa, spices, and tobacco; but that in Africa their native land, they are among the most industrious people in the world, highly cultivating the lands, and that ere long they and their country must hold the balance of commercial power by supplying as they now do as foreign bondmen in strange lands, the greatest staple commodities in demand, as rice, coffee, sugar, and especially cotton, from their own native shores, the most extensive native territory, climate, soil, and greatest number of (almost the only natural producers) inhabitants in the universe; and that race and country will at once rise to the first magnitude of importance in the estimation of the greatest nations on earth, from their dependence upon them for the great staples from which is derived their national wealth."

"How surprising! What a different requisition this places us in to the whites. And are there really hopes of Africa becoming a great country, Colonel Montego?"

"Nay, Madame, not only 'hopes' but undoubted probabilities, and that too at no distant day. The foundation of all great nationalities depends as a basis upon three elementary principles: first, territorial domain; second, population; third, staple commodities as a source of national wealth. The territory must be extensive, population numerous, and the staple such as the world requires and must have; and if the productions be not natural, they must be artificial. This will be seen in the case of Great Britain, which being but a small island, extended her dominions by conquest, thus adding an immense population, and taking advantage of her coal, established manufactories to supply the world with fabrics, in addition to her natural mineral productions, also made available by art. Africa, to the contrary, has five thousand miles of latitude, and four thousand longitude, with two hundred millions of homogenous population, all of whom readily assimilate themselves to civilized customs, and their continent, as shown before, producing the greatest staples of wealth to the world. Do you now understand it, Madame Cordora?" [36]

"Indeed I do, Señor Placido; and although I thought I had no prejudices, I never before felt as proud of my black as I did of my white blood. I can readily see that the blacks compose an important element in the commercial and social relations of the world. Thank God for even this night's demonstrations, if we do no more. How sensibly I feel, that a people never entertain proper opinions of themselves until they begin to act for themselves."

"This is true, Madame," added Placido, "and I might call your attention further to the fact that by a comparison of the races, you may find the Africans in all parts of the world, readily and willingly mingling among and adopting all the usages of civilized life, attaining wherever practicable, every position in society, while those of the others, except the Caucasians, seldom acquire any but their own native usages."

"And these are really the people declared by American Laws, to 'have no rights that a white is bound to respect'? Why have we so long submitted to them?" said the Madame with a burst of indignation, taking her seat amidst demonstrations of intense emotion.

"It is indeed a sad reflection," said Blake, "to contrast the difference between British and American jurisprudence. How sublime the spectacle of the colossal stature (compared with the puppet figure of the Judge of the American Supreme Court), of the Lord Chief Justice when standing up declaring to the effect: that by the force of British intelligence, the purity of their morals, the splendor of their magnanimity, and aegis of the Magna Charta, the moment the foot of a slave touched British soil, he stood erect, disenthralled in the dignity of a freeman, by the irresistable genius of universal emancipation."[37]

"Let us then," said Placido, "make ourselves respected."

"So far as Cuba is concerned, we are here for that purpose," replied Blake.

"And if we say it shall, it will be so!" added Madame Cordora.

"Then it shall be so!" declared Blake.

"Then," concluded the Madame, "it will be so!" when the Council closed its grand and important session of several hours, to meet again at the residence of Carolus Blacus, father of Blake the leader of the great movement.

CHAPTER 62
Fearful Misgivings

In the fullness of enjoyment at the Palace of the Queen's nativity, the celebration continued the entire evening, only ceasing with the ushering in of a most delightful morning.

It was not until sometime subsequent to supper in the servant's hall during the fete, that the absence of a number of domestics employed about the palace was discovered, especially the head of the cuisine, Gofer Gondolier. This favorite servant on all previous occasions when others failed, was usually chosen to supply the place of some absent musician, in which his skill on the Spanish guitar, or African bango, especially the latter instrument, in which he had few, if any equals, was fully put to the test. He was a special favorite of the Lady Alcora, who preferred his execution to any other person. In consequence of

the absence of nearly all of the amateur musicians, the presence of
Gofer had been particularly desirable.

As an outfit for the evening, an undress military suit from the
wardrobe of the Captain General, selected by his own hands, was
intended by the Countess to be presented to Gondolier.

On commanding to the presence that evening the caterer of the
palace, her ladyship was told that he was not to be found.

"Are you certain of this?" asked the Countess.

"I is, your 'adyship; case I looked—I hunted 'im good."

"Did you enquire of the butler?"

"No ma'm you ladyship, I didn't."

"Why, Hober, did you not do so?" enquired Lady Alcora.

"Case twarnt no use."

"How do you know when you did not enquire?"

"Case dare's a big party at Madame Cordora's in P——s street
tonight, an' Gofer's gone at it."

"At Madame Cordora's! Are you certain?"

"Yes, ma'm, I is," definitely replied he.

"I see," impatiently murmured the Countess to herself, having
ordered the servant away, "this explains the whole matter. And even
Gofer must be taken off to play for them! Indeed, things are fast
changing, when not only are the blacks preferred to the whites, but
even the civilities of the palace are slighted and its domestic offices
neglected, and that too by a class wholly dependent upon and existing
by the sufferance of the whites and clemency of the government. Tell
me, Hober," she further enquired as the servant re-entered the
apartment, "did you hear Gofer say that he was going to the Cordora
mansion?"

"Yes ma'm you ladyship."

"What for; a party did he say?"

"Yes ma'm you ladyship, but dat am not what 'im call 'im."

"What was it then?"

"It am somethin like 'sorry,' or sich name like dat."

"Ah, soiree!" explained the lady.

"Yes, you ladyship, dat am it."

"Ah, holding a domestic council, Lady Alcora?" playfully asked the
Captain General, who had just entered.

"No, your excellency; not holding a domestic council, though counseling with a domestic. But I very much fear, if all that's told be true, that if not already so, 'domestic councils' may become a reality in the colony," seriously replied the Countess.

"Please explain, Lady Alcora, as I do not comprehend you!" anxiously asked the Count.

"Why your lordship, it would seem that tonight, there is being held a great soiree at the fine mansion of Madame Cordora, the wealthy widow mulatress, where doubtless a grand scheme will be disclosed for a general rebellion of the Negroes."

"Can't be possible!" exclaimed the Captain General. "Where in the world did you learn this?"

"From our servant here, Hober."

"How could he know these things! I'm sure it would be very difficult for him to learn them," replied the Count.

"You are mistaken, Count Alcora, as he learned them among our servants, several of whom taking advantage of the fete tonight have gone there; among them our caterer, Gofer Gondolier, the chief of the cuisine," explained the Countess.

"Are you certain of this, Lady Alcora?"

"I am."

"Probably he only went for a short time as caterer, or carried some little notion of his own preparation."

"No seh, 'e didn'; w'en 'e goed, 'e took wid 'im 'is big new carvin' knife. I seed 'im and hearn 'im say 'e goin' to use it on de wite folks, too," interrupted Hober in explanation.

"Say that over again, Hober; let the Count hear you!" said the Countess.

"I distinctly understood him," replied the Count; "but regard it as merely a freak of vanity to show himself by exhibiting among the Negroes evidence of his ingenuity by showing his invention; and an idle boast about using it on the whites would not be out of place to swell his importance."

"I am fearful that you attach too little importance to this matter, Count Alcora, and could I without committing myself to ridicule do so, I would like to reveal a singular dream to you."

"Well, my lady," humorously said the Count, "as there are many revelations which I am incapable of comprehending, I shall make no objection to recording yours on the catalogue. Pray tell me, what is your revelation?"

"It is the more singular, as I know of no external cause for it," replied the Countess.

"Do let me hear it quickly!" playfully continued the Count, "as you have excited my organ of wonder."

"I dreamed," related the Countess, "of being in the interior of Africa surrounded entirely by Negroes, under the rule of a Negro prince, beset by the ambassadors of every enlightened nation, who brought him many presents of great value, whilst the envoy of Her Catholic Majesty sat quietly at the foot of the African Prince's throne. I cannot get this impression from my mind, it seems so indelibly fixed."

"Having had the revelation," with ludicrous seriousness said the Count, "now to a comprehensive interpretation of it. By your permission I will give it to you, Countess Alcora. It simply means that we shall have in Cuba several large cargoes of choice Negroes from Africa, out which your new plantation is to be stocked and when seated upon it in your new villa, very likely among them will be some Negro prince, catering to your orders. I take no fee for the interpretation."

"Count Alcora! I crave your clemency," impatiently replied his lady, "when I say to you, that as the executive, you set too little estimate upon what seems to be important. I have had another presentiment: this is no dream but a wakeful reality."

"What is it my lady? I am anxious to hear."

"Why, that the Negroes of Cuba are maturing a scheme of general insurrection!"

"How so? Why just now this conjecture, Countess Alcora? Will you let the idle vanity of an elated Negro cook frighten you out of your wits? I am really astonished at you, Countess. Tush!" rebuked the Count.

"No, Count Alcora, it is not this but something antecedent from which I draw my conclusions," replied the Countess.

"Have you discovered anything? Pray do tell me if so, and let us be done with this unpleasant dreamy conversation," said the Captain General.

"I have, and I would that I could make the same influence on your mind concerning them, that the things which I saw made on mine."

"What were they, Lady Alcora?" now seriously enquired the Count.

"I'm sure I shall fully appreciate any advice you may be pleased to communicate."

"I thank your excellency. I shall freely relate to you the facts. Today while at the amphitheatre exhibition, I observed on the part of the colored officers of the day—those in your confidence—a recognizance of the common Negroes and mulattoes in the pavillion; and on the parade ground in the sports of the Negro chase, so soon as that part of the amusements were announced, I saw an immediate change not only in the countenances, but the conduct of all the Negroes and mulattoes present. And never before had I witnessed anything indicative of insubordination as their manner, when the chase was ordered and the hounds let loose in chase of the Negro prizes. Even Colonel Montego, one of your aids mounted on horseback near your side when the word was given, 'let go the dogs!' involuntarily started a pace forward, pressing his teeth upon his lip, and placing his hand on the hilt of his sword for a moment, looked a rage of vengeance at the whites."

"Do you tell me this," exclaimed the Count with alarm.

"This is not all, Count Alcora," continued the lady. "Intensely watching with a steady countenance the chase of the dogs, when a Negro was caught and uttered a scream of agony; just as the shout of applause from the multitude rent the air—involuntarily drawing his sword partly from the scabbord, with a suppressed voice, though full in my hearing, exclaimed: 'by the Holy Virgin, 'tis too bad!' gritting his teeth till they chattered. Recollecting himself and adjusting his sword, turning to me he dissemblingly remarked—'a well executed chase Lady Alcora; very well done! Fine animals, those dogs!' But I had seen and heard all, and determined to advise you of it."

"Thank you, thank you, my dear Charlotte. I have found you in more than one instance a valuable adviser. I shall hereafter modify my actions by your counsels. Let us repair to the drawings rooms," said the Captain General, supporting his lady on the left arm.

Previous to returning to the drawing rooms, precaution was taken to dispatch a servant spy to the mansion of Madame Cordora, to reconnoiter the premises, and if possible discover the true state of affairs. On nearing he observed a universal stir and passing to and from the mansion into the beautiful enclosure and shrubbery. To facilitate his errand, the spy attempted an entrance by a narrow court back way, but found it obstructed by Negroes on guard some distance from the gate in among the shrubbery, who approaching, in a gruff manner, demanded his errand.

"I is got a message from de Captin Genal an' de Countess, for Madame Cordora, an' I wants to see 'er," replied the domestic.

"She's engaged and can't be seen!" impatiently replied the guardian black, seeming to anticipate the message.

"I mus' see 'er, case de Captin Genal tole me!" insisted the palace messenger.

"Curse the Captain General and his message!" was the imprudent retort. "Be off, you can't see her!"

Hastening to the palace, the eager domestic related with compound addition to the governor and lady, all that he had seen and heard.

Becoming by these startling facts seriously impressed, the dawn of the morning induced the numerous guests to leave the palace to the quiet contemplation of the distinguished inmates, whose troubled souls now sought solace in the refreshing slumbers of retirement.

CHAPTER 63

The Captain General and Lady

"Indeed," said the Captain General, pacing the floor with hands locked behind him, "I cannot, my dear, dismiss from my thoughts last evening's surprise. I have been anxiously meditating upon the whole thing, and scarcely know what course is best to pursue towards the rebels."

"Let me suggest to your excellence, I pray you, not use the word 'rebel,' " said the Countess. "Whatever my apprehensions I would not have you take it for granted, and anticipate that which has no reality. I would make no issue where there is no occasion for it, but first ascertain the true state of the case, and then act with decision, and if need be promptness and vigor."

"Thank you for the advice; but what better evidence could I desire than that already obtained? It does appear to me that it is a plain case. However, in my course I'll be governed by your opinion."

"Not at all, Count Alcora; I would not in the least control you, but only desire to prompt your memory."

"But I solicit your opinion, Lady Alcora, and will not be content without it. I pray you therefore, speak freely to me!"

"I have said," resumed the Countess, "be cautious of the word 'rebel.' Let us take a common sense view of the case, and first enquire whether there was on the occasion an entertainment at the mansion of Madame Cordora; its character, and how far it will verify the report and implicate them in the crime of rebellion."

"You think then there is no cause for suspicion?"

"That is not the idea, General Alcora. We should first carefully investigate, and nor form hasty conclusions. And for the credit of the colony and your administration, let us not rest so grave a charge as 'rebellion' on so light a testimony as that of the stammering jargon of a slave. Madame Cordora and associates are persons of reputation and affluence in the community, and cruel would it be to arraign them on the evidence of an envious Negro servant. Besides, rumor has it that the poet Placido is betrothed to her daughter, the beautiful Ambrosina, and it might have been a celebration of the nuptials. Whether or not the circumstances justify investigation——"

"How, my lady," pointedly enquired the Captain General, "will you account for your dreams and presentiments?"

"That, your excellency," she quickly rejoined, "is of minor consideration. Having once had your interpretation of them, I consider that case disposed of."

"Well, your counsel is ever the same—judicious and available, Lady Alcora," concluded the Captain General.

Thus he affected to be satisfied, but in such an emergency Count Alcora was not the man to remain passive, especially at the hazard of his government. Whilst seeming to be satisfied, he set immediately industriously at work using every covert means in his power, not only to ferret out, but with a determination to implicate if possible some of the suspected parties; the first effort being to entrap by stratagem on his return, the head of the culinary department, Gofer Gondolier.

They could not be reconciled to the disappointment met with by the noncompliance of many of the guests supposed to be at the Cordora mansion, with the invitation to the Palace fete. The Captain General had long suspected something wrong among this portion of the population, and with the facts before him, must have some victim as a peace offering to appease his vengeance.

His domestic had eluded his vigilance, misled his confidence, baffled his intelligence, and betrayed his trust, and who if not made an example of, was evidently destined to become if not the leader, an agent of a dire mischief throughout the island. It was clear to him that his Negro was one of the promoters of a bold design to wrest from Spain the Island of Cuba, and instead of a Castilian, establish a Negro government. This was the shock which electrified every nerve and dormant fiber of his system; the stimulant which exciting him to frenzy, induced him to neutralize every agency in the fearfully approaching issue, as far as it could be known; and Gofer was the only offender known to his excellency.

Despite the admonitions of the Countess, the Captain General summoned before him his faithful servant and spy, Hober, to repeat the whole story as previously related, touching the conduct of the culinarian at the soiree of Madame Cordora, the wealthy mulatto.

Promptly obeying the orders of his master, the but too willing servant tremblingly stood before him.

"I is ready, Count, to tell you anything, dat I thinks will please you lordship," obsequiously bowing, proffered the debased slave.

The Countess gave a significant smile, whilst the Captain General looked seriously rebuked.

The story of the slave was concise and piquant, and absorbed for five minutes or more the breathless attention of the master. Whilst secreted in the shrubbery of the palace grounds, he overheard the conversation of Gondolier and several other servants previous to their going to the soiree. Gofer was to obtain at the instance of the Countess, the privilege of introducing into general use his patent Cuban carver, to give to every black the opportunity of having in their possession a formidable deadly weapon, without the violation of law, suspicion, or even objection of the whites. In the general rebellion that was to ensue, firearms at the commencement were to be prohibited, as the slaughter which was to commence in the dead of night could be prosecuted with silence, and thereby prevent a premature alarm.

"Now, Hober, my man, tell me, like a good fellow, all you know about this thing—keep nothing back," said the Captain General with emphasis, anxious and determined to criminate some persons.

"Wy, yo' lordship, da is to begin soon!"

"When? Speak out, my man, speak out!"

"Da is all to begin on one night!"

"How, my man? Let us hear all about it."

"Da is all to be hid, in an' out o' doors, one black for every white in each house on all de plantations, an' all at once at de same time, each one is to seize a white and slaughter 'im."

"Immaculate Madonna, hear that! Go on, my man, go on!" impatiently exclaimed the governor.

"Ag'in daylight, da ain't one white to be left alive. In di same way dat de whites is all to be seized, one for each, da is to have one to set fire to each house in all de towns at da same time, an' every white dat makes 'is escape is to be ketched an' killed as 'e runs into de country to escape de fire!"

To all this did the Captain General sit and listen with an eager ear, till his emotions nearly equalled those of the guilty monarch, manifested at the interpretation by the Jewish captive of the blazing inscription upon the walls of Babylon.

Just as the servant concluded, the Count was startled by a sudden interruption, which presented in the person of the Countess.

"Do I intrude, your excellency?" she enquired, slowly approaching.

"No, my lady! I have just been giving some order to the servant," replied he with an uncontrollable sigh.

"Are you indisposed, Count Alcora? I'm sure you look worn," said his lady.

"Nothing more, my dear, than fatigue from the loss of sleep last evening," replied the Count with a conciliatory tone.

"We are summoned to coffee. Come, let us walk!" said the Countess taking his arm, who with pallid cheek and somewhat faltering step—the servant in the lead—supported her to the coffee table.

CHAPTER 64

The Confrontment

And is he gone?—Byron

Early that morning as usual, Gofer Gondolier was found in the cuisine department. Mild, affable, pleasant, and cheerful, he went about his duties, as though the past evening his rest had not been taxed in the expension of a night, certainly to him, the most eventful in the political record of history.

After the family had been seated, as was his custom to walk to the door and take a peep into the ordinary, this morning there was no delinquency.

When the Countess turned her face in the direction of the door, with his accustomed politeness, Gofer quite raised from his head the black silk slouch cap which he wore, bowing with that civility becoming his position, and due the distinguished personage in whose presence he then was.

There was observed in the countenance of the Captain General a slight emotion, but with decided effect he managed to suppress it, and looked at Gofer with a smile, such as he had never before witnessed from that personage, which gave him an impression such as he had never experienced. Stepping backwards he bowed himself out of the noble presence.

Shortly after repast, before executing his design, the Count deemed it advisable to acquaint the Countess of his intended course toward the caterer.

To this she decidedly objected as impolitic and unwarrantable, which, from its rashness, tended to thwart his designs. She suggested instead, that nothing should be done or said until the application made to her by Gondolier for the license of a general use of the carving knives, which might give the occasion and pretext for an accusation against him.

To this Count Alcora readily assented, and reclining for a rest, the Countess immediately left his presence.

Scarcely had she emerged from the chamber when Hober entered, bearing the intelligence that Gofer was preparing to leave the palace. Startled with emotion she quickly imparted it to the Count.

Fearing corruption among the rest of the servants, it was thought advisable to dismiss him at once, which having been done, in less than half an hour the faithful Gondolier was lost—as doubtless the Captain General hoped forever—among the transient inhabitants of the busy thoroughfares of the city.

It was but a short time, however, till the Countess had good reason to believe that the story against Gofer was a base fabrication, originated through jealousy by their own slave Hober, who, envying the position of the free black, designed to succeed him in the cuisine department.

This fact went far in changing the feelings of the governor toward him, and reduced in his opinion the felon and rebel to a mere peccadillo offender.

CHAPTER 65

What of the Negroes?

After leaving the palace, making the most of his time, sauntering through the streets, vacantly gazing at almost every person and thing, Gofer Gondolier continued wandering till evening caught him far up in the city. His first impulse was, in consequences of the restrictions, to hasten back in search of lodgings, but being directly in front of a large and fashionable "restaurateur" thronged with white men in the full enjoyment of an evening's pleasure; stopping to look in at the windows, he thus reflected, "Freedom should ever be potent to repeal and annul the decrees of oppression, and repel the oppressor. The instant a person is claimed as a slave, that moment he should strike down the claimant. The natural rights of man are the faculties of option, heaven bequeathed, and endowed by God, our common Father, as essential to our being, which alone distinguish us from the brute. The authority of the slaveholder ceases the moment that the impulse of the slave demands his freedom, and by virtue of this divine attribute, every black is as free as the whites in Cuba, and I will resist this night, and henceforth every attempt at infringement on my inherent privileges." Acting upon these promptings, Gofer left the front of the restaurateur, continuing his rambling through the town.

This evening Blake and Placido had several appointments in different parts of the city, one of which was at the residence of Andro Camino. Looking at his watch, Placido with a smile observed:

"As our time is limited we had better go!"

Though said as a jest, the emphasis with which it was expressed was full of meaning. They immediately left the house.

According to an ordinance of the city, at the firing of the great gun at Moro Castle at nine o'clock in the evening, every Negro and mulatto was compelled to be within doors, or if caught out fifteen minutes after, to be imprisoned in the calaboose until the sitting of the police court at ten o'clock next morning, subjected to a fine or whipping according to the decision of the magistrate.

In the enforcement of this ordinance, there were some exceptions made at the discretion of the police who arrested or persons who tried the case. The wealthy, professional, and literary classes among them were usually shown favors by the officers of the law, in consequence of their influence over the Captain General.

But subsequently to the demonstrations of the Grand Negro Councils, these ordinances were violated and set at defiance by Negroes and mulattoes of all grades and classes, with impunity, passing at all times and places.

Leaving the residence of the newly appointed Quartermaster General Blacus, father of the Chief, where for a short time business had called them, they took the nearest way to reach the upper part of the Almeda, the great fashionable thoroughfare of the city.

Leisurely promenading among the moving mass, deeply engaged in conversation on the momentous subject of their political and social condition as a race, and position in community as a class, at the instant when Placido named the injustice and despotism of the city ordinances toward them, the great gun fired its evening alarm.

The grim howl of this municipal watchdog had scarcely ceased growling in the air, when two Irish gendarmes came hurriedly up to them saying, "An' who do yez e'long to?" when Blake and Placido, looking first at each other, then at the Irishmen, uttered not a word.

Mistaking their silence as an evidence of guilt and fear, "Faith," continued one of them, "an' sure yeh ain't no pass, an' must go to de calaboose! An' sure nagurs hain't no business out fornint de firin o' de gun. Come along wid us to de guard house, an' sure yez'll be well taken care of!" each taking hold of one of the party.

As the policemen laid hands upon them, a blow in quick succession from a powerful unknown source, struck down their arms in paralyzed suspension at their sides.

At his timely and unexpected inference, Blake and Placido were not less surprised than the affrighted gendarmes themselves. On turning to discover the perpetrator, to their surprise, Gofer Gondolier with clenched fists in the attitude of defence, stood gritting his teeth behind them. Somewhat recovering, and recognizing the person of their assailant—

"Och, jabers! An' he b'longs to de palace!" cried one.

"He is dat same! An' is'nt it mese'f dat knows 'im well? Troth boys, an' we'll not be afther hurthen ov yez! An' sure yez'll be afther taken a bit uv a joke!" concluded the other, to which Gondolier made no reply. "Good night gentlemans, good night!" saluted the Irishmen as the party left.

Gondolier indeed was well and popularly known to the police and keepers of the public houses, many of the latter being greatly indebted to him as the chief caterer at the palace, for their knowledge of some of their most choice dishes which filled their daily bills of fare. His position, together with this, gave him a license throughout the city which probably no other black enjoyed. He was accustomed to pass at all times and hours of the night, in every part of the city, without hindrance or molestation. His presence was thus most timely, and of the greatest importance to the two black officers.

CHAPTER 66

Chit-Chat

In the midst of revolutionary movements, there are sometimes the solutions worked out of other problems than that of the political destiny of a people. It was so in the present issue.

The frequent coming together in general council formed attachments, doubtless, but little thought of previous to the occasion which induced their meeting. The consummation of conjugal union is the best security for political relations, and he who is incapable of negotiating to promote his own personal requirements might not be trustworthy as the agent of another's interest; and the fitness for individuals for positions of public import, may not be misjudged by their doings in the private affairs of life.

With the fullness of some such convictions, there were many billets-doux exchanged, arrangements made for a chit-chat or "tete a tete" between parties, on matters entirely separate from those touching the general welfare.

Of these, Gofer Gondolier became enamored of Abyssa Soudan, and General Juan Montego betrothed to Madame Cordora. So sincere were they in these obligations that the time for their fulfillment was set as early as the approaching Sabbath morning.

Among them, a great event was expected to ensue, when every step taken should have been well measured, timely, and in the right direction, tending in its course to the accomplishment of the great and desirable end to be attained.

The political relations of the colony were peculiar, and singularly mischievous and detrimental to the best interests of this class of inhabitants. The four great divisions of society were white, black, free and slave; and these were again subdivided into many other classes, as rich, poor, and such like. The free and slaves among the blacks did not associate, nor the high and low among the free of the same race. And there was among them even another general division—black and colored—which met with little favor from the intelligent.

The leading characters had long since observed all these social evils, and fully matured the scheme and policy for their remedy. Hence, the better to verify this policy, Montego communicated to Gondolier the design and intention of Madame Cordora and himself consummating at the same time at the same sacred hymeneal altar with him and Abyssa, the holy sacrament of the marriage feast.

This, as might have been expected, was received with great favor among the high and low classes, especially the slave portion of the black inhabitants, and their social relation was now regarded as a mutually fixed reality.

After this, many rumors obtained circulation with no little credence, that other hearts than those were mutually throbbing, and other hands than theirs were intended to be joined in a pledge of union forever.

CHAPTER 67

False Alarm

On Saturday morning after the encounter of Gondolier with the gendarmes, a report spread rapidly that an unsuccessful attempt of the

Negroes at insurrection had been quelled on the evening of the Queen's nativity by the decisive and timely action of the National Guards. One white was said to have been killed; another mortally, a third and fourth seriously wounded.

The gendarmes who had cowered before the stout arm of Gondolier, determining to be avenged for his temerity and daring, gave credence to the rumor to excite the prejudice of the whites against the blacks.

This day the troops marched to and fro the city, and out of ranks freely mingled among the people, designedly to keep them in awe. On the corner of every street and byway could be seen in crowds, the white inhabitants standing discussing most earnestly the topic of the day. By noon there was much sensation, and against the middle of the afternoon the excitement became so general and intense that it was with eminent peril that any free black could pass along the public highways.

Although the Mayor had full authority over the matter to prevent a popular outbreak, the Captain General was compelled to interfere by summoning the parties to appear forthwith before his excellency in the fort of Moro Castle. This had a tendency to appease and to some extent allay the excitement to await the result of an investigation.

As the viceroy rode through the streets, the people followed in crowds around him, and only stopped from necessity at the Castle gates, standing on the quay during the investigation.

The two gendarmes were the first called to answer to their names, and who took their places on the stand with assurance of a verdict against the Negroes. Having laid complaint before the chief of police, their affidavits had been filed for future reference, which unexpectedly to them was brought in comparison with the charge now made before the governor.

By this there was too much discrepancy to justify a verdict for the plaintiff, the gendarmes being unable to identify the criminal, though they insisted that two white men had been attacked, and felled to the ground by a Negro desperado.

The case after a strictly summary hearing was finally dismissed by the Captain General, who ordered the discharge of the complainants from office, and the story of the insurrection to be contradicted, as a base fabrication got up at the instance of two profligate gendarmes.

From circumstances transpiring but a day or two before at the palace, the Captain General had his own opinion of the matter, but unsustained as it was even by their own testimony, he deemed it advisable at such a time to decide as he did.

The difficulty now having been adjusted, and the inhabitants again quieted, the Negroes were permitted to pass through the streets without molestation or unusual attraction.

Taking advantage of this brief respite, and determined to make the most of the time, invitations to the friends of the parties were immediately sent to attend the marriage ceremonies of Montego and Madame Cordora, Gondolier and Abyssa Soudan—at the earliest dawn on Sabbath morning at the church of the Ascension, to be celebrated the next evening after at the house of Carolus Blacus.

Cheerfulness and high hopes once more impelled the progress of the black inhabitants, and in their esteem the name of Count Alcora stood first among the greatest of Cuban executives. Every little Negro learned to lisp his name, and the black stevedores at the seaside rung its praise in the packing of his cargoes. Even the old black matron as she sat under the verandah, sung a morning chant to the name of—

The Great Alcora,

whilst the old black invalid, basking in the sun, had not to cheer his hopes but—

God help de Captin General!

Congratulating themselves whenever they met through the day on the merciful escape they had, each for that evening retired to his home, though well advised, determined to profit by the opportunity offered them in the policy pursued by the highest authority in dismissing the trial for insurrection.

CHAPTER 68

Sunday Morning

Early this morning, before the peep of dawn, ere the great bell of St. Xavier had sounded the first knell of her loud summons to the altar of supplication, the wedding party, brides and bridegrooms, with numerous friends and attendants, might have been seen directing their course toward the church of the Ascension.

Scarcely could be seen at this early hour any others, save in different directions noted by their Franciscan caps and long white surplices, numerous visiting priests hastening to the various places for the performance of their official duties.

So dim was the faint inkling light which just began to dawn, that those sons of the holy order presented more the appearance of spectres than men; spectres disturbed from their resting place by a consciousness of wrongs done and left unrepented of while inhabiting their "earthly tenement." Doubtless were they such; for, professing death to the world, its cares and fleeting allurements, sensibly mindful were they of having "left undone" many things that they ought to have done, whether or not they were fearfully conscious of "having done the things they ought not to have done."

Presently the darkness was dispelled by that soft and mellow light peculiar to a West India sky, which ushered in a beautiful cheerful morning. The priests, but faintly discovered before, could now be distinctly seen, and appeared rather impressive at so early an hour in the morning.

"Behold the men of God!" reverently whispered Abyssa.

"Who made them men of God?" sarcastically asked Montego.

"Are they not God-fearing men?" innocently inquired the simple, religious African.

"To be 'God-fearing' is to do the will of God," continued he, "and these men have neglected the letter of the law 'Whatsoever ye would that men should do unto you, do ye even so unto them.' These are the words of His divine injunction, every letter of which these men have neglected either to carry out themselves or to enforce. They are, in the stern language of the holy prophet, 'dumb dogs and will not bark.' Were they not, there never would have been occasion for the

279

gathering, organization of the Council, nor such a meeting as we must have tomorrow evening at General Blacus' residence."

"Then they can't marry us!" replied Abyssa, which provoked a general merriment from the company.

In this general good humor Gondolier heartily joined, and nodding his head significantly to one side, observed that it was the only good thing he believed they did do, and thought that the blacks might try them that time. The merriment was long continued.

Montego explained to Abyssa that the acts of the priests in performance of the marriage ceremony were right, because done in accordance with the law of God, and acknowledged by the laws of the land, but not more sacred than if performed by a civil magistrate, or any other person set apart by law for such purpose. He preferred the priests for the simple reason that he thought them better men than the magistrates. Hastening on they entered the church at a very early hour.

On entering, the vestibule was dark, and had not the numerous variegated tapers emitted from the farthest extremity their scintillating rays to the center, the body of the building itself must have been equally gloomy.

Slowly and solemnly did they advance till directly in front of the altar, where a silly looking adult vestry attendant standing with half-open mouth, by motion and gesture admonished them that the place whereunto they approached was a sacred spot.

Stopping directly in front of a massive golden flesh-colored lifelike statue representing the Savior of the world, upon either side of which was suspended a malefactor in supplication; they bowed in the name of the Eternal Three. Still looking upon the truthful picture of a skillful hand—the delineations of the well-developed muscles of trunk and extremities; the stern and ghastly, though mild, pitying, and forgiving expression of the face—a mouth which she almost imagined she could see and hear bid her sorrows cease—in the fullness of native goodness and simplicity of African devotion, no longer able to restrain her feelings, falling upon her knees before the altar, clapping her outstretched hands, with face upturned toward heaven, Abyssa cried out:

"Glory to God!"

At this moment a body of twelve priests arrayed in robes imposing, accompanied by numerous attendants bearing in their hands many colored lighted candles, entered, the leading divine saying:

"Arise my child from grief to joy! The first miracle wrought by our blessed Savior was on an occasion of this nature; a marriage feast in Cana of Galilee. Be not sorrowful then but rejoice and be exceeding glad, for where Christ is"—pointing to the crucifix before her—"there is no sorrow."

"Thank God!" responded Abyssa, when the right hand of the simpleton instinctively was lifted to enjoin silence in the house of God and presence of the holy order, as he stood with gaping mouth, holding in his left hand a burning wax candle.

The ceremony was short, pointed and impressive, relating mainly to religious duties and a preference for the Roman Catholic church, concluded by the placing of a plain gold ring on the forefinger of the right hand of each of the brides.

"This ring which I place on your finger," said the priest, "is a type of our holy religion; in substance as pure as the incorruptible gold; in character like him"—again pointing to the crucifix—"who propagated it, it must endure forever. Here you see a cross surmounted by a ring"—holding up a Maltese cross in the centre of a ring—"which is steadfast in its position, as you see the cross on our spires. But not so with other religious denominations. Upon their churches you behold a weathercock which turns every way the wind blows. This shows that there is nothing steadfast in their professions, they changing whenever it suits them. I pronounce you man and wife in the name of the Immaculate Conception."

It was surmised that the rings supplied were obtained from a stock in trade kept for the purpose in the church, as at the conclusion of the ceremony the gaping simpleton hinted by the summons of his beckon that there was yet another duty to be attended to; when Placido and Castino, following the priests in the vestry, returned three doubloons each less in their pockets.

On his fact becoming known to the married party as they retired through the aisle, Gondolier observed in a whisper:

"These 'men of God' make most ungodly charges for their services; a doubloon apiece for the two little gold rings the ladies got."

The remarks were fully appreciated and equally enjoyed. When the party emerged into the streets, it seemed as if all the beauty and fashion of each race were crowding the streets, en masse, making their way instead of to the Cathedral, the head of the See, the church of the Ascension appearing to be their aim.

Jet, topaz, and lily colored maidens, graceful and comely, the pictures of innocence and virgin purity, majestic and stately matrons, grave and dignified men, as well as children, composed the mighty throng, but by far the fewest of them being the whites. This fact elicited general observation.

"Singular," remarked Montego, "that there should be this morning such a large number of the blacks out, and comparatively so few of the whites."

"Enough of them," replied Gondolier, "to watch over us and keep us in our place. These few came out as our masters and overseers."

"But seriously," enquired Madame Montego, "I have always observed it. Why so many more of our people than the whites attend church?"

"Because," replied Placido, "we are really more religiously inclined than they."

"I have also often wondered why it was that we are so much more submissive than they," resumed Madame Montego.

"Let us for the present defer this discussion," prudentially admonished Placido, "and resume it on tomorrow evening at the quartermaster's residence."

CHAPTER 69

Entertainment at Carolus Blacus

Monday was another day of promise to the oppressed race of Cuba. For although there was on this occasion no general public demonstration, yet so completely were they organised, and systematic their plans, that whatever might be going on among them in Matanzas those in Havana were conversant with it, and that which might take place in Havana was at once known to those of Matanzas, Principe, Trinidad and St. Jago de Cuba, Fernandina and every part of the colony.

Many who visited the city from a distance on the occasion of the

Queen's nativity, having entered the seclusion and received commissions in the Council, went forth to establish confidence in all parts of the island. Even Louis Chevaro, of Principe, was one of the foremost of these.

Early in the evening they began to gather, which occasion was unlike that of the soiree at Madame Cordora's, where many being unacquainted, doubts and fears prevailed, not only for their fidelity to each other, but also of their acceptance on account of their humble social position as inferiors and domestics in society.

But to this they came under very different circumstances, having at the other been redeemed from the degradation of captivity, chosen among the self-reliant of their people, received into seclusion and acknowledged as equals in the Council.

The repast was simple, though substantial and wholesome, the warm table beverages being coffee and chocolate. The assembly was complete, every person being in his place, and of the whole sent out, not one invitation probably had been neglected. Among them there were cheerfulness and even gaiety, though solemnity and dignity prevailed.

At the appointed hour, a servant entered the drawing room announcing that the Council Chamber was in readiness, when Gondolier immediately arose following him into an off wing extending back the most distant from the street, which being so completely enveloped with closely clinging creepers and thickly studded shrubbery, that light could not be discerned from an uncurtained window; at the door of which he took a seat armed with a cutlass and his fearful Cuban carver. Shortly after the Council was in session.

"Preceding all great undertakings," said Blake, "Divine assistance should be invoked. Let us this night, as on former occasions, as the first step in so momentous an undertaking, ask the aid of heaven," when they immediately fell upon their knees with their heads bowed low to the floor, burying their faces in the palms of their hands.

In this position they remained in silent prayer for half an hour, when silence was broken by Abyssa Gondolier, the captive woman of Soudan, in the following unique supplication, which emanating from any other source could hardly be approved of:

"Make bare thine all conquering; uncover thy impenetrable shield;

sway thy matchless scepter; put our enemies to flight before Thee that not one have courage to stand, and at every stroke of the weapon may they fall as dead men before us! Look down we beseech Thee upon us, the least protected, by reason of our weakness, of Thy humble children. We have been captured, torn from friends and home, sold and scattered among strangers in a strange land; yea, to and fro the earth. Sorely oppressed, mocked and ridiculed, refused and denied a common humanity, and not even permitted to serve the same God at the same time and place, in the same way and manner as themselves. Change, O change, we beseech Thee, this state of things! Give us success in this, our most important undertaking and hour of trial, and enable us we beseech Thee to go forth and conquer even unto a mighty conquest!"

"Amen!" responded the Council in conclusion, rising to their seats.

Though simple in manner and language, and humble in source, yet so earnest and impressive was this prayer, that many of the principal persons present were moved with deep emotions of sympathy. Sensibly touched with the unexpected scenes around her, the simple, good-hearted Abyssa wept aloud, clasping her hands exclaiming—

"O Lord, look down on one of the least of these thy despised children, and protect her from harm!"

"Ef he don't I will!" exclaimed Gofer, her husband, who, until then, stood outside of the door, but now entered the room with his terrible weapon glittering in his hands, eyes flashing and teeth gnashing for vengeance on his oppressors.

"Thank God," said Blake, "for this prospect! It much reminds one of the singular days of miserable happiness spent at times while in bondage, agonizing together in our religious meetings in the huts of the slave quarters of Mississippi and other plantations. But bright as we at times, from our faith and dependence on God, then considered our prospects, there is here a much brighter and happier one in view. When faith and hope were our only dependence, expecting God to do everything for us, and we nothing for ourselves, now with the same faith and hope and dependence on God we have learned and know what He requires at our hands, and stand ready in obedience to this divine command to do it. Let us then, for God's sake, profit by this knowledge, self-reliance, with faith and dependence on God. What is now before the Council; God has been praised—what comes next?"

"Our policy is the first consideration," replied Placido.

"What is that policy?" inquired Blake.

"That is for the Council to determine," replied he.

"The rules laid down, whatever they may be, should be plain, simple, and at once comprehensible to every black person, however illiterate," said Blake.

"That's the idea at once expressed," sanctioned Placido with emphasis.

"Shall we not discuss the point raised returning from the church of the Ascension—the equality of the black and white races?" inquired Madame Montego.

"I cannot see the utility of it, Madame Montego," replied Placido.

"A useless expenditure of time, Madame, it would seem to me," added Blake. " 'Ethiopia shall yet stretch forth her hands unto God; Princes shall come out of Egypt'; 'Your God shall be my God, and your people my people,' should comprehend our whole policy."

"That's the word of God," said Placido.

"I'm sure God's word is His will," added the Madame.

"We would what God wills," responded Placido.

"Then let God's will be done," said Blake.

"A word from the President of the Council and Commander in Chief would be in place at this time in defining his own position and intended course of policy," suggested Montego.

"In the name of God, the cause of my brethren and suffering humanity," said Blake, rising to his feet in answer to the call, "I can only promise for the confidence and trust reposed in me, that guided and directed by Him in whom I have ever trusted, the will and desires of my head, the most elevated feeling of my heart, and the best-directed efforts of my hands shall ever be united in endeavors to carry out, as the humble representative of my race, every just measure which comes within the province of my duty."

The pithy speech ended, Placido, supported by Antonio Blacus, Justin Pampo, and six ladies, among whom were Ambrosina and Seraphina, also Julia Chevaro, the wife of the Principe quadroon planter; taking their stand on the orchestra prepared for the occasion at the extreme end of the drawing room, commenced in the most stirring strains the following ballad composed for the evening and event:

Yes; strike again that sounding string,
  And let the wildest numbers roll;
Thy song of fiercest passion sing,
  It breathes responsive to my soul!
A soul whose gentlest hours were nursed
  In stern adversity's dark way,
And o'er whose pathway never burst
  One gleam of hope's enlivening ray.

If thou wilt soothe my burning brain,
  Sing not to me of joy and gladness;
'Twill but increase the raging pain,
  And turn the fever into madness!
Sing not to me of landscapes bright,
  Of fragrant flowers and fruitful trees,
Of azure skies and mellow light,
  Or whisperings of the gentle breeze.

But tell me of the tempest roaring
  Across the angry foaming deep,
Of torrents from the mountains pouring
  Down precipices dark and deep.
Sing of the lightning's lurid flash,
  The ocean's roar, the howling storm,
The earthquake's shock, the thunder's crash,
  Where ghastly terrors teeming swarm.

Sing of the battle's deadly strife,
  The ruthless march of war and pillage;
The awful waste of human life,
  The plunder'd town, the burning village
Of streets with human gore made red,
  Of priests under the altar slain,
The scenes of rapine, woe and dread,
  That fill the warrior's horrid train.
Thy song may then an echo wake,
  Deep in this soul, long crush'd and sad,
The direful impressions shake,
  Which threaten now to drive me mad.

Again the whole assemblage bowed in silent devotion.

Their justification of the issue made was on the fundamental basis of original priority, claiming that the western world had been originally peopled and possessed by the Indians—a colored race—and a part of the continent in Central America by a pure black race. This they urged gave them an indisputable right with every admixture of blood, to an equal, if not superior, claim to an inheritance of the Western Hemisphere.

The colored races, they averred, were by nature adapted to the tropical regions of this part of the world as to all other similar climates, it being a scientific fact that they increased and progressed whilst the whites decreased and continually retrograded, their offspring becoming enervated and imbecile. These were facts worthy of consideration, which three hundred years had indisputably tested. The whites in these regions were there by intrusion, idle consumers subsisting by imposition; whilst the blacks, the legitimate inhabitants, were the industrious laborers and producers of the staple commodities and real wealth of these places. They had inherited those regions by birth, paid for the soil by toil, irrigated it with their sweat, enriched it with their blood, nothing remaining to be done but by a dependence in Divine aid, a reliance in their own ability, and strength of their own arms, but to claim and take possession.

"On this island," said Blake, "we are the many and the oppressors few; consequently, they have no moral right to hold rule over us, whilst we have the moral right and physical power to prevent them. Whatever we determine shall be, will be. What say you, brethren, shall we rise against our oppressors and strike for liberty, or will we remain in degradation and bondage, entailing upon unborn millions of our progeny the insufferable miseries which our fathers endured and bequeathed to us?"

"Liberty! Liberty or death!" was the frantic response of every voice.

"Then," concluded he, "freedom is ours!"

The manifestations succeeding this conclusion were indescribable and such only as an abjectly oppressed and degraded people determined to be free were capable of giving. Applause, shouts, cheers, sighs, heaves, groans, and tears, all with intense feelings of restraint, were there exhibited. They looked each other in the face, then at their Chief, wringing their finger ends and pressing the palms of their hands.

"Arm of the Lord awake!" cried some.

"Glory to God!" cried others.

Their course henceforth being decided on, they determined that nothing should daunt their courage nor obstruct their way.

"What hope of assistance have we from our sister islands?" inquired Madame Montego.

"None at all," replied Placido.

"Nothing from the British colonies, all of which are free?"

"Not any. Because although our brethren there are all free and equal in the law, yet they are a constituent part of the body politic, and subject alike to the British government and laws which forbid any interference in foreign affairs by any of her Majesty's subjects."

"Are not our people the most numerous part of the population of these islands?"

"They are."

"Why then do they not at once rise up and assert their independence?" continued Madame Montego.

"Simply because under the circumstances, this is not particularly desirable, if they were able to do so, which they are not. What they most desire is freedom and equality politically, practically carried out, having no objection to being an elementary part of the British body politic."

"This I can fully comprehend—it is plain," replied the Madame, "but why should we who also owe allegiance to our mother-country, Spain, be more justifiable than they in striking for liberty and independence?"

"The cases are entirely different," explained Placido. "The British islands have all been fully enfranchised by that nation, all the inhabitants being equally eligible to positions: whilst here in Cuba we are the political and social inferiors of the whites, existing as freemen only by suffrance, and subject to enslavement at any time."[38]

"Is there no remedy for these evils?"

"We have petitioned and prayed for a redress of grievances, and not only been refused but spurned and ridiculed with greater restrictions placed upon us. And bad as things were before, since the advent of these Americans in the colony, our people have scarcely an hour of peaceful existence. Should we under such circumstances strike for liberty, it must also be for independent self-government, because we have the prejudices of the mother-country and the white colonists alike to contend against. Whereas, were we, as we should be, enfranchised by Spain we would then only have the opposition of Cuba and Porto Rico, and should be loyal to Spain."

"This is all very plain, Señor Placido. One question more and I shall be satisfied," said the Madame. "What aid may we expect from Hayti—she is independent?"

"Hayti is a noble self-emancipated nation, but not able to aid us, excepting to give such of us shelter, as might find it necessary or convenient to go there."

"What of Liberia?" enquired Maggie Blake. "I'm sure while living in Mississippi I heard a great deal about the greatness of Liberia. When I went north, I often heard the white folks say it was the greatest country in the world; that the Negroes were better off there than the whites were in America."

"They are too weak, and too far off, dear Maggie, to render us any aid at present, though making praiseworthy efforts to develop their own nationality, and the staple products of their native Africa. The whites did not believe what they said, nor even what is really true concerning the advantages of that country."[39]

"Brethren," said Blake, "you must 'tread the winepress alone' so far as earthly aid is concerned, only looking above to Him who 'tempers the storm to the shorn lamb' and directs the destiny of nations."

"God's will be done!" responded Montego.

"Amen!" added the woman of Soudan.

"Let us then," replied Placido impromptu,

On God and our own strength rely,
And dare be faithful though we die;
But trusting in the aid of Heaven,
    And willing with unfaltering arm,
The utmost power which God has given—
Conscious that the Almighty power
    Will nerve the faithful soul with might,
Whatever storms around may lower,
    Who boldly strikes for the true and right.

They closed this most portentous gathering with the doxology of "Gloria in excelsis," and "Praise God from whom all blessings flow."

CHAPTER 70

Momentous Step

The time for this important gathering was chosen on the auspicious occasion of the day of Special Indulgence granted by the Bishops to the colonists, and set apart as a general holiday, which presented another favorable opportunity for bringing together many of the Negroes and mulattoes from a distance to the metropolis.

The place of meeting was, as before, the residence of Madame Montego, the Cordora mansion, the attendance being general and full. Solemnly they sat in their places, with anxiety depicted in every countenance, not a whisper being heard among them.

"What is the order of the evening?" enquired the Chief on taking his seat, who was the first to break silence.

"We should like to have an expression from each member of the seclusion, and cannot have a more acceptable precedent than that of the Chief himself," replied Placido.

"I have but little to say," said Blake, rising. "You know my errand among you; you know my sentiments. I am for war—war upon the whites. 'I come to bring deliverance to the captive and freedom to the bond.' Your destiny is my destiny; the end of one will be the end of all. On last Sabbath, a day of rest, joy and gladness to the whites, I was solemnly and sadly impressed with our wretched condition. While passing through the great cemetery amidst the busy throng of smiling faces and anxious countenances of the whites; the soul-impressing odors of the flowers and inspiring song of birds; the sound of the unfettered rolling sand on the beach and untrammeled winds of heaven; and then beheld the costly ornaments and embellished tombs erected at the expense of unrequited toil, sweat and blood wrung from our brother slave still laboring on in misery, inexpressible suffering and wailing, though Sabbath it be, sending up to heaven in whispers of broken accents, prayers for deliverance, all in the sight of these happy throngs and costly catacombs—I could not suppress the emotion which swelled my breast, nor control my feelings when I cursed their bones as they lie mouldering in their graves. May God forgive me for the wickedness, as my conscience admonished and rebukes me. In contemplation of our condition, my heart is sorrowful to sadness. But my determination is fixed; I will never leave you. An overwhelming power of our oppressors or some stern adversity, brethren, may force you to forsake me, but even then will I not leave you. I will take me to the mountains, and there in the dreary seclusion of the wilderness, though alone, will I stand firmly in defence of our cause. Buckle on your armor then, and stand ready for the fight! Finally, brethren, I may eventually go down to a disappointed and untimely, but never to a coward's or a traitor's grave! God's will be done."

To this impressive and solemn speech there was a universal shout of response, when Gofer Gondolier next spoke by request:

"I haven't done nothin', I hadn't no chance; but I'm anxious to do somethin', an' ef the general there hurry up this thing an' give me a chance, I'll show 'im what I kin do. I'm no speaker, but whenever there's any carving to be done, give me a chance; I'm your man. I've nothin' more to say, only that I owe 'em somethin' for what they done to her"—pointing to Abyssa, his wife—"an' I'm ready to pay 'em back with interest."

"You should 'pray for them that despitefully use you,'" admonished Abyssa.

"I will," said Gofer as he passed out with a significant nod of the head to one side, eloquent with meaning.

"Are we now certain each for himself," asked the Chief, "that he is ready to enter into this solemn responsibility of self-emancipation from an otherwise interminable bondage? If you have so decided and determined, I desire each to so express himself audibly and distinctly, that the name may stand on our secret record to be seen and read by future generations."

"I am," was the universal response, each rising separately to give his name.

"How," inquired he, "what am I to understand by it? Are you for or against?"

"For war!" was the shout sent up with a thrill.

"Then let us pray," said he—all falling upon their knees with their heads again low to the floor, Blake offering up this petition:

"O God of clemency, in humble petition we again prostrate ourselves before Thee, to acknowledge our feebleness and unworthiness to come before Thee. We are more and more sensible that without thy divine aid, we can do nothing. O, guide and direct us in this the greatest of undertakings: be a leader in our wilderness traveling; director in our wilderness wanderings; chief in our wilderness warfare; benefactor in our wilderness sojourning; and light in the midst of the darkness in which we are now enveloped. O, fit and prepare us for the work that is before us—a mighty undertaking: go with us to the battlefield—be our buckler and shield, sword and spear, and strengthen us for the conflict; and be with such of us who fall in the struggle, through the dark valley and shadow of death. Be our great Captain, I pray thee; for it is written in thy holy word, 'the Lord is a man of war, for the Lord is his name.' If thou art for us, Lord, none need be against us. These things and thy name shall be ever praised, and have all the glory!"

"Amen!" was the response, all rising to their seats.

"In the name of God, I now declare war against our oppressors, provided Spain does not redress our grievances!" proclaimed Blake.

"In God's name, then," responded Placido, "let us prepare for war."

"By God's help, I second the motion!" sanctioned Montego, the vote being taken standing, with great sensation.

The greatest enthusiasm prevailed, though prudently controlled within due bounds; and among other preparatory arrangements the regimentals of the general officers were at once to be obtained. Those of Blake, Placido, Montego and staffs were to be ordered from the French capital.

Again summoning the council to a solemn seclusion, the Chief at length addressed them, reminding them that it was the last opportunity they would have for a regular meeting in seclusion. The time, he impressed them, was fast elapsing, and Nature being exact and regular in all her fixed laws, suspended nor altered them to suit no person, circumstance, nor thing. That the time to strike was fast verging upon them, from which, like the approach of the evening shadow of the hilltops, there was no escape. It would overtake them whether or not they desired it, though in accordance with its own economy, would be harmless and unfelt in its action and progress.

This period was familiar and regular action of nature which suggested the occasion and proffered the auspices.

"Glorious circumstance!" exclaimed the Chief, a regular daily visitant, whose hints and suggestions have never, until recently, been comprehended. "No longer shall they be neglected, but eagerly accepted of, as sixty or ninety days hence, at most, will verify our appreciation of them. Nature, after all, in uncorrupted purity, is the best and most reliable friend of man.

Equality of rights in Nature's plan,
To follow nature is the march of man.

Then let us determine to be ready, permitting nothing outside of an interposition of Divine Providence to interfere with our progress. Whenever an emergency demands it, I shall call a special council in seclusion; until then, let confidence, the most implicit, govern and control all of your actions toward each other, when a united effort must crown our portentous struggle with success. And may God protect us, and defend the right!"

After singing the solemn hymn of "Old Hundred" to the words of

Before Jehovah's awful throne,

and offering up a solemn prayer by Montego, these people full of hope the highest and expectation the most sanguine, separated for their homes and lodgings near three o'clock in the morning, amidst the most intense feelings and unswerving determination to make a bold and fearless effort to break the shackles of bondage and throw off the galling yoke that so long and grievously tormented them.

CHAPTER 71

Fearful Apprehensions

Another report obtained currency that the Negroes were about to rise, through what medium—whether the legitimate consequence of conscious guilt and fear, or the revelations of a servile black—never was known.

As a natural consequence, all Havana was thrown into consternation—effect following causes as the report gained currency— until the whole colony in a very short time was aroused to the most fearful apprehensions. As is usual on such occasions, the Captain General placed the city under martial law, enforced restrictions upon the Negro population, ordered the military to be in readiness for a moment's warning and commenced a rigid inspection of all the military departments.

The Negroes and mulattoes were eyed with suspicion, and instead of the accustomed nine o'clock alarm, every hour during the night a gun from the castle thundered the terrible warning, executing the order throughout the prevailing excitement.

On one of those eventful evenings in the upper Almeda, just after the alarm of the gun, a black man who had been seen in close conversation with a white was arrested, and exhibited a "pass" purporting to have emanated from a foreign functionary in the city.

The next day the place was fermented with excitement, the highways being thronged with people eagerly discussing the subject and anxiously speculating thereupon.

Among the absurdities to which this report gave rise, none were greater than those which found their way into the Havana morning journals one of which was "El Diario," hawked about the streets and eagerly brought up by the news-seeking population to the effect that "Dr. M——n, the British consul, having been caught, tried, found guilty and afterwards confessed to having been concerned in a Negro insurrection in Cuba, was to be hanged, shot or garroted"; while another report had him "imprisoned," "publicly whipped," and "transported to the mines in Spain."[40]

In the meantime this functionary was really seized and thrown into prison, which act threw the authorities into a dilemma much more perplexing than that of the British Consul.

Whilst the Captain General in fearful suspense was pondering with much embarrassment, and devising schemes to extricate himself from the difficulty of an almost fatal error commited by a stupid blunder, a timely relief was offered by a note received from the minister for Foreign Affairs in Great Britain, politely suggesting that the immediate and unconditional release of H.B.M. Consul for the port of Havana was desirable, concluding with that affability for which the distinguished nobleman who then occupied the Foreign Office, and other British statesmen, are remarkable. This was opportune, proving a most fortunate and happy pretext for an honorable escape from the fiery ordeal which awaited them by the terrible displeasure of England.

The first sail from Havana to Great Britain bore to the Minister for Foreign Affairs the assurance that an apology had been made to Her Majesty's Consul for the rash conduct of two hasty officials who would receive at the hands of the government due attention for their indiscretion.

This speculation was happily disposed of, the Spanish adventurer escaped with little loss of capital in a bold and precipitious investment, though at one time the stock had considerably depreciated at the political exchanges.

The whole matter doubtless had been schemed by interested American slave dealers in the Negro brokerages of the Southern states, a number of whom may always be found in Cuba watching the foreign slave trade for the purpose of purchasing souls to drive on their plantations. It is confidently believed upon good authority that the American steamers plying between Havana and New Orleans, as a profitable part of their enterprise, are actively engaged in the slave trade between the two places.[41] These facts, though seen and known by all employees and passengers of such vessels, are supposed to be a legal traffic of masters removing their slaves.

The excitement consequent to the arrest and the imprisonment of the British Consul had not yet ceased throbbing in the public heart when a new issue was made of an entirely different character. In this speculators and political jobbers might with impunity make the most reckless investments without a fear of loss, the article being a home commodity.

One evening while the Captain General and lady sat musing on the rear corridor of the palace, a gentleman, who subsequently proved to be a loyalist and one of the first persons of education and wealth, came with hurried steps to the door where meeting a guard, enquired for his excellency, who being apprised, immediately repaired to the antechamber.

"Has your excellency heard the news?" with quick breathing, inquired the gentleman.

"Of what import; señor?" asked the Captain General.

"Concerning the insurrection, sir!" replied he with evident fatigue by the hurry of his errand.

"Which one of them señor?" replied his excellency. "Since rumor recently has been so abundant in her productions of insurrectionary reports, we must be certain before proceeding to an investigation, what we have before us."

"The last one, your excellency," seriously said the gentleman.

"Ah! Then that one has been happily settled to the honor of our country. The Consul has been released, an apology made, the British Government reconciled, and Spain satisfied."

"Your excellency," with surprise replied the man, "I have no reference whatever to that affair, but something more recent."

"Ah!" again exclaimed the governor gravely, "I thought you had reference to that, since it is the last of which I had any knowledge."

"May it please your excellency!" anxiously importuned the gentleman. "The intelligence of this has just come to light."

"Indeed!" responded he in a manner which greatly embarrassed the messenger. "How many plantations sacked and what the number of whites killed?"

"Your excellency," impatiently replied the bearer of dispatches, inwardly feeling what he dared not outwardly express, "it has not yet come to a strike, but has been discovered in the plot."

"Yes, yes! That materially alters the case," indifferently continued the Count. "Like all the others it may only exist in the imagination of those who fabricate and vend these alarms for political purposes, keeping the public mind in a continual state of uneasiness and excitement."

"I hope that your Excellency does not mistake me?" in a subdued tone enquired the disheartened loyalist. "I am no political newsdealer, huckstering gossip for speculative purposes. I am chairman of a delegation of the proprietors of large estates near Matanzas, appointed as a messenger and bearer of despatches to communicate with the government."

"Ah ha! Something new in reality then?" with some anxiety enquired the governor. "What is the true state of the case?"

The gentleman at once proceeded to relate the facts that some thirty miles in the interior from Matanzas, the wife of a respectable planter had doubtless from impressions made upon her mind by the reality, become a maniac, making the most startling disclosures. An insurrection was to have commenced on their own plantation, she having been a party to the scheme. Talking incessantly, she raved and screamed, frequently startled, calling for a black chief to protect her. When to dispel the phantom a black girl child had to be placed in her bed, with the assurance that it was the child of the Negro chief sent in advance of him, when she immediately became quiet and apparently reconciled. She had imagined herself in a horrible seclusion or cave surrounded by black serpents, when being attacked by a huge monstrous serpent, was only protected from certain death by the timely interposition of one of those divine black spirits.

"How long has she been thus affected?" enquired the Captain General after patiently hearing the history of the case.

"During the last three days and nights, your excellency."

"What do you desire at my hands?"

"Protection of troops—and if thought advisable, the presence of your excellency."

"What have her physicians done in the case?" continued to inquire the governor.

"They can do nothing at all, Count Alcora," positively replied the planter.

"Neither can I," gravely rejoined he; "and would willingly send up troops to restore her to rationality, but see no good reasons for detailing at the bedside of a crazy woman a corps of military to frighten her out of whatever mind there might be yet remaining. As to myself, I can see no good to result from my entering the bedchamber of a maniac, dressed up in regimentals. If her greatest hallucination now be black ghosts, it would only change the illusions to white ones. You, sir, will hereby inform your constituents, that it is neither the desire nor duty of the executive of this colony to carry the national troops in battle array to divert the phantoms of a prostrated maniac," when, making a polite bow, he withdrew.*

*So frequent were these complaints to the Captain General that he often gave them a summary dismissal.

The planter so unsatisfactorily dismissed, with sullen countenance left the palace gritting his teeth with a determination of being avenged for the neglect and want of care shown to his neighborhood, a loyal district.

The Count was a proud and haughty Castilian, and the planters near Matanzas generally being Americans, a restless, dissatisfied class, ever plotting schemes to keep up excitement in the island, thereby having continual cause for complaint; he hated them as only a member of the Cortez Council could do a colonial "patriot," as the American party termed themselves.

For this contempt, however, the country paid dearly, as they made it the immediate cause of dissatisfaction and complaint against the administration of Count Alcora, and also the home government.

They complained that the Creoles had not the right of franchise, being ineligible to positions of honor the council being selected by the Captain General, and all the offices of consequence being filled by persons directly from Spain—persons whose every relation was foreign to the interest of society and detrimental to the progress of the colony. Spain, they insisted, was a foreign country, having no right to rule them. They were Creoles, and of right ought to be their own rulers.

To these complaints the Captain General, as also Spain, paid a deaf ear, replying that in general these "Creole" statements originated in the principal commercial cities in the United States, by such speculators as frequent the exchanges in Dock, Wall and State streets, backed by the brokerages of Baltimore, Richmond, Charleston and New Orleans. They had openly declared that Cuba and Porto Rico must cease to be Spanish Colonies, and become territories of the United States.

All this did the Spaniards hear and know with a degree of tolerance, patience and forbearance worthy of a cause having higher claims upon their magnanimity. But the Captain General and true loyalists were becoming impatient, who with his Executive Council were maturing a decisive course toward them.

CHAPTER 72

King's Day

It was now in January, the sixth day of the month, on the occasion of "El Dia de los Reyes," or "King's Day," at Havana, to witness and enjoy which, many of all classes, both strangers and residents, white and black, had come from different parts of the island to the city.

Should the disaffected party persist in their seditious indications on this occasion, the Captain General intended at the head of an army of Negroes to put the rebels to a merciless sword.

The demonstration consisted of a festival—physical, mental and religious—by the native Africans in Cuba, in honor of one of their monarchs; being identical, but more systematic, grand and imposing, with the "Congo Dance," formerly observed every Sabbath among the slaves in New Orleans.[42]

I am indebted for the following description of the grand Negro festival to a popular American literary periodical, given by an eyewitness to the exhibition:

"For the week preceding the sixth of January, the native African servants of Havana are in a state of intense excitement. Their masters and mistresses are begged for every spare feather, flower, bit of tinsel, ribbon, or finery of any description whatever; their pocket money is spent on the conventional trash consecrated to the occasion; and every leisure moment is consecrated to preparing for that great day on which they may at least fancy for a few hours that they are free. In all the year, this is the only day the black can call his own; the law gives it to him, and no master has the right to refuse his slave permission to go out for the whole day. At last the important day arrives; the dawn is ushered in by salvos of artillery from Moro Castle—the Negroes pour out of the city gates in crowds to assemble at the places where they are to dress—dainty dressing rooms are they—and the delicate ear is agonized by sounds proceeding from the musical instruments of Africa. They generally assemble according to their tribes. The Gazas, the Lucumis, the Congoes, and Mandingos, etc., in separate parties. One party ordinarily consists of from ten to twenty. There are about half a dozen of principal actors, and the rest hang around and are ready to do any extra dancing or shaking that may be required. Women there are too, in plenty—their dresses 'low in the neck and high in the arms,' covered with gay ribbons and tinsel flowers—that dance all day long for the pure love of the fun, joining first one party and then another, constant to none, and therefore have no right to a portion of the money collected.

"Their place of rendezvous on the King's Day being the grand square or Plaza de San Francisco, called after the church and convent of that name.

"There are three principal personages that appear, with but slight variation of costume, in every group, no matter to what tribe it belongs. They are always chiefs, princes or prophets, or if these elevated individuals are not sufficiently numerous to head the numberless parties, the highest in rank is always chosen to wear the regal African paraphernalia. . . . The king is dressed in a network of red cord, through the interstices of which glisten oddly enough square inches of the royal black skin. Round his waist is an immense hoop, with a thick drapery of horsetails with every color of the rainbow, with many hues not found therein.

"Another has a hideous mask surmounted by horns. He is the prophet of the tribe, and is sometimes supposed to be gifted with magical powers—a full belief in charms being a part of the Negro's native creed. . . . This Obesh or Jumbo butts with horns, yells, and performs various antics that impress deeply the surrounding Negroes. If a white person pretends to be alarmed at the unearthly sounds or sights, it is, of course, a great triumph.

"Around the feet of the principal performers are fastened branches of horsehair, that divide the mind between Mercury and a bantam cock.

"Placing themselves in the attitudes of kangaroos, they go through a series of shuffling, screwing, and shaking that utterly defies any description. It cannot be called dancing, for Sorocco would disown it; neither can it be called convulsions, for the doctors would pronounce them perfectly healthy. St. Vitus himself would be puzzled what to call it, though he could not but be gratified at the favor of his votaries.

"All day long they keep up a movement of some kind, either dancing or waltzing to an almost incredible degree. The parties roam all over the city, stopping in front of the principal houses, or before

the windows in which they see ladies and children. They have also
their favorite corners, and there they will go through with fifteen or
twenty minutes violent agitation, during which the perspiration pours
off their faces, and one unaccustomed to the sight is momentarily
expecting to see them fall exhausted to the ground, perhaps never to
rise again. The only stoppage, however, is when that elaborately
dressed personage with a cane, so beruffled and beringed, hands round
the box to the spectators for "pesetas" and "medios." He is the
steward of the party, and after all is done, he produces the money
which pays for the room in which they hold their ball at night—all
night indeed, for they keep it up till morning.

"Large sums of money are often collected in this way; and gold
occasionally finds its way in; but the Negro improvidence of character
makes it of very little consequence whether they have much or
little. . . .

"The inside of the hall is extraordinary, but not pleasing. A piece of
parchment stretched over a hollow log beaten with bones, or a box or
gourd filled with beans or stones, rattled out of all time, comprise
their instruments. The songs are quite in keeping with the instruments
and performers. On this day they are allowed to use their own
language and their own songs, a privilege denied them on other days,
lest they might lay plans for a general rising.

"As it is the sights, the sounds, the savage shrieks, the uncouth yells
suggest very uncomfortable thoughts of Negro insurrection. One
cannot help thinking of the menace of the Spanish Government that
Cuba shall be either Spanish or African, and when we see these savages
in their play more like wild animals than human beings, the idea what
their rage would probably be, makes the boldest shudder. It would be
easy on King's Day for the Negroes to free themselves, or at least to
make the streets of Havana run with blood, if they only knew their
power; Heaven be praised that they do not, for who can count the
lives that would be lost in such a fearful struggle?

"The whites of Havana are rejoiced when the day is over. Apart
from a certain uneasy feeling of distrust which the government shares,
for it doubles it guard everywhere, the cessation of all business, and
the circumstance that the streets are not safe after an early morning
hour, make one such day quite enough for a year. The tintamarre is
such, that the head must indeed be strong that escapes a furious

aching by nightfall. To a stranger the first few hours are amusing enough in their novelty, but he speedily wearies of the scene, and is not apt to wish for a repetition of it.

"In 1849, Roncall, the Captain General then in power, took advantage of the Dia de los Reyes to give the Creoles of Cuba a significant hint of what they might expect from the government if they gave any alarming degree of aid to the revolutionary operations of General Lopez.[43] He prolonged for three days the privilege of the day to the Lucumis, the most warlike of the tribes of the African slaves in Cuba. The hint was well understood, and many a Creole family shuddered and trembled within doors at the fearful illustration thus exhibited under their eyes of the standing threat that Cuba must be Spanish or African.

"As night comes on all the scattered parties begin to crowd back again to their starting places; they replace the paint and feathers they have danced off, and repair the ravages of the day. Let it be remembered that all this dancing has been done under a tropical sun, and that the January of Cuba is sometimes like our June, or even July. All is then wound up by a ball. The money derived from the sale of licenses for Negro balls forms no contemptible item in the income of the Queen Mother Christiana."

CHAPTER 73

Increased Alarm

On the evening of "King's Day" the disaffected whites sought by device to aggravate a tendency to insubordination of the blacks, hoping thereby to destroy confidence in them and turn the suspicions and rigor of the Captain General from themselves to the Negroes.

To accomplish their designs, no act however derogatory to manhood and justice, equity and honor, was too atrocious for them to perpetrate.

During the African ball this evening, a party of the rebels called at a restaurateur, where getting among them a stupid, demented slave whom for hours they kept stimulated with spirits, then aroused to a state of intense excitement by dreadful tales of horror, they placed him in a close carriage, had him taken to the door of the hall in which the ball was held, and when at the height of their amusement he was ushered into the hall crying, "Blood, blood, blood! Rise, Negroes, rise!" when being soon forced out he continued thus to scream in the street.

Soon was the city in the greatest consternation; the streets in a few minutes filled with troops, and the National Guards were seen in every direction. The sound of the bugle, rattling and ringing of arms, hasty dashing forth and back of expert horsemen, made the scene one of portentous warning.

The frantic black was shot as he ran through the street; fell bleeding, and arrested, the ball immediately surrounded, the inmates arrested and confined in Moro Castle. Arrests were continued during the night, with reports the most extravagant. And although the free black and colored inhabitants were generally safe in their own houses, but few enjoyed sleep that evening.

Early next morning the sound of the reveille was heard and the troops hastening to their posts, while the city was alive with the excited inhabitants anxious to catch every word of passing gossip. The Captain General, ever on the alert and always suspicious of the dissatisfied rebellious American settlers, was early at his post— determined, as was his wont in criminal transactions, to make summary work of the whole affair.

The first step in the proceedings was to hear the story of the wounded black, shot by the gendarmes, wherein the Americans objected to the testimony of a Negro being taken before white men's.

This the Captain General declared was done in due deference to the Americans, that it might not be said that they had been disparaged by a Negro giving evidence against them. As no white man had yet testified, the Negro's testimony was against none. He would, therefore, take the Negro's first and theirs afterwards. There was nothing out of the usual course in those proceedings, except the order of taking the testimony, which gave them the advantage. Negroes in Cuba had the right of testimony; but a slave could not rebut the evidence of a freeman whatever his color, and all free persons in evidence, stood equal before the law.

There had been nothing on the part of the Negroes done out of their usual course on the celebration of King's Day. By all the evidence, even that of the gendarmes themselves, there was nothing to convict them of an overt act. But the testimony of the carriage driver and the wounded Negro implicated a number of white Americans as being conspirators assembled at the Hotel de Americana Norte for the purpose of getting up a "patriot" demonstration, by turning the attention of the authorities to the Negroes.

"We'll force the Captain General to terms whether he will or not. Can we but once get him at issue with the Negroes, his only dependence will be cut off, and if not they'll be too feeble to be either formidable or dangerous," said one.

"The Negroes," said another, "the only formidable enemy in the event of a patriot movement we should have to contend against, must be got out of the way. That can only be done successfully by getting the government down on them. This once effected, we are safe, as they will never again place confidence in those who once go against or deceive them."

"Never!" was the reply. "The Spaniards have taken great pains to prejudice them against us Americans by impressing them with the fear that should we be successful in taking the island they will not be allowed King's Day, nor any of the privileges they now enjoy under Spanish rule."

"Then," said a fourth, "the sooner the government is brought against them the better. Let it be done, by all and every means in our power, and I know of no more favorable time than this evening."

"Yes, this evening, by all means!" exclaimed a voice, "as we can't tell what may take place against another King's day. Let it be done at once, as we have a Negro in readiness to make the alarm."

"Come then and let us be at it!" exclaimed the crowd, rushing into the dining apartment where the black was confined.

This the gendarmes testified that they heard, and following closely in their wake saw the slave put into the carriage, three of the Americans entering with him, drove to the doorway leading to the dancing hall, taken out by whites standing near the door, the three Americans remaining inside, when he rushed forth exclaiming the insurrectionary words.

Instantly releasing the blacks from confinement and proclaiming the city again under martial law, the Captain General caused the arrest and imprisonment of every white in the least suspected of seditious designs. A "coup de main" upon the American hotel seriously implicated the proprietor and all the white inmates, resulting in a destruction of the establishment.

But a short time was required to counteract the report of attempted insurrection of the blacks, which like a flash of light spread over the city. The report of their release from Moro Castle by order of his excellency the governor took the community by surprise, producing great dissatisfaction, but soon became reconciled in the security they enjoyed from the calamity of a servile Negro insurrection.

Few people in the world lead such a life as the white inhabitants of Cuba, and those of the South now comprising the "Southern Confederacy of America." A dreamy existence of the most fearful apprehensions, of dread, horror and dismay; suspicion and distrust, jealousy and envy continually pervade the community; and Havana, New Orleans, Charleston or Richmond may be thrown into consternation by an idle expression of the most trifling or ordinary ignorant black. A sleeping wake or waking sleep, a living death or tormented life is that of the Cuban and American slaveholder. For them there is no safety. A criminal in the midst of a powder bin with a red-hot pigot of iron in his hand, which he is compelled to hold and char the living flesh to save his life, or let it fall to relieve him from torture, and thereby incur instantaneous destruction, nor the inhabitants of a house on the brow of a volcano could not exist in greater torment than these most unhappy people.

Of the two classes of these communities, the master and slave, the blacks have everything to hope for and nothing to fear, since let what may take place their redemption from bondage is inevitable. They must and will be free; whilst the whites have everything to fear and nothing to hope for, "God is just, and his justice will not sleep forever."

The general orders issued by the government were stringent, bearing directly and heavily upon all Americans resident or transient in the colonies. All who visited the island were required at quarantine to obtain from an officer a passport for landing, couched in Spanish, French and English. For this during the restrictions two Spanish dollars each were paid, ordinarily the price being only fifty cents Spanish, by which police regulation large sums were realized to the revenue on the arrival of every steamer, especially the California mails touching there, the passengers of which were generally curious to go on shore.

The government continued its rigors, sparing none on account of age, position, or family; the high and low, rich and poor, all faring alike; consequently many were made to feel the force of the strong arm of the law: among whom were several connected with some of the first families of the United States.

Thus, the expense to those who connived at the prerogatives of the Castilians, Spanish colonists, and Negroes was far greater than they had reckoned in their calculation; the first installment being paid under a pressure, it was reasonable to suppose that the full share when demanded would be hard to meet.

For the time it had the desired effect of checking the extravagant political experiments and military adventures in Cuba, the stock becoming depreciated, shares were rated far below par, so that the brigand jobbers were at a loss to meet the second installment of rebellions.

For a time political brokers suspended operations in all of the conclave exchanges in the United States, whilst their marauding agents in Cuba repudiated not only the claims against them, but really denied their own identity. The concern proving a bankruptcy, ruined many more in the fall with themselves by the final execution of Lopez on the garrote with his many American followers.

CHAPTER 74

American Tyranny—Oppression of the Negroes

The severe ordeal through which the rebel party had recently passed tended only to awaken in them against the blacks feelings of the bitterest resentment. Smarting as they were by the wound, still bleeding from the disappointment lately received under trying circumstances, they determined on taking a stand in which, could they not succeed in attaining political equality with the Castilians, at least would enjoy the satisfaction of knowing that they stood above the Negroes. This superiority, they were satisfied, was not to be attained by the elevation of themselves but by putting the Negroes down.

For weeks subsequent to the evening of the last King's Day, the blacks had to withstand the most trying difficulties. Every place of public entertainment, saloon, hotel, coach, cabin passage or what not—the greater part of which being controlled by Americans—were closed against Negroes and mulattoes.

On entering the public market, did a white but appear at a shamble or a stand, though the black was first, he must await the serving of the white, and at his or her bidding, stand back at a "respectful" distance; and on passing along the sidewalk, at the command of a white, every black man was compelled to uncover his head, and leave the pavement for the street. The rule applied to the sidewalks was afterwards restricted upon both sexes. On entering shops and storehouses their hats had always to be raised, and females on entering such places were subject to the coarsest of treatment.

Every day brought to the ears of the unhappy blacks fresh news of some new outrage, but as yet this had not been extended to the better class among them. They were doomed, however, to enjoy but a short respite of this kind, as one evening the whole population was thrown into a ferment of feverish consternation.

Placido, in passing along one of the principal thoroughfares, stepped into a book dealer's establishment, the proprietor of which was an American, formerly of Baltimore to whom the poet was, of course, unknown. He was known to have Negro blood; it was enough to know that he was a mulatto. "Take off your hat, sir," abruptly ordered the bookseller.

The surprise came so suddenly that the poet stopped short in front of the counter in a kind of gaze of bewilderment. Before he could recover himself the man had leaped over the counter, knocked off his hat, kicking it into the street and seized him by the collar of the coat. Though physically weaker, the poet grappled with him, until nearly exhausted he let go his grasp.

As the dealer relinquished his hold, the sacred fire of Heaven which burnt divinely in the poet's soul, blazing as fearfully from his eyes as a lightning flash from a thunder cloud, he gave him a look of godlike defiance.

"Do you look so at me, you black villain! Insulted are you—angry, hey? I'll please you!" The poet still said nothing, but kept his eye firmly fixed on him, terrible as wrath. "Look pleased, sir," indignantly continued he, "look pleased, I say, laugh, I bid you; you black rascal, laugh!"* when dealing him a well aimed blow he sent the bard of Cuba staggering prostrate upon the pavement in the street.

*A similar circumstance really transpired in Wheeling, Va., between a white man called a "gentleman" and a black man.

A respectably dressed white man passing at the moment, supposing the person to have stumbled and fell accidentally, ran quickly to his relief, but on observing him to be colored, although stunned and bleeding upon the earth, he hurriedly passed along without extending a finger of assistance.

The wounded part immediately inflaming and swelling, became discolored and painful, accompanied with lightness of head and dimness of vision. Putting up his hand to the part, and feeling the extent of the cruel mutilation, the left molar bone being badly wounded, picking up his hat, with sacred eloquence in touching tones he exclaimed,

> How long, O gracious God! how long
>   Shall power lord it over right?
> The feeble trampled by the strong
>   Remain in Slavery's gloomy night!

When, walking feebly on, he turned into the first byway, lest, ere he reached his humble abode he might meet with other summary corporeal abuse, and the majesty of heaven again be compelled to yield before the mandate of hell.

The divine aspirations escaping the poet's lips reached his oppressor's ears, and the wretch who with perfidy had just stricken him to the earth, was now touched with sympathy at the outrage perpetrated by his own hand.

"Listen, listen!" admonished he. "He's a praying! He must be a Negro preacher. I'm sorry I used him so badly. I'll try after this to be more careful. I knew several of them while doing business in Baltimore, and always found them good religious black men. They are good customers, always buying costly and large works on divinity, and other books whether or not they read them. They are indeed clever black fellows, and know their place. Which way did he go?" Going to the door he looked every way, but the sorrow-stricken poet was out of sight.

On entering his study, where sat in waiting Blake, Montego, Antonio, Blacus, and Gofer Gondolier, the mutilated and crippled bard exclaimed:

"At last has it come! At last has it come!" falling exhausted upon his couch.

"Good heavens! Placido, what is the matter?" cried Blacus, to which there was no reply.

"My God! What is the matter?" exclaimed Montego.

"Enough's the matter!" interposed Gondolier. "These devils of 'patriots' as they call themselves, have been murdering him as sure's you're born, just as they'll do the whole of us if we don't begin first."

"Gondolier, I'm surprised!" replied Montego. "And——"

"So am I," interrupted he. "General, pardon me—but I do hate them reptiles so!"

"You are wrong, Gondolier. We should not 'hate' our fellow man, as God made us all," admonished Montego.

"I don't care if he did, General; they hate us, an' I'll do them as they do us. They don't care if God did make us: they don't treat us any better on that account," rejoined Gondolier.

"They don't all hate us; there are some good ones among them, as well as other people."

"Good ones, hey! I don't know where you'd find them; I'm sure it wouldn't be among the whites of Cuba. But we're neglecting our murdered brother there, disputing about them serpents which the Scriptures told us long ago should have their heads mashed," said Gondolier.

"Never mind, he dozes now," admonished Montego in a whisper, looking round at the couch where lay the bleeding poet.

"We must know something more about this," said Gondolier, "find out who these devils is that have been beating out his brains."

Justin Pampo, the black surgeon, was called in, who, on examination, pronounced a serious contusion of the cheek, with slight concussion of the brain. On recovering sufficiently to relate his grievances, a thrill of terror and almost irrepressible indignation were manifestly felt.

"This is certainly a serious state of affairs; and that, too, without a medium of redress," said the surgeon.

"Yes," replied Gondolier, "and we ought to by this time be able to redress our grievances. Some men are born to command and others to obey; and it is well that this is the case, else I might be a commander; and ef I was, I might command when orders should not be given."

"This is you failing, Gondolier," said Montego; "and one good reason why you should not hold command. I want no better under-officer, as orders received would be strictly executed."

"Yes, General, I know my 'failing,' and it's useless to talk to me about 'policy' and nonsense when a bloodhound is tearing out my vitals. 'Discretion' at such a time. Give me a revolver, knife, club, brickbat, or anything with which to defend myself, and I'll put a varment to flight. If a tiger, hyena, or any other wild beast should attack you, ought you to take its life immediately, or stop to argue the best method of getting rid of danger? 'Self-preservation is nature's first law'; an old truth my grandmammy taught me many years ago when a child sitting in the chimbly corner. I haven't forgot it yet," rejoined Gondolier starting from his seat toward the door.

"I am now satisfied that we must do something," concluded Montego.

Placido was removed to the residence of Carmino, the architect and civil engineer, when a council of the seclusion was ordered to be held.

The consternation succeeding the spread of this intelligence was indescrible. Females who heretofore held up their heads as ladies of the first rank in society, lost their personal pride and seemingly self-respect, and might thenceforth be seen with dejected spirits, downcast countenances, shying along, giving the entire sidewalk at the approach of every white, frequently going into the street. Men of position and means had also begun to lose their spirits, and children cowered at the sight of a white child.

Among the restrictions in the new Negro laws, the blacks, without regard to age or sex, were compelled to salute all white children, by the appellation of "master" and "mistress." Though the people generally despaired, their leaders were firm; and the maltreatment of one of the ablest and best men among them had well nigh cost the whites in exchange for the proud edifices of their extensive city, a smouldering heap of ruins. Succeeding this despair there was a reaction. A new vigor seemed ever to actuate, and a new impulse given to these faithful men and women determined to be free.

"I will never submit—I will never submit to the base and degrading restrictions! I'll die first!" indignantly exclaimed Madame Montego as she sat with other ladies at the bedside of the disabled and suffering Placido.

"We will not," replied Madame Carmino. "We are Creoles, and, take our people generally, are the most numerous part of the population. I don't see why we should be put down by a set of intruders."

"We will not submit!" added Carolus Blacus. "This, ladies, you may depend upon."

"Thank God," exclaimed Madame Montego, "there is yet some hope!"

Blake during the whole of these scenes was grave and sober, having nothing to say; Montego was thoughtless with determined look, while Gondolier occasionally gave his head a significant nod to one side which all present comprehended.

That evening the seclusion met in Council against the most intense sensation. The bedside of Placido was visited by every member again and again, with sighs, tears, prayers and expressions of vengeance by Gofer Gondolier, who had no scruples in assuming to himself this particular duty of political dispensation. The Council sat the whole evening, the members dispersing after daylight the next morning.

That day early in the afternoon Ambrosina Cordora, the daughter of Madame Montego, and Seraphina Blacus took a promenade through a portion of the Almeda. When in a thronged part of the thoroughfare, Ambrosina accidently came against a lady with whom there was a gentleman. Politely bowing she made acknowledgements for the balk, which the lady acknowledged with a bow and passed on. The man, however, gave her a rude push with an oath and other hard language.

On returning she passed by a store (a fancy dry goods shop) in which sat the man whom she had encountered with the lady, who proved to be the proprietor of the shop. Snatching up a horsewhip, which seems to have been secured for the purpose, running out and seizing her by the breast of the dress rending it in tatters, he dealt upon her person over the arms, neck, head, and face the most cruel punishment, to the sad disfiguring of her features for the time. Her cries brought no white persons to her relief—the blacks dared not have attempted it.

With the clothes half torn from her person, the distressed young woman made as hasty retreat as possible to her home, rushing into the house, falling upon the neck of her mother with a screech, as that lady sat in the drawing room in conversation with a number of others, just then recounting their sufferings as a class.

"O! My God, my God!" screamed the mother. "What does all this mean?"

"I see it! I see!" exclaimed Madame Sebastian, "'tis but a

continuance of the outrages commenced on Placido. O gracious Heavens, is there no remedy for this!"

"If this is the way we are to be treated, " said Maggie Blake, who was then residing in the Montego family, "for my own part I would rather be dead at once! O, must I again become a slave! Is there no mercy in Heaven for us!"

"O! This is dreadful, dreadful!" exclaimed Madame Blacus, wife of Carolus. "In God's name what's to become of us!"

"God only knows!" responded Madame Barbosa, throwing herself carelessly upon a sofa.

"Lord have mercy on us!" implored Abyssa Gondolier, clasping her hands, the tears streaming down her cheeks as she looked upon the tattered, torn, and abused beautiful girl, still clinging to the neck of her distressed mother. "Have mercy on——"

"Ef He don't I will!" interrupted Gondolier who just entered in time to catch the exclamation of his wife, he having learned of the outrage previously in the streets.

"I wish I was dead, so I do!" sobbed the poor girl, amidst the most distressing weeping.

"God——!"

"Stop, Gondolier, don't blaspheme! Remember upon whom we depend for aid," interrupted Madame Montego as he stood with eyes fixed upon her maltreated child. "Offend not Him who gave us being."

"Thank you, Madame, for the advice; I won't! All honor and praise be to God! But we have a race of devils to deal with that would make an angel swear. Educated devils that's capable of everything hellish under the name of religion, law, politics, social regulations, and the higher civilization; so that the helpless victim be of the black race. Curse them! I hate 'em! Let me into the streets and give me but half a chance and I'll unjoint them faster than ever I did a roast pig for the palace dinner table."

"Yes, Gondolier, I know your desires; but we must be prudent and use no rashness at such a time as this especially. 'He that killeth with the sword, will be slain with the sword,' remember," admonished Madame Montego.

"Madame Montego, your gospel talking is very good," replied Gondolier, "but the same book tells me, 'whosoever sheds man's blood shall his blood be shed.' As they shed the blood of our brother two days ago by dashing him on the pavement, and the blood of our sister here today by a horsewhip, I would like to shed theirs with a knife," replied he.

"We must not exasperate, nor even aggravate the whites, Señor Gondolier," remarked Madame Barbosa, "as we must guard against making bad worse."

"I wish I was a man, I'd lay the city in ashes this night, so I would," retorted Ambrosina.

"Stop, my child," admonished the mother, "if you were a man suited to such an undertaking, you would have better sense than to attempt it at an improper time."

"Yes, yes, my child, you must think of these things and not desire that which would only precipitate us into more trouble," added Madame Blacus.

"One thing I do know, if our men do not decide on something in our favor, they will soon be called to look upon us in a state of concubinage; for such treatment as this will force every weak-minded woman to place herself under the care of those who are able to protect them from personal abuse. If they have no men of their associations who can, they must find those who will!—O, my God, the thought is enough to drive me distracted—I'll destroy myself first!" said Ambrosina, startling every person present.

"You speak rationally, my child, regarding yourself, that is just what white men desire to do, drive colored women as a necessity to seek their protection that they may become the subjects of their lust. Do you die first before thinking of such a thing: and let what might come, before yielding to such degradation as that I would be one of the first to aid in laying the city in ashes!" replied the mother.

"What say you to this, General?" exclaimed Gondolier, pointing at the girl, who renewed her lamentations with those of her mother, as Montego, who hearing of the circumstance had hastened to the mansion and just entered the room.

"By yonder blue heavens, I'll avenge this outrage!" said Montego, embracing the mother and daughter as they sat wailing.

"I thank God, then there is still some hope! My lot is cast with that of my race, whether for weal or woe," exclaimed Ambrosina, with brightened countenance; when Gondolier, rejoicing as he left the room to spread among the blacks an authentic statement of the outrage:

"Woe be unto those devils of whites, I say!"

Notes to Text

1 Natchez-under-the-Hill was also renowned as a center for gambling and prostitution and housed a transient population of boatmen, wagoners, and professional gamblers. These activities, however, were in decline by the 1830s. See D. Clayton James, *Antebellum Natchez* (Baton Rouge, La., 1968), p. 169.

2 "Hut" is Delany's equivalent of Harriet Beecher Stowe's "Cabins." Solomon Northrup, however, had previously described slave quarters as "huts" in his *Twelve Years a Slave* (Auburn, N.Y., 1853; reprint ed., Baton Rouge, La., 1968), pp. 6, 188. Delany may also have been influenced by the name "The Hut" given the small cottage in which he lived at Chatham, Canada West, in the late 1850s. (My appreciation to Victor Ullman for this information, which Mr. Ullman received in an interview with Stanley J. Smith, Ingersoll, Ontario.) See also Delany's letter to the Rev. James Theodore Holly from the "King Street Hut," Chatham, January 15, 1861, in the *Chatham Tri-Weekly Planet,* January 21, 1861, p. 3.

3 This attitude was shared by at least two of the many ex-slaves who wrote narratives. See *Narrative of the Life and Adventures of Henry Bibb, an American Slave* and *Narrative of William Wells Brown, a Fugitive Slave*—both reprinted in *Puttin' On Ole Massa,* edited by Gilbert Osofsky (New York, 1969), pp. 147, 166, 215.

4 Compare this song with Harriet Tubman singing "Farewell, oh farewell' as she began her flight from slavery. Sarah H. Bradford, *Scenes in the Life of Harriet Tubman* (Auburn, N.Y., 1869), p. 18.

5 Ballard is referring to the Dred Scott decision of 1857 in which the Supreme Court held blacks not to be citizens of the United States and which also declared the Missouri Compromise of 1820 unconstitutional. Ballard's final statement—"that persons of African descent have no rights that white men are bound to respect"—is almost a direct quotation from Chief Justice Roger B. Taney's opinion. The distinction between suffrage and franchise was one Delany frequently drew. See, for instance, the report of a lecture he gave in Monrovia, Liberia, July 27, 1859, in *The Weekly Anglo-African,* October 1, 1859, p.2.

6 The original version of this chapter, as it appeared in *The Anglo-African Magazine,* read "little Joe." Delany corrected this for the serialization of the complete novel in *The Weekly Anglo-African.*

7 An incident of this sort was not merely the product of Delany's imagination, as the narratives of Solomon Northrup and Peter Still indicate.

However, Harriet Beecher Stowe claimed the kidnaping of free blacks was not common. See her *Key to Uncle Tom's Cabin* (Boston, 1854; reprint ed., New York, 1968), p. 345; Northrup's *Twelve Years a Slave* (Auburn, N.Y., 1853; reprint ed., Baton Rouge, La., 1968); and Kate E. R. Pickard, *The Kidnapped and the Ransomed, Being the Personal Recollections of Peter Still and His Wife, Vina . . .* (Syracuse, 1856).

8 Fort Towson was located about seven miles from the Red River in Oklahoma, then Indian Territory, in 1824 and was abandoned in 1854. It was a mile east of Doaksville, which was the trading center, site of the Indian Agency, and, in the 1850s, the capital of the Choctaw Nation. The Choctaws first moved to this area in early 1831 after having been pushed from their lands east of the Mississippi by white settlers in violation of the Treaty of Dancing Rabbit Creek. The Chickasaws ceded their lands east of the Mississippi to the United States in 1832, and in January 1837, the two tribes signed a treaty at Doaksville by which the Chickasaws purchased a tract of land from the Choctaws for $530,000 and in turn secured citizenship within the Choctaw nation. Friction developed as a result of the Chickasaw's minority status within the ostensibly united nation, and the two tribes separated in 1855. Some of the Choctaws had been slaveholders in Mississippi, and a few of the leaders brought their slaves to the large cotton plantations they established upon their new lands along the Red River. Both the Choctaws and the Chickasaws were strong supporters of the Confederacy during the Civil War. See W. B. Morrison's paper, "Fort Towson," in *Chronicles of Oklahoma,* III (June 1930), pp. 226-227, 231; Angie Debo, *The Rise and Fall of the Choctaw Republic* (Norman, Oklahoma, 1934), pp. 59-60; Grant Foreman, *A History of Oklahoma* (Norman, Oklahoma, 1942), pp. 13-14, 24, 36; and Annie Heloise Abel, *The American Indian as Slaveholder and Secessionist* (Cleveland, 1915), pp. 155-157.

9 Culver is referring to the Seminole Wars of 1817-1818 and 1835-1842 in which blacks and Seminoles fought side by side in Florida. See Kenneth W. Porter's paper, "Negroes and the Seminole War, 1817-1818," in the *Journal of Negro History,* XXXVI (July 1951), 302-322, and his "Negroes and the Seminole War, 1835-1842," in the *Journal of Southern History,* XXX (November 1964), 427-440.

10 Delany probably was referring to Chartres Street in New Orleans.

11 Delany had previously recognized the extent of black and mulatto participation in New Orlean's commercial life in his *Condition, Elevation, Emigration, and Destiny of the Colored People of the United States, Politically Considered* (Philadelphia, 1852; reprint ed., New York, 1968), p. 109. For more recent accounts of the fluidity and relative "openness" of New Orleans ante-bellum society, see Joseph G. Tregle, Jr., "Early New Orleans Society: A Reappraisal," in the *Journal of Southern History,* XVIII (February 1952), 32-36; and Roger A. Fischer, "Racial Segregation in Ante Bellum New Orleans," in the *American Historical Review,* LXXIV (February 1969), 926-937, esp. pp. 928-930, 934.

12 Delany may have been the first to comment on the sorrowful songs of the

Mississippi boatmen. Compare this description with that given by W. E. B. Du Bois in his essay, "Of the Sorrow Songs," in *The Souls of Black Folk* (originally published, 1903; paperback ed., Greenwich, Conn., 1961), pp. 181-191—especially p. 183, where Du Bois writes that spirituals and other black music "are the music of an unhappy people, of the children of disappointment; they tell of death and suffering and unvoiced longing toward a truer world, of misty wanderings and hidden ways."

13 This may not necessarily be a derivation from Stephen Collins Foster's "Old Folks at Home," first published in 1851. Since Foster (1816-1863) grew up in Pittsburgh and married the daughter of Dr. Andrew McDowell, a local physician under whom Delany began his study of medicine in the 1830s (Frank A. Rollin, *pseud., Life and Public Service of Martin R. Delany,* . . . [Boston, 1868], p. 46), it is conceivable that Foster learned the song from Delany, or that both drew upon a common source.

14 Delany's portrait of the Brown Fellowship Society, organized in Charleston in 1790, is essentially accurate. See E. Horace Fitchett, "The Traditions of the Free Negro in Charleston, South Carolina," in the *Journal of Negro History,* XXV (April 1940), 139-152. Delany's antagonism toward mulattoes who practiced color prejudice persisted throughout his life. See his letter to *The North Star,* June 22, 1849, p. 2, in which he denounced "Quadroon Societies" and "Dead-Head Societies" as "ridiculous feints at superiority of descent" and as emanating "from slavery, ignorance and arrogance." After the Civil War, he repeated this attack, claiming the societies to be "a relic of the degraded past." *The New National Era,* August 31, 1871, p. 3.

15 Following Nat Turner's rebellion of 1831 in Southampton County, Virginia, there were reports of large numbers of fugitives hiding out in the Great Dismal Swamp which ran from Southampton into North Carolina. See Herbert Aptheker, *American Negro Slave Revolts* (New York, 1943), p. 308; and Edmund Jackson, "The Virginia Maroons," in *The Liberty Bell: By Friends of Freedom* (Boston, 1852), pp. 143-151. Delany's remembrance of Nat Turner as a symbol of slave resistance was not unique. See Benjamin Quarles, *Black Abolitionists* (New York, 1969), pp. 128-129, 235; and *The Weekly Anglo-African,* October 29, 1859, p. 3.

16 Charleston and Charlestown were both in that part of Virginia which is now West Virginia. John Brown was hanged at Charlestown on December 2, 1859, following his unsuccessful raid at Harper's Ferry. The raid had been preceded by a Provisional Constitutional Convention at Chatham, Canada West, in May 1858, at which Delany was active. See the *Chatham Tri-Weekly Planet,* November 5, 1859, p. 2. Delany's description of Charlestown above is equally appropriate for nearby Harper's Ferry.

17 Abolitionist forces in Kentucky made an unsuccessful attempt to elect to the 1849 state Constitutional Convention candidates favoring gradual emancipation. Although abolitionists retained some support in Kentucky, gradual emancipation remained an unfulfilled goal. J. Winston Coleman, Jr., *Slavery Times in Kentucky* (Chapel Hill, 1940), pp. 314-317.

18 Didacticism of this sort was not untypical for Delany. Moreover, his emphasis on the North Star as the guiding light for the fugitive slave was not unusual as a cursory glance at slave narratives demonstrates. See the narratives of Henry Bibb and William Wells Brown in *Puttin' On Ole Massa,* edited by Gilbert Osofsky (New York, 1969), pp. 131, 133, 146, 205, 217.

19 A similar stratagem was depicted by William Wells Brown in *Clotel; or, the President's Daughter* (London, 1853; reprint ed., New York, 1969), pp. 168-170, and in a speech by Brown to the New England Anti-Slavery Convention reported in *The Liberator,* June 4, 1858, p. 2.

20 This is almost identical with the song Harriet Tubman and a group of fugitives were reported to have been singing while approaching the Suspension Bridge leading from New York State into Canada. See Sarah H. Bradford, *Scenes in the Life of Harriet Tubman* (Auburn, N.Y., 1869), pp. 32-33.

21 As the "mulatto gentleman" is a minister (see text, pp. 155-156), Delany could well be describing the Rev. William C. Monroe, a black Episcopal minister in Detroit who was active in Delany's emigration movement in the 1850s and who sailed with Delany in 1859 to Liberia, where he died a few months after arrival. See also, pp. 188-189 of the text.

22 Compare this scene with Henry Bibb's comment concerning the importance of the marriage ceremony for fugitive slaves. This is in Bibb's narrative in *Puttin' On Ole Massa,* edited by Gilbert Osofsky (New York, 1969), p. 78.

23 This is clearly Phillip A. Bell. See text, p. 188, where Delany uses the initials "B.A.P." as further identification. Bell ran an intelligence office (which was both a mail drop and an employment office) in New York in the early 1850s. Delany included a brief sketch of Bell in *The Condition, Elevation, Emigration, and Destiny of the Colored People of the United States, Politically Considered* (Philadelphia, 1852; reprint ed., New York, 1968), pp. 102-103. Bell served as an editor of *The Colored American* in New York in the late 1830s, and during the Civil War he edited *The Pacific Appeal* in San Francisco.

24 Albertis is referring to the process of "coartacion" by which the slave was given the right to purchase his freedom with funds earned outside of his master's jurisdiction. Although more difficult on the plantation than in urban areas, coartacion, in the words of Herbert S. Klein, "was never seriously challenged and it steadily fed energetic and able Negro slaves into the free colored population." Klein, *Slavery in the Americas; A Comparative Study of Virginia and Cuba* (Chicago, 1967), pp. 98-99, 154, 196-200; quotation on p. 199.

25 Compare this description with that of the historian Joseph G. Tregle, Jr., who has written that "The whole behavior of the Negro toward the whites, as a matter of fact, was singularly free of that deference and circumspection which might have been expected in a slave community. It was not unusual for slaves to gather on street corners at night, for example, where they challenged whites to attempt to pass, hurled taunts at white women, and kept whole neighborhoods disturbed by shouts and curses. Nor was it safe

to accost them, as many went armed with knives and pistols in flagrant defiance of all the precautions of the Black Code." "Early New Orleans Society: A Reappraisal," in *Journal of Southern History*, XVIII (February 1952), p. 33.

26 "B.A.P." is clearly Phillip A. Bell and the Detroit minister is the Rev. William C. Monroe. See text, pp. 155-157.

27 Placido was the pen name of Gabriel de la Concepcion Valdes (1809-1844), a freeborn mulatto of uncertain ancestry. After receiving a limited formal education, he was apprenticed to a portrait painter and then, around 1823, as a typesetter in the shop of Jose Severino Boloña, a printer and poet and later publisher of the *Diario de la Marina de la Habana*. Shortly thereafter, Placido became known as a poet although he had replaced typesetting with the more remunerative trade of carving tortoise shells. In the late 1830s, Placido, then living in Matanzas, published poetry in the local daily. In 1843 he was arrested on suspicion of plotting an insurrection but was released. He was again imprisoned in early 1844 and was condemned to death on the charge of high treason—partly because many of his poems appeared seditious and partly because it was believed that prominent blacks such as Placido were capable of inciting insurrections. He was executed by a firing squad June 28, 1844. See Frederick S. Stimson, *Cuba's Romantic Poet; The Story of Placido* (Chapel Hill, 1964). Delany had previously recognized the heroic proportions of the Cuban poet in *The Condition, Elevation, Emigration, and Destiny of the Colored People of the United States, Politically Considered* (Philadelphia, 1852; reprint ed., New York, 1968), p. 203. William Wells Brown also wrote about Placido; however Stimson claims the sketch of the Cuban poet-rebel in Brown's *The Black Man, His Antecedents, His Genius, and His Achievements* (New York, 1863) confused Placido with the full-blooded black poet, Juan Francisco Manzano (1797-1854) who had been born into slavery. Stimson, p. 100. William G. Allen, a black professor at New York Central College at McGrawville, apparently did likewise. See his sketch in *Autographs for Freedom*, edited by Julia Griffiths (Boston, 1853), pp. 257-263.

28 Delany used this poem—which he may have written himself—at the close of an article, "Annexation of Cuba," in *The North Star*, April 27, 1849, p. 2.

29 The advantages of employing the American flag on slave merchants has been confirmed by both contemporary and historical accounts. See "The Slave Trade in 1858," in *The Edinburgh Review*, CVIII (July and October 1858), p. 294; *Arthur F. Corwin, Spain and the Abolition of Slavery in Cuba, 1817-1886,* (Austin, Texas, 1967), p. 94; and Lawrence F. Hill, "The Abolition of the African Slave Trade to Brazil," in the *Hispanic American Historical Review*, XI (May 1931), pp. 179-181, 184-186. See also Hugh G. Soulsby, *The Right of Search and the Slave Trade in Anglo-American Relations 1814-1862* (Baltimore, 1933).

30 This was undoubtedly one of many bitter parodies of patriotic songs. For instance, the 1843 Anti-Slavery Almanac contains a song beginning "Oh, Hail Columbia, happy land!/The Cradle Land of Liberty/Where None but

Negroes Bear the Brand/Or Feel the Lash of Slavery . . ." (My appreciation to Dorothy Sterling for calling this to my attention.)

31 It was not uncommon for European merchants on the coast to have African wives. See, for example, Thomas J. Bowen, *Adventures and Missionary Labors in Several Countries in the Interior of Africa, from 1849 to 1856* (Charleston, S.C., 1857; reprint ed., London, 1968), p. 86.

32 Delany's companion on his African trip, Robert Campbell, also described this slaver. See Campbell's *A Pilgrimmage to My Motherland* . . . (New York, 1861), p. 133.

33 Mendi or Mendeland was a portion of the African coast that was then adjacent to the Colony of Sierra Leone. In 1839, a group of Mendi blacks on the slaver *Amistad* traveling from Cuba to Puerto Rico, overwhelmed their captors and took charge of the vessel. Attempting to sail back to Mendi, the blacks followed the advice of the Spaniards whose lives they had spared and finally sailed to the New England coast where they were captured and jailed in New Haven, Connecticut. After lengthy litigation (including a successful argument before the Supreme Court by John Quincy Adams), the Africans returned home in early 1842, accompanied by missionaries sent by the Amistad Committee which had been formed to defend the liberated slaves. The committee eventually merged with two other groups to form the American Missionary Association which, in addition to many other activities, conducted a Mendi mission until 1883. C. P. Groves, *The Planting of Christianity in Africa* (London, 1954), II, pp. 64-67. Interestingly, the *Mendi* was the barque which carried Delany to Liberia in 1859.

34 This is consistent with Herbert S. Klein's observation that "Given the dark complexion of most Spaniards, it was often enough to be a moderate mulatto to be considered physically white, especially when the cultural and economic roles demanded such a definition." *Slavery in the Americas: A Comparative Study of Virginia and Cuba* (Chicago, 1967), p. 195n.

35 The banjo developed from the African bango. Delany was conscious of other African survivals as his borrowed account of the Congo Dance indicated. See text, pp. 300, 302.

36 Delany made many of these points in a letter in which he expressed his clear preference for African emigration as opposed to Haytian emigration. See *The Weekly Anglo-African*, February 1, 1862, p. 2.

37 Blake is referring to William Murray (1705-1793) first Earl of Mansfield and chief justice of the King's bench for thirty-four years. In the Somersett case of 1772, Murray ruled that slaves were free the moment they set foot upon British soil.

38 This may very well have been written after Delany returned from Africa and England and during a period when he was cooperating with the African Aid Society of England, which was committed to aid Delany in establishing a colony of Canadian blacks in the Niger Valley. See the introduction to this edition, pp. xv-xvi.

39 This reflects Delany's more moderate views at the time of his African trip.

See, for example, *The Colonization Herald* (Philadelphia), July 1860, p. 478 (erroneously numbered p. 476).

40 The British consul here probably was patterned after David Turnbull, an abolitionist who served as the British consul to Cuba from November 1840 until June 1842, when he was recalled at Spain's request. As superintendent of liberated Africans, Turnbull returned to Cuba in October 1842 with some British free blacks. He was soon charged with plotting rebellion. The blacks were shot, and Turnbull, after being imprisoned, was eventually deported. Arthur F. Corwin, *Spain and the Abolition of Slavery in Cuba, 1817-1886* (Austin, Texas, 1967), pp. 75-77. Cuban officials believed Turnbull and Placido were close friends; this, however, has never been adequately documented. Frederick Stimson, *Cuba's Romantic Poet: The Story of Placido* (Chapel Hill, 1964), p. 79.

41 Historians as diverse in their views as W. E. B. Du Bois and Ulrich B. Phillips have testified to the illicit importation of slaves after the trade had been outlawed in 1808. See Du Bois *The Suppression of the African Slave-Trade to the United States of America 1638-1870* (New York, 1896), pp. 180-183; Phillips, *American Negro Slavery* (paperback ed., Baton Rouge, 1966), p. 147. A contemporary account can be found in *The Cotton Supply Reporter* (Manchester, England), October 15, 1860, p. 282. In addition to smuggling slaves, there were efforts in Louisiana in the late 1850s to legalize the foreign trade. See James Paisley Hendrix, Jr., "The Efforts to Reopen the African Slave Trade in Louisiana," in *Louisiana History*, X (Spring 1969), 97-123.

42 William Wells Brown has vividly depicted the New Orleans Congo Dance in *My Southern Home: Or, The South and Its People* (3rd ed., Boston, 1882), pp. 121-124.

43 Narciso Lopez, a native of Venezuela, came to the United States in 1849 as a Cuban exile intent upon overthrowing the Spanish regime. After centering his headquarters in New Orleans in the summer of 1849, he soon received the backing of Southerners dedicated to the annexation of the Spanish island as well as other groups interested in the liberation of Cuba. In late summer, 1851, he led an assault on Bahia Honda on the west coast of the island but was captured and garroted. Lester D. Langley, *The Cuban Policy of the United States: A Brief History* (New York, 1968), pp. 26-31; see also this text, p. 306, for a reference to Lopez's execution.